Their eyes met. Something passed between them. Something that stopped his breath, stopped his heart, and made the floor shift under his feet.

He was hot, hard, and poised on the edge of a precipice, struggling to hold on. Struggling not to touch her. But this might be a battle he could not win.

His heart pounded, restraint making his muscles flex. The weight of inevitability came crushing down on top of him, a weight too heavy for even him to hold off. He wanted her so intensely he could taste her on his tongue.

Her eyes fell to his mouth. Her lips parted. She leaned closer.

The subtle invitation was too much to resist; the battle was lost. His mouth fell on hers with a deep groan. For a moment it was just like the first time he'd kissed her. He felt the same unexpected ripple of shock at how good she tasted. How soft her lips were. How the innocent tremble of her mouth under his made him ache to be the one to teach her about passion.

But then it changed, because this time he didn't pull back. This time he didn't fight the urge to deepen the kiss. This time he slid his arm around her waist, dragged her up against him, and let himself sink into the honey softness of her mouth to taste her fully. This time he caught the tremble of her lips with his and showed her how to open for him, how to take his tongue in her mouth and let him stroke her.

Aye, he stroked her. With long, slow pulls of his tongue until she stroked him back. The first flick of her tongue against his made him groan. His knees almost buckled.

It was incredible.

Bone melting.

Blood heating.

Mind blowing.

By Monica McCarty

The Raider
The Hunter
The Recruit
The Saint
The Viper
The Ranger
The Hawk
The Chief

Highland Warrior
Highland Outlaw
Highland Scoundrel

Highlander Untamed
Highlander Unmasked
Highlander Unchained

The Raider

A HIGHLAND GUARD NOVEL

MONICA McCARTY

BALLANTINE BOOKS • NEW YORK

A Ballantine Books Mass Market Original

Copyright © 2014 by Monica McCarty

Published in the United States by Ballantine Books, an imprint of Random House, a division of Random House LLC, a Penguin Random House Company, New York.

BALLANTINE and the HOUSE colophon are registered trademarks of Random House LLC.

ISBN 978-0-345-54393-6
eBook ISBN 978-0-345-54394-3

Cover design: Lynn Andreozzi
Cover illustration: Franco Accornero

Printed in the United States of America

www.ballantinebooks.com

9 8 7 6 5 4 3 2 1

Ballantine mass market edition: March 2014

To my very own strapping lad.
(Yes, Dave, stop looking around, I *am* talking about you.)

And to all the readers on Facebook,
thanks for your enthusiasm, encouragement,
and expertise on subjects far and wide.
You'll see one of the examples here
(oats, that's all I'm saying!).

THE HIGHLAND GUARD

Tor "Chief" MacLeod: Team Leader and
  Expert Swordsman
Erik "Hawk" MacSorley: Seafarer and Swimmer
Lachlan "Viper" MacRuairi: Stealth, Infiltration, and
  Extraction
Arthur "Ranger" Campbell: Scouting and
  Reconnaissance
Gregor "Arrow" MacGregor: Marksman and Archer
Magnus "Saint" MacKay: Survivalist and
  Weapon Forging
Kenneth "Ice" Sutherland: Explosives and Versatility
Eoin "Striker" MacLean: Strategist in "Pirate" Warfare
Ewen "Hunter" Lamont: Tracker and Hunter of Men
Robert "Raider" Boyd: Physical Strength and
  Hand-to-Hand Combat
Alex "Dragon" Seton: Dirk and Close Combat

  Also:
Helen "Angel" MacKay (née Sutherland): Healer

FOREWORD

The year of our lord thirteen hundred and twelve. Since Robert the Bruce first made his bid for the crown six years ago, he has defeated not only the English but also the powerful Scottish noblemen who stood against him. After a much-needed reprieve from warfare for Bruce and his men, in late summer 1310 the English marched north to invade Scotland, this time under the leadership of Edward II.

But the second Edward is nothing like his "Hammer of the Scots" father, and the English campaign was a disaster. Bruce refused to take the field in pitched battle. Instead, with the help of the elite warriors of the legendary Highland Guard, Bruce waged a "secret war," using the pirate tactics he had perfected, harrying the English with surprise attacks and skirmishes, and wreaking havoc on the soldiers' morale.

After unsuccessfully attempting to track down Bruce, Edward and his army withdrew to the English Marches to wait out the winter in Berwick-upon-Tweed before marching on the rebels again. But the English king's second campaign was delayed when in the summer of 1311, after ten months in Scotland and the Borders, trouble with his barons required him to return to London.

. Bruce immediately took advantage of Edward's withdrawal and went on the offensive, for the first time taking his war deep into the English countryside. Like the Vikings before them, the fierce Scot raiders struck terror in the heart of the enemy. The names of their leaders will go down in history. Men like Thomas Randolph, James "The Black" Douglas, Edward Bruce, and Robbie Boyd will earn both fame and fortune, beginning the fierce campaign that will eventually bring about the end of the war.

Prologue

Gud Robert Boyd, that worthi was and wicht
(Good Robert Boyd that worthy wise and strong)
—Blind Harry, *The Wallace*

Kildrummy Castle, Scottish Highlands, October 1306

Killed? Rosalin nearly choked on a bit of beef.

"Are you all right?" her brother asked, leaning over to pat her on the back.

After a burst of coughing, she took a sip of sweetened wine and nodded. "I'm fine." Seeing his concern, she managed a smile. "Really. I'm sorry for the disturbance. You were saying something about the prisoners?"

Her attempt at nonchalance didn't fool him. He frowned. He'd been speaking in a low voice to her guardian, Sir Humphrey, on his other side, and the conversation obviously hadn't been meant for her ears. She blinked up at him innocently, but Robert, the first Baron de Clifford, hadn't become one of the most important commanders in the war against the rebel Scots because of his rank and handsome face—although he certainly possessed both. Nay, he'd risen so high in King Edward's estimation because he was smart, loyal, and determined. He was also one of the greatest knights in England, and she was fiercely proud of him.

Even if he was entirely too perceptive.

"An unfortunate accident, that is all. Part of the wall collapsed when the prisoners were dismantling it. Two of the rebels were crushed by the stone and killed."

Her heart jumped to her throat and a small cry of distress escaped before she could help it. *Oh God, please don't let it be him!*

Aware of her brother's watchful gaze, she attempted to cover her too concerned reaction with a maidenly, "That's horrible!"

He studied her a little longer, and then patted her hand. "Do not let it distress you."

But she *was* distressed. *Deeply* distressed. Although she certainly couldn't tell her brother why. If he learned about her fascination with one of the rebel prisoners, he would send her back to London on the first ship, as he'd threatened to do when she'd arrived unexpectedly a week ago with her new guardian, Sir Humphrey de Bohun, Earl of Hereford.

"*Christ's Cross, Rosalin! This is the last place in Christendom suitable for a young girl.*"

But the opportunity to see Cliff had been too tempting to resist. With her in London and her brother fighting the Scottish rebels in the North, it had been nearly two years since she'd seen him, and she missed him desperately. He, Maud (Cliff's wife of eight years), and the children were all the family she had left, and if she had to venture into Hades to see them, she would. Maud would have made the journey with Rosalin and the earl's party, but she'd just discovered she was with child again.

"I don't understand why the wall is being dismantled in the first place," Rosalin said. "I thought we won the war?"

Her distraction worked. Cliff loved nothing more than to talk about England's great victory. Robert Bruce's bid for the crown had failed. The outlaw king had been forced to flee Scotland, and the English were now occupying most of Scotland's important castles, including this one, the former stronghold of the Scottish Earls of Mar.

"We did. Robert Bruce's short-lived rebellion is at an end. He might have escaped the noose set for him at Dunaverty Castle, but he won't find refuge in the Western Isles for long. Our fleet will find him." He shrugged. "Even if they don't, he only has a handful of men left under his command."

She lowered her voice to a whisper. "But aren't they Highlanders?"

Her brother laughed and tweaked her nose. Though sixteen—nearly seventeen—was much too old for tweaking, she didn't mind. She knew just how fortunate she was to have a brother who cared for her so deeply. Not many fourteen-year-old boys would have bothered themselves with a four-year-old sister on the death of their parents, but Cliff had always watched out for her. Even when they were both made wards of the king, he always made sure she knew she was not alone. If he sometimes acted like more of an overprotective father than a brother, she didn't mind. To her, he was both.

"They aren't bogeymen, little one. Or supermen, no matter what you might hear at court. They might fight like barbarians, but when they meet the steel of an English knight's sword, their blood runs as red as any other."

As she wasn't supposed to be watching the prisoners, she refrained from asking why they were kept so heavily guarded then.

Her brother turned back to Sir Humphrey, and Rosalin bided her time, waiting for the long midday meal to come to an end before racing up to her chamber in the Snow Tower.

Usually she delayed her return to her chamber as long as possible. Cliff had permitted her to stay in Scotland at Kildrummy only under the condition that she keep to her room except for during meals and chapel (he didn't want there to be any chance of her coming into contact with one of *them*), and the small chamber had begun to feel like a prison. (When she protested that it wasn't fair, the other ladies in Sir Humphrey's party weren't being confined, he replied that the other ladies were not his sixteen-year-old sister!) But right now all she could think about was the window that looked over the courtyard and shield-shaped curtain wall. The same curtain wall that had collapsed and killed the two prisoners.

Her heart raced as fast as her feet as she climbed the seven—*seven!*—flights of stairs to the top level of the luxurious tower. The Scots might be "rebellious barbarians," but they certainly knew how to build castles, which was one of the reasons King Edward was so anxious to have Kildrummy destroyed. The "Hammer of the Scots," as King Edward was known, was making sure no other rebels could use the formidable stronghold as a refuge in the future.

Bright sunlight filled the room as she drew open the heavy door of the lord's chamber and tore past the enormous wooden bed, the half-unpacked trunks carrying her belongings, and the small table that held a pitcher and basin for washing. Heart now in her throat, she knelt on the bench under the window, leaned on the thick stone sill, and peered through the fine glazed window to the courtyard below.

She knew it was wrong, and her brother would be furious to discover her fascination with the rebel prisoner, but she couldn't help it. There was something about him that stood out. And it wasn't just his formidable size or his handsome face, although she had to admit that was what had attracted her initially. Nay, he was . . . *kind*. And noble. Even if he was a rebel. How many times had she watched him take the blame (and thus the punishment) for one of the weaker men? Or shoulder more than his share of the burden of the work?

He couldn't be . . .

She refused to finish the thought and scanned the cobble courtyard and wall area between the southeast tower and newly constructed gatehouse where the prisoners were working.

In the crowd of men near the wall there were no more than a handful of the rebels, but they were being guarded by at least a score of her brother's men. Given the state of the prisoners, it seemed an overabundance of caution. Perhaps when the castle was first taken over a month ago such a show of force might have been warranted, but stripped of their crude leather warcoats and weapons, after weeks of imprisonment with barely enough food and water to keep them alive, and being worked nearly to death all day, the raggedy-looking prisoners appeared ill equipped to mount much of a resistance.

Except for one.

She looked and looked, the panic rising in her chest. Where was he? Had he been one of the men crushed?

Hot tears prickled her eyes, and she told herself she was being ridiculous. He was a prisoner. A Scot. One of Robert the Bruce's rebels.

But he was also . . .

Her heart slammed, and she let out a small cry of relief, when the powerfully built warrior stepped out from behind the wall.

Thank God! He was all right. More than all right, actually—he was spectacular.

She sighed with every bit of her almost-seventeen-year-old heart. The women at court teased her mercilessly about her naivety and innocence. "You're such a child, Rosie-lin," they'd say with a roll of the eyes when she dared to venture into their conversations (the nickname sounded much nicer coming from her brother than from them).

Well, she certainly wasn't feeling like a child now. For the first time in her life, she was feeling like a woman utterly entranced by a man.

And what a man! He was the fodder of legend and bard's tales. Tall and broad-shouldered, his dark hair hanging in long tangled waves around a brutishly handsome face, he was one of the strongest, most imposing-looking warriors she'd ever seen.

As if to prove her point, he bent down to pick up an enormous stone. Her breath caught and her heart started to flutter wildly in her chest. Despite the coolness in the room, her skin warmed with a flush. The damp linen shirt stretched across his broad chest with the effort, revealing every ridge, every bulge, every sharply defined muscle straining underneath—of which there were an abundance. Even weakened by imprisonment, he looked strong enough to tear apart a garrison of soldiers with his bare hands.

She revised her earlier opinion: Perhaps the large number of soldiers keeping watch was prudent after all.

Only when he disappeared around the other side of the wall did she remember to breathe again. A few minutes later, he reappeared and it would start all over again. Every now and then, he would exchange a word or two with one of the prisoners, before one of the guards broke it up— usually with the flick of a switch.

He spoke most often to a tall, blond-haired man, though he wasn't as friendly to him as he was with the third red-haired man. He was also tall, but that was where the similarities ended. More than any of the other prisoners, the red-haired man was showing the effects of the hard labor. He was gaunt and pale, and every day he seemed to grow more stooped.

The Scot—that is how she thought of the impressive warrior—did what he could to help him when the guards were not looking, by shouldering some of his rocks or taking his place in line to wield the hammer. She'd even seen the Scot pass the other man the precious few ladles of water they were allowed during their brief breaks. But the man was fading before her eyes.

She turned away from the window. She had to stop. She couldn't do this. It made her feel so helpless. She knew they were rebels and deserved to be punished, but the man was going to die. That he would probably be executed anyway when the work was done didn't matter. No one should suffer like that.

She picked up her needlework, but she put it down a few minutes later and returned her gaze to the window.

She couldn't look away. She had to do something. But what? Her brother had warned her not to interfere.

The answer came to her the next morning after church. As she was leaving morning prayers, she caught sight of a serving woman carrying a large bowl and a few pieces of bread toward the prison—a paltry amount for so many men.

That was it! She would leave them extra food.

It took her a few days to come up with a plan, but eventually she was ready to put it in motion.

Sneaking extra bits of beef was the easy part. She wrapped them in the cloth she kept at her lap while she ate, and then tucked the bundle in the purse at her waist before she left. Getting the food to the prisoners, however, was the challenge.

She'd watched the prisoners enough to know their routine. Every morning the guards led them out through the small courtyard between the chapel and the damaged Great Hall to the main courtyard. They were lined up and given instructions before being permitted to collect the carts, which were stored on the side of the bakehouse. The carts were what she was aiming for.

That night, when the castle was quiet, she donned a dark cloak and snuck out of the tower. Keeping to the shadows, she worked her way around the yard, careful to avoid any guards who might be on patrol. But it was remarkably quiet. With the rebel forces crushed, there was little threat of an attack. She quickly deposited her bundle in one of the carts and made her way back up to her chamber.

The next morning she watched from her window as one of the men returned with the cart, immediately went to the Scot, and surreptitiously passed him the bundle. The Scot looked around, as if suspecting a trick, but when one of the guards barked an order at him—presumably to get to work—she saw the faint twist of a smile.

That smile was all the encouragement she needed. Her nighttime excursions continued for a week, and she swore the dark red-haired man grew stronger. Many of the men seemed to walk a little taller.

She knew her brother would be furious if he discovered what she was doing—and she hated the idea of a secret between them—but she told herself it was but a small gesture and could do no harm.

But she was wrong. Terribly wrong.

Rosalin yawned as one of the attendants who'd accompanied her from London finished twisting her long plaits under the veil and circlet. "You look tired, m'lady," the older woman said, a concerned look in her eye. "Are you not feeling well?"

After eight nights the loss of sleep was catching up with her, but Rosalin managed a smile. "Well enough, Lenore. Nothing a few extra hours of sleep won't cure. I fear I've been staying up with my brother and the earl—"

A shout from the courtyard below made her stop what she'd been about to say.

"I wonder what that is all about," Lenore said.

But Rosalin had already jumped from the chair and raced to the window. Her heart stopped, a strangled cry escaping from between her lips before she could smother it with her hand. The red-haired rebel was kneeling in the dirt, holding his side where one of the soldiers must have struck him. The cloth and pieces of beef and bread that she'd smuggled out to them last night were strewn on the ground in front of him. The soldier was shouting at him, using his fists and the back of his hand to punctuate his words.

It wasn't hard to guess what he was asking.

The red-haired man shook his head and the soldier hit him again—this time with so much force his head snapped back and blood sprayed around him like a bubble that had popped.

He crumpled to the ground.

She cried out in horror, and Lenore tried to pull her away. "Come away, m'lady. Those vile beasts are not fit for your eyes. Brigands and barbarians, that's what they are. I hope your brother draws and quarters every one of them!"

Rosalin barely heard her words. She shook her off, crying out again as she sensed—she *knew*—what the Scot would do. He roared forward, tossing off the two soldiers who'd been holding him as if they were poppets. His fist slammed into the jaw of the soldier who'd beaten his friend. The soldier had barely hit the ground when the Scot was over him, driving his powerful fist into him again and again like a battering ram until the soldier lay motionless on the ground.

It seemed there was a stunned pause before the courtyard erupted in chaos.

Lenore gasped in horror from behind her. "The prisoners are attacking!"

"No. Oh God, no," Rosalin groaned softly as the melee ensued. *What have I done?*

The Scot fought like a man possessed, like one of those berserkers of Norse legend. Using nothing but his hands, he fended off half a dozen of her brother's men. Each time one of them tried to get hold of him, he made some kind of quick maneuver and twisted out of the man's grasp. Usually the soldiers ended up on their backs. The blond-haired prisoner had managed to grab one of the hammers used to take down the wall and had taken a position at the Scot's flank. Together they were a two-man army.

One by one the other prisoners were subdued, but the two men seemed as if they could hold off capture forever.

But of course they couldn't. Without armor and proper weaponry, all it took was one well-placed pike in the side of the blond-haired warrior, and one powerful hit of the hammer on the ribs of the Scot, and the English had regained the upper hand.

Her heart was pounding. Tears were streaming from her eyes as her brother's soldiers surrounded the two men.

God in heaven, they are going to kill them!

Without thinking of what she was doing, only knowing she had to put a stop to the fighting, she raced down the stairs, heedless of Lenore's worried cries behind her. She reached the yard only moments after her brother and his men, two of whom prevented her from going farther than a few feet beyond the tower door. "You shouldn't be here, my lady," one of the men said. "Go back to the tower. This will all be over soon."

That was exactly what she feared.

"I need to see my brother." She tried to look around one of the men, but with the crowd of people who'd flooded the courtyard she couldn't see anything.

She heard her brother's voice from up ahead. "What is the meaning of this?"

A series of English voices responded with "stealing food," "find out," and "Scots attacked."

"Your man was beating a man to death for something he could not answer. He would have killed him had I not stopped him."

The sound of the deep, powerful voice reverberated through her like a clap of thunder, jolting in its intensity. It was her Scot; she knew it.

Her brother said something she couldn't hear and a few more English voices went back and forth.

Then her brother spoke again. "Take him to the pit, where he won't incite a damned riot."

"Is this your English justice, Clifford?" that deep voice sneered. "Killing a man for defending someone who could not fight back? I could have taken a dozen of your men with me—next time I will."

Rosalin tried to push through again, but one of the men—a knight who she thought was named Thomas—forcibly held her back. "Your brother won't like you being here, my lady. You need to get back to the tower."

"But what will happen to them?"

He gave her a quizzical look. "Why, they'll be executed, of course."

The blood drained from her face. She must have looked like she was going to faint, because he called another one of the soldiers over and together they steered her back into the tower.

Rosalin waited for what seemed like hours for her brother to return to his solar. Her hands twisted anxiously in her lap. The glass of wine that she'd drunk for courage tossed in her stomach.

She dreaded the conversation ahead of her but knew it could not be avoided. She couldn't let those men be killed because of what she'd done.

It was dark when her brother finally entered the room. He looked surprised to see her. "What are you doing here, Rosie-lin? I thought you'd be readying for the evening meal." He frowned, seeing the distress on her face. "Is something wrong?"

She blinked up at him, feeling the heat gather in her throat and behind her eyes. "It's all my fault!" Unable to hold back, the tears and emotion came pouring out. "I gave them the food. I didn't think there would be any harm and they looked so hungry. I was only trying to help." She latched on to his arm, tears streaming down her cheeks. "You can't punish them."

The jumbled confession took him a moment to sort through, but when he did, his face darkened. It wasn't often that her brother was angry with her, and she hated it. "Damn it, Rosalin, I told you to stay away from them! Do you have any idea how dangerous those men are?"

"I do. I swear I didn't go anywhere near them." She explained how she took the scraps of food to the cart at night. He seemed to relax a little, and his expression wasn't quite as thunderous. "I only wanted to ease their suffering. I didn't mean for this to happen."

He gave her a long, steady look. "You never meant for things like this to happen, which is exactly why you don't belong here. Your heart is too soft for war. These men are not one of your scullery maids with blistered hands or a serving wench who needs to spend more time with her sick baby rather than tend her duties."

"But Katie's hands were so chapped they were bleeding, and it wasn't fair that Meggie lost a week's pay because she missed a few hours—"

Her brother held up his hand, stopping her. "That's what I'm trying to say. These men are hardened killers—they are not deserving of your kindness."

She bowed her head, unable to meet his gaze. "I had to do *something*."

She heard him sigh and a moment later, he wrapped his arm around her and drew her to his side. Relief that he'd forgiven her only made her sob harder. "I'm so sorry."

He murmured soothing words and rocked her against him until she quieted. It reminded her of the night her father had died, and the night less than a year later when their mother had followed. "You can't stay here, little one. I should have sent you home right away, but I was selfish. I missed you, and seeing your face was like a breath of spring air in this cesspit."

She looked up at him, eyes burning. "You are sending me away?"

Please, not that. Anything but that.

He nodded solemnly. "Aye, but only for a while. I will come see you in London as soon as I am done here. The king will wish a report, and I can give it to him personally. I will bring Maud and the children. You'd like that, wouldn't you?" She nodded; he knew she would. He smiled teasingly. "Besides, I want to see all these suitors Hereford has been telling me about."

Heat crawled up her cheeks. That was one of the reasons she'd come. The attention at court had become impossible and none of the men interested her. No man had interested her until . . .

"Does that mean you will spare them?"

It took him a moment to follow her leap in conversation. His mouth tightened—whether from anger or the unpleasantness of the topic, she didn't know.

"Your misguided charity changes nothing."

"But it isn't fair—"

He cut her off in a voice that brokered no argument. "This is war, Rosalin. Fair doesn't enter into it. They nearly killed three of my men. Whatever the provocation, prisoners cannot be allowed to fight back. Ever. Especially these prisoners. They are not worth your tears."

"But—"

He cut her off again, his face getting that implacable, we're-done-talking-about-it look. "I will hear no more on the subject. These men have been given only a temporary reprieve from the executioner's axe. But they have proved too dangerous even for that. They are brigands who fight without chivalry and honor. Their leader is a vicious scourge who would slit your pretty neck without thinking twice. Do you understand?"

Her eyes widened. Her brother spoke with such conviction, but his words did not jibe with the man she'd watched the past couple weeks. Knowing that Cliff would not be gainsaid, all she could do was nod.

He smiled. "Good, then we will hear no more of this. What's this I hear about your taking after our illustrious ancestor?"

Rosalin blushed at the gentle teasing about her embarrassing nickname. Their infamous great-great-great-aunt Rosamund Clifford had captured the heart of King Henry II and had gone down in history as "The Fair Rosamund." Apparently, the men at court had taken to calling her "The Fair Rosalin."

She tried to play along with her brother's teasing, but she could not forget the horrible fate awaiting the men in the prison, especially the one languishing in the pit prison, who'd been forced to defend his friend because of her.

All through the evening meal and the long hours of the night it stayed with her. She could think of nothing else.

It was wrong. The word echoed over and over in her head no matter what she tried to do. Eventually the voice grew too loud to ignore. Sometime in the small hours of the night, she rose from bed, donned a pair of slippers and a dark hooded cloak, and slipped out of her chamber. She didn't know whether she could do anything, but she knew she had to try.

This was partially her fault, and rightly or wrongly, if she didn't do something, she would feel responsible for the deaths of those men for the rest of her life.

But it was one man's death that would haunt her. The man she'd watched for over two weeks, the man who'd sacrificed himself, who had selflessly given his food and shouldered more of the burden for his friend, did not deserve to die. She knew it deep in her soul with a certainty that could not be ignored. War or not, it was wrong, and she had to try to make it right, even if . . . even if it meant letting him go free.

Once the treacherous thought was out, it felt as if an enormous weight had been lifted from her shoulders. She knew what she had to do—or try to do, if it were possible.

Exiting the Snow Tower, she paused in the shadows to get her bearings. She didn't have a plan. All she knew was that the Scot had been moved to the pit prison, which was located below the old keep next to the burned-down Great Hall. She'd walked past it every night on making her deliveries—quickly, as the forbidding old stone building hadn't been used in some time and seemed very dark. But there was a torch there now, burning from its iron perch beside the doorway. Drawing a little closer, she kept tight to the shadows of the wall and watched.

Dear God, what was she doing? She couldn't help but feel the impossibility of her plight. How was a sixteen-year-old girl going to break anyone out of a pit prison without help? Without a plan? She couldn't very well just walk in there, open the door, and pull him out.

Could she?

What about the guards? Even though she couldn't see anyone right now, and the pit prison offered little chance of escape, there had to be at least one.

There was. A soldier appeared from the direction of the warden's tower, where the prisoners were being held, walked back and forth a few times in front of the entry to the old keep, and then disappeared. About five minutes later he did it again. After two more times, she had to hope it was a pattern. The next time he left, she waited until he was around the corner and then darted into the entrance of the keep.

It was pitch black and cold. *Very* cold. Chill-run-down-your-spine cold.

There are no such thing as ghosts . . . no such thing as ghosts.

But if the dead were ever inclined to walk the earth, this would be the perfect place to do so.

After giving her eyes a few moments to adjust to the darkness, she moved around the room, looking for the entrance to the pit prison, finding it in a small stone antechamber off the main entry. The room was no more than three or four feet wide, with a small wooden door covering one corner of the stone floor. She heaved a sigh of relief, seeing that the door had a simple latch rather than a lock.

How many minutes had gone by? Two, maybe three? Very carefully she slid the iron latch, her heart stopping more than a few beats when it squeaked—loudly. She froze, but when no one came rushing in with a sword drawn, she slid the latch fully out of the way and grabbed the edge of the wooden door to lift.

It was heavier than it appeared, and she struggled, but finally managed to open it. A rush of cold, dank air pushed her back for a moment, but eventually she kneeled over the hole and peered down into the darkness. It was dead silent. At first she didn't see anything, but then she saw the unmistakable glow of white gazing up at her.

She startled.

"Morning already?" he sneered. "I was just getting comfortable."

God, that voice! Deep and powerful, it seemed to reverberate through her bones. "Shhh," she whispered. "The guard will be coming back."

Though she knew it was impossible, she swore she could see him stiffen with surprise.

"Who are you?"

"Shhh," she pleaded again. "Please. The guard will hear you."

Leaving the door open, she raced out of the small antechamber and plastered her back to the wall next to the entry. Holding her breath for what seemed like eternity, she waited for the guard to approach. With each footstep her heart stopped, starting only when she heard the fall of the next. When the footsteps finally moved away, she ran back to the room.

"We have to hurry," she whispered. "He'll be back in a few minutes."

The Scot didn't waste time questioning her, taking charge in the coolly efficient manner of a man accustomed to the role. "They lowered me down with a rope tied to a latch in the wall. See if it's still there."

His voice was closer now, and she realized he must be standing right below her. Probably only a few feet separated them. She shuddered or shivered, she didn't know which, but turned around to do his bidding. She found the iron peg in the stone wall and sure enough, an old, frayed piece of rope was tied around it. Picking up the end, she moved back to the opening.

Seeing her shadow return, he asked, "Did you find it?"

"Yes."

"Throw it down."

She hesitated; suddenly the full import of what she was doing hit her.

After a long pause he spoke. His voice was harder—with disappointment maybe? "Change your mind?"

Had she? *No.* She wasn't wrong about him. But still, it was one thing to watch a man from a window and admire him and another to have him right next to you. "If I help you, you have to promise to leave without hurting anyone."

"I will not leave my friends behind to die."

She'd anticipated that. It was one of the reasons she was here—a noble leader would not leave his men. "But you will give me your word you will not hurt any of the guards?"

He made a sharp sound that might have been a laugh. "My word is good enough for you?"

"It is."

He paused as if her answer surprised him. "Very well,

you have my word that I will do my best to see that no one is killed."

He spoke the words with the solemnity of a vow. She had no reason to trust him, and yet she did. Enough to drop the rope.

She moved back, and in a shockingly few moments he was standing in front of her. *Looming* in front of her, actually. His large, muscular frame seemed to fill the entire room. Jesu, he was even taller and more formidably built than she'd realized! Instinctively, she shrank back, every one of her brother's warnings suddenly running through her mind.

Cut your throat . . . Vile barbarian . . . Vicious brute . . .

He stilled. "You've nothing to fear, lass. I will not harm you. I owe you my life."

Some of her fear dissipated. He might be built like a brute, but the man inside was noble of heart. She just wished it weren't so dark. She wanted to see his face up close, but she couldn't make out much more than shadows. Her other senses worked perfectly, however, and mingled with the dank air of the pit, she caught the musky edge of a well-worked body that was not as unpleasant as she would have expected.

"Who are you?" he asked.

She shook her head. "It's not important."

"Why are you doing this?"

She wasn't sure she knew herself, but standing here with him, she knew it was right. "It was my fault. I didn't mean for anyone to get hurt—I was only trying to help."

"You brought the food." He said it as if the last piece of a puzzle had just been fit into place, and it still didn't make sense.

She nodded.

"How old are you, lass?"

Something in his voice caused her to throw up her chin and straighten her spine. "Eighteen," she lied.

She could almost hear him smile. He couldn't be more than a handful of years older than she, but he made her feel so *young*. Even in the darkness it seemed as if he could see right through her. As if he knew her reason for helping him. He was probably used to women admiring him. Used to young, starry-eyed "lasses" who made themselves silly over him.

But it wasn't like that. She was righting a wrong. Mostly.

"No matter what your age, what you are doing is a kindness, and I thank you for it. What happened is not your fault, though I won't say I regret your thinking so, since otherwise I would still be in that pit."

He stopped, hearing something.

Oh God, the guard! She'd been so distracted by *him* that she'd forgotten about the guard. The soldier must have heard something and was coming to investigate. Before she realized what was happening, the Scot grabbed her, pulled her against him, and put his hand over her mouth.

She gasped soundlessly, first with shock and then with ice-cold fear. She felt as if she'd been enveloped in steel. Every inch of him was hard and unyielding, from the chest plastered against her back to the rock-hard arm tucked under her breasts. She tried to squirm free, but he tightened his clamplike hold, stopping her. When he enfolded her hand in his big, callused one, a strange warmth engulfed her. Not realizing what he was trying to do, she startled—at least she thought the shudder running through her was a startle. Capturing her fingers, he gently folded back four fingers and then three.

Suddenly, she understood. She pointed one finger. One guard. He nodded and slowly released his hand from around her mouth. She realized that he'd grabbed her only to prevent her from making any startled sound.

Her mind might know that, but her heart was still slamming against her chest with the aftereffects. Yet she knew that was not the only reason. She was suddenly aware of him. Aware of him in "a woman who's being held by a man for the first time" kind of way. He might be made of steel, but he was warm. Very warm. And no man had ever held her so intimately. She had the sensation of being tucked in against him, every part of their bodies fitted in snug and tight. She was sure it was highly improper, and she would be shocked later, but right now all she could think was how incredible it felt. Like she was warm and safe and nothing would ever hurt her.

He inched them against the wall, turning her toward it to protect her with his body. She could feel the muscles in his body tense as torchlight flooded the main chamber of the keep. The light drew nearer and nearer. The guard was coming this way!

She couldn't breathe. Both from fear and from being pressed up against a stone wall with a steel one behind her.

"What the hell?"

The soldier had noticed the open pit. He walked into the room and held the torch over the pit. The Scot sprang into action. He moved so fast, the soldier never had a chance. A sharp blow to the soldier's throat and a jab to the stomach pushed him back. He managed a cry of surprise before he fell into the hole. The torch went black and a moment later, the door was slammed shut.

The Scot spun her around to face him. "I have to go. They'll come looking for him."

She nodded wordlessly, still stunned by how fast it had happened.

"You will be all right?" he asked. "I will do what I can to make it seem as if we had no help."

"I will be fine." She paused, wanting to say something but not knowing what. "Please, you had best go quickly."

But she didn't want him to go. She wished . . . she wished she had a chance to know this man who'd captured her heart.

Perhaps he'd heard her hesitation—and guessed the reason for it. He turned to do as she bid, but then he, too, hesitated. Before she realized what he was going to do, he cupped her chin in his big hand, tipped her head back, and touched his lips to hers. She had the fleeting sense of warmth and surprising softness before it was gone.

"Thank you, lass. One day I hope we shall meet again, so I can repay you in full."

She watched with her heart in her throat as he disappeared into the darkness. She brought her hand to her mouth as if she could keep the moment there forever.

It had been a kiss of gratitude. The barest brushing of mouths, with no intent of passion. Even brotherly—on his part, at least. But in that one instant, she felt a spark of something big and powerful and magical. Something extraordinary. Something wonderful.

She might have stood like that until morning, but a sound from the pit prison below roused her from her dreamlike state.

Rosalin raced out of the keep and back up the stairs to her chamber, knowing that she might live with the repercussions of this night forever, but she would never regret it.

One

❧

Hannibal ad portas (Hannibal is at the gates)

Cranshaws, Scottish Marches, February 1312

The English would pay.

Robbie Boyd, King Robert the Bruce's authority in the Borders, stared at the blackened shell of the barn and vowed retribution.

His mouth fell in a grim line, the bitter taste of memory as acrid as the smoke burning his throat. He would never be able to see a razed barn without thinking of the one that had served as his father's funeral pyre. It had been the then seventeen-year-old Robbie's first lesson in English treachery and injustice. In the fifteen years since, he'd had many more.

But it would end. By all that was holy, he would make sure of it. No matter what it took, he would see Scotland freed of its English "overlords." No more sons would see their father's burned body hanging from the rafters, no more brothers would see their sister raped and brother executed, and no more farmers would see their farm razed and cattle stolen.

He didn't care if he had to fight for another godforsaken fifteen years, he wouldn't rest until every last English occupier fled from Scotland and the Lion—the symbol of Scotland's kingship—roared free.

Freedom was the only thing he cared about. Nothing

else had mattered from the first day he'd lifted his sword to fight alongside his boyhood friend, William Wallace.

Recalling the manner of his friend's death, Robbie's jaw hardened with the steely determination born of hatred. He turned from the smoldering timbers—the latest example of English "justice"—to face the villagers who'd cautiously begun to approach the manor house.

"Who did this?" he asked, the evenness of his tone not completely masking the ominous warning underneath.

But he already knew the answer. Only one man would be bold enough to defy him. Only one man had refused to renew the truce. Only one man had sent Robbie's missive requesting a parley back in embers.

A few of the villagers looked around before the village reeve, a farmer by the name of Murdock, cautiously stepped forward. The trepidation among the villagers wasn't unusual. As one of the most feared men in the Borders—hell, in all of Christendom—Robbie was used to it. Though his notoriety served its purpose in striking fear in the enemy, it wasn't without complications. It had sure as hell made keeping his identity secret as one of the members of Bruce's Highland Guard a challenge. Eventually he knew someone was going to recognize him, even with his features hidden. He'd become too well known.

"Clifford's men, my lord," Murdock explained. "They took everything. The cattle, the grain—even the seed—before setting the barn afire."

Clifford. God's bones, I knew it! Robbie's gauntleted fists clenched at his side, rage surging through him in a powerful rush.

It wasn't often that he lost his temper. As his size and reputation alone caused hardened warriors to shake in their boots, it served no purpose.

But there were two things guaranteed to test his control: one was the English knight who stood behind him, Alex "Dragon" Seton, his unlikely partner in the Highland

Guard, and the other was the English knight who'd imprisoned him six years ago and seemed to be thwarting him ever since, Sir Robert Clifford, King Edward's new Keeper of Scotland—in other words, Scotland's latest bloody overlord.

Devil take the English whoreson, Clifford would pay—for this and for old scores as yet unsettled. It was a reckoning long overdue. For six years, the bastard had eluded him, and now Clifford's defiance—his refusal to know when he'd been beaten—was threatening to ruin everything.

"*Take care of it, Raider,*" the king had said.

Robbie had a job to do, damn it. Bruce had put him in charge of enforcing the peace in the lawless, war-torn Borders. His war name of "Raider" attested to his experience in the area. The king was counting on him to bring the English barons to heel, and *no one* was going to stand in his way.

When King Edward left Berwick Castle last summer, forced to abandon his war against the Scots to attend to brewing trouble with his barons, Bruce had gone on the offensive, leading a series of well-executed raids into Northern England. For the first time, the English had gotten a taste of the devastating war the Scots had been experiencing for years. The raids had not only shifted the war from the burdened Scottish countryside to England, but also served to replenish the drained royal coffers by exacting payment from the Northern English barons in exchange for a truce.

The other barons had renewed their truces, but Clifford, the new governor of Berwick Castle, refused their "offer," and was continuing to resist. His resistance could encourage others to do the same, and Robbie sure as hell wasn't going to let that happen.

Bruce would have his truce and Clifford's cooperation; Robbie would bloody well see to it.

James Douglas, one of the three other warriors who'd accompanied Robbie and Seton on this "simple, straight-forward" mission (as if such a thing existed) to collect the feudal dues owed the king, muttered an expletive, echoing his thoughts a bit more crudely.

If anyone hated King Edward's new "Keeper" more than Robbie, it was Douglas. Clifford had made his name and fortune by the war in Scotland in part by laying claim to Douglas's lands.

"There is nothing left?" Douglas asked the farmer, his face growing dark with anger.

The Black Douglas hadn't earned his epitaph only for the color of his hair but also for his fearsome reputation. Mistaking the source of his rage, Murdock's hands shook as he tried to explain. "Nay, my lord. They took every-thing. Claimed it was the cost of dealing with 'the rebels.' They would have burned the entire village if we refused. We had no choice but to give it to them. It's the same ev-erywhere. Clifford's men raided the entire Eastern March from here to Berwick. The reeve at Duns sent a warning this morning, but it came too late."

Robbie swore. *Damn the bastard to hell!*

"Was anyone hurt?" Seton asked.

The farmer shook his head. "Nay, praise God. It's only the barn they destroyed—this time. But the fire was a warning. It's because they know we were dealing with Bruce that they came."

"The Bruce is your king," Robbie reminded him point-edly. In this part of Scotland, so near the English border, the people often needed it. Though Bruce had established his kingship north of the Tay, there were many in the south who reluctantly called Bruce king and whose sympathies still lay with the English.

Speaking of Scots who acted like Englishmen, Seton, whose lands in Scotland lay near here, jumped to the farm-er's defense. "I'm sure Murdock meant no offense to the king. He was only pointing out the difficulty for those who live surrounded by English garrisons with no one to defend them."

Boyd looked at him sharply, not missing the implied criticism. Seton often bemoaned the "damned-if-they-do, damned-if-they-don't" situation of the people who lived so near England. But everyone had to make a choice: for England or for Scotland; there was no straddling both sides of the line. Seton still didn't understand that he couldn't live in both worlds.

"Damnation." Douglas swore in frustration. "The king is counting on that grain and cattle. What the hell is he supposed to feed his men?"

The Bruce and a good portion of his army (and the Highland Guard when they weren't on other missions) had been laying siege to Dundee Castle for the past three months. With Edward in London and the threat of war abated, Bruce's focus had shifted to clearing the entrenched English garrisons from Scotland's castles.

It was the only way the war could truly be won. All the victories and momentum of the past few years wouldn't mean shite if the English continued to occupy their castles.

And they were making progress. Linlithgow had fallen after the raids last year, and Dundee was close. But all of it would soon come to a quick end if Robbie didn't do his job. The king was without funds, and with the required hundred days of free feudal service of many of the soldiers nearly up, if the siege were to continue, they had to find coin to pay the men and food to feed them.

It wasn't much of an overstatement to say that the future of the war rested on Robbie's shoulders. And if the path to victory depended on securing protective truces from the English barons who'd raided Scotland for years, he was damned glad to do it.

"The king will have his food," Robbie said flatly. *And his damned truce with Clifford.*

Douglas guessed what he meant, a slow smile spreading over his dark visage. Seton did as well, but his reaction was to clench his jaw as if he wanted to argue but knew it would do no good. Maybe he'd learned something the past seven years after all.

Clifford had thrown down the gauntlet, and Robbie sure as hell wasn't going to let it go unanswered.

Murdock, however, didn't understand. "But how? There is nothing left and they will only come again. You have to do something."

Robbie leveled his gaze on the farmer. "I intend to."

"What?" the farmer asked.

He would fight fire with fire, and strike in a place his enemy could not ignore. Something rare appeared on his face when the corners of his mouth lifted in a smile. "Take it back."

Berwick Castle, English Marches, One Week Later

"It isn't fair, Aunt Rosie-lin."

Rosalin looked down at the small, upturned face, at the cherubic features twisted with hurt, disappointment, and disbelief, and felt her insides melt.

Cliff's seven-year-old daughter, Margaret, had come bursting into Rosalin's solar almost in tears a few moments ago. Rosalin tried not to show her shock at her niece's attire. The poor thing was fighting so hard not to cry, she didn't want to push her over the edge.

Sitting down on the edge of the bed, she patted the space beside her. "Come sit, Margaret, and tell me what has happened."

Sensing that she'd found a pair of sympathetic ears, Margaret did as she bid, hopping up and settling in on the fluffy feather mattress next to her.

"It's Meg," she corrected, wrinkling her nose with distaste. "No one but Father calls me Margaret."

Rosalin's mouth twisted, trying not to smile. Instead,
she nodded solemnly. "Forgive me, *Meg*."

The little girl rewarded her with a tremulous smile, and
Rosalin melted a little more.

"That's all right," Meg assured her, patting her hand as
if their ages were reversed. "You only just got here, and
you haven't seen me since I was little."

Rosalin pretended to cough.

Meg's tiny, delicately arched brows drew together over
an equally tiny nose. "Are you sickly?"

Rosalin couldn't hide that smile. "Nay, Meg. I'm perfectly hale."

The little girl studied her. "Good. Andrew is always
coughing, and he isn't allowed to play outside. He's no
fun."

Rosalin felt a sharp stab in her chest but tried not to let
her fear show. Cliff's three-year-old son Andrew had always been frail. Though no one spoke of it, he was not
expected to see beyond his childhood.

Glad that the little girl was no longer close to tears, even
if she couldn't say the same, Rosalin asked, "So why don't
you tell me why you are wearing breeches and a lad's surcoat?"

Meg looked down as if she'd forgotten. "John said I'd get
in the way."

Rosalin didn't follow. "In the way . . . ?"

Meg gave her a little frown of impatience, as if she hadn't
been paying proper attention. "Of riding lessons. Father
gave John a horse for his saint's day last week, and today
he begins his training with Roger and Simon. It isn't fair.
John is two years younger than I am. I want to train like a
knight, too. He can barely pick up the wooden sword
Father gave him. How's he supposed to kill bloody Scots if
he can't lift a sword?" Rosalin coughed again and made a

note to tell Cliff to have care of his language around Meg. "He shouldn't have told Father when I borrowed it. No one likes a tale-teller."

Rosalin was having a hard time keeping up, so she just nodded.

The little girl's face crumpled. "Roger wouldn't let me stay, even when you can see my skirts won't get in the way. I don't want to sew with Idonia and Mother. Why won't they let me train with them?"

Because you're a girl. But as it didn't seem the right time to explain the harsh truth of the sexes, Rosalin gathered the sobbing child in her arms and sighed. She understood her pain. She, too, had wanted to be with her brother— probably even more so, since he was all she had. Learning that she couldn't simply because she was a girl had been a bitter draught to swallow.

Riding, practicing swordplay, and running around outside had seemed vastly preferable to sitting inside with a needle and lute. Of course, that was much too simplistic a view of their respective roles, but at Meg's age, she had seen it the same way.

After a moment, the little girl looked up at her, her long, dark lashes framing big, blue eyes damp with tears. She might look like her pretty, dark-haired mother, but Rosalin saw Cliff's stubbornness in the firm set of her chin. "Will you talk to him?"

"Talk to whom?"

"Father. He'll listen to you. Everyone says he's never refused you anything."

Rosalin laughed. "I assure you, he's refused me plenty. I wanted to ride and practice with a sword, too."

Margaret's eyes widened to almost comical proportions. "You did?"

"Aye. And I thought it just as unfair as you when he told me no."

The smile that spread across the little girl's face was al-most blinding. "You did? He did?"

Rosalin nodded, then paused for a moment to think. "What would you say if I took you on a ride tomorrow and let you practice by holding the reins?"

It clearly wasn't what Meg hoped to hear, but after a moment of disappointment, she decided to take what she could get and negotiate for better terms. Perhaps the little girl was like her aunt in that regard.

"For how long?" Meg asked.

"As long as you like."

"Where can we go?"

Rosalin paused, considering. She didn't want to venture far. "Your mother said there was a fair at Norham tomor-row. Would you like to go to that?"

Meg nodded enthusiastically and a moment later, she was running from the room, eager to lord her upcoming adventure over her siblings.

Rosalin called her back. "Meg!"

The little girl turned around questioningly.

"Wear a gown," Rosalin said with a smile.

Meg broke out in a wide grin, nodded, and skipped away.

A few hours later, Rosalin tracked down her very busy brother to inform him of her plan. She stood outside the door of the solar while he finished with his men.

As the newly appointed governor of Berwick Castle, Cliff had taken over the royal apartments and was using one of the receiving rooms as a council chamber.

She was so proud of him. Not only had the king left him in charge of the war, making him Keeper of Scotland, he'd also appointed him governor to one of the most important castles in the Marches. The castles of Berwick in the east, Carlisle in the west, and Roxburgh in the middle formed a key defensive band across the border to prevent the Scots from invading England.

She bit her lip. At least the castles *had* done so until last summer. Robert Bruce's raids into Cumbria and Northumberland had devastated the countryside, striking terror in the hearts of the English, from which they were still clearly recovering. Fear hung in the air, and the names of his fierce raiders were bandied about in terrified whispers, as if saying them aloud would conjure up the devil himself.

Douglas. Randolph. *Boyd.*

A sickly feeling swam over her. *Don't think of it . . .*

"Two thousand pounds?" she heard Cliff say, clearly furious. "He must be mad. Send the man away. I'll hear no more of their demands."

Rosalin waited until the men shuffled out, and then entered.

Seeing who it was, Cliff looked up and smiled, lifting some of the weariness from his face. "Ah, Rosie, I'm sorry to have kept you waiting."

"Is everything all right?" Clearly, it wasn't. Her brother was much changed since she'd seen him last. The war had taken its toll. He was still handsome, but he looked older than his two and thirty years. And harder.

He waved off her concern. "Nothing that can't be handled." He motioned for her to sit. "So what is it that you need?"

She could see him trying not to smile as she explained. By the end, he was shaking his head. "I know you told her she was too young to ride, but really, Cliff, she's seven years old. I don't see any good reason why a seven-year-old girl is too young and a five-year-old boy is not."

Leaning back in his chair, Cliff studied her over the length of the big wooden table that he used as a desk. "You've been here two days, and she's already found her champion? I wondered how long it would take her to find her kindred soul."

Rosalin's brow furrowed, not understanding. "Kindred soul?"

"You don't see it?" He laughed. "For God's sake, she's just like you, Rosie-lin, always rushing to someone's defense, always trying to right every wrong."

She frowned, taken aback. "I don't do that."

That only made him laugh harder. "God, it's good to have you here. I've missed you. I'm sorry I haven't been able to visit you more in London."

"You've been busy." It was an understatement. In the past five years, since Robert Bruce had returned from the grave to rise like a phoenix from the ashes of defeat, her brother had barely had a free moment. She'd seen him only twice in the six years since that one fateful trip to Scotland.

"I wasn't sure Sir Humphrey would ever give you leave to visit," he said dryly.

She hadn't been sure either. The earl had insisted that it was too dangerous, and . . .

Heat rose to her cheeks. "I think he was waiting for me to . . . ah . . . decide."

Cliff's expression changed. "And you have decided? This is whom you wish to marry? I will not have Hereford force you. I don't care if you are the ripe old age of thirty—I'll not have you tied to a man you don't care for."

"Two and twenty isn't as ancient as all that." She laughed. "Nay, you need not worry that Sir Humphrey has forced me into anything. He's been very patient. Although between you and me, I think both he and the king despaired that I would ever pick anyone."

"And you're sure Sir Henry is the one?"

Something in his voice caught her attention. She studied his face, but her brother hid his thoughts well. "Do you not like him, Cliff?"

"The question is not whether *I* like him, but whether *you* do, little one."

"I do," she said with a soft smile. "Very much."

Though she'd known Sir Henry de Spenser for only a few months, he had bowled her over with his gallantry and charm. If the lauded English knight was also tall, dark, and muscular, she was sure the resemblance to a certain Scot rebel was coincidental.

"Then that is all that matters," he said firmly. She frowned and would have asked him more, but he added, "I must admit that as glad as I am to see you, I am relieved you will be returning with Maud and the children to Brougham at the end of the month to prepare for the wedding."

Her formidable sister-in-law had insisted that they return to the Clifford stronghold in Cumbria (where Rosalin had been born and the closest thing to home for her), which was farther south and thus safer from "barbarians." It was some some distance from Berwick, but Cliff would be able to visit occasionally.

"Has it become so very bad?" she asked.

He hesitated, but then apparently decided to tell her the truth. "Aye. The Scots have grown bold with Edward gone, and someone needs to stop them or—"

He stopped, his jaw clenched hard.

"Or what?" she asked.

"Or they won't be stopped."

Her eyes shot to his. It seemed inconceivable that the rebels could actually *win*. She bit her lip. Her brother tried to keep her insulated from the war and the politics, but something made her start to ask, "Do you ever wonder if . . ."

Embarrassed by what she'd been about to say, she didn't finish the question.

But Cliff guessed. "I don't wonder, Rosalin. My job is to follow orders and do my duty to the king."

Feeling suddenly disloyal, she felt a fierce rush of pride in her brother. He was dutiful *and* loyal—one of the greatest knights in England—and she loved him. Of course he was doing what was right.

"Go on your ride to the fair, Rosalin, and take your little crusader with you. Roger is riding out with some of my knights; you can go with them. I think he will be proud to show his aunt his new squire's skills. Norham is as safe as Berwick. Not even Bruce's phantoms would dare anything near one of the most heavily garrisoned castles in the broad daylight."

Two

❧

Despite her brother's warning, Rosalin never dreamed it would be this bad.

Only three miles separated Berwick-upon-Tweed from Norham, but the moment they left the outskirts of the great burgh, they might as well have entered a different world.

The bucolic countryside she remembered from when she'd passed through Berwick on her journey south from Kildrummy Castle was nearly unrecognizable. Every tree, every blade of grass, every building bore the black-charred scar of razing. But it wasn't only the land that had been devastated, it was the people as well. She could see the fear on the peasants' grim, forlorn faces as they gazed up from their work to watch the large party of knights, ladies, and men-at-arms ride by.

It broke her heart. "My God, who did this?"

She didn't realize she'd spoken her thoughts aloud until her thirteen-year-old nephew Roger, who was riding beside her, answered. "King Hood himself. The usurper led his men through here last September. He started with the Earl of Dunbar's lands, then came over the Cheviot Hills into Northumberland, raiding and harrying as far south as Harbottle and Holystone for nearly two weeks between the feast of the Nativity of Mary and St. Cissa's Day, before scurrying back into his brigand's foxhole."

Rosalin had heard about Robert Bruce's raids while she

was at court at Whitehall last summer not long after King Edward returned to London. Cumberland had suffered a similar fate the month before, she recalled. But she'd never imagined . . . *this*.

Cliff had been safe at Brougham at the time with Lady Maud, so Rosalin hadn't sought out every detail as she usually did. She didn't want to take the chance of hearing *his* name.

"These poor people," she said. "Was there no one to defend them?"

Roger's mouth hardened, and her heart squeezed. He looked so like Cliff had at that age: tall and golden-haired, the lean build of youth already hinting at the formidable knight he would become. Also like Cliff, Roger was stubborn, determined, and fiercely proud, with a hefty dose of confidence. He had that air of invincibility seen in most young men who were training for knighthood but had yet to see battle.

"Most of the garrison at Berwick and Norham had left with King Edward the month before. No one expected Bruce to invade—or do it so quickly. Father had yet to be appointed governor of the castle."

Roger was too politic to criticize Cliff's predecessor, Sir John Spark, but Meg wasn't. "Don't worry, Aunt," Meg said, turning around to look up at her. "The cursed rebels won't show their vile faces around here again. Not with Father in charge."

Roger and Rosalin exchanged a look, trying not to laugh. But obviously he wasn't the only one to have inherited Cliff's pride.

Roger leaned over and ruffled his sister's hair fondly. "You've the right of it, brat. Father has the area well defended. Bruce wouldn't dare attack. Hell, I'd wager even the Black Douglas and the Devil's Enforcer Boyd would turn tail and run before facing Father's men."

Rosalin's heart slammed against her ribs at the mention

of *his* name. It wasn't an infrequent occurrence, as the name of Bruce's ruthless enforcer seemed to be mentioned nearly as often as Robert Bruce, Bruce's phantoms, or the Black Douglas.

Everyone had heard of Robbie Boyd. He was one of the most hated, reviled, and feared men in England.

The familiar guilt rose inside her, twisting her stomach in knots. She hadn't known . . . she hadn't realized that the man she was releasing was Robbie Boyd. Even at that time, he'd already made a name for himself, having fought alongside William Wallace in the early days of the war. It was said that Wallace trusted him so implicitly, he left Boyd in charge of his army in his stead, even though Boyd was not yet twenty years old at the time.

Setting one of Wallace's key commanders free was bad enough, but in the intervening six years it had become so much worse. While fighting for Bruce, Boyd's reputation had grown to prodigious proportions. Even far from the war in London they spoke of him with a strange mixture of terror, awe, and revulsion.

Unknowingly, she had helped free one of Scotland's most notorious rebels. Every story she heard—and there were a lot of them—weighed on her, making her question whether what she'd done was right.

At first, she hadn't second-guessed herself. The man she'd watched for weeks couldn't be as black-hearted as they said. There was good in him—he had a noble heart—she was certain of it. But over the years, as the stories took on a more sinister cast, her certainty wavered. Had her attraction to him blinded her to the truth? Had the star-filled gaze of a young girl in the throes of her first infatuation made her see things that weren't there?

She didn't want to think so, but the certainty she'd once known had long since faded.

Her only consolation was that her brother never suspected her role in the infamous prisoner's escape. Boyd had kept his word—on both counts. He made it appear as if his men had overpowered the soldiers and then freed him, and he hadn't killed any of her brother's men. Ironically, that had become the part that troubled her brother the most: why had one of the most fierce, ruthless warriors in Scotland not killed men when he had the chance? Especially after Boyd's forbearance in killing had not been rewarded before. Her brother didn't like inconsistencies or mysteries, and for years she'd lived in fear that he would discover her part in the escape.

Hunting Boyd down had become personal for Cliff. That he had once held one of Bruce's fiercest brigands and let him slip through his fingers was the one stain on an otherwise unblemished military career.

Cliff would be furious if he ever learned the truth. And worse, he would be disappointed—something she couldn't bear to contemplate. Her brother was the one constant in her life, and his approval—his love—meant everything to her. He could never learn what she'd done.

"I hope they try," Meg said. "Then Father will slay them and take their heads and stick them on the gate, and everyone will see them as they pass into the castle and know that Father is the greatest knight in England. Nay," she turned around so Rosalin could see her fierce little face, "in Christendom."

Roger laughed and ruffled her hair again before riding forward to join his friends. Rosalin hoped that would be the end of it, but unfortunately the men proceeded to recount some of the more horrific stories and deeds attributed to the Black Douglas and Robbie Boyd. The story of what had become known as the Douglas larder was the worst. All those men killed, tossed in the tower, and then burned? She shivered.

How could a man with the boyish nickname of Robbie do such horrible things? It couldn't be true.

Eventually she had to ask Roger to stop—he was upsetting his sister—but in truth it was she that he was upsetting. Meg, who had been devouring every word, protested, but Rosalin distracted her by letting her hold the reins for a while and teaching her how to make the small movements of her hands to steer the horse.

It took less than a half hour to reach the village. While Rosalin and Meg and the two attendants who'd accompanied them were left to explore the many stalls of the fair lined up along the high street of the village, Roger and the rest of her brother's men rode up the hill to the castle to meet with the commander of the garrison, presumably to discuss what they always discussed: war and Robert Bruce.

It was a chilly morning, and as the day drew on, it became even colder as the gray skies descended around them. Though she and Meg both wore hooded cloaks, Rosalin decided to purchase a couple of extra wool plaids for the ride back to Berwick.

Cognizant of the time approaching for them to meet Roger and the other soldiers, she quickly picked two weaves in soft blues, greens, and grays. She had just finished bundling them both up when she heard a strange shout.

Normally, she wouldn't have paid it any mind—fairs were often loud and boisterous—but something about it sent an icy chill trickling down her spine.

Meg must have sensed something unusual as well. "What was that?"

They were standing at the far end of the high street, near where they were supposed to meet Roger, and it was difficult to see through the crowds and stalls to the other end of the village where the sound had come from. "I don't know, sweeting. Probably nothing."

But it wasn't nothing. No sooner had she spoken than more cries rang out. In an instant, the already chaotic and crowded fair broke out into utter pandemonium.

She grabbed the arm of a woman who was running past her. "What is happening?" she asked.

The woman's face was white with fear. "An attack, m'lady. The rebels are raiding the fair!"

Stunned, Rosalin immediately released her arm and the woman disappeared in the sea of people who'd flooded the street and were pouring toward them. It couldn't be an attack. Not in the middle of the day. Not in *Norham*. Not even the Scots would dare flout her brother's authority like that.

But they had—were. Oh God, what was she going to do?

She froze, having never been so scared in her life. A shout of "fire!" only added to the fear.

Suddenly, she felt a sharp tug on her hand. "Aunt Rosalin?"

Gazing down into the small, trying-not-to-look-frightened but obviously terrified face of her niece, Rosalin's head instantly cleared. She schooled her features, showing none of the fear she felt inside. Meg needed her. "There is nothing to worry about, sweeting, the bad men won't hurt—"

She stopped. Her mouth gaped. *Dear God in heaven.* Behind the sea of moving people, she caught her first glimpse of the invaders and everything she'd been about to say—everything she *thought* she knew about warriors, knights, and soldiers—fizzled out like a torch dunked in water.

She would have made the sign of the cross if she thought it would protect her. But nothing could protect her from these men.

Brigands. Pirates. Barbarians. She'd thought the names for the Scot warriors an exaggeration. But they weren't. The raiders looked nothing like the gleaming mail-clad English knights with their colorful surcoats and banners. They wore darkened helms and crude black leather warcoats, some riveted with bits of steel. A few wore mail

coifs, but those, too, were blackened. But most terrifying
of all were the weapons that seemed strapped to every inch
of their massive chests. She'd never seen so many poleaxes,
swords, hammers, and spears in her life.

If the knights were figures of faerie tales, the Scots were
creatures of nightmares. They looked rough, violent, and
utterly deadly. No wonder the Scot raiders had been compared to the Vikings. The terror her ancestors must have
felt watching the longboats approach their shores must be
the same her countrymen felt now seeing the wild Scots
ride across the border.

She could see only a handful of them, but it was enough.
All thoughts of getting out of the way or hiding fell to the
wayside.

"We have to get to the castle," she said to Meg and the
terrified servants. Behind the castle walls they would be
protected. Norham Castle was one of the most impenetrable strongholds in the Borders, nearly as impenetrable as
Berwick Castle. "We'll be safe there," she assured the
wide-eyed little girl. "With Roger and the rest of the men."

Unfortunately, Roger wasn't in the castle.

No sooner had Rosalin grabbed Meg's hand and plunged
into the crowd, the two attendants following, than she
heard the fierce pounding of hooves ahead of her.

Oh God, no, please don't let it be . . .

But her prayer wasn't answered. In the blur of knights
and men-at-arms riding past them, she caught sight of her
nephew near the rear of the party. They must have been
already approaching to meet her and Meg when they realized what was happening.

How many of Cliff's men had accompanied them? She
hadn't counted earlier. Twenty? Maybe a few more?

Against how many of the enemy? She didn't know; she
just prayed it would be enough.

The crash of steel on steel was deafening—and much
closer than she'd anticipated. A few women in the crowd

let out terrified shrieks. One of the serving women started to cry behind her. The smoke was thickening, turning the skies to night.

Rosalin glanced down the street and not forty feet away, her brother's men were exchanging blows of their swords with the attackers. She heaved a sigh of relief, seeing that the Scots were outnumbered by about two to one. And thankfully, Roger, at the rear, was nowhere near the fighting.

But her relief didn't last long. Within an instant, two of her brother's household knights fell beneath the enemies' swords. She cried out in horror. Some of her brother's fiercest champions had just been cut down like butter.

She forced her gaze away. Though she desperately wanted to watch and make sure Roger was all right, she had to get Meg to safety.

Rosalin tried to forge through the crowd that had slowed as people turned to watch—as she had—the unfolding battle happening just a short distance away. A few voices rang out around her, offering encouraging words, if a bit colorfully, to the English soldiers. She forced herself not to look as she concentrated on getting Meg to safety.

Meg, however, was still watching. They'd just reached the place where the road funneled into the village and headed up the hill to the castle when she let out a cry and tried to pull away.

Rosalin turned around. "What is it, Meg? What's wrong?"

The little girl pointed toward the village. "The brigand has Roger."

Rosalin's heart dropped like a stone. Through the swarm of people still trying to fight their way out of the village, through the dust of battle, through the black smoke and flames now engulfing the village, she could see that Meg spoke true. Roger had been unhorsed, and he was being held up by the scruff of his neck like a pup by one of the rebels.

An eye for an eye. Clifford was going to lose his mind.

Robbie smiled from behind the cold steel of his darkened helm as he watched one of Northern England's most important villages go up in flames. He felt nothing but satisfaction for a job well done. Pity had been burned out of him a long time ago.

Maybe it had been his sister's rape, or his brother's execution, or the miles and miles of Scottish scorched earth he'd seen left in the wake of an English army, the bodies of people who'd dared to disagree with their English overlords, torn apart by horses, the heads of his friends on gates, or any of the other countless atrocities he'd witnessed since the first, when he'd seen his father's burned body hanging from the rafters. But somewhere in the past fifteen years, his hatred for all things English was complete.

And no one epitomized England for him more than Robert Clifford. *Sir* Robert Clifford, he amended. Clifford was just one more English bastard in a long line who wore his knighthood like a cloak of hypocrisy, as if he could hide the injustice of tyranny behind a shimmering shield of chivalry.

It wasn't just the opportunistic attempt to conquer their land and usurp the throne of a sovereign nation—although that was enough. Never far from Robbie's mind was the friend who'd lost his life under Clifford's command. Thomas Keith, his kinsman and boyhood companion, had escaped from Kildrummy prison only to die two days later. For Thomas, their rescue had come too late. The beating that he'd suffered at the hand of Clifford's soldier had proved too much.

Robbie frowned as another memory struck. He supposed there was one exception to his hatred of all things English. He could still remember his shock at looking up from that hellish pit where he'd thought to spend his last night and realizing that not only was his savior a woman, she was also *English*. He had assumed their guardian angel (what his men had taken to calling the person bringing them food) was one of the Scottish serving lasses who'd remained at the castle when it was taken.

Another memory followed. This one of the softest, sweetest lips he'd ever tasted. Lips that had been completely *wrong* for him to taste in the first place. Thanks to the cloak and the darkness he'd seen her face only in shadows, but if the lass had been eighteen, he'd drink the swill the English called brandy for a week.

Even after six years, he still couldn't say why he'd done it. Maybe because she was so young and innocent, and he'd been living in hell for so long. Maybe because he'd realized why she'd helped him and had been unexpectedly touched. It wasn't the first time a young lass had thought herself enamored, but it sure as hell had been the most opportune. He'd wanted to thank her. He still did. But after all these years of trying to find out who she was, he almost wondered whether he'd imagined her.

Strange that he still thought of her at all, especially when the memory invoked thoughts of what had been some of the darkest days of his life.

Thanks to Clifford.

But Robbie would bring the English baron to heel in the end, of that he was damned sure. The arrogant bastard wasn't going to be able to ignore this. Such a bold attack right in the heart of his "realm" was a direct affront to Clifford's authority and would prove to him there was nothing they wouldn't dare. It would bring him to the table. He'd sign the damned truce and pay the two thousand pounds just like all the others.

Carrying off an attack of such magnitude in the shadow of one of the largest English garrisons in the Borders was a daring proposition even for one of the elite members of the Highland Guard. But Robbie had planned everything down to the smallest detail. He always did. It was part of why Bruce's war had been so successful. They'd learned from Wallace's successes and not only built on them but improved them. The terrifying, wild "pirate" raids of which the English accused them had become extremely disciplined and well-organized professionally waged attacks.

And so far everything was proceeding exactly as he had planned. Well, except for the soldiers. But his men were dealing with the unexpected resistance. Quite quickly, it appeared—even though they were out-manned by at least two to one.

He smiled again. This might not be a mission dangerous enough for the Highland Guard, but the men Robbie had brought with him were his own, and he'd taught them well.

Though tempted to join the fun himself, he was in charge and had to stand back and make sure nothing went wrong.

With one eye on the battle taking place down the street, he watched while two of his men loaded the grain, goods, and coin that would fund the king's army for the next few months onto the sumpter horses they'd brought for that purpose. With the exception of a few chickens, they didn't bother with the livestock. It would only slow them down, and unlike their typical raids conducted well away from any castle, for this they were going to need to disappear fast.

He stiffened as Seton, who'd been overseeing the men setting the fires, approached. From his angry stride, Robbie guessed what he was going to say.

"I thought you said no one would be hurt."

Robbie clenched his jaw. "I gave the same orders as the king: no one is to be hurt unless they resist. It's a mercy, I'll point out, not often returned by your English countrymen.

But as you can see," he pointed to the soldiers, "they are resisting."

Seton's face was hidden behind his helm, but Robbie saw his eyes narrow at the word *countrymen*. Though raised in Scotland, Seton had been born in England, where most of his family's lands were, and Robbie never let him forget it.

But they'd been partners for too long for Seton to be so easily baited. "I told you this was a bad idea. It's too dangerous. But Clifford tweaked your pride, so now you have to tweak his. Even if we all end up swinging from the gibbet."

Robbie's jaw clenched even harder. He was well aware of Seton's feelings on the matter. What had started out as an ill-fated partnership between them in the Highland Guard had never materialized into anything else, despite their leader Tor "Chief" MacLeod's intent. They'd learned to tolerate each other, work together, and rely on each other when they had to, but they would never see eye to eye.

If anything, the tension between them had gotten worse since their unfortunate pairing in the early days of the war. Seton's dissatisfaction with how they were winning this war had been growing for some time. But if they'd played knights the way Seton wanted, they'd still be outlaws "lost" in the damned Isles.

"This isn't about pride," Robbie said, annoyed in spite of his vow not to let Seton get to him. "I'm doing my job. Bruce needs the food and the truce. If you have a problem, take it up with the king."

"I intend to."

The two men faced off against each other, as had happened too many damned times to count. Finally, Seton stepped back—as had also happened too many times to count. Seton might have been born in England, but being raised in Scotland had given him some sense. He knew better than to challenge Robbie. His reputation had been well earned.

Seton shook his head, gazing at all the destruction around him. "Where the hell is the justice in this?"

The question hadn't been directed at him, but he answered anyway. "An eye for an eye—that's the only justice the English understand. Looking for anything else only makes you naive."

"Better naive than dead." Seton held Robbie's gaze. "Or as good as dead."

Robbie's eyes narrowed. *What the hell did he mean by that?*

Before he could ask, Seton said, "We have what we need. We should go in case any more of Clifford's men are about."

It took Robbie a moment to realize what Seton meant, but when he looked back down the street at the soldiers his men were battling, he recognized what he hadn't noticed before: the arms of some of Clifford's household knights.

God's bones, this was even better than he could have hoped for! A raid right in the heart of Clifford's dominion *and* defeating a force of his men?

He smiled. "Don't worry. We'll be leaving soon enough. The men are almost done."

He instructed the two men loading the horses to finish up, helping to fasten the last sacks himself.

Seton had left to gather the rest of the men, when one of Robbie's men came racing toward him. Despite the helm, Robbie recognized him instantly from his slight build. Malcolm Stewart, a distant kinsmen of his, might be only seventeen, and half the size of most of the men around him, but he fought with the heart of a lion.

"Captain," he said anxiously. "We have a problem."

"What kind of problem?"

"Sir Alexander has Clifford's son."

Robbie stilled. In the din of the battle taking place all around him, he thought he hadn't heard him right. "What did you say?"

"Lord Fraser has Clifford's son."

Robbie muttered a curse as if it were a prayer. He couldn't believe it. Was it possible? Could fortune have shined on him so brightly? "What the hell is the problem? Take him!"

Having Clifford's son as a hostage would leave the English commander no choice. Clifford would have to accede to their demands.

Robbie couldn't have planned for anything more perfect.

"That's not the problem. The problem is the lady, Captain. She won't let go of the boy and Sir Alexander doesn't want to hurt her."

As much as he liked MacLeod's young brother by marriage, Alexander Fraser was a knight and like his English counterparts, chivalrous to a fault.

Robbie scanned the battle. Not seeing them, he realized that they must be away from the main part of the army. "Take me to them."

But they'd taken only a few steps before Robbie heard a sound that told him their fortune had just changed.

"The gate!" Seton shouted in warning.

Robbie swore. "I see it."

The English garrison had apparently decided to leave the comfort and protection of their stone walls and come to their countrymen's aid, probably because of the lad.

Robbie and his men had overstayed their welcome. But he had no intention of leaving the boy behind. He could see him now—and the plaid-cloaked problem. The woman had her back to him, but she was clutching the boy, trying to pull him away from an obviously uncomfortable Fraser, who was doing his best to try to detach her from the boy without being too rough and equally obviously having a difficult time of it.

The woman was tenacious; Robbie would give her that.

She wouldn't let go. He'd recalled a few of the sort at the Highland Games.

He swore again, glancing at the hill. The soldiers from the castle were closing in quickly.

His mouth fell in a hard line. They didn't have time for this. He would take care of the problem himself.

Three

Rosalin had to do something, as clearly no one else could. The one knight who was close enough to come to Roger's aid was deep in a fight for his own life. Her brother's men— battle-hardened knights and men-at-arms—were being cut down as if they were wet-behind-the-ears squires. Roger *was* a wet-behind-the-ears squire. He wouldn't last longer than it took the warrior to swing his massive two-handed sword.

She knelt down and took Meg by the shoulders. "I'm going to get Roger."

"I want to go—"

Anticipating the little girl's instincts—probably because they were her own—Rosalin cut her off. "I need your help. I need you to run as fast as you can up that hill and tell them that they must send soldiers. Tell them that Lord Clifford's son is in danger. Can you do that?"

Meg nodded uncertainly.

Not willing to rely on the child to keep her promise, Rosalin saw her safely entrusted to the arms of the sturdier of the two attendants, with a stern warning to not let her go until they'd reached the safety of the closed gate.

Rosalin didn't think she'd ever run so fast. She prayed every second it took her to wind her way through the crowd and cross the distance to her nephew. *Don't let me be too late . . .*

"My father will kill you for this! He will see all of your rebel heads on spikes!"

She nearly sighed with relief, hearing Roger's voice— even if she wished that indelible Clifford pride would show more discretion in issuing threats to large, menacing-looking barbarians with sharp swords. Her too confident, thirteen-year-old intent-on-being-a-fearsome-knight nephew was going to get himself killed.

Pushing her way past the last few fleeing villagers, she was at last able to see him. The Scot was still holding him by the neck, with Roger's sword at his feet, having dis-armed the youth rather than kill him. *Thank God!*

"Let me go, damn it!" Roger thrashed around, pulling on the hand of the man holding him.

"Let him go!" Rosalin shouted, echoing her nephew's demands. Racing forward, she threw herself between them.

She didn't know which one of them looked more sur-prised. Beneath the steel helms she could see both sets of blue eyes widen.

The rebel recovered first. "Get back, my lady," he said, in the same surprisingly refined Norman French that she'd instinctively used. Although she was fluent in the English more typically used by people in the North and Borders, French was the language of nobles and the court. "I don't wish to hurt you."

"Then let go of him!" she said fiercely, latching on to her nephew and trying to free him from the warrior's hold.

Her appearance incited a renewed frenzy in her neph-ew's effort to free himself. Together they fought against the much larger warrior and struggled to free Roger from his vise-like grip.

They almost succeeded. Roger saw just as she did that the warrior wasn't going to draw his weapon, not with her there (apparently there was some vestige of chivalry even in barbarians), and they used it to their advantage.

A fierce Viking game of tug-of-war ensued, with Rosalin trying to insert herself between Roger and the warrior. If his frustrated swearing was any indication—at least she assumed it was swearing from his tone, as it was spoken in Gaelic—their efforts were taking a toll.

Finally, she freed Roger's habergeon from the warrior's grip (he'd been holding the mail shirt and not Roger's neck as she'd thought) and was about to pull him free, when she heard a horse galloping up behind her.

She turned and caught the heart-stopping, blood-chilling flash of an enormous shadow looming over her right before darkness smothered her. Instinctively she cried out and raised her hands to claw at the thing covering her head. It was coarse and scratchy and smelled of grass. Nay, grain, she realized. Barley.

The vile beast had put a sack over her head!

She fought to rip it off, realizing her mistake too late. She'd let go of Roger. Only for an instant, but it was enough. The terrifying shadow barked some kind of order in Gaelic, presumably to the warrior who'd been holding Roger, and an arm circled around her waist. At least she thought it was an arm, though it felt more like a steel hook. With her as the fish!

She gasped, too shocked to scream, and in one smooth motion, he lifted her off the ground and none-too-gently slung her over his lap.

Her ribs and stomach met the rock-hard muscles of his thighs with enough force to jar the air from her lungs in a hard whoosh.

All at once the reality hit her. She was being abducted. Fear raced through her veins, setting off every primitive instinct inside her. To fight. To flee. To live.

She screamed and thrashed about wildly in his lap, trying to get free, not caring that they were riding faster than she'd ever ridden in her life. She'd take her chances with the ground. It would be more forgiving.

Her captor swore, the crude oath recognizable in any language, and one big hand covered her bottom to hold her more firmly against him.

The shock of a man's hand on such an intimate part of her body made every muscle in her body still.

She forgot to breathe.

She could feel the size of his palm, feel the length of every finger, as his gauntleted hand held the soft flesh. His grip was firm, not rough or threatening in any way, but still her blood went cold with terror.

"Don't move," he warned in a low voice, the gravelly lilt of the Gael lending a shiver-inducing edge to his English. "You won't be of much use to the boy if your head is splattered on the rocks."

Roger! Oh God, he was right. As desperately as she wanted to get away, she could not do so without Roger.

But it wasn't just the barbarian's words that sucked the fight right out of her. It was also her sudden awareness of the part of him wedged against her stomach. The very big, very hard part of him that reminded her that for a woman, there were fates far worse than abduction.

Every scary story she'd ever heard about the Scots picked that moment—the very worst moment—to come back to her. Rape, torture, and God knew whatever other hideous manners of death they might devise filled her head with ghastly images and made her do as he bade. For now.

What the hell was wrong with him? Obviously, Robbie had neglected certain areas of late if the frantic wiggling of a woman—and an *English* woman at that—was enough to get a rise out of him.

It was bloody embarrassing. Shameful even. He shuddered to think of the shite he'd hear from MacSorley if he ever found out. Erik "Hawk" MacSorley could always be counted on to lighten the mood during the tense, dangerous missions of the Highland Guard, but Robbie preferred when it wasn't at his expense. And Robbie, who hated all things English, stiffening like a lad with an Englishwoman would be sure to qualify.

With so many willing Scottish women throwing themselves in his path, he had never considered looking south of the border. His reputation as the strongest man in Scotland fostered at the Highland Games over the years was not without its benefits. With the exception of Gregor MacGregor, whose war name of "Arrow" attested to his skill with a bow rather than his reputation as the most handsome man in Scotland, Robbie had more female admirers than anyone. Besides, if he'd ever seen an attractive Englishwoman (and right now he couldn't recall one), as soon as she opened her mouth any spark of lust would surely die a cold, quick death.

Hell, the woman strewn over his lap was probably old enough to be his mother if, as he initially suspected from the simple plaid, she was one of Clifford's servants.

His gaze fell to the hand that still gripped the surprisingly curvaceous and firm, plaid-covered bottom, peeking out from beneath the edge of the burlap sack he'd requisitioned from some of their spoils to drop over her head. He frowned, reconsidering. Perhaps not so old after all.

Guessing what it was that had stopped her wriggling, he removed his hand. He was tempted to tell her that her fears were unfounded. He did not abide the rape of women, and God help the man in his command who thought otherwise. But he doubted she would believe him. And as he'd learned from fighting this war, fear could be a powerful weapon. If it kept her still until he could be rid of her, it would be worth it.

And he planned to do exactly that—be rid of her—as soon as it was safe. Chancing a glance behind him, he saw that the English soldiers giving chase from the burning village were not too far behind. But that wouldn't last.

With the woman secure, he urged his mount faster across

the flat fertile valley of the Tweed River. It wasn't long before the ground started to rise and they entered the altogether different terrain of the Lammermuir Hills. The hills and forests of the Borders—like those of the Highlands—were Bruce territory. The English might control the castles, but the Scots controlled the countryside. The light, agile, and sturdy hobby horses Robbie and his men used had been bred for this type of terrain, and it wasn't long before their English pursuers faded into the distance behind them.

He slowed, but it wasn't until another hour had passed, and they were deep in the forested hills, that he finally signaled his men that it was safe to stop.

They needed to water the horses, and despite the fact that she hadn't moved an inch since his warning, he was damned uncomfortable and eager to rid himself of the lad's fierce protector. Fraser could take the woman for a while, as it was he who'd neglected to deal with her properly in the first place. Not that Robbie had fared much better, he had to admit. As much as he disdained all the chivalry shite, he had never struck a woman before. He supposed he could have left her standing there when she'd finally detached herself from the lad, but it had seemed more expedient just to take her. Hell, if she was that attached to the boy, she might even be of some use.

If Robbie's eye had strayed a few too many times to that surprisingly taut bottom, he told himself it was only deprivation. Deprivation that would be dealt with as soon as he returned to camp. He'd neglected Deirdre of late, but would make it up to her. God knew he had reason to celebrate.

Clifford's son . . . Nay, not just his son. From his size and age, the boy had to be his *heir*.

He still couldn't believe the means of bringing Clifford to his knees had fallen right into his lap.

His gaze fell to that bottom again. Well, at least *something* had fallen into his lap.

Dismounting, Robbie would have pulled her off after him, but Seton grabbed him by the arm and swung him around to face him. "What the hell do you think you're doing? We're making war on women and children now?"

Robbie shot him a warning glare, not just for the hand on his arm (which was quickly dropped), but also for speaking in English.

"Not here," he replied in Gaelic. He motioned to Malcolm, who had ridden up beside them. "See to the woman and the boy."

He headed toward the loch, his fists clenching tightly. He should have known his partner would object. But if Seton wanted a fight, Robbie would be damned happy to give him one.

After being bounced around on a horse for what seemed like hours, while simultaneously trying to keep her body from slamming against her captor's (which was about as forgiving as a stone wall), Rosalin could have wept with relief when the brute finally called what she assumed was "halt" in Gaelic.

Every bone in her body ached—even her teeth, which were still rattling from the constant jarring. Her ribs had taken the brunt of the abuse, and if they weren't broken they certainly felt like it. And her poor stomach seemed to have been turned permanently upside down. She was glad she hadn't eaten anything at the fair, or the sack over her head could have been much worse. It was smothering enough without sharing it with the contents of her stomach.

Rolling her forward off his lap with all the consideration of a sack of flour, her captor dismounted.

Rosalin wanted to offer some kind of protest. She'd never been treated so ignobly in her life. But she was brutally aware that far worse could be yet to come. So she kept her protests to herself and lay still, waiting.

What would he do with her—with them?

Fear and apprehension tensed her already bruised and battered limbs. But instead of more manhandling, she heard the angry voice of a man who spoke in clean, clear, crisp English and seemed to be challenging her captor's decision to take them.

She didn't need to understand the harsh reply to know that the challenge was not a welcome one.

Something prickled at the back of her neck—and it wasn't a scratchy thread of hemp from the sack. Without the buffering sound of the wind and pounding of hooves, she was able to hear her captor's voice clearly for the first time. There was something about the deep, rough tones that made her ears prick and her spine tingle. Something that made a tiny warning bell ring inside her head. Something that tickled the fringes of a memory.

But then it was gone, and she realized it was probably just an innate sense of self-preservation. The primitive instinct of a hare who hears the flap of the falcon's wing for the first time and senses danger. And there was no doubt that a man with a voice like that was dangerous.

She stiffened when hands grabbed her again. But it was clear they were not the hands of the same man who'd taken her. The grip was far less firm and confident, and the man seemed to struggle with her weight as he half lifted, half slid her off the horse.

The sack must have caught on part of the saddle, because it did not come with her. No sooner had her feet touched the blessed solidness of *terra firma* than she felt the welcome rush of fresh air into her lungs. She blinked as the darkness of the sack gave way to the light of day, or at least what remained of it. The short days of winter were not helped by the heavy gray mist, and though it was probably only a few hours past midday, the light had dimmed to an eerie twilight.

Still facing the horse, Rosalin's legs nearly gave out when the man released her.

"Sorry, my lady," he said, catching her arm to steady her.

She turned at the surprising sound of his voice and found herself gazing into the ruddy, freckle-faced countenance of a youth of no more than eight and ten. Compared to the terrifying-looking brutes she'd seen before, his friendly, boyishly handsome face and thin, nonthreatening build allayed some of her immediate fears of rape, death, and dismemberment.

From beneath his steel cap, his eyes widened in shock, and he took a step back.

It took her a moment for her to realize why. Rosalin had never cursed her face, but she did so now. Hastily, she drew on the hood that must have slipped off in the struggle with the sack and sank back into its dark woolen folds.

But the boy was still staring at her shadowed face, slack-jawed.

"Malcolm, what the hell's the matter with you, lad? The captain told you to take care of the hostages."

From beneath the safety of her hood, Rosalin glanced at the newcomer. But she had barely taken in the fierce-looking warrior before he thrust her nephew forward and all her attention shifted to the boy.

"Roger!" she exclaimed, rushing forward to catch him in her arms. "Thank God! Are you all right?"

After a relieved squeeze, she held him out to look at him, having to tilt her head back to meet his gaze. Though only three and ten, he was already taller than she. She drank in ever inch of his dirty face and rumpled golden hair. He'd lost his helm and his surcoat was torn and heavy with mud, but he appeared unharmed.

"I'm fine," he assured her. "Are you?"

She nodded, tears of relief squeezing her throat with emotion.

Thankfully, the warrior had moved off during their reunion, but she was conscious of the youth watching them.

His mouth was now closed, but he was still staring at her with a slightly dazed expression on his face.

In other circumstances it might have been rather sweet, but right now all she could think about was if this was the boy's reaction, what would the men do when they saw her? Ruffians. Outlaws. Men who lived beyond the law would not hesitate to . . .

She shivered. Dear God in heaven, she had to do something!

Glancing around, she saw that they were standing in a small clearing near a stream a few dozen yards from any of the other warriors. To her profound but grateful shock, none of the ruffians were paying them any mind while they tended their horses. Obviously, no one thought them a threat. She was sure Roger would be greatly offended, but she was thrilled with their good fortune.

Knowing they might not get another opportunity like this, and that the sooner they escaped the better (her brother's men couldn't be that far behind), she didn't waste any time.

"Catch me," she muttered under her breath to her nephew. She started swaying dramatically. "Oh!" she gasped. "I don't feel . . ."

She let her words fall off and promptly swooned, crumpling like a poppet of rags.

Her startled nephew barely caught her before she hit the ground.

The young warrior rushed forward. "What's wrong with her?" he said anxiously.

"I don't know," Roger answered. "I think she fainted."

Rosalin moaned dramatically and fluttered her eyes open wide. "Water," she croaked pitifully, looking right into the young warrior's concerned gaze. "Please."

"Here, have some whisky," he said, holding out the skin he'd ripped off from around his shoulders.

The shudder she gave was not feigned. It smelled horrible, like bitter peat. She shook her head and clutched his arm. "Please."

Feeling ridiculous, she batted her lashes a few times.

It worked.

"I'll be right back," the young warrior said, running toward the edge of the stream just visible through the trees.

Rosalin took her nephew by the hand and quickly got to her feet. "Let's go."

Without a backward glance, they plunged through the trees in the opposite direction and ran as if the devil were on their heels. He was.

Four

Robbie moved far enough away to ensure they were not overheard, before stopping by the edge of the burn to deal with his irate partner. Seton had removed his helm, and Robbie did the same, tossing it down on the ground to run his hands through the itchy, damp waves that were plastered to his head in sweat and grime.

Not caring that his red-faced partner looked like he was hanging on to the last shreds of his control by a very thin string, and that it would only likely add to his irritation, Robbie knelt by the stream. With both hands, he cupped the icy water, splashing it on his face and over his head a few times. Damn, that felt good. He hated the suffocating full-faced helms he wore on regular missions, much preferring the nasal helms he wore with the Highland Guard. But the style had become associated with "Bruce's phantoms," and he wasn't going to push his luck.

Shaking the water from his hair, he stood and faced Seton, whose expression had only grown darker at Robbie's apparent nonchalance.

Crossing his arms, he eyed Seton intently. "You had something to say?"

Seton's gaze narrowed and his mouth tightened white. Seven years of *Highland* warfare may have toughened up the young knight, but he still had a difficult time keeping a rein on his temper—or at least not showing it. "Damned right, I have something to say. I sure as hell didn't sign up to make war on women and children."

Robbie refrained from asking him why he *had* signed up—other than the fact that his dead hero brother had been Bruce's closest companion.

"That 'boy' is Clifford's heir, and a squire old enough to wield a blade at Fraser. The woman got in the way and will be released as soon as it is feasible. As to why, I should think that would be fairly obvious. The taking of hostages is common enough on both sides." He paused, unable to resist adding, "Even for English knights."

It was the truth. Hostage taking, particularly of an heir to serve as surety, had been an established practice undertaken throughout Christendom for centuries. Both sides did it. Not even Seton could argue with that.

"Hostages are given, not taken," Seton said stubbornly.

"As I did not feel like waiting around to ask someone, I'd say the distinction is meaningless. But feel free to return to Norham and wait for Clifford so you can negotiate. Although I would think from previous experience that you might not like the way those negotiations turn out."

Seton knew better than to wade into that cesspit. The manner of their capture at Kildrummy was still a sore point even after all these years. His teeth clenched until the muscle in his jaw ticced. "I don't like it."

"You don't have to like it," Boyd replied bluntly. "The king wants Clifford's truce, and the boy will ensure that this time Clifford negotiates in good faith."

His partner didn't say anything, although it was clear he wanted to.

Suddenly, Robbie understood what it was, and in spite of the current tension between them, it packed a surprising sting. "Hell, Dragon, after all that we've been through, you can't think I'd hurt the lad?"

Seton pinned his gaze to his, his mouth pursed in a hard

line. "I don't want to think so, but I know how much you hate his sire."

Robbie's fists squeezed at his side. "Aye, I want vengeance, but against Clifford, not a green squire. Despite my reputation to the contrary, I do not slaughter innocents or make war on those weaker than me."

His partner should know that.

Perhaps Seton realized it as well. "Everyone's weaker than you," he said dryly.

Robbie managed a small smile at the jest, and what he suspected was meant as an apology. "You know what I meant." He couldn't abide bullies. Perhaps because of his strength, he was even more conscious of fighting worthy opponents.

Seton bent down, picking up his helm and handing it to him. "You intend to let the woman go?"

Robbie tucked the helm under his arm. "I wouldn't have taken her in the first place, but she'd latched on to the boy and Fraser was having a difficult time separating them. I figured the boy would put up less of a fight if I took her."

"Who is she?"

Robbie shrugged. "I don't know. Probably a servant—a nursemaid, perhaps."

"She isn't a nursemaid," Fraser said, approaching them from the trees where they'd left the horses. MacLeod's young brother by marriage, Sir Alexander Fraser had become one of their regular companions in the war along the Borders.

Robbie frowned. "How do you know?"

"One look at her face." He shook his head. "If I had a nursemaid who looked like that, I would never have left the nursery."

So the nicely shaped bottom wasn't an aberration. Still, Robbie was sure Fraser exaggerated.

"I wasn't aware that beauty precluded servitude, but I'll

take a Scottish serving maid over an English Rose any day," Robbie said.

"My partner here is convinced nothing of any worth grows below the Roman wall," Seton added.

"Aye, well, be prepared to change your mind," Fraser said.

Suddenly curious, Robbie glanced through the trees to where he'd left the hostages. The dense trees and thickening mist prevented him from seeing anything. He scanned the area around him, frowning when he saw Malcolm kneeling by the stream, apparently filling up his skin with water. The young warrior stood and started back up the hill.

"Who is watching the boy and the woman?" he asked Fraser.

"I thought you told Malcolm to. I left Clifford's whelp with him before I came to find you."

Robbie swore.

"What's wrong?" Seton asked.

But Robbie was already striding toward the horses. He reached the clearing only moments after Malcolm, who was standing there stunned, looking around.

"Where are they?" Robbie demanded.

Malcolm's face paled. "The lady fainted. I went to fetch her some water. I was only gone for a few minutes."

Robbie swore again. He was really beginning to regret not being the type of man who would knock a lass out of the way.

The young warrior shirked back in the face of his anger. Robbie didn't need to tell him that he'd made an enormous mistake. And he would be reprimanded—but later. Right now, all Robbie was focused on was getting the hostages back.

He quickly organized his men into a search party. In a low voice that contemplated no other result, he ordered, "Find them."

"Hurry!" Rosalin grabbed Roger's hand, pulling him into the river behind her. "They're coming."

The icy water splashed at her knees as they raced toward the felled tree. She was almost too scared to notice how cold it was—almost. Heart pounding, every few feet she glanced around behind her, expecting to see the beasts snapping at their heels.

Knowing they wouldn't be able to outrun a dozen warriors on horseback, Rosalin had ignored the instinct to run and instead used the precious few minutes of lead time they had to search for a place to hide. Not an easy task in the barren wintry countryside, but as opportune hiding places went, the felled tree was better than she would have dared hope.

Propped up on one end by a rock, the tree must have been there for some time, as the inside was partially hollowed out. Moss and ferns had grown over the log almost like a blanket, creating a space underneath that was just large enough for her to crawl under.

Roger didn't need to be told what to do. He practically dove into the hollowed-out tree as she did the same underneath the mossy curtain.

It was just in time. No sooner had they scampered into position than she heard the sound of voices.

"They couldn't have gotten far."

Her heart stopped, recognizing the deep voice of her captor. Shivering, and not just from the cold, she waited for them to approach.

"Damn, I wish we had Hunter with us," another man said. She couldn't be sure, but she thought it might be the man who'd objected to their abduction.

"The ground is too hard, and there are too many tracks," the deeper voice said. "I can't tell which are theirs."

That voice . . . a chill ran down her spine. There *was* something familiar about it.

She quickly pushed the thought away. It couldn't be. Her

captor's voice was deep, but hard and humorless, with a clipped, authoritative cadence. The prisoner's—Boyd's—had been softer. Kinder. He'd sounded like a man who knew how to smile, not a harsh, unforgiving brute.

"Do you think they crossed the river?" the second man asked.

"I don't think so," her captor replied. "We would see some dampness on the ground where they came out."

"Unless they decided to swim farther downstream."

"If they did, they won't have gotten far—not if they don't want to freeze to death. You take some men and go on the other side of the river. I'll try down this way."

"Captain, here!" she heard a shout, possibly from the young warrior whom she'd tricked. "Tracks!"

"Go," her captor said. "I'll see what Malcolm has found."

He moved out of hearing distance for a while, and all Rosalin could hear was her heart pounding and the chattering of Roger's teeth.

"Do you think they're gone?" he whispered.

"Not yet," she replied. She sensed her captor with the hard, uncompromising voice wouldn't have given up that quickly.

A few minutes later, she heard footsteps and froze. Well, as she was actually already frozen, she just stopped breathing.

"Do you see anything?"

Now her heart stopped. It was the young warrior, and by the sound of it, he was standing right by the felled tree.

"Keep looking," her captor shouted from farther away. "They're here, damn it. I can feel it."

The anger and frustration in his voice gave her an unexpected burst of hope. *Sweet heaven, this might actually work!*

From her place scrunched up under the log, Rosalin watched through the blanket of moss as one of the barbarians walked right by the tree on the opposite side of the hollow. Fortunately, he didn't stop, probably assuming that no one could hide inside. "I don't see anything. They must still be running."

It *was* the young warrior. Malcolm, her captor had called him.

Her captor swore, and although it was a word rarely uttered in her presence, she was thrilled to hear it, as it only buoyed her hopes further.

"Let's get back on the horses," her captor replied from closer than before. "We'll backtrack and see if we can find another set of tracks. They can't have just disappeared."

They'd done it! She couldn't believe they'd actually done it.

A frantic scurrying sound from above, followed by a sharp "ouch" from Roger, put an end to her celebration. A moment later, Roger shot out of the tree and was quickly followed by a brown creature about the size of a cat with a bushy tail. Apparently, their log was already occupied— by a pine marten!

She rolled out from under the log after Roger, praying that the men chasing them hadn't heard. But one peek over the log quashed that particular fantasy.

"There!" The young warrior shouted from about forty yards away. "There they are."

Panic shot through her. Grabbing Roger's hand, she started toward the woodland ahead. "Run!"

Racing over the uneven terrain, she had to release her nephew's hand so she wouldn't take him down the hillside with her if she slipped. It was also clear that she was slowing him down.

The footsteps behind them were closing in. Whatever chance they'd had of escape had disappeared with one angry pine marten, but she had to at least try. "The rocks," she gasped, already breathing heavily. "Hurry."

Roger shot off. Rather than follow after him, she

stopped, hoping to slow their pursuers enough to give her nephew time to hide. She hadn't anticipated the man right on her heels. He lunged for her, catapulting them both back into the dirt and mud.

She cried out from the force of the ground slamming against her back, and then, an instant later, from the big, solid leather-clad slab of granite that landed on top of her—the *very* big and very solid slab of granite.

The air was knocked out of her lungs with a hard jolt. She couldn't breathe. But in that stunned moment her gaze locked on that of her captor's, and she felt an altogether different kind of jolt. One of recognition.

She gasped with all the air she had left in her lungs. Dear God, it *was* him! Robbie Boyd. The Scot she'd released from prison all those years ago. The handsome, strapping young rebel who'd so captured her young girl's heart. She was certain of it. Even from a tower window, the strong lines of his face had been burned indelibly on her consciousness. His dark hair was shorter, and his eyes were blue, not brown as she'd assumed from his dark coloring, but God in heaven it was him.

Her heart leapt. In that one instant of recognition, all the youthful fantasies came rushing back to her in a crashing romantic wave. If she'd secretly dreamed of meeting him again, it seemed her dreams had come true. "It's you," she whispered.

The softly spoken words seemed to break the strange spell that had momentarily entranced them both. Recognition was clearly one-sided. His gaze hardened and his mouth pulled into a tight, angry line. Suddenly, the veil of her memories cleared, revealing not the young warrior of her memories but the cold, merciless man before her now.

The romantic wave crashed, taking her heart to the ground with it.

If she'd ever doubted the stories she'd heard of Robbie Boyd, one look told her they were all true. He appeared every inch the ruthless enforcer. Every inch one of the most feared men in England. Every inch the black-hearted devil who'd laid scourge across the Borders.

He'd changed. She wouldn't have thought it possible, but he looked even more imposing. The distinctive height and muscular build was the same, but six years of war had honed it to a razor-sharp edge, erasing any vestiges of youth. There was a hardness, a solidness, an imperviousness to him that hadn't been there before. He looked like a man who did nothing but fight.

His features were the same, though she would no longer call him handsome. It was far too gentle and civilized a word. And there was nothing gentle or civilized about the terrifying-looking barbarian staring down at her. From the bone-chilling ice-blue gaze to the line of dark stubble that shadowed his blunt jaw, he exuded wild and untamed menace. Fiercely good-looking—perhaps that was more apropos.

He was older than she'd initially thought—probably close to Cliff's two and thirty—and he wore the years of battle in every line and scar on his face. And in the fierceness of his expression. It was as if every bit of good humor had been leached out of him.

Her eyes slid to the mouth that was hovering only inches above hers. It seemed impossible to believe that the wide, sensual lips that had so briefly touched hers in her first kiss could have become fixed in such a cold, hard line.

But she did remember, and in spite of the circumstances, a flush of awareness ran through her. A flush that turned to a full-fledged shudder as she became aware of the intimacy of their embrace, especially the part of him that was wedged between her legs.

Over the years of battle, Robbie had been hit on the head a few times by a war hammer. The stunned, discombobulated, slightly dazed feeling was about the same as when he first saw the face of the woman beneath him.

"Beautiful" seemed too pedestrian a word for the masterful perfection of her delicate features. Big, dark-green eyes framed by long, feathery lashes, porcelain-white skin as flawless and powdery as freshly fallen snow, high cheekbones tinged a delicate shade of pink, a slight, straight nose, a softly pointed chin, and a mouth so cherry-red and sweet it took everything he had not to taste it.

Long, wavy tresses of softly spun silk were splayed out in a golden halo behind her head. He'd never made a poetical allusion in his life, but this woman could inspire even the most prosaic of men to think of angels and goddesses descending from the heavens.

When their eyes met, he actually startled. The force of the connection had all the subtlety of a lightning rod prodding at the base of his spine.

There was something about the way she was looking at him that made him feel as if she knew him. But hers was a face he would have remembered, even in the crowds of women who thronged around him at the Highland Games.

Then she spoke, and he was reminded why he didn't know her: she was English.

His head cleared just enough to make him aware of other things. Such as the warm softness of the body underneath him, the fullness of the breasts crushed against his chest, and most significantly, the opportune placement of his cock nestled in that sweet little juncture between her legs.

Ah hell. Now that he was thinking about it, he couldn't stop thinking about it. How good it felt. How good she felt under him. How it had been over a week since he'd had a woman.

The wave of desire that hit him was so hot, so powerful, so intense that it took him aback. It rushed up between his legs, lengthening a part of him that was far too big to hide.

Apparently, his previous reaction to the lass hadn't been an aberration.

Damn, Fraser was right. This lass made him reconsider some of his preconceived notions about being attracted to an Englishwoman. He stood corrected. He stood very hard and very thickly corrected.

She made a sound—a gasp of shock that reminded him of the less-than-appropriate circumstances for him to be stiffening like a lad with his first maid. He didn't want to terrify the chit. And the sudden paling of her skin and widening of her eyes told him that she was terrified. But he could have sworn he'd also glimpsed a flicker of awareness on her part that mirrored his own.

Before he could disentangle himself and assure her that she wasn't in any danger—especially *that* kind of danger from him—he felt a hard poke in his back that skidded off to the side.

"Get off my aunt, you cursed barbarian!" *Bloody hell*, he realized, his head clearing. That wasn't a poke, it was the stab of a blade! Robbie barely managed to twist his body out of the way before the boy could strike again. "I'll kill you if you touch her."

Robbie sprang to his feet just as Malcolm was pulling the lad off. "Sorry," the young warrior said. "He got to you before I could stop him."

Robbie wasn't about to chastise Malcolm for his own mistake. A mistake that could have cost him his life. It was a good thing Robbie had been wearing his thick, leather *cotun* and the lad wasn't more adept with a dagger. Christ, the strongest man in Scotland could have been killed by a squire! If Hawk heard about this, Robbie would never hear the end of it.

But he'd been so struck by the lass, an army could have come galloping up behind him and he wouldn't have heard it. Glimpsing Seton and his men only a few feet away, he realized they practically had. The lass—

All at once the truth struck him cold. *Aunt*.

Bloody hell. Any flash of desire he might have experienced was quickly doused when he realized that not only had he taken Clifford's heir, he'd also taken his sister.

His mouth tightened as he stared at the woman slowly getting to her feet and shaking the dirt and leaves off her skirts.

"*Aunt?*" he demanded, as if she'd somehow tricked him.

"Lady Rosalin?" Seton asked in a slightly stunned voice that told Robbie he'd seen her face and had been similarly affected.

Ignoring Robbie's question, she looked at Seton and nodded.

Of course. Robbie should have guessed. The beauty of Clifford's sister was well known. The English called her the Fair Rosalin, alluding to Clifford's illustrious ancestor.

For once, Robbie was forced to acknowledge that the English stories that he'd assumed were exaggerations were true—perhaps even understatements. The lass was one of the most beautiful creatures he'd ever seen. The quintessential English Rose. His jaw tightened. But there was enough resemblance to Clifford to remind him of exactly who she was: the sister of the man bent on destroying them, conquering their land, and seeing them subjugated.

Clifford's sister, bloody hell! He felt his face darken as blood surged through his veins in a hot rush. Somehow his attraction to the lass made it worse. It felt like a damned betrayal. In this case, his own.

God knew she was probably as arrogant and condescending as her brother. Aye, no doubt she was a spoiled, cosseted brat who'd never suffered a moment of hardship or strife in her life.

Beautiful or not, how could he have forgotten—even for an instant—that she was *English*? She might look sweet on the outside, but she was undoubtedly just as ugly as her brother on the inside. Beauty, in this case, was surely deceiving.

He stared at her coldly, calculatingly, forcing himself to

see not the perfection of her features but the resemblance to his enemy and the added benefit she would bring him. Their raid had reaped far greater bounty than he could ever have dreamed.

"It seems fortune has shined on us twice today," he said, as much for her benefit as that of his men's who'd gathered around them. "Not only have we caught Clifford's heir, but his beloved sister as well." Clifford's affection for his only sibling was well known. Apparently the bastard had a weakness for the women in his life. At one time Robbie had, too. But unlike Clifford's sister, his hadn't escaped the brutality of war. His mouth fell in a hard, unrelenting line as the familiar anger stirred inside. "I'd wager we have double the means to ensure a truce, don't we, lads?"

He was answered with a flurry of "ayes" from all his men except for Seton, who managed to shake off his stunned trance for long enough to turn on him. "I thought—"

"The situation has changed," Robbie said, cutting him off with a look of warning. If Seton was going to insist on voicing his objections—not that it would make a difference—it wasn't going to be now. He wasn't going to give up a boon like Clifford's sister without consideration. A whole hell of a lot of consideration.

"What do you mean to do with us?" she asked. Her voice trembled, although he didn't miss the way she angled herself in front of the lad as if to protect him.

Something about that voice bothered him. It wasn't just that having a woman—even if she was Clifford's sister—scared of him didn't sit well, it was something else. Something he couldn't put his finger on that made him feel as if a ghostly voice were whispering a warning in his ear, but he couldn't make out the words.

He pushed the odd feeling aside and answered her question. "You and the lad will be taken someplace safe to wait while a messenger is sent to your brother." He shrugged. "Whatever happens after that is up to him."

Her eyes widened, and despite her obvious fear she managed, "You can't do that!"

He would admire her courage later, but right now all he could see was the slight stiffening of the spine and offended lift of the chin that reminded him too much of her condescending brother. He leaned toward her threateningly. He was trying to emphasize his point. It wasn't because she smelled so damned good. Although that was what hit his senses, engulfing him in her soft floral scent. Roses, of course. A big, heady, blooming bouquet of them. He managed not to inhale—just.

"I assure you, *my lady*, I can. Your brother's authority does not run here. If I were you, I would remember that." Her eyes widened further, and he had to force himself to stand his ground. *Clifford's sister* . . . He quashed whatever foolish impulses were leaping inside him. But bloody hell, he wished she would stop looking at him like that. "Consider yourself fortunate that you are not being punished for attempting to escape."

Her eyes scanned his face with an intensity that made him uneasy. She almost looked close to tears. "What happened to you?"

His brow furrowed. It was an odd comment to make, but he'd never understood the English. "War," he said simply, turning away. She'd delayed him long enough. "Tie up the lad and separate them," he said to Malcolm, who was still holding Clifford's whelp.

That should prevent any further problems.

"No!" she shouted, grabbing his arm and swinging him back around to face her. He ignored the slam in his chest and spike in his temperature caused by her touch. His skin tightened. Actually, all of him tightened.

Fear forgotten, her eyes flashed angrily. "You can't do that. He's only a boy. I won't let you hurt him."

The fierceness of her voice made him smile. This was more like it. He liked her better like this. It made it easier to remember her brother.

The source of her impassioned defense, however, didn't look as pleased. The boy was too old to have a woman defending him, and the red in his cheeks suggested he knew it. "Let them tie me up, Aunt Rosalin. I don't care. They won't hurt me. Father will kill them if they dare harm either one of us."

Not a complete whelp, at least. After watching him wield that sword at Fraser earlier and the attempt he'd squandered with a bad plunge of his dagger, Robbie had wondered. But he had no more patience for the lad's bravado than he had for the aunt's. "Your father wants to kill us anyway. I assure you it is not the threat of Clifford that will keep you safe."

"Then what will?" she demanded.

Steeling himself, he met her gaze again. Not that it helped. Every muscle in his body still squeezed. What the hell was wrong with him? It wasn't as if he'd never seen a beautiful woman before. His eyes dipped. And noticed a spectacular set of . . . He forced his gaze up and schooled the lust from his body. This lack of focus wasn't like him.

"My good humor," he replied. "So I suggest you do not try it again." Her hand dropped and he felt his pulse return to normal. "But a word of caution about attempting to escape. Your brother's raids have not exactly endeared him to the people around these parts, and you might not like who finds you. But as long as you are under my protection, no one will harm you."

"Is that supposed to ease my mind?"

Sarcasm. He liked that, too. He was really seeing Clifford now. "I don't give a damn whether it eases your mind or not."

"You have nothing to fear," Seton interjected gallantly.

"You and the boy will be safe for the short time you are here. I will see to it personally."

Seton might as well have stepped between them and lifted his shiny shield—the effect was the same. He'd just declared himself their champion and made Robbie the enemy.

It was a role he'd been cast in before, so there was no reason it should bother him. There was no reason he should want to rip that shiny shield from his partner's hand and hold it up himself. There was no reason he should care if she looked at Seton with gratitude.

Except it wasn't Seton she was looking at, it was him— with the oddest expression on her face. "Please," she said softly. "Don't do this. I'm asking you to release us."

The look made him feel uneasy. It was that feeling that she knew him again. That she was searching for something in his face, but it wasn't there. That she was waiting for something.

"Why the hell would I do that?"

Her eyes never left his. "Because you owe me."

He tried to laugh, but it didn't ease the tension coiling inside him. The feeling that something was very wrong, and that whatever it was, he wasn't going to like it. "What could I possibly owe Clifford's sister?"

She lowered her voice, but he heard the one word that changed everything. "Kildrummy."

Five

❧

The blood drained from Robbie's face. *Kildrummy.* A memory stirred. His heart started to pound.

Nay, it wasn't possible.

It couldn't be . . .

But he felt a sinking feeling in his gut. The knowledge of what that ghostly voice had been trying to tell him. Of why she was looking at him as if she knew him and expected him to know her as well.

He swore and closed the distance between them in one long stride. With the back of one gauntleted finger—gauntlets designed to protect him from blades in battle, not silky-soft skin, although right now he was rather glad of the latter—he tilted her face back and forth in the misty twilight.

She didn't shirk from his touch or try to pull away, holding her finely carved features up to his scrutiny, almost daring him to deny the truth.

Dread churned like a portent of doom in his gut. But he *knew.* The shadowed lines of her chin and nose left no doubt: it was the young lass who helped free him from prison all those years ago. The lass who from behind her hooded cloak he'd assumed to be a servant. The lass whom he'd tried to find for years so he could repay her. Though it seemed inconceivable, the sweet, young girl whose velvety lips had trembled under his with a chaste kiss had been Clifford's sister.

The truth slammed like a hammer across his chest, the blow powerful enough to fell even the strongest man in Scotland.

Suddenly, it all fit. He recalled overhearing some of the guards discussing the girl's unexpected arrival with Hereford's party, and how she'd been locked up tight in one of the towers like some bloody princess who would be sullied by just breathing the same air as the vile Scots.

It had never crossed his mind that their guardian angel might be Clifford's precious sister. No wonder Robbie's enquiries hadn't turned up anything. He'd asked about the half-dozen young serving women in the Earl's party, not the ladies.

Their eyes met. "You said you would repay me if we ever met again," she said.

Seton being the only one close enough to overhear, and the only one who would understand of what she spoke, he uttered an expletive under his breath.

For once he and his partner were in agreement. Robbie dropped his hand from her face and stepped back, not trusting himself. Something was building inside him that he didn't recognize. A different kind of anger. A wild, frenzied maelstrom harnessed by the barest of tethers.

It wasn't right, damn it! Why did it have to be her? The one good memory he had of that godforsaken time was now destroyed by the knowledge that his angel of mercy, the sweet young girl who'd freed him from that hellhole, was sister to the man who'd put him there.

"Release us," she entreated, her soft voice tugging on a part of him long forgotten.

His conscience, damn it.

Damn her for doing this to him! For ruining everything. For making him indebted to a bloody *Clifford*. His mouth fell in a hard line, his fists clenching against the storm of emotions surging inside him.

He needed to think. But he couldn't do it standing here

with her looking up at him. Turning away from that expectant gaze, he started back to his horse. "Get them mounted up," he said to Seton. "We'll need to ride hard if we are to reach the gathering place in time."

Norham wasn't the only raid this day. Douglas and Randolph were waiting for them near Channelkirk.

He didn't need to look at her. Her harsh gasp of disbelief said it all.

Seton was just as astonished but not as restrained. "You mean you aren't going to release—"

Robbie stopped him with a glare that was probably as black as he felt inside. Just once he wished his partner didn't have to question everything he did—or didn't do. "Damn it, not now. Clifford's men are probably right on our tails. If we don't get out of here right now, we'll be the ones who need releasing."

How could I have been so wrong?

Rosalin watched him stride away and felt the last flicker of uncertainty in her go out. All the doubts fostered by years of stories and rumor had proved true. The cold expression on his face when he realized her identity, and his refusal to release them, left her no doubt that whatever good she'd once imagined in Robbie Boyd was long gone.

It was her worst fear realized. She'd made a mistake in releasing him, and her shame knew no end. She couldn't bear to think about how many of her countrymen might have died because of her misplaced compassion. Because she'd thought she was righting a terrible wrong and couldn't look away. The noble rebel that she'd created in her mind was nothing more than a merciless brigand without any semblance of honor.

After what she'd done for him and all she'd risked, he'd turned his back on her—literally.

Whatever vestiges remained of her foolish young girl's heart crumbled to dust. Had she really thought the connection forged by one reckless act somehow bound them? Had she really expected him to release them because of some debt he'd probably never thought to have to repay?

She had. She'd never believed the man she'd watched could be so ruthless.

"What were you saying to that rebel, Aunt Rosalin? It almost looked like you knew him."

Malcolm had released Roger, and he'd come up to stand beside her as the blond-haired warrior sorted out their riding companions. Rosalin hated lying to him, but she could hardly explain. "How would I know him?" How indeed. "I simply asked him to release us."

"But don't you know who that is? That's the Devil's Enforcer, Robbie Boyd. One of the most ruthless men in Scotland—and said to be the strongest. Father had him imprisoned at one time, and he would have been executed if he hadn't managed to escape. He and Father hate each other. The Devil's Enforcer won't release us without exacting payment from Father."

"I see that now," she said quietly. "But I had to try."

They didn't have the opportunity to talk further, as the brigands had decided on their riding arrangements and they were separated. Roger's hands were tied, and he was forced to ride with the warrior who'd first captured him at Norham. Fraser, she thought someone had called him. If he was part of that great patriotic family, she knew she would find no sympathy from him. She was placed in the charge of a stony-faced, red-bearded older warrior—apparently named Callum, although he'd not spoken a word to her—who bore a strong resemblance to young Malcolm. If it was his father, as she suspected, he's apparently taken her tricking of Malcolm personally.

Within a few minutes, she was plopped up on the saddle before him, and they were on their way. To where, she could only guess. She wished she'd paid more attention on the journey south from Kildrummy with Sir Humphrey. Her head had been filled with romantic fantasies (which seemed especially cruel in light of what had just happened), and she hadn't taken note of many landmarks. She'd seen so many churches and castles, they'd all started to blur. She knew the general location of the major burghs and cities, but she doubted the rebels would go anywhere near those. By her best estimation, they were northwest of Norham and Berwick in the hills and forests, headed west into more of the same.

She knew Bruce and his men controlled the countryside and operated from their base in the Ettrick Forest . . .

Her heart dropped. Good God, was that where they were going? Rosalin didn't believe in ghosts, but the stories of Bruce's phantoms who reputedly had their lair in the vast Royal Forest made her wonder. Her brother's men would be hard-pressed to follow them into such hostile and dangerous territory.

Which made the need to escape as soon as possible even more imperative. But as she could not do so without Roger, she would have to bide her time. They could not ride halfway across the Borders to Ettrick without resting.

She hoped. But these men looked tough and rugged, and used to riding bone-jarring and bottom-numbing distances. They'd probably pick up the horses and carry *them* when they got tired.

Although she was considerably more comfortable than she had been when she was strewn over Boyd's lap in a sack, as the day faded and became swallowed up by the mist, she increasingly suffered the effects of her walk through the river. Her wet slippers had turned to ice, and her feet along with them. Soon, her shivering became uncontrollable.

Not that anyone noticed. The gruff old warrior behind her barely seemed to acknowledge her presence. Stiff-backed, eyes fixed straight ahead, he completely ignored her. The other warriors did as well.

Boyd and the handsome blond-haired warrior, who also looked familiar, had stayed behind initially (presumably to scout for any soldiers who might be pursuing them) and had only just reappeared.

Not that she would expect sympathy from *him*. He hadn't looked in her direction once. So much for the special connection. If she needed proof of how one-sided that connection was, she had it. What had she expected—one look and somehow he would know her? That he would fall on his knees and pledge his undying devotion to her for what she'd done?

He hadn't seen her face, so how could he know her? And he wasn't a knight in a faerie tale; he was a rebel. A brigand. A scourge. A man who fought without rules or honor.

And she was a fool.

Rosalin wrapped the plaid around her tighter and tried not to think about how tired she was, or how cold she was, or how miserable she was.

Unsuccessfully. Her throat tightened and a hot sheen of tears burned behind her eyes. But she wouldn't cry. She wouldn't. No matter how much she wanted to. No matter that she'd been abducted, manhandled, hunted, nearly crushed to death, found out a man she thought was a hero was no more than a merciless brigand, and was probably being taken into what undoubtedly was the most terrifying place in Christendom. She had to stay strong for Roger.

Perhaps she wasn't completely without sympathy. The blond-haired warrior glanced in her direction, but he was careful not to meet her gaze. From their tense conversation, she wondered if it might be about her. Whatever the two men were talking about, it was clear they weren't in agreement.

She was so cold, she was about to break down and ask the recalcitrant old warrior for something warm to wrap around her feet, when Boyd swung his mount around and glowered in their direction. Ripping the plaid off from around his shoulders, he threw it toward them. "Damn it, Callum, wrap her in this. She'll bring the entire English army down on us with all that chattering."

Callum caught the plaid and draped it over her, tucking it under her feet, which were slung to one side. Rosalin burrowed into its heat with a contended sigh.

Apparently, Boyd did not want or expect her thanks, because he'd already turned around.

Considerably more comfortable, she told herself not to read anything into the less than graciously made gesture. But there was a strange intimacy to being wrapped in his plaid. The thick wool fibers still held the warmth of his body, and if she inhaled just a little, she caught the faint edge of pine and heather and something distinctly masculine. It felt like he was surrounding her and made it difficult for her not to think about foolish things.

She tried instead to think about Sir Henry. He would be arriving at Berwick soon. She shuddered to think what he would do when he found out about her abduction. She hoped he didn't do something rash. Her nose scrunched up. Strange that although she didn't know him that well, that was her first thought.

The sky was as black as pitch by time they finally stopped. Though they'd been riding for a few hours, with the rough terrain, heavy loads, and having to slow their speed with the horses over the hills, she guessed they hadn't gone more than ten or fifteen miles.

Callum dismounted and helped her down without looking at her.

Despite his less than friendly expression, she asked, "Where are we?"

"Ask the captain," he replied, already walking off.

She intended to. Right after she checked on Roger. But seeing her nephew standing with "the captain" a few feet away, she marched over toward them both. After a quick glance to assure her Roger was all right, she turned to Boyd. Not without reluctance, she unwrapped the plaid from her shoulders and handed it to him. "Thank you," she said.

"Keep it," he said indifferently. "You'll need it tonight."

"Won't you be cold?"

He gave her a long stare. "I didn't go swimming in a river."

It hadn't been swimming, but given the subject was her attempted escape, she decided not to argue semantics. She looked around in the torchlit darkness, seeing what appeared to be a small sheltered corrie in the forest with a stream running between the two mist-shrouded hills. It would be hauntingly beautiful if she weren't cold, abducted, and suspecting that it would serve as her bedchamber for the night. "Where are we?"

He waited a long beat before replying. "St. Cuthbert's Hills."

"I've never heard of it."

The way he shrugged suggested he was well aware of that, which was probably why he'd told her. It was probably a local way of referring to the place that would have no meaning to anyone not from the area.

"Is that near Edinburgh?"

His piercing blue eyes narrowed. She still couldn't quite get used to the sharp contrast of his light eyes with dark hair, and she felt something like a shiver race over her skin. It was unsettling. *He* was unsettling.

"If you are thinking about attempting another escape, I would not advise it. These hills are dangerous, my lady. You never know who you might come across."

As if to punctuate his words, a group of riders approached from the other direction. "Ah, here they are now," Boyd said.

Apparently the newcomers were expected.

A few moments later a man jumped off his horse, pulled off his helm, and strode toward them. He was a big man. Maybe even an inch taller than Boyd, though not as heavily muscled. She doubted few men were as heavily muscled as Boyd. Not that Boyd was bulky. Just strong-looking. Not that she'd been staring at him. She was a woman of two and twenty now, not some impressionable sixteen-year-old to be taken by an impressive-looking physique. Even if it *was* the most impressive-looking physique she'd ever seen. There had to be an ounce of fat on him somewhere, although she certainly couldn't see it.

She turned—not forced—her gaze back to the other man. He wore the same black leather warcoat and chausses as the other men, but it was as fine as anything Cliff might wear. Neatly shaved and free of dust and dirt, he appeared considerably more civilized than Boyd and his band of rough-looking brigands.

"You're late," Boyd said. "Any problems?"

The dark-visaged newcomer shook his head. "Nothing that couldn't be handled." Noticing her, he barely covered his surprise. He slowly lifted a brow and turned back to Boyd. "What about you? Your haul looks much more interesting than mine. Have you finally decided to *take* a wife? Your methods might be a little old-fashioned, but the results seem to have been worth it." He let out a low whistle. "You're fortunate I'm a happily married man, but don't let Randolph see her—you know how partial he is to blondes."

"Sod off, *Sir* James. The lass is a hostage, as is the lad."

"Sir"? Thank goodness! At last, a knight! Perhaps she would find someone to champion their cause for release. Although something about the way Boyd had emphasized "sir" made her think there was more to it.

"This sounds even more interesting," Sir James said. "Who are they?"

"Clifford's sister and heir."

Sir James's expression changed so quickly, it was as if a dark thunderstorm had clapped down over them all. She took a step back, feeling the hot blast of menace directed toward them.

"Lady Rosalin. Young Roger," Boyd said with mock formality. "Meet Sir James Douglas. Perhaps you've heard of him? He's the rightful owner of the land Clifford has spent nearly fifteen years attempting to occupy."

Rosalin gasped. Her blood turned to ice, and her heart slammed to the ground as fear crept over every inch of her skin. Instinctively she reached for Roger's hand and pulled him back toward her and Boyd, whom she'd just as instinctively sought out. Only moments ago he'd seemed like their worst nightmare. But now they knew otherwise. Their worst nightmare was standing right before them. The Black Douglas. Her brother's worst enemy, and the man who hated him more than anyone.

With one glance, Robbie told Douglas to back off. He'd experienced a strange thump in his chest when she'd unconsciously moved to him for protection, and had to fight an unexpected—and unwelcome—urge to put his arm around her. When Seton shot him an odd look, however, Robbie wondered whether he'd fought the urge as well as he thought he had.

Whether it was the shock fading or his warning glance, he didn't know, but Douglas's expression changed. A sly curve slid up his mouth. "By God, this is perfect. What a boon! We finally have the means to bring that English bastard to his damned knees. With his sister and heir in our possession, he'll dance a damned jig atop the parapets of Berwick Castle if we want him to."

It was the same reaction Robbie had had, but for some reason coming from Douglas it sounded different. Perhaps it was because of the effect the words had on the lass and the boy. They both visibly paled and huddled a few inches closer to him. That odd thump expanded in his chest.

He turned to Seton, and with a glance told him what he wanted him to do.

"Come, my lady," Seton said, leading her away. "You must be hungry. Let's find you and young Roger something to eat."

The look of gratitude she gave his partner made Robbie almost wish that he'd voiced his order. He frowned at the odd reaction. Knight errant was Seton's role, not his. But the lass seemed to be provoking all kinds of odd reactions in him. When he returned from scouting earlier, he'd felt like he was crawling out of his damned skin every time he saw her shiver.

"Seton," he called out. His partner turned around questioningly. "Have Malcolm build a fire."

Seton didn't say anything, but Robbie read the speculation in his gaze and quickly put a stop to it with a hard stare. It wasn't that unusual a request, damn it. It was a cold, misty night. Even if they were a little exposed for a fire, the English wouldn't track them into the hills and forests at night—or in the day, for that matter. It was near villages and English garrisoned castles where they had to be careful.

"Whatever you say, *Captain*."

Boyd didn't miss the sarcasm in Seton's tone. His partner was still smarting from the fact that Bruce had put Robbie in charge. This was *his* mission, and therefore—as he'd told his partner many times over the past few hours—he didn't have to listen to Seton's opinion on what they should do.

He'd been in no mood to hear about Seton's damned code of honor, and how they "had" to release her and the boy. How it was only "right" after what she'd done for them.

The only "right" thing was winning this damned war.

That was all Robbie should be thinking about. His sole focus should be on doing whatever was needed to secure Clifford's agreement and then collecting the money. If the lass and boy would help him in that regard, nothing else should matter. Honor wasn't going to win the damned war.

But no matter how many times he told himself that, he couldn't stop hearing her voice. *You owe me.* He did, damn it.

Honor—or what he had left of it—warred with duty. He owed her a debt, but he couldn't just hand over the means to bring Clifford to heel.

He watched her hurry away with Seton, trying not to wonder what they were talking about. Or why she'd suddenly turned and given Seton a tentative smile.

Bloody hell! His fists clenched. Did she have to look like that? If he'd ever seen a more beautiful woman, he couldn't think of one. Lady Rosalin Clifford was stunning. Breathtakingly stunning. By all rights, Clifford's sister should have a forked tongue, horns, and all sorts of other manner of devilry. Or perhaps warts and moles, like a troll or witch.

Actually, she did have a mole. A very small one that looked like a freckle. And its placement on the edge of a very sensually curved upper lip didn't make him think of witches or trolls, but of something else entirely. An unwelcome heat and heaviness tugged in his groin. He liked having his cock sucked just as much as any other man—which was to say a whole hell of a lot—but never had the mere thought of it made him hard.

Clifford's sister. He still couldn't believe it. He couldn't reconcile the sweet lass who'd saved him with the cosseted, spoiled English beauty she had to be. He was sure that once some of her fear dissipated, and she realized he meant what he said about them coming to no harm, she would start making demands and issuing orders. Her expression would change from looking as if he'd just torn up the pages to her favorite faerie tale and burned them before her eyes to haughty and condescending. She would look down that adorable little nose of hers not with disappointment and disillusionment, but with cold hatred.

She couldn't possibly be as sweet as she looked. Not with a brother like that.

He frowned as Seton jerked off his plaid to cover a low boulder for her to sit on. Dragon and his damned knightly sensibilities. Even after seven years of fighting like a "pirate," he still thought he was bloody Lancelot. It was how he'd earned his war name. Dragon was a jest, referring to the wyvern on the Seton arms that he'd so stubbornly held to wearing in the early days of their training—before he was forced to admit how ridiculous it was to wear mail and a surcoat doing the kind of fighting they would be doing.

"What in Hades is wrong with you?"

It took Robbie a minute to realize Douglas was talking to him. Hell, how long had he been staring? Too long, if the man's narrowed gaze was any indication.

"I would have thought you would be more excited," Douglas added. "We have Clifford by the bollocks."

"I am," he assured him, forcing the dark scowl from his face. "Did you receive the money from the good bishop?" Douglas had gone to Bewley Castle to meet with the Bishop of Cumbria.

But Douglas wouldn't be so easily put off. "You seemed almost protective of the lass. I'll admit, she's a beauty, but I wouldn't have thought you would be so easily deceived. The English bitch is Clifford's sister, for Christ's sake."

Robbie had to be more tired than he realized, because he was feeling quite a few of Seton's knightly sensibilities right now—as well as the sudden urge to slam his fist through his friend's teeth. For what? Calling her a bitch? It wasn't anything Robbie hadn't said many times before about their enemy: English dog, English bitch—it was as common as saying it looks like it might rain or the skies are dreich today.

Which didn't explain why his teeth were grinding. "I don't need you to remind me who she is"—he could think of nothing else, damn it—"but the lass is under my protection and will be until she is released."

"Why the hell would you release her? King Edward still holds Bruce's wife, daughter, and sister. Why should we not do the same with our 'overlord's' family?"

Robbie was just about as interested in hearing Douglas's opinion on the subject as he was Seton's. Nor was he going to explain himself.

He glanced over at Seton and the lady in question just in time to hear the soft tinkle of her laugh. Every muscle in his body tensed. The lad, Roger, was laughing, too. Both were stretching their feet out by the crackling fire, looking quite cozy.

"Hell, if you want the chit, why don't you just keep her for yourself? Think how furious Clifford would be to learn that his precious sister is in Robbie Boyd's bed."

The image was sharper than Robbie would have wished, and included sweaty, naked limbs twisted in well-rumpled bedsheets. He clenched his jaw until the muscle started to tic. "I don't want her, and I sure as hell don't want a wife."

Douglas smiled slyly. "I wasn't thinking of her as your wife. You can't marry an Englishwoman." He shuddered dramatically. "Make her your leman."

"I said I don't want her, damn it!"

"Aye, I can see that," Douglas said with a laugh—the bastard. "That's why you keep looking over at Seton like you want to kill him—even more than usual, that is." He lifted a brow. "Oh, look who just showed up! Didn't take him long to find her. I told you he had a weakness for blondes."

Robbie glanced over just in time to see Sir Thomas

Randolph, Bruce's nephew and nearly as much of a pain in his arse as Seton, bending over her hand like a gallant courtier and not the ruthless warrior he was—that they all were.

"My wife informs me that women find him attractive. I don't bloody see it," Douglas said with disgust. Obviously, Joanna Douglas was keeping her notoriously competitive husband on his toes by teasing him about his rival. Robbie was really beginning to like his friend's new bride. She was tougher than she looked. "Maybe it won't be you taking her to bed after all," Douglas added.

Robbie thought his head might explode. "No one is taking her to bed, damn it. She isn't going to be here long enough."

Six

It took Rosalin a while to figure it out. Once she did, she had to wait for Sir Thomas to engage Roger in conversation so they would not be overheard.

She'd met Sir Thomas, Robert Bruce's nephew, a number of times at court when he'd temporarily changed sides a few years back. The gallant, handsome knight hadn't changed at all—he was still a charming rogue. His friendly presence had relieved some of the tension of encountering the Black Douglas.

But it wasn't Sir Thomas with whom she wished to speak in private. "You were there, too," she said softly to the blond-haired warrior who'd championed them earlier.

She hadn't realized it before only because he'd changed so much. The tall, lean, boyishly handsome youth with the sun-bleached hair had added sufficient bulk and hardness to his build as to almost be unrecognizable. He was no longer a youth but a man full-grown—quite impressively, she might add. With his blue-eyed, golden-haired good looks, he seemed like every girl's fantasy of a knight in shining armor.

Except he was a brigand.

He looked surprised but nodded. "Aye, I was there."

He handed her another oat bannock fresh from the iron plate or "girdle," as he called it, cooked over the campfire. Though she was starving and would have eaten anything, the simple fare was surprisingly tasty. She suspected the oats had been mixed with some of the fat from the strips of pork she was also offered.

"I remember you." Indeed, had she not seen Boyd first, she probably would have found herself watching him. "I used to see you and Boyd talking all the time. You were friends even then." His mouth tightened a little as if he might disagree. "There was another man as well. He had red hair."

"Thomas," he said. "A childhood friend of Boyd's."

"What became of him?"

He gave her a sad look. "He died two days after we escaped."

Rosalin's heart squeezed, more stricken by his answer than she would have believed. Learning that her efforts to save him hadn't been enough made what she'd done seem so much worse. "I'm sorry."

He nodded. "He was a good man."

She did not doubt it. "Might I know your name?"

"Sir Alexander—Alex—Seton, my lady."

He was a knight? She must have shown her surprise. One side of his mouth lifted in a wry smile that held a hint of sadness. "I know it doesn't seem that way, but we are not all brigands."

There was more than a little bitterness in his tone, which she thought it better not to explore. At least not yet. But it was clear that if she hoped to find a friend from among the rebels, this man would be her best prospect.

Suddenly, she realized what else he'd said. Her eyes widened. "Seton? Were you related to Sir Christopher?"

He looked down at the fire, prodding it with a stick. "He was my brother."

He said it matter-of-factly, but she sensed the deep emotion underlying the simple words.

Her shock was complete. Like Wallace, Sir Christopher Seton had been one of the great Scot heroes in the early days of the war. Losing Sir Christopher's brother would have been nearly as big a blow to Cliff as losing Robbie Boyd. "My brother didn't know?"

Sir Alex shook his head. "Circumstances . . . Well, suffice it to say I had reasons for not making my name well known at the time. In the chaos and confusion of the surrender, no one made the connection. I was lucky. Others were not."

The sick feeling in her stomach grew along with her guilt. Now she had not only the release of Robbie Boyd on her list of grievous betrayals of her brother and country, but Sir Christopher Seton's brother as well.

He must have guessed her thoughts. "Thank you for what you did for us, my lady. I owe you my life. We all do."

His gratitude was so graciously given, she could not refuse it. She bowed her head. "You are welcome." Her gaze slid over to Boyd, who was still locked in conversation with the Black Douglas, and she shivered reflexively. "I wish all felt as you do."

She turned back to Sir Alex in time to see his mouth harden. "I tried, my lady. If it were my command, you and the lad would have never been taken." He paused, a tinge of resentment sneaking out. "But it isn't my command."

"Thank you for trying. Is there nothing more that can be—"

She stopped, stiffening, as a dark shadow fell across her. Good gracious, how had he gotten there so quickly?

She didn't need to look to know who it was. The strange hum along her skin and spike in her pulse identified him. She resisted the urge to glance up and confirm it, guessing that her disinterest would bother him.

If the sharpness of his voice was any indication, it did. "Time for bed, my lady."

There was nothing suggestive in his tone, but her stomach did a little flip anyway. She smothered a sharp intake of breath but wasn't able to stop her face from paling. She looked up at him and knew from the glint in his eyes that he'd guessed her thoughts and was taking devilish pleasure in discomfiting her.

Why was he so angry with her? The dark look he directed at Sir Alex made her wonder if it had something to do with him.

"I'm not tired yet." It couldn't be much past seven o'clock. She stretched her feet close to the fire. "And my shoes aren't dry."

"If you wish to be returned to see your brother in the morning, you will go to bed now."

Her shocked "What?" was drowned out by the half-dozen or so louder ones coming from the men around her. She didn't know who was more stunned: her, Sir Alex, or the Black Douglas.

"You are releasing us?" she asked incredulously.

"Not 'us,' you."

The Black Douglas exploded. "You can't release her! Clifford will give his left arm for the chit."

Rosalin's gaze had immediately slid to her nephew on Boyd's pronouncement. Although Roger was trying valiantly not to show his fear among the enemy warriors, she saw his face pale. Her heart went out to him. Despite the height and armor, he was still only a boy. As terrified as she was, she would not leave him.

"No!" She didn't realize how loudly she'd spoken until all the men turned in her direction. With so many eyes upon her, heat rose to her cheeks. "I won't go," she said in a more moderate tone. "Not without Roger."

Robbie struggled to control his temper. Something he seemed to be doing quite a bit around Lady Rosalin Clifford. The lass was as bad as Seton.

Though he'd overheard only the last few words, it wasn't hard to figure out what they were talking about. He might be impressed at how quickly she'd identified a sympathetic ear if he weren't so furious about it. The last thing he and

Seton needed was more discord between them; it was even more reason for the lass to be on her way.

He should have guessed after the way she'd refused to let go of the boy in Norham that she would be difficult about this. Her protectiveness toward the lad was commendable, but God's breath, did she have any idea of the concession he was making in letting her go with nothing in return? Douglas wouldn't be the only one who was furious—the king, too, would have some questions. Questions Robbie would be hard pressed to answer without revealing what she'd done for him. Something that he suspected she might not want known.

But the lass was right. He did owe her. And Robbie Boyd always paid his debts. That was one thing *all* the English could bloody well count on.

He would still have the lad. Clifford would pay with or without the lass.

He tamped down the urge to tell her that the matter wasn't open for debate and instead turned to Seton. "Take the lad to the cave and get it ready for the night. I want two men posted at the entrance at all times in four-hour shifts."

Robbie saw the frightened exchange of glances between the lass and lad and wasn't as immune to their unwarranted fear as he wanted to be.

"But—"

He didn't let her finish. "Your aunt will be along shortly," he said to the boy, relieving them both. "Lady Rosalin and I have something to discuss." He looked at Douglas and Randolph. "Alone."

The boy looked to her, and she nodded. "Go. I'll be fine. The captain has given us his word that no harm will come to us."

From the way her gaze flickered to Douglas's, Robbie suspected she'd said it just as much for his friend's benefit as for his.

With obvious reluctance the boy did as he bade, casting

worried glances over his shoulder until he disappeared into the misty darkness.

Randolph and Douglas followed with nearly as much heel digging. "You and I will talk later," the latter said in a voice that promised a reckoning.

There were perhaps a handful of men in this world who would not be intimidated by a threat from the Black Douglas; Robbie was one of them. He met his friend's gaze unflinchingly. Douglas might not like it, but that wasn't going to stop him from letting the lass go.

The exchange, however, had a different effect on Lady Rosalin. The fear that she'd been making such an effort to contain returned full force. She watched Douglas walk away as if he were a snake coiled and ready to strike. As soon as he was gone, she turned to Robbie. "What does he mean to do with us?"

He sat opposite her on the stump vacated by Seton. "Nothing. You are under my protection. You have nothing to fear from Douglas."

She made a sharp sound that was halfway between a laugh and a choke. "Does *he* know that?"

Robbie almost smiled before he caught himself. "Don't worry about Douglas. I'll take care of him."

She eyed him warily, clearly not sure whether to believe him.

He had to fight the urge to reassure her, which was sure as hell not anything he'd ever felt compelled to do with a hostage before. Of course, he'd never had a woman as a hostage before. A woman who was so beautiful it was hard to look at her without his blood heating.

What the hell was wrong with him? She was *English*, damn it. Clifford's sister. The enemy.

His mouth tightened. "Go home, Lady Rosalin. I've given you what you asked for. I suggest you take it."

"I asked for you to release *both* of us. I will not leave

Roger here alone." *With you*, she didn't need to add. Her gaze turned imploring. "Please, won't you just let us go?"

He couldn't, even if he wanted to. This was too important. He'd been handed a way to bring Clifford in line, and he sure as hell wasn't going to throw it back—not all of it, at least. The king was counting on him.

"You heard Douglas. You should consider yourself fortunate that I've decided to let you go. Your brother is causing trouble. Your nephew will ensure it stops."

"Then keep me and let him go."

"No."

"Why not?"

"The boy is more valuable. You might be his sister, but Roger is his heir."

"To most men, perhaps, but not my brother. He loves me. He'll do anything—"

She stopped, probably realizing she shouldn't be saying that.

"The lad stays."

She looked up at him, her big green eyes luminous in the misty moonlight. "Won't you have pity? He's only a boy. Just thirteen last month."

He steeled himself against the sheen of tears in her eyes. An onslaught he'd never faced in battle, and one that was proving more effective than any sword. *God's breath!* He squeezed his fists. "That 'boy' would have put a blade through my back or slain any one of my men if given the chance. I'll remind you that I wasn't the one to put him in the battle." It was hard as hell being cold and matter-of-fact with her looking at him like that. He relented—just a little. Her devotion to her nephew and attempt to protect him were admirable. "Your fears for the lad are unfounded. He does not need you here to defend him. He will be perfectly safe."

"And I am to believe that from you?" Her eyes met his. "Your reputation is well known, my lord."

There was just enough English haughtiness in her tone to set his temper right back on edge. "Perhaps you should have thought of that earlier."

It took her a moment to realize to what he was referring. When she flinched, he almost wished he could take it back.

"I didn't know who you were." Her eyes searched his with an intensity verging on desperation that made him want to look away. She wanted something from him that if it ever had been there was long gone. "At the time, I thought I saw something worth saving. Something noble and honorable. Apparently, I was wrong. A man who would use a woman and child to his advantage—as a weapon in war—is without honor. A knight would never—"

"Bloody hell! You English and your damned knights!" For a moment, staring into those fathomless green eyes, he'd been in danger of forgetting who she was. "You don't need to tell me what a knight would do. I know all about English chivalry. If you think your countrymen are like heroes in some troubadour's tale, you are dead wrong. Your king put a sword in my hand when I wasn't much older than your nephew, and he invited my father and some other local chieftains to a parley—under a truce—and then treacherously slaughtered them all."

Her eyes widened and blinked, slowly.

"Whatever I have done," he continued, "I assure you, your countrymen have done far worse. Should I remind you of the two women who were hung in cages from English castles for over two years? Where the hell is the chivalry in that? Bruce's queen, sisters, and daughter are still imprisoned by your king. The English have done everything they can to destroy and impoverish us: razing our countryside, taking our castles, raping our women, and killing our people for over fifteen years. So if winning this war and seeing my country free from English occupation and subjugations means I have to use a squire to do so, you can be damned sure I will do it. There is very little

I wouldn't do to win, so perhaps you'll remember that before you start spouting off about rules and codes of which you know nothing."

She drew back at the onslaught but did not cower. "My God, you are nothing more than what they say: the Devil's Enforcer. Bruce's hired muscle. A brigand and a thug."

He'd been called a hell of a lot worse, but somehow her words pelted like stones—deeper and sharper than he would have thought possible.

Furious, he stood and hauled her up beside him. It was a mistake. Standing close to her was like being caught in a fierce undertow. His senses flared as wildfire ignited through his blood.

Their eyes held. He swore he could see the tiny flutter of her pulse at her neck and had to fight the urge not to reach down and caress it with his thumb.

He couldn't tell whether she was scared or aroused.

She sucked in her breath and awareness crackled between them. The soft parting of her lips answered his question: *aroused*. Hot with it. Soft with it. Ripe with it.

His eyes fixed on her mouth. A desire so fierce and strong rose inside him, every muscle in his body went rigid. He was a hairsbreadth from lowering his mouth down onto hers.

What the hell was he doing?

He let her go and took a step back. "If I were you, I'd be hoping you were wrong in your estimation of my character. A less-than-honorable man might think about taking you up on your invitation."

Her eyes widened, the vivid emeralds sparking with indignation. Lady Rosalin Clifford might look sweet and docile on the outside, but as he'd seen with her defense of her young nephew, the little kitten had the claws of a she-tiger when stirred. Usually he preferred women with more of an edge—experienced women who knew what they wanted. He'd assumed sweet meant boring. It was a mistake he wouldn't make again. Her combination of sweet and fierce was oddly arousing. Maddeningly arousing.

"An invitation? By God, you must be mad! I don't know what you think you saw, but I assure you, I am no longer a naive, starry-eyed maiden susceptible to a generous display of flexing muscle." She smiled sweetly, her gaze skimming over some of those flexing muscles. "I outgrew oversized barbarians when I turned seventeen."

Claws *and* a sharp tongue to go along with it. Part of him admired her spirit, while another part of him wondered whether she spoke the truth. Had he imagined it?

His eyes narrowed at something else. *Seventeen.* Christ, how the hell young had she been?

The kiss that neither of them wanted to mention hung between them.

"You weren't eighteen," he said flatly.

Her small smile had a distinct devilish glint, as if she knew how much the answer would bother him. "Nay, just sixteen."

He grimaced and swore. Which meant she was only two and twenty now. Compared to his two and thirty, she was a child. God knew, in those ten years he'd seen a lifetime of pain and suffering.

Suddenly, in the eyes of this beautiful girl brimming with youthful innocence and radiance, he felt very tired and very old.

"You have until the morning to reconsider. But if I were you, Lady Rosalin, I'd take the offer. 'Tis not one you are likely to get again. I do not think you will find the hardships of war to your liking."

She stayed. Not that there had ever been a question on her part. Rosalin wouldn't leave Roger to face the brutes and brigands on his own. They were in this together, and together they would get through it. Preferably without having to spend another wretched night sleeping on a dirt-floored cave with little more than a plaid for cover.

Boyd was right. She didn't like the "hardships" of war, especially living like an outlaw without even the most basic of necessities. She'd thought travel before difficult, but then the long stretches of riding had been broken up by stops at castles—or at the very worst an inn—with her own bedding and plenty of servants to attend her every need. Here, she didn't even have a pitcher to wash her face or a comb to run through her hair.

She supposed she should be grateful that she wasn't sleeping outside surrounded by a bevy of brutish barbarians but was instead in a cave alone with Roger. But it was hard to be grateful for small mercies when they were imposed with such harshness.

Boyd's coldness toward her stung. She didn't know what she'd expected him to be, but it wasn't this horrible and unfeeling brute. He'd hardened to stone—just like that muscled body of his. He seemed a shell of the man he'd once been, consumed by vengeance and intent on vanquishing the enemy at any cost. Finding out she was Cliff's sister had seemingly erased whatever good favor she might have curried by releasing him. She wasn't surprised that he hated her brother or the English; she was just surprised by the depth of that hatred and that it included her.

How dare he act like this after what she'd done! To Hades with the blighter. She supposed one good thing had come out of all this: he'd certainly cured her of any romantic fantasies. She would marry Sir Henry when this ordeal was over and never look back.

As it was clear he had no intention of releasing Roger, her thoughts turned toward escape. Although she and Roger had been permitted to be together in the cave, the moment they woke and tried to go down to the stream to wash, they were separated. Roger was taken to rejoin the rest of the group, while she was permitted a few moments—a *very* few moments—of privacy in which to tend her needs, wash her face and teeth in the icy water, and run her fingers through her hair before braiding it with the one frayed ribbon she had left. On second thought, she left her hair loose and tucked the ribbon in her purse, which hung from the thin leather girdle belted around her waist. She had an idea.

The best part of the morning, however, was when she was led back to camp and learned that over half the men had departed, including—to her and Roger's great relief—the Black Douglas. Apparently, they were taking all the ill-gained pirate plunder from the raids to Robert Bruce in the North. She and Roger were being taken elsewhere. Their captor was far less forthcoming about that, but from the southwesterly direction they'd been riding, the daunting Ettrick Forest still seemed a likely destination.

The second-best moment of the morning had been learning that horses had been arranged for her and Roger, so she would not be forced to ride tandem with the stoic and taciturn Callum. It also gave her an opportunity to begin implementing her plan.

Working carefully, to ensure no one could see what she was doing, Rosalin slid the frayed pink ribbon from her purse and began pulling threads free, dropping them every furlong or so. If her brother and his men were tracking them, the threads would leave a trail for them to follow. But without the sumpter horses and extra goods, they were traveling at a much faster pace. She would have to try to find a way to slow them down.

Her first effort had the unexpected benefit of irritating her captor. "Again?" he demanded, glaring at her as if she were a child. "You just went before we left—*thirty minutes* ago."

The blush staining her cheeks wasn't feigned. How like him to be ungallant enough to question her! She lifted her chin. "I must have had too much ale to drink while breaking my fast."

Grumbling the entire time, he called for a stop. After Sir Alex helped her down, she took her time finding a bit of privacy in which to pretend to relieve herself. By the time she returned, Boyd's irritation had turned to full-fledged chomping-at-the-bit impatience. He didn't say anything, just glared at her. She smiled sweetly. "Thank you."

He grumbled something unintelligible about "lasses," and they were off again. She wondered how many times she'd be able to get away with the ploy before he became suspicious and put an end to it. If she could get past the embarrassment, the next time he questioned her, she planned to plead her woman's curse. Surely that would properly mortify him. Maybe she'd top it off by asking him to go find some rags for her to use?

She smiled, thinking the embarrassment would almost be worth it to see the formidable countenance pale with male horror.

By all rights she should be terrified of the man, certainly not thinking of ways to irritate him—even if it was for a good cause, to slow them down. But for some reason, despite his reputation, his harshness toward her, and his intimidating physicality, she sensed he would not hurt her.

Her attempts at conversation with the other men were brusquely cut off by all except Sir Alex. He was no more forthcoming than Boyd, but at least he curtailed her questions with a smile.

She spent most of her time keeping an eye on Roger, and when the opportunity arose, attempting to keep his spirits up. "Just think of the stories you will have to tell when this is all over," she said. "I'm sure the other squires will be hanging on every detail."

Her nephew seemed to consider this, and after a moment his sagging shoulders lifted just a little. "I hadn't thought of that. Do you think they will be impressed?"

Rosalin tried not to smile, knowing how important it was for boys of his age to impress their peers—boys of any age, she might add. "I should think so. Not many English squires have come face-to-face with the Black Douglas and the Devil's Enforcer. Not to mention nearly plunging your dagger into his back and drawing your sword against a knight of Sir Alexander Fraser's stature. Aye, you will have quite the stories to tell. I daresay, you will have the young lasses at the castle interested as well." She gave him a side-long look. "Although you probably aren't interested in the lasses?"

His red face told her differently. He hesitated, looking as if his surcoat were tied too tight. "Actually, there is a lass at Norham who might be interested."

She lifted a brow. "I thought there might be. Cliff wasn't much older than you when he first met your mother."

Roger looked at her in surprise. "Really?"

She nodded. "I remember thinking it was so romantic." Then she added for Boyd's benefit, as she suspected he was listening to every word, "Of course I was young and prone to silly romantic fantasies at the time. Your father and mother were very fortunate; most youthful romances only lead to disappointment." She saw Boyd stiffen and knew her barb had struck. Suddenly, remembering who she was really talking to, she turned back to her nephew with a smile. "But you shall have plenty of time for that, and un-less I've missed my mark you are very much like my brother in another way. He seemed to have every young girl in the Marches half in love with him."

Roger blushed, and the opportunity for further conversa-tion was lost when Boyd—not coincidentally, she suspected—quickened their pace. Every now and then, Boyd or one of his men would break off to scout ahead or behind to make sure they weren't being tracked.

Rosalin was making more of an effort to remember iden-tifying landmarks for their next opportunity to escape, but as they seemed to stick to the forests and hills and avoid any size village, only the occasional church or house in the distance provided any break in the monotony of rusty heather-covered hillsides and ghostly gray forests. In the spring it would undoubtedly be beautiful, but right now it just looked cold and forbidding.

God in heaven, she wanted to go home!

She was just about to demand another stop to tend her needs when she glimpsed black billows of smoke in the trees to the east a few furlongs in the distance. "Hold," she said, pulling back on her reins.

Boyd, who was riding right in front of her at the time, swung his horse around and glared at her. "I don't know what your game is, my lady, but if this is another one of your breaks, you're going to have to wait."

Despite the fact that he was glowering at her again, and she was just as angry at him, something caught in her chest when she looked at him. He might have tried to blame it on her, but invitation or not, he'd been about to kiss her last night, and every time their eyes had met since, she couldn't forget it. There wasn't a pretty bone in him, but he was gorgeous enough to make her stomach drop. His masculine appeal was undeniable. Looking at him made her heart flutter just as frantically as it had when she was sixteen. Apparently, she *was* still attracted to oversized barbarians.

Usually she preferred clean-shaven men, but rough and stubbly was beginning to grow on her. There was something about the shadow of whiskers darkening his already formidable jaw that made her feel shivery and a little wicked.

Realizing he was waiting for her to respond, she had to shake off the daze. "I don't have to stop again. It's just that I saw smoke." She pointed. "Over there."

He didn't even glance over. "I saw it."

"And you are not going to investigate?" she said incredulously. "It looks like a building could be burning."

His expression darkened. "Probably more than one.

There is no need to investigate. Given the proximity to the garrison at Thirlestane, I'd say it was more English looking to fatten their stores by raiding the local villagers."

She paled, understanding now why her question had angered him. But she didn't let it deter her. "Should we not go and see if they need help?"

"It's too late for that. Given the color and thickness of the smoke, the English are long gone by now."

"Perhaps so, but fighting English isn't the only reason to stop—they may still need our help. We cannot just ride by and do nothing."

He gave her a long look. "Why do you care? These are not your people. Hell, the order for the raid probably came from your brother."

She flushed indignantly. "It most assuredly did not." She hoped. "And they might not be 'my people' as you say, but they are people and thus deserving of compassion." She lowered her voice and met his gaze, daring him to deny her. "I would not turn my back on anyone in need, even starving rebel prisoners."

He did not take the dare. "Very well, but do not blame me if you do not like what you find."

Seven

❦

Rosalin didn't like what she found at all. It was horrible—every bit as devastating as what she'd witnessed at Norham. How could people do this to one another? But war and the horrors committed in its name were something that she'd never understood. Her brother was right. Her heart was too soft for this.

Perhaps it might be different if she hadn't been raised so far away. In London, she didn't have raids, devastation, and suffering with which to contend. The kind of hatred Boyd possessed was foreign to her, but perhaps also justified if what he'd said was true.

Had his father really been killed so treacherously? Though Cliff had tried to keep her insulated from the war, she recalled hearing a story about the Barns of Ayr, which sounded much like what Robbie described. She also recalled the brutal retaliation by Wallace and the Scots.

But it was his reminder of the fate of the Countess of Buchan and Mary Bruce, who'd been imprisoned and hung in cages from Berwick and Roxburgh castles, that made her realize what a naive view she'd had of chivalry. Barbaric acts had been done by both sides—knight or brigand.

From the crest of the hill looking over the small valley below, she could see the burned-out shells of two stone houses, with a third still burning. Four wooden outbuildings had been reduced to a black skeleton of charred posts and fallen beams. A fifth was burning, with two more in danger of catching fire. At least three dozen people—mostly women and children—were racing back and forth to the river, frantically filling buckets to put out the roaring flames in what seemed to be a task of Herculean proportions.

Boyd was already shouting orders in Gaelic as they charged down the hillside. From what she could discern, half the men were put to the task of helping the villagers put out the fires, while he and the other half-dozen men went to work clearing the dead grasses and shrubs from around the handful of buildings, presumably to stop the flames from spreading farther.

She and Roger hadn't been forgotten. In English, which she suspected was for her benefit, Boyd ordered Malcolm to take them down by the river where it was safe and to not let them out of his bloody sight. Unlike his father, Malcolm did not appear to harbor any bad feelings toward her. She'd apologized for taking advantage of his gallantry, which seemed to surprise him as much as embarrass him.

For what seemed like hours, but was probably only a fraction of that, they watched from a safe but frustrating distance as the men worked tirelessly and efficiently to put out the fire and stop it in its tracks. It was an impressive sight to behold. The same fierce intensity she'd noticed in the Scots' fighting was displayed in their well-coordinated and strategic attack on the flames.

Unbidden, her eye kept straying to the captain of this pack of unlikely heroes. It was clear the single-minded determination that she'd noticed earlier to win the war at any cost helped to make him an exceptional leader. He was focused, decisive, and confident. Watching him like this, she could almost believe that he hadn't changed as much as she'd thought. That there were still vestiges of the noble warrior for whom she'd risked so much. That maybe she hadn't been completely wrong about him.

The Scots appeared to be well on their way to winning the battle when disaster struck. The wind, which to that point had been a light breeze, shifted and started to gust, whipping up the flames with renewed frenzy.

A handful of villagers screamed as one of the walls of what appeared to be a barn started to fall back on them. They were saved only when some of Boyd's men rushed forward to hold it back long enough for them to get out of the way.

"We should do something to help," Rosalin said.

"The captain said to stay here," Malcolm replied dutifully, although it was clear he agreed with her and would much rather be with the other men than guarding them—apparently his punishment for allowing them to escape.

The sound of another crash, this one much closer, caused Rosalin to jump.

"What was that?" Roger asked.

Malcolm pointed to the burned-out stone house closest to them. As it was the largest of the buildings by far, it probably belonged to the reeve—the most important man in the small village. "The last bit of roof has collapsed. One of the beams must have fallen."

She was about to turn away, when she heard something. "Do you hear that?"

"What?" Malcolm said.

"Listen." They stood silently for a moment, but with the wind, the roar of the fire, and the shouts of the villagers and men fighting the flames, it was hard to pick anything out.

Malcolm frowned. "If this is another one of your tricks—"

"There!" she said. "Did you hear it? Someone is crying for help."

"I didn't hear anything."

But Rosalin was already racing toward the burned-out cottage where the roof had just fallen.

"Wait, my lady! You can't go in there. The captain said to wait here."

"Hurry!" she said, not listening. "It sounds like someone is hurt."

Without waiting to see whether they were behind her, Rosalin raced into the building. What appeared to be a hollowed-out shell of stone from the outside was a dark, smoldering maze of beams, posts, roof trusses, thatch, and furniture inside. She had to cover her mouth with the wool of her plaid to stop the smoke from choking her.

"Hello!" she cried out.

"Here!" a faint voice replied.

She followed the direction of the sound and in the farthest corner of the building came to a tangled pile of wood in front of a partially collapsed stone wall. Wedged in what appeared to be a space in that wall was a man who was penned in by rocks and still burning lumber. It was hard to see through all the smoke in the darkness, but he appeared to be barely alive under all the rubble.

"Here!" she shouted back to Malcolm and Roger, who she could hear calling for her. "He's over here."

The two made there way to her, their coughing growing louder as they drew nearer. They were both looking at her as if she were a madwoman. "He needs our help. He's stuck."

"What was he doing in here in the first place?" Roger asked.

It was a good question—one they could ask him when they got him out. "I don't know," she said. "Here, help me with this post—" She yelped in pain as her hands touched the hot wood.

"We'll do it," Roger said. "You don't have gauntlets. Try to move some of the rocks out of the way."

Rosalin nodded and went to work on some of the smaller rocks. Recalling a man who'd lifted rocks with much more ease, she couldn't help wishing Boyd were here to help them. He would make quick work of—

She heard a loud creak as the boys moved one of the larger pieces of charred framing out of the way. She looked up just as what remained of the roof came crashing down on them, along with the main beam that formed its spine.

She screamed a warning, but it was too late. Malcolm wasn't able to get out of the way in time and the beam crashed down in front of him.

"Malcolm!" She tried to lunge toward him but was prevented by a virtual wall of building material that had landed between them. She could no longer see the first man at all.

Fearing the worst, she was relieved when the ash and dust settled enough for her to see Malcolm move. "Are you all right?"

"I think so," he said groggily. "Help get this off me."

Protecting her hands as best she could with the wool of her plaid, she and Roger tried to lift the enormous beam, but it wouldn't budge. It had probably taken a half-dozen men to move it into position when the building was constructed. "It's no use," she said to Roger. "We'll have to fetch help."

Their eyes met. She could see what he was thinking, probably because the thought had quickly crossed her mind as well. She shook her head. They might not get another chance to escape, but she wouldn't leave Malcolm and the villager like this.

Roger nodded. "I'll be right back."

Out of the corner of her eye, she saw something that made her pulse spike and every nerve ending in her body flare with panic. The fire was no longer smoldering. The falling beams and roof had stirred the embers and reignited the fire.

"Roger!" she shouted. He turned back. She glanced in the direction of the flames, which were no more than a twenty feet away. "Hurry!"

Robbie's lungs were burning. He was hot and tired, and every inch of his skin felt gritty with soot and smoke, but he faced the fire with the same win-at-all-costs determination with which he faced the English. He was surprised how good it felt to be doing something to help that wasn't fighting. It had been a long time since he'd lifted anything but his sword in the defense of his countrymen. But the English weren't going to destroy this village today. Not if he had anything to say about it.

With the break line in the brush established, he was about to start helping Seton carry water when he glanced down by the river and stilled.

Malcolm, Roger, and Lady Rosalin were gone. Letting off a string of oaths, he ran. If she'd tricked the lad again and tried to escape, he was going to tie her up for the rest of the journey and throw her back into that sack.

He was halfway there when he saw Roger Clifford emerge from the burned-out shell of a longhouse-style building. The boy's eyes stuck out like two white discs in his soot-streaked face, and his golden hair that was so like his aunt's was matted to his head. He was wheezing heavily as he stumbled toward him. "Hurry!" he managed in a cracked voice. "N-need help."

Robbie grabbed him by the arm, more to hold him up than in anger. "What happened? Where are your aunt and Malcolm? Are they in there?"

The boy nodded and Robbie took off into the burning building, a flurry of expletives firing in his head. His ears were pounding with a sound he didn't recognize. It took him a moment to realize it was his heart.

What the hell could have possessed her to go into that

building? He was furious. Beyond furious. Out-of-his-mind furious. But most of all he was bloody scared. Enough to admit it.

He ducked through the doorway into the smoky cavern. Covering his mouth with his arm, he blinked through the black haze, his eyes immediately tearing.

"Rosalin! Malcolm!" he choked, trying to see through the maze of smoldering destruction. It looked as if one of Sutherland's black powder explosions had gone off in here.

"Here!" a distinctly feminine voice replied. "We're back here."

Ploughing through the stacks of beams and posts as if they were twigs, he made his way toward them. It wasn't difficult. All he had to do was follow the line of flames that seemed to be heading right for them.

For as hard as his heart was pumping, his voice came out remarkably calm when he looked down into her tear-stained, soot-streaked face. "What happened?"

His voice didn't sound like his own. He hadn't known it was possible for him to speak so . . . tenderly.

Her tiny chin trembled and for a heart-wrenching instant, he thought she might fall apart. If she had, he knew he would have pulled her into his arms. He wouldn't have been able to stop himself.

But she took a deep breath and held her emotions in check. "I heard a man crying for help, and when we came in to help him, Malcolm got stuck when a beam fell on us."

It was strange how a heart that was pounding so fast could suddenly come to a dead stop. He waited a beat or two for it to start again. He wouldn't think of her lying under that beam crushed. He wouldn't. But he started to get a sick, twisted feeling in his gut anyway. He felt something he'd never felt before: weak-kneed.

"Captain? Is that you?"

Malcolm's voice brought him back. "Aye, lad. I'll have you free in a minute."

She looked behind him. "Did no one else come with you?" Her voice shot up in panic. "We aren't going to be able to move it in time."

Obviously, she'd been trying to do just that.

"Move back." He quickly took stock of the situation and realized he needed to have care. One wrong move and the entire pile of rock and beams would come down on Malcolm, crushing him instantly.

Turning his back to the beam, he grabbed the squared edge and using his legs, started to lift. But damn, the thing was heavy, even for him. "See if you can scoot out from under it," he said from between clenched teeth, every muscle straining.

"Almost," Malcolm said. "Another inch or two."

Robbie clenched harder and lifted. His arms burned against the weight. But Malcolm was able to slither his way out. Very carefully, Robbie lowered the beam back into place.

And not a moment too soon. The flames were only a few feet away now. "Come on," he said. "Let's get out of here."

"But what about the man?" Rosalin said. "We can't just leave him."

Robbie clenched his fists, fighting the anger and fear that made him want to lash out. "Where?" he said tightly.

"Behind that wall." She pointed to a space that had obviously been built into the wall as a hiding place. Suspecting for what, and exactly why the man was there, Robbie was tempted to leave him for being so reckless. But a few moments later, he'd moved the debris out of the way enough to drag him out. Not wanting to tell her that it was too late, he lifted the dead man over his shoulder with one arm, and with the other wrapped around her waist tucking her up tightly against him—trying not to notice how good she felt—he led them out of the burning trap.

As soon as they hit the fresh air, Malcolm collapsed on the ground coughing. Rosalin stayed on her feet but bent over to do the same, while Robbie let his arm slide from her waist and dropped the body of the villager, then grabbed on to the nearest tree so he didn't topple over. His lungs and arms were on fire.

Seton, Fraser, Callum, and two more of his men were almost on them. The lad had obviously managed to alert them to the danger. Seton immediately rushed forward to assist Lady Rosalin, as did Callum with Malcolm. "What happened?" his partner asked.

For once, Robbie wasn't annoyed by his solicitousness. The lass needed tending, and he could barely stand.

It took a few stops and starts for the story to come out. But between Malcolm, Roger, and Rosalin, the details began to emerge. It was hard enough to believe she'd raced in to try to help someone she didn't know, but when Lady Rosalin reached the point where Malcolm became stuck behind the debris, the men looked at each other in astonishment.

Robbie voiced what all of them were thinking. "You could have left him there and escaped."

She met his gaze. "He would have died," she said, as if the explanation were obvious.

For her, he realized it was. She wouldn't leave a man behind to die, not even an enemy. He should know that better than anyone. Something inside his chest shifted. It was as if a big rock had been pushed out of the way, revealing a small opening.

Callum looked at him as if the world had just been declared round. "But she's *English*," he said in Gaelic.

"I know." Robbie was at just as much of a loss for an explanation. It didn't make any sense to him either. This one small lass seemed have more honor in her than the entire English army put together.

Yet the more he watched her, the more he believed it wasn't an act. She was just as sweet and kind as she looked. He'd noticed how she'd distracted her nephew earlier to keep his spirits up and her natural friendliness toward his men—even in the face of their brusqueness (in most cases, outright rudeness). When she'd demanded to come see what could be done in the village, he thought it was a trick. But it wasn't. It had obviously been motivated by honest concern. For *Scots*. She'd run into that burning building to help someone who was her enemy.

It defied belief.

But it was more than that. Beneath the sweetness he detected a fierce sense of right and wrong that reminded him of someone, although he couldn't put his finger on who.

When she reached the part where he arrived, he tried to stop her, but she wouldn't let him. "I've never seen anything like it," she said. "I don't know how you lifted that by yourself."

It wasn't the first time he'd heard admiration and awe in a lass's voice, but it was the first time he felt his face growing hot. Bloody hell, he was blushing!

"You should see him at the Highland Games, my lady," Malcolm offered. "The captain can throw a stone three times as heavy as anyone else. No one has ever come close to beating him. Why, he can defeat ten Englishmen using just his hands—"

"That's enough, Malcolm," he said sharply. "The lady doesn't want to hear about all that."

She looked like she was about to disagree, when she glanced to the man lying on the ground at his feet. Her eyes filled with tears. "He's dead, isn't he?"

He nodded.

She looked up at him. "Why would he have done something so dangerous?"

Robbie reached down and pulled a purse from the man's

clenched fingers. "For this. He had it hidden in a space in the wall, along with some grain and other goods. He'd probably put it there when the English came and then tried to get to it once he thought it was safe."

"All this for a few coins and some grain?" she asked incredulously.

Robbie's jaw hardened. "Aye, it was foolish, but it was probably all he had to feed his family. These people will have nothing left."

The realization affected her. There was no denying the real compassion and sadness in those too expressive eyes of hers.

"But you saved some of them," she said. "The fires are almost out."

The way she was looking at him . . .

For a minute, he felt like he'd donned some of Seton's shining armor.

Bloody hell.

Robbie glanced over to where the rest of his men and the villagers were throwing the final buckets of water. But she was right. They had.

Something had changed. Rosalin didn't know what, but over the next hour, while Robbie and his men helped the villagers put out the last of the fires and see what could be salvaged from the rest, she detected a difference in the men's attitude toward her.

Once they'd stopped staring at her as if she had suddenly grown a second head, they actually spoke to her. And not just in grunts and unintelligible words in Gaelic. Men who she didn't think knew a word of English were suddenly addressing her as "my lady."

Even Callum. Well, perhaps *especially* Callum. Just as personally as he'd taken her tricking of Malcolm, it seemed he'd seen her refusal to leave his son in the burning building as the establishment of some kind of bond between them. She couldn't tell whether he was pleased about it or not, but he'd taken his son's place in guarding her and seemed to have nominated himself as her protector.

When some village children cautiously approached and started touching her soiled but very fine gown, he'd shooed them away and told them not to get the lady's gown dirty with their grubby hands. Considering how inelegantly she'd been handled the past twenty-four hours and how filthy she was already, such admonishments were quite laughable. But cognizant of how serious he seemed to be, and his Scot pride, she smothered her smile and told him she didn't mind just this once.

The children had been entranced with her and had asked some of the most humorous questions, at which she'd struggled hard not to laugh. They must have asked her ten times if she was *truly* English. That she didn't have the face of a gorgon, or devil's horns and tail, was apparently incomprehensible.

It was when talking to the children—a few of whom had lost everything—that she'd had an idea.

Callum hesitated, giving her that strange look again. "You want to give them our food?"

"Aye, do you think some could be found that might be spared?"

He stared at her for a long time, his ruddy, weathered features inscrutable. "I'll ask the captain."

From their post by the river, Rosalin watched the older man walk over to where Boyd stood with some of the villagers. Boyd's head turned in her direction, and even from the distance the intensity of his gaze made her shiver. A few moments later, he nodded, and Callum strode toward the trees where the horses had been tied and started to go through the bags.

With Callum occupied and Roger conscripted to help the other men with the cleanup, Rosalin kept herself busy answering the children's questions while trying not to let her eyes stray to the man who seemed the center of attention in the village.

She frowned. For one small village, there certainly were a disproportionately large number of young women. And every one of them seemed to be traipsing after Robbie Boyd like he was some kind of hero.

To them, he was, she realized with a start. This man reviled as a devil on one side of the border was lauded as a hero on the other. It was strange what a difference perspective made.

The women were practically tripping over each other trying to get him to notice them. Good gracious, had they never seen a handsome man before? She could see the stars shining in their eyes from here.

Why did she care, anyway? She'd outgrown barbarians, hadn't she? Besides, he'd made his feelings toward her perfectly clear: they were enemies. She would not forget it.

Escape was what she should be thinking about. Not tall, broad-shouldered brutes with excessively muscled bodies.

Tearing her gaze away from the man commanding so much feminine admiration, she focused her attention on the children. When they moved off, she asked Callum if she might wash up before they left. After a quick glance to where Roger stood with Malcolm and another young warrior (he knew she wouldn't try to escape without her nephew), he nodded and told her to be quick about it.

She hurried down toward the river, heading to the left, where it bent and a copse of trees would protect her from view and give her the privacy she needed.

She hadn't lied. She *did* want to wash and soak her hands in the cold water, but she also needed to replenish her supply of ribbon for the trail she was leaving for Cliff. The last few strands of pink were in her purse, but her chemise was decorated on the neck and sleeves with small, light-blue bows of satin ribbon. The costly garment imported from France had raised even her indulgent brother's eyebrow, but she didn't think he'd mind its destruction under the circumstances.

Indeed, most of her once luxurious clothing was in shambles. Removing the plaid and cloak, she shook them out as best she could, set them down on a log, and then brushed the dirt and soot off her dark blue wool *cotehardie* edged at the hem, neckline, and cut sides with gold embroidered ribbon. But she feared not even a good brushing and hanging would save the pretty garment after such abuse.

She grimaced, lifting her skirt up to examine the rest. The lighter blue wool kirtle underneath was in much better shape, except for the muddy hems where it hung below the *cotehardie*. But she didn't think to remove her over-gown; she needed every layer for warmth.

The fashion for both gowns was tight in the sleeve and bodice, and it wasn't without some difficulty that she was able to loosen the laces of the *cotehardie* on the front and the kirtle on the side to reach the chemise underneath.

After pulling off as many of the ribbons as she could reach, she tucked them into the purse still at her waist. Then, kneeling beside the river, she dipped her hands into the icy water and cupped it to her face. It was cold but invigorating. She washed and scrubbed until the water came back clear and not gray with soot.

It felt so good to be clean that she considered dunking her head in and washing her hair, but she didn't want to risk the chill of wet hair while they were riding. She did, however, take the opportunity to wash her upper body as best she could with the loosened garments. She was so engrossed in her task, she didn't hear him approach.

"It's time to go. The men are . . ."

His voice dropped off. It took her a moment to realize why. She'd jumped up when he startled her and turned without thinking. His gaze had fallen on her chest and appeared to have become stuck, along with his tongue.

A quick glance down told her why. Her chemise was soaking wet from her washing. Her very thin, very transparent, very revealing chemise, which was now molded to her breasts, revealing every curve, every contour, every point in perfect detail. She might as well have been naked.

She sucked in her breath, which was a mistake, as it only made her breasts rise to even more prominence.

He made a sound low in his throat that was almost pained, but it made every inch of her skin blaze with heat.

She made a move to cover herself, but he grabbed her wrist. "Don't. God, please don't."

Heat blasted her again. It poured off him in a hot, molten wave, making her nipples tighten.

He groaned, a deep, intensely masculine groan that sent a rush of something hot and damp between her legs. It pooled there, growing warm and achy.

His face was harder than she'd ever seen it—sharper— more dangerous somehow. It was as if all the civility had been stripped away, leaving nothing but the fierce, primitive male underneath.

He stared at her breasts as if he had never seen anything more desirable. As if he could barely hold himself back from touching them. From *ravishing* them.

Their eyes met, and she felt the shock of it radiate like a bolt of lightning up her spine. No one had ever looked at her with such raw lust, possession, and heat.

The air was charged with something she didn't understand. The fierceness of the emotions crackling between them was too overwhelming.

Men had wanted her before, but never like this. This was different. This was wild, dangerous, and uncontrollable. This was desire unlike anything she'd ever experienced before and, for a moment, it scared her.

He scared her. She might have thought she knew him, but Robbie Boyd, hardened warrior, was not the noble rebel she'd watched as a girl. She was alone with one of the most feared men in Scotland. A man who by all accounts was a scourge, brigand, and barbarian. She was completely at his mercy, and the precariousness of the situation—and her vulnerability—slid down her spine in a terrified chill.

Eight

❧

It took Robbie a minute to realize he was scaring her.

Before that he was lost. From the moment she'd turned, with every inch of that damp linen molded to her chest, he hadn't had one rational thought in his head. With all the lustful thoughts swirling around, there hadn't been room for anything else.

Hell, there hadn't been room for much else since the moment he'd first laid eyes on her. Even his dreams had been filled with her. Images that had made him wake up hard and restless this morning. Images that had come back to him during the day, too many times to count. Images that it turned out were nowhere near as spectacular as reality.

This image was going to haunt him for the rest of his life. Every pair of breasts he saw from now on would suffer from the comparison.

The funny part was that she didn't even fit what he'd thought of as his ideal. To be blunt, he liked them big and lush, with sweet, juicy nipples. He liked to bury his head between the soft mounds of flesh, to watch them bounce, jiggle, and sway as he drove in and out. He liked them to pour over his hands as he gripped from behind (aye, he especially liked that), to suck the hard peak of a substantial nipple into his mouth and draw it between his teeth and tongue.

Not that he opposed variety. But if he'd had an ideal, that would have been it.

Until now. The two perfectly rounded mounds of flesh before him were not generously proportioned by any means. They would fit in his hands with nary an ounce of flesh spilling over. But the shape was exquisite—masterful in its detail—putting any Grecian sculptor to shame.

They were high, round, and firm, and perfectly proportioned to her slim ribcage and waist. Her nipples were small and a dusky shade of pink. When they hardened under the heat of his gaze, they weren't much bigger than two pearls. Not much to pluck between his teeth, but he could still practically taste the tiny points on his tongue, and it took everything he had not to reach out and rub one under his thumb. To circle the wrinkly edge and pinch the delicate tip gently between his fingers and see if it felt as perfect as it looked.

It would be. God, he knew it would be.

He felt like a child who'd just opened a door and found a room full of sugary confections waiting for him to gorge on. And God, she was sweet. Sweet and so damned ripe, it took his breath away.

Her skin was like freshly poured cream, smooth and velvety white. In God's way of devising the perfect torture for a man, he'd matched the naughty little freckle on her lip with one above her left breast. He didn't know which he wanted to put his mouth on first. But it was all he could think of.

Blood pounded through his veins. He throbbed hard with need. Seeing her like this had stripped away all pretense of control. His attraction to the lass went beyond rationality. His body didn't care if she was English, if she was Clifford's sister, if touching her would be the biggest mistake he ever made in his life. All his body wanted was to smooth his hands over every inch of her soft skin until it was just as hot as his, until her cheeks flushed and lips parted with pleasured breaths, until her hips pressed against his in silent entreaty, until he opened her with his fingers—and maybe even his mouth—and made her slick and wet for his entry. And until he came into her with a hard thrust and made her his. He wouldn't stop thrusting until she came, until she screamed his name and every last shudder of her release had ebbed from her spent body.

He'd never felt anything like this, and the force of it overpowered him, dulling everything else around him.

Until he saw her eyes widen. The effect of that was like a dousing of ice water. He was brought back to reality with a hard jolt.

"Christ, I'm sorry." He took a step back. "I don't know what—" He stopped and cleared his throat, trying to let the strange tangle of emotions in him calm before he said something he shouldn't. "I didn't mean to frighten you."

He turned away, giving her a chance to fix her gown and his blood time to cool. Only then did he allow himself to look at her again.

She couldn't seem to cover herself quickly enough. She'd donned not only her gowns, but her cloak and plaid, and was still eyeing him warily.

He didn't blame her. What the hell had come over him? He'd never so completely lost himself. He'd never allowed himself to lose focus of what was going on around him. He'd never allowed himself to be that distracted by a woman. Never. He was always in control. But something had come over him, and she'd seen it.

But damn it, no matter what had come over him, he would never force himself on any woman, and he needed her to know it. "I am many things, but a rapist is not one of them, Rosalin. Believe what you will of what they say about me, but know that. I will never force you and would kill any man who tried."

The latter came out with a ferocity that surprised him, provoking questions he didn't want asked. Such as why the hell did he feel so protective toward her?

She lifted her gaze for a moment, and then dropped it again. "All right."

"I mean it."

She looked up at him again, this time meeting his gaze. He could see that some of her fear was gone, but not all of it.

His mouth tightened with anger. Not at her, but at the subject he was about to broach. He hated talking about the past. Hated thinking about what had happened to his sister. He couldn't recall ever talking about it—even to his Highland Guard brethren who knew what had happened. But he would raise the vile specter this one time to make her understand. "My only sister was raped."

She gasped. Her eyes locked on his, as if she knew the flat matter-of-factness of his tone hid a deep, searing pain—a wound that would never be healed.

She put her hand on his arm, and he stared at it, feeling his chest tighten.

"I'm sorry. That must have been horrible. But she is lucky to have a brother who cares for her so deeply."

Cared. She meant it as a kindness but didn't know how much pain her words caused. He'd loved his sister more than anyone else in the world. Pretty and vivacious, always with a smile on her face, she hadn't been much older than Rosalin the last time he'd seen her. "A hell of a lot of good it did her. I wasn't there to protect her when the English garrisoned the King's Inch castle in Renfrewshire and invaded our village. When the captain learned she was the sister of the rebels Robbie and Duncan Boyd, he decided to make an example of her. He didn't use her once, but over and over. He made her his whore and raped her until she couldn't bear it anymore and threw herself off a cliff into the sea to end her suffering."

She covered her mouth with her hand in horror. "Oh God, Robbie, I'm so sorry. But the fault lies with the soldier, not you. If you could have helped her, you would have."

Her confidence in him did nothing to ease his guilt. His help had come too late for Marian. But the soldier had paid for his deeds. Slowly, painfully, and ultimately with his life. Robbie's fists clenched at the memory.

"I tell you this not to earn your sympathy or your pity," he said, "but so you understand that I would never hurt a woman like that."

Her eyes met his, this time without a trace of wariness. "I see that now. Thank you for telling me. No wonder . . ." Her voice dropped off. "You've lost so much. I'm sorry about your father and sister. And about your friend."

His brother Duncan and his mother, as well. She'd died of a broken heart not long after his sister's death. He frowned. "My friend?"

"Thomas." She must have noticed his stiffening, because she hurried to explain, her hands twisting in front of her. "Sir Alex told me he died not long after you left Kildrummy. I understand why you would blame me for it—it was my fault he was beaten for leaving the food."

He grabbed her arm to put a stop to the anxious hand twisting. "I don't blame you. As I told you that night, what you did was a kindness. The food gave him a chance."

Her breath hitched at his touch. He shouldn't be touching her. Men didn't simply go around touching ladies whenever they felt like it. But his impulses with her had never been normal. He dropped his hand, oddly unsettled.

"Then why are you doing this? What have I done to deserve your hatred?"

He frowned. This wasn't about her, it was about her brother. "I don't hate you."

He didn't, he realized. That was part of the problem. The war was black-and-white for him. The English were the enemy, and they deserved his hatred. But she . . . she made him see gray.

"Well, you are certainly doing a wonderful job acting like it. All these years that I wondered what it would be like if we ever met again, I never imagined it would be like this."

The touch of sarcasm in her voice sparked some of his own. "Did you think I'd be happy to learn that my rescuer was the sister of my worst enemy? The man I despise above all others? The man who was responsible for our capture and the execution of many of my friends?"

It wasn't until her eyes widened that he realized he was shouting.

He swore and raked his fingers back through his hair. He knew he shouldn't take his frustration and anger at the situation out on her, but he couldn't seem to help himself. Something about this lass made him want to pull her into his arms at one moment and lash out like a lion in a cage the next.

"My brother was only doing his duty. He—"

He stopped her again, taking her by the arm and turning her to face him. "Don't, Rosalin. Don't attempt to defend your bastard of a brother to me. He is a subject upon which we will never agree."

Rather than be put off by his anger, she seemed amused. "Do you know he says the same thing about you?"

He let her go, some of his anger dissipating. "I can imagine." Robbie was sure Clifford had plenty of choice things to say about him. He eyed her speculatively. "He doesn't know what you did?"

She shook her head. "The food, but not the rest. If he ever found out . . ." Her voice fell off, and he could see her distress. "I couldn't bear his disappointment."

Her brother's opinion obviously meant a lot to her. Apparently Clifford's well-known affection for his only sibling wasn't one-sided.

"He will never hear of it from me." He supposed it was the least he could do. But if Clifford's opinion mattered so much, why would she have risked so much to help him?

She'd admired him, he knew. But was there something else? "Why did you do it?"

"It was wrong," she said simply. "And I couldn't stand by and watch my brother put men to death for something that wasn't right."

He laughed; he couldn't help it. "Clifford has never let something like right and wrong get in his way of killing Scots."

It was her turn to stiffen, that patrician English beauty turning sharp and icy. "Are you accusing my brother of being a *murderer*?"

His gaze turned just as hard. "I suppose it depends on your definition. He operates under the color of law—*English* law, which I assure you has very little justice for Scots." Before she could attempt to defend her brother again, he said, "Come, they will be waiting for us."

She was quiet for a moment as they walked through the trees. When she finally spoke, he wished that she hadn't. "Did you ever think of me?"

Her voice sounded small and uncertain. He should have said no, but he found himself answering honestly. "I wondered who you were." He thought about the kiss and found himself adding with a wry grimace, "And I wondered how old you really were."

He glanced over in time to see a soft flush spread over her cheeks. But then she bit her lip, and he felt a surge of heat to his groin and had to look away. "Why did you kiss me?"

Robbie stopped in his tracks, but he recovered quickly and increased their pace. Christ, of all the questions to ask. She hurried alongside him, casting him expectant glances.

He sighed and answered slightly exasperatedly, "I have no bloody idea."

The answer seemed to please her. A small smile turned

her mouth and he realized he could stare at that smile for hours. A smile like that could be distracting.

But it disappeared quickly as they walked through the village to where the men were waiting, and he returned the wave of one of the women.

"Are you married?"

The question took him aback. "Hell—" He stopped. "Nay," he said more calmly.

"Why not?" Her mouth pursed. "If those women are any indication, it certainly can't be from lack of opportunity." She sounded oddly annoyed by the observation. "And you must be over thirty."

"By two saint's days," he provided. "I am not married because I do not wish to be. There is no place in my life for a wife or children."

He hadn't meant it as a warning, but it had come out as one.

They were nearly within hearing distance of the men waiting for them, but she asked, "You don't want a family?"

Truthfully, he didn't think much about it. That part of his life had never been important to him. He was too focused on the task at hand. Besides, look what had happened to his sister. A wife of his would be in danger. Aside from the threat were it ever to be known of his place in the Highland Guard, he was too well known.

"Maybe when the war is over. But until then, nothing else matters." He paused and held her gaze so there would be no mistake. He wasn't going to be distracted by anyone. "Nothing."

Time was running out. Rosalin's heart pounded anxiously, knowing that every mile they rode was bringing them closer to the forest that she'd come to think of as the place of no return. Though no one had as yet confirmed their destination, their southwesterly direction left her no doubt. She and Roger had to try to escape before they were swallowed up in the impenetrable Ettrick Forest, the dark and terrifying lair of thieves and *phantoms*.

After emerging from yet another hilly forest onto a track that might almost pass for a road by Scotland standards, she let another pale blue bow of ribbon slip from her fingers and had to resist the urge to glance over her shoulder. Was Cliff tracking them? Was that why Boyd was pressing them so hard? It seemed his urgency to reach their destination matched hers *not* to reach it.

She stared at the powerfully wrought back of the man who alternated between scouting and riding at the head of the band of warriors. Had he been as unsettled as she by what had nearly happened at the river? His desire for her had been so well hidden, she'd never imagined that kind of intensity. It seemed to have surprised even him. Clearly he wanted her, but it was equally clear that attraction wasn't going to change anything. She was his hostage—a means to an end—that was all.

Her own attraction to him was just as confusing. The glimpse of the noble warrior that she'd seen today, and the insight into what drove him in what he'd revealed about his sister, didn't change anything. He might not be the coldhearted devil she'd first thought, but he was focused and determined to win the war to the exclusion of everything else. He'd devoted his life to the fight for freedom. Dear Lord, he was the same age as her brother, who'd been married since he was eighteen and had six children.

"*Nothing else matters*," Boyd had said. She believed him.

But it wasn't just her unease about what had happened earlier and the realization that she was still ridiculously attracted to him that fueled her urgency to escape. Although she did not believe he would needlessly hurt her or Roger, she knew he would not hesitate to use them as a weapon against Cliff, and that she would not allow.

Nor would she risk her nephew's life on "needlessly." Just look at him! Poor Roger looked as if he were about ready to fall from his horse. He was exhausted after the travails in the village and the seemingly endless hours of riding over rough and brutal terrain. He wasn't alone; she was exhausted as well. They weren't hardened warriors. But every time she'd tried to raise the subject with Boyd on one of their infrequent stops, he dismissed her pleas and seemed to grow increasingly angry.

They'd been riding for a few hours when she glimpsed what appeared to be the parapet of a castle and surrounding village before Boyd once again led them into the trees and hills (which she'd become certain must cover ninety percent of this godforsaken countryside). What she wouldn't give for a proper English road! Her backside was going to be bruised for weeks after the abuse. Fortunately, the pain in her hands had subsided.

A short while later, near dusk, Boyd called for them to stop. She watched him ride off with one of the other warriors, presumably for more scouting. His diligence made her wonder whether Cliff was close.

After Callum helped her down, she approached Sir Alex where he stood talking to Malcolm and Roger. Though the two boys were both tall and slim, with only a few years separating them, the differences between them could not be more glaring. Malcolm had the hard, wiry strength and endurance of a warrior. He looked like he could ride for another day or two, whereas Roger looked as if his legs might collapse at any moment, though he was fighting hard to hide it. Her heart went out to him, knowing how much the proud youth would hate the idea of looking weak in front of the enemy.

"Will we be camping here for the night?" she asked hopefully.

Sir Alex gave her a sympathetic smile. "I'm afraid not. We've only stopped to water the horses."

Rosalin tried to ignore the disappointment on Roger's face, not wanting to draw attention to it before the men. "But it will be dark soon. Surely we must take time to eat something?"

"But you gave all our food away," Malcolm said, with obvious surprise.

Rosalin turned to him. "I did?"

The boy nodded. "Aye, back at the village."

She hadn't realized they'd been left with so little after the Black Douglas had taken the plunder from the raid. No wonder Boyd had looked at her so strangely when Callum had brought him her request.

"We wanted to travel lightly and didn't anticipate the delay in the village," Alex said, gallantly trying to ease her guilt. "We would have been back at camp by now."

But Rosalin did not regret her actions. The burned-out villagers would need the food more than they did. She could go a night without food. Her belly rumbled. Even if her stomach protested.

"If we had time, we could hunt something," Malcolm said helpfully. It seemed Sir Alex wasn't the only brigand prone to gallantry; Malcolm was also concerned that she not feel guilty.

She gave him a grateful smile that made the lad turn as red as his hair, before turning back to Sir Alex. "We will reach camp soon?"

"Not for a few hours. Maybe longer in the dark."

She couldn't stop the groan. Roger, too, looked like a pup who'd just been kicked.

"Sir Alex, if you have a moment there is something I should like to talk to you about—in private."

He nodded and sent Malcolm and Roger off to tend the horses. He motioned for her to take seat on a rock nearby, but she shook her head. As tired as she was, the prospect of sitting on hard rock was not appealing. "Do you mind if we walk a little? I should like to stretch my legs."

They headed toward the stream, but instead of joining the other men, he led her in the opposite direction. When they reached the water's edge they stopped. In addition to forests and hills, there were streams or burns, as the Scots called them, everywhere. They were pretty, she realized. Even in the barren bowels of winter, the dark waters cutting through the small valleys of russet moorland, flanked by tree-covered hillsides, evoked a peacefulness at odds with the wild, war-torn countryside.

"I did not want to say anything in front of Malcolm, but you must see how tired my nephew is—though he'd die before admitting it. He's not used to riding for this long over this kind of terrain. I don't know how much longer he can take it." She glanced up at him pleadingly. "I don't know how much longer *I* can take it. Is there not a place nearby where we might stay for the night? An inn, perhaps?"

His mouth thinned. "I'm sorry, my lady. I would not have you forced to endure any of this. These are no conditions for a lady—or a lad." He smiled, but it was without humor. "But you've seen how little sway my opinion holds around here."

The bitterness in his tone was undeniable. She hadn't been mistaken in identifying Sir Alex as a potential ally. She had, however, underestimated the level of his disaffection. Whatever disagreement there was between him and Boyd, it ran deeper than she'd realized.

She didn't understand it. By all appearances the men were close companions who'd fought together for years. Half the time they didn't even use words to communicate—just glances. So why the animosity and resentment?

She hated taking advantage of Sir Alex's gallantry like this, but she had to do something to slow them down. Something to give Cliff a chance to catch up to them or for them to escape. The village and the castle she'd seen weren't all that far away. If they could stop . . .

"Please, Sir Alex?" The shimmer in her eyes wasn't completely feigned. She truly was exhausted. "Is there nothing you can do?"

"Seton!"

The deep voice from behind startled her. She dropped her hand from Alex's arm, not realizing she'd put it there, and turned to find Boyd standing right behind them.

"How do you do that?" she snapped guiltily. Which was ridiculous, as she had nothing to feel guilty about. He'd refused her appeals, so she'd brought them to a more sympathetic source.

"Do what?"

"Sneak up behind people."

"Practice," he said, his eyes dark with something she didn't recognize. "Return to your nephew. I need to speak to *Sir* Alex."

The way he emphasized *sir* sounded like a slur.

She was tempted to argue, but something about his expression gave her second thoughts. She looked at Sir Alex questioningly, and he nodded. For some reason, her appeal seemed only to make Boyd more irate. From the way his eyes darkened and his nostrils flared at Sir Alex, he looked like a bull ready to charge. She wouldn't want to be standing in the young knight's shoes right now.

She hoped whatever had provoked his anger toward the other man didn't have anything to do with her.

She gave Alex an apologetic look and started to walk off, but Boyd stopped her. "Lady Rosalin."

She turned.

"You dropped something."

Instinctively, she looked to the ground, but he reached out, took her hand, and turned it palm side up. A moment later it was filled with blue bows and threads of pink satin.

She gasped, her eyes flying to his. But his expression was as hard as granite and utterly unreadable.

"Be more careful where you leave things," he said icily. "We wouldn't want anyone to follow us."

She swallowed slowly, her mouth dry, and nodded.

Robbie barely managed to wait long enough for her to be out of earshot before rounding on his partner. He leaned toward him, his muscles flaring for battle. "Stay the hell away from her, Dragon."

He knew he was overreacting, but the black emotion that was surging through his blood right now wasn't rational or controllable. It seemed to come over him every time he saw Lady Rosalin conversing with his partner. In other words, about every time he turned around. But it had really gone wild, nearly blinding him with rage, when he'd returned from picking up more of her damned ribbon to see their two golden heads bowed together and her hand on Seton's arm.

Seton didn't move a muscle, giving no indication that he perceived the threat. Instead, he gave Robbie a long, steady look. "No. I don't think I shall. I rather like Lady Rosalin."

"What do you mean you like her?" Robbie exploded. "Have you forgotten who she is?"

Seton shrugged indifferently. "We have much in common—as you are always pointing out. Or have *you* forgotten?"

"So now you are English?"

"Haven't you been telling me that for seven years? Maybe I've decided to start listening to you."

"What the hell is that supposed to mean?"

"It means I'm done trying to defend my loyalties to you. I'm done trying to prove that the blood I've shed over the past seven years is just as Scottish as yours. It means that if I see a lady who has been ripped away from her family and everything she's ever known, who is scared and needs help, I'm going to try to put her at ease—even if she happens to be English."

Robbie was so stunned for a minute he didn't know what to say.

"What is this really about, Raider?" Seton paused, scanning Robbie's irate face, bunched shoulders, and tight fists. "You know what I think? I think you're *jealous*. I think you want her, and you can't stand it that she might prefer me to you."

Robbie had never struck his partner before—though God knew he'd been tempted more than once—but he was a hairsbreadth from doing so. He wanted to sink his fist through that knowing smirk so desperately his arms twitched. Mostly because he knew it was true.

He *was* jealous. For the first time in his life the ugly emotion was twisting him up inside, and he couldn't stop it.

He was attracted to her.

Hell, attracted was putting it mildly. All he had to do was look at her and he was picturing her naked and under him again. Picturing her cheeks flushed and her lips parted as he made her cry out—nay, *scream*—with pleasure. Aye, the fair Rosalin—the perfect English Rose—screaming his name as he made her come again and again was something he just couldn't get out of his head. But he'd be damned if he'd admit it to Seton.

"Sod off, Dragon. The lass has obviously identified you as an easy mark, and I'm just trying to make sure you don't do anything foolish."

"If being sympathetic to her plight makes me an easy mark, then I guess you are right. The lass needs someone to protect her."

A fresh spike of rage set his teeth on edge. "Nay, she doesn't. She has me. I will protect her."

"Then I suggest you start doing so. Have you taken a look at her and the lad? They are so exhausted they can barely stand. You've dragged them halfway across Scotland in less than a day and a half with little food—"

"Whose fault is that?" Robbie snapped.

Seton gave him a look that said he knew very well that Robbie had been touched by her kindness and didn't begrudge the loss of a meal. "What if one of them falls ill? What will you tell Clifford then?"

Damn it, he wasn't blind. Seton wasn't telling him anything he couldn't see for himself. The conscience he'd unfortunately found tugged every time he looked at one of them. "I don't give a shite what Clifford thinks, but I was coming to tell you that Fraser has ridden ahead with Keith and Barclay to Kirkton Manor to see about arranging a room for the night."

The old laird was of unquestionable loyalty, and the accommodation was perfectly situated to ensure she wasn't tempted to make another escape attempt. Though they weren't in the forest yet, they were close enough and firmly in Bruce territory, despite the garrison at Peebles Castle a few miles back.

Seton smiled. "Good to know you aren't a completely unfeeling bastard."

Robbie's eyes narrowed, having the distinct feeling he'd just been maneuvered. "Aye, well I might have let you know of my plans sooner had I not been forced to backtrack for ribbon."

Seton's grin deepened. "You have to admit, it was rather clever of her."

A wry smile lifted one corner of his mouth. "Aye, well it's a good thing Fraser noticed it or we might have led Clifford right to us. I should punish her for it."

"But you won't."

It wasn't a question. Maybe Seton knew him better than he wanted to think. God knew they'd been partners for a long time. Seton knew more about him than anyone. He frowned. Even more than his brother Duncan had.

"Maybe not," he agreed. "But I'll let her think about it."

Seton laughed. "I don't think it will work. With all the dark looks you've been casting her, the lass is strangely unintimidated by you. Perhaps she knows something the rest of us don't?"

"I don't know, Dragon. I think I stopped intimidating *you* a long time ago—or you wouldn't be such a pain in my arse."

It was an acknowledgment of sorts. A recognition that despite the imbalance between them at the start, the scales had started to even. They might never agree on the war and how it should be won, but as a warrior and a partner, Seton had his respect.

Seton nodded. Though a small acknowledgment, Robbie could see it meant something to him.

After a moment, his partner asked, "Do you want to tell them the good news or should I?"

They both knew there was more to the question than first appeared. He could let Seton continue in the role of champion or . . .

Robbie held his partner's gaze. "I'll do it."

He didn't know what kind of claim he'd just made, but he knew that he'd made one.

Nine

❧

The sight of a pillow nearly made her weep. The fact that one small, lumpy, linen-covered pillow could bring her to tears was a testament to how tired Rosalin was and how grateful—and surprised—she was that Boyd had agreed to let them stop for the night.

Although once she saw the place, she understood. The old wooden tower turned fortified farmhouse was auspiciously situated on the edge of a steep ravine. With the only entrance well guarded, escape would be nearly impossible. *Nearly*. But she was determined to try. With her ribbon plan foiled, it was up to her.

She and Roger had devoured the small bowl of bland beef pottage and day-old crust of bread they'd been given by the farmer as if it were ambrosia, before being escorted up the two flights of stairs to their garret chamber by Boyd.

It was as she'd anticipated when she'd first seen the building: they were given the room at the top of the house overlooking the ravine. If the height and position of the room weren't enough, as an added deterrent to escape Boyd would be sleeping right outside their door.

Their host had been surprisingly thoughtful, providing not only water to wash but paste to clean their teeth and—she said a prayer of gratitude—a comb to run through their hair. A small iron brazier in the corner provided a pleasant warmth to the room that made it easier to ignore the earthy smell of peat.

There was a small bed tucked under the one shuttered window in the room, and through an adjoining door a few mattresses were tucked under the eaves for servants.

It was the bed and window that had given her the idea. After they'd washed and readied for bed, she shared it with her nephew.

Roger looked at her with increasingly widened eyes. "You want to do *what*?"

Cognizant of the man on the other side of the door, she put her finger up to her mouth to warn him to keep his voice low as she continued to explain her plan. "Like Queen Matilda," she whispered. "Do you remember how she escaped Oxford Castle? If we tie the bedsheets together to make a rope, we can tie one end to the bedpost"—she hoped it was strong enough to hold them—"and climb out the window."

When Queen—or Empress—Matilda was under siege by King Stephen at Oxford, she'd escaped in a similar fashion by being lowered down the wall by her men, famously wearing white to blend into the snow-covered surroundings.

"Didn't you see the ravine? It must be forty feet from here to the ground."

"Then we will have to use lots of sheeting." She took the solitary candle in the room and cracked the shutter enough to look outside, ignoring the cold blast of air that seemed to remind her of the warmth and safety of the room she planned to leave. Peering down into the fathomless darkness, she tried—unsuccessfully—not to shiver. "See, it doesn't look that bad. I don't see anyone guarding it."

"For good reason," Roger pointed out. "Who in their right mind would climb out this window?"

Rosalin knew he was right and was just as scared as he was, but they had to at least try. This might be their only chance. She wouldn't let Boyd use them against Cliff. "It won't be that bad. You'll see. And once we are down, it's not that far to the castle we passed earlier."

Roger nodded. "I saw it, too. I wish I knew where we are. But if you are right that they are taking us to Ettrick Forest, it is probably Melrose, Selkirk, or even Peebles—all of which are held by the English."

She nodded. "Your father is probably racing to one of them right now."

Roger seemed to be warming to the idea. "Perhaps you are right. We have to at least try. It will be much harder to try to find our way out of the forest. If we do this, though, I have one condition."

She tried not to smile at his authoritative posturing and nodded.

"I will go first."

"Absolutely not—" She started to object, but he cut her off.

"If something goes wrong, I can jump farther than you."

If something went wrong, jumping was the last thing they needed to worry about. She wanted to refuse, but she could see that stubborn look of Cliff's on Roger's face. She considered him for a moment. "Very well, but you will give me a promise as well. If something goes wrong, you will not stop and wait for me but go for help."

He held her gaze and nodded. Neither of them was pleased with the conditions, which she supposed was the indication of a good negotiation.

Sweeping an errant lock of hair from his forehead, she gave him a tender smile. "Get some sleep. We will have need of it. I will wake you when it is quiet."

Roger nodded, too tired to argue. "I'll sleep in there." He pointed to the garret. "You take the bed." He frowned uneasily. "Or maybe I should sleep at the foot of your bed. I don't like how he looks at you."

Rosalin wasn't sure she did either, but the look on Roger's

face was so concerned and the instinct to protect her so sweet, her heart squeezed.

Yet it was her job to protect him. "I don't think that will be necessary." Cognizant of his pride, she added, "Though I thank you for the offer. But he will not hurt me like that."

After what she'd learned today, she knew rape was the one thing she need not fear from Robbie Boyd.

Either her confidence had impressed him or Roger had reached a similar conclusion on his own. He looked at her pensively. "You like him, don't you, Aunt Rosie-lin?"

She hoped her shock at his perceptiveness didn't show. "I . . ." She bit her lip. "I don't know what to think," she finished honestly.

Roger frowned as if he, too, were undecided. "He is not what I expected. He doesn't act like a brigand—at least not all the time. But Father hates to even hear his name mentioned. So I'm sure he must have done a lot of bad things."

Rosalin thought for a moment, pondering all that Boyd had confided in her today. "I'm sure he must have, but lots of bad things have been done in the name of war by both sides. It's hard to find someone all good or all bad. People are usually somewhere in between."

Roger seemed troubled by what she'd said but nodded. Like most people, he wanted to see in black or white, not shades of gray. But Rosalin was beginning to see that Robbie Boyd was very gray indeed. Behind the ruthless shell lingered some of the man she remembered. Perhaps he was not the black-hearted, merciless brigand, but not the noble knight on the white steed either. Probably the same could be said of Cliff.

As she didn't dare close her eyes, Rosalin kept herself occupied for the next few hours by preparing the strips of sheeting she and Roger had made before he went to bed. Working by the sliver of moonlight coming through the cracked shutter, she twisted them into plaits and tied the ends together. When she was done, she'd constructed a strong, forty-foot-long rope.

Fortunately, the wooden bed was sturdily built. Tying one end of the sheeting to the thick post, she let the other end drop out the window. They might have to drop the last few feet, but it should be long enough.

When the sounds from below had completely died down, and she was certain everyone was sleeping, she woke Roger.

Moving about the room like ghosts, they climbed atop the bed and carefully drew the shutters wide. Giving the rope a hard tug, Roger stepped onto the sill and looked down. His face paled, and his Adam's apple bobbed, but he didn't hesitate. They exchanged a look, and he started down. She held her breath, wanting to reach out and grab him. He must have sensed her turmoil. "Remember your promise," he whispered.

She stilled. "You, too."

And then he was gone. For five agonizing minutes she watched the rope strain against his weight. A few times the bed creaked and her heart dropped to the floor. But it held. It held! And finally—finally!—the rope went slack. He'd reached the bottom.

She peered down, unable to see him, but didn't hesitate. Tugging the rope as he'd done to test its strength, she started to climb onto the sill. But before her foot touched the wood, disaster struck. The shutter hadn't been open all the way, and she accidentally knocked it with her elbow, causing it to clatter against the outside wall—loudly.

She froze as the sound seemed to reverberate through the quiet night like a church bell. Maybe he wouldn't hear . . .

Movement and the sound of the door rattling told her otherwise. Thank God she'd thought to latch it.

"Rosalin. Open the door."

She looked outside and her heart lurched, almost as if it

were trying to tell her to jump. To go after her nephew and do whatever she could to escape.

But she had to give Roger a chance. Quickly untying the rope, she let it drop and drew the shutters closed. Her hands were still on the latch when the door banged open.

Restless and on edge, Robbie hadn't bothered to try to sleep. Instead he sat with his back propped against the door and attempted to concentrate on Kirkton's fiery whisky rather than the woman firing his blood.

It wasn't working. He was so attuned to her in the chamber behind him, his pulse jumped every time he heard a noise.

But this noise was different. It wasn't footsteps or whispered voices or the sound of the bed creaking as she rolled around; it was a loud slam that was out of place in the middle of the night. So when she didn't respond right away, he didn't hesitate to snap the paltry latch with a hard slam of his shoulder against the door and burst inside.

A blast of cold air hit him. The window had been open. A fact seemingly confirmed by her current position, kneeling on the bed with her hands on the shutters. She turned to him with a startled gasp. He thought he detected a flash of panic in her eyes, but it might have been just surprise. "What are you doing in here?"

He closed the door behind him and strode toward her. "I might ask you the same thing."

He was close enough to see the flush heat her skin and the pulse in her neck begin to quicken. She was nervous. But whether it was his presence in her chamber, the fact that he stood close enough to smell the mint of the rub she'd used to clean her teeth, or something else, he didn't know. "Why were the shutters open?"

He was watching her closely, closely enough to see the flutter of that quickened pulse before she replied. "The room was warm, so I cracked one of the shutters. It must have blown open while I slept. I'm sorry to have woken you, but as you can see, there is no cause for your concern."

A quick sweeping glance of the room seemed to confirm her words. The iron brazier was stocked with peat and burning in the far corner of the room, the small table set out with the items he'd asked Kirkton to procure for her next to it, candle on the nightstand, bed against the window . . .

Everything was where it should be.

But something wasn't right. He reached for the latch of the shutters behind her. She hitched her breath as his hand crossed right in front of her, grazing her chest. He jerked at the contact, every nerve ending snapping to attention, but didn't look at her.

Leaning over, he peered outside. It was a mistake. Her soft feminine scent, which to that point had been faint and gently teasing, turned deep and penetrating, engulfing his senses and making him feel as if he were drowning.

How anyone could smell that good after two days in a saddle and being trapped in a burning building, he didn't know. It must be some secret women's magic to drive men insane.

His body was pulled as tight as one of MacGregor's bowstrings as he quickly scanned the darkness. Though he didn't see anything, his instincts were telling him that something was wrong, and they'd saved him too many times for him to ignore them.

The boy. "Where's Roger?"

Though it was dark, he could see her eyes flicker before darting to the adjoining garret. "Sleeping."

He started to move toward the door, but she stopped him with the soft press of her hand on his arm.

Jesus! His blood hammered. She was too close. Touching him.

"Please, don't wake him. He's so tired and needs to rest."

Their eyes met. Something passed between them. Something that stopped his breath, stopped his heart, and made the floor shift under his feet.

He was hot, hard, and poised on the edge of a precipice, struggling to hold on. Struggling not to touch her. But this might be a battle he could not win.

His heart pounded, restraint making his muscles flex. The weight of inevitability came crushing down on top of him, a weight too heavy for even him to hold off. He wanted her so intensely he could taste her on his tongue.

Her eyes fell to his mouth. Her lips parted. She leaned closer.

The subtle invitation was too much to resist; the battle was lost. His mouth fell on hers with a deep groan. For a moment it was just like the first time he'd kissed her. He felt the same unexpected ripple of shock at how good she tasted. How soft her lips were. How the innocent tremble of her mouth under his made him ache to be the one to teach her about passion.

But then it changed, because this time he didn't pull back. This time he didn't fight the urge to deepen the kiss. This time he slid his arm around her waist, dragged her up against him, and let himself sink into the honey softness of her mouth to taste her fully. This time he caught the tremble of her lips with his and showed her how to open for him, how to take his tongue in her mouth and let him stroke her.

Aye, he stroked her. With long, slow pulls of his tongue until she stroked him back. The first flick of her tongue against his made him groan. His knees almost buckled.

It was incredible.

Bone melting.

Blood heating.

Mind blowing.

About the best damned thing he'd ever felt. And with every stroke it got better. Hotter. Even more incredible.

The role of tutor was not one Robbie had assumed before—preferring experienced women in his bed—but he found himself reveling in it, enjoying her soft moans of awakening as if they were his own.

He liked knowing that this was new to her. That she'd never let a man kiss her like this before. That he would be the one to inflame her passion for the first time.

He felt an unexpected wave of tenderness that gave him the strength—even when other parts of his body were urging differently—to go slowly.

Just a kiss, he told himself. Nothing he hadn't done countless times before.

But he was fighting new sensations of his own. Kissing her was . . . *different*. It wasn't just that she tasted incredible, that her lips were about the softest damned things he'd ever felt, that the tentative stroke of her tongue against his had made him as hard as if she'd licked his cock, or that he felt like he was burning up and drowning at the same time, it was also the sense of peace that came over him. Real peace. For the first time in a long time—hell, he couldn't remember the last—the restlessness inside him eased. At that moment, he knew he was exactly where he was supposed to be.

He felt a pleasure so engulfing it seemed to drown out everything else. All he could think about was how soft her cheek was in his hand, how she smelled like rosewater, how good she felt pressed against him, and how he could go on kissing her like this forever.

If only he weren't so hot. If only his blood weren't roaring through his veins and his heart weren't hammering in his chest. If only those soft little mewls of pleasure weren't reaching down to grab him by the bollocks and giving him a tug. If only her hands weren't on his shoulders, her nails digging into the muscles, a visceral marking of her grow-

ing pleasure. If only her breasts weren't crushed against his
chest and his cock weren't throbbing hard against her
stomach. And if only her hips hadn't started to move.

Aye, especially that. The tentative press, the sweet grind,
the slow circling of her hips against the part of him that he
was doing his damnedest to ignore set off something loose
inside him. The faint voice in the back of his head that
wanted to make her his turned to a loud roar. The knowledge that she wanted him as much as he wanted her
snapped whatever rein he had on his control.

Rosalin hadn't meant it to happen, but when it did, it felt
so inevitable—so destined—that she wondered that it had
taken so long.

The magic and wonder, the sense of stunned shock,
she'd felt the first time his lips had touched hers was nothing to the perfect myriad of sensations that crashed over
her when he kissed her, *really* kissed her.

She felt enveloped in heat, drowned in the heady taste of
whisky, and possessed by emotions she didn't fully understand. Fierce emotions. Poignant emotions. Intense emotions
that made her breath catch, her heart jump, and her body
feel as if it were melting into a pool of heat.

She'd been kissed since that first time, but never like this.
Never so thoroughly, in a way that took her breath away.
Never with such all-encompassing need, such possession,
such skilled seduction, and such tenderness.

That was the biggest surprise of all. That this fierce warrior, this ruthless enforcer, this man who stormed and pillaged his way across the countryside, could kiss so *tenderly*.
That the soft strokes of his mouth and tongue could en-
treat and not command. That this man of incredible
strength could be so gentle. She would never have believed
it. But here she was half-kneeling on her bed, half-cradled
against his chest, being kissed as if she were the most precious thing in the world.

His hand cradled her jaw, the big callused fingers that could grip the hilt of a sword with such deadly purpose caressing her cheek with the gentle stroke of a mother to a newborn babe, as he coaxed her mouth open to the deft plunges of his tongue.

Deft and slow, and knee-weakeningly sweet. The shock she might have felt at the intimate invasion was blunted by the sensation of utter rightness. There was nothing more natural or perfect than the warm slide of his tongue against hers.

Each stroke seemed calculated to draw her in deeper. To make her shudder and moan. To make her want more. She couldn't stand it.

But clearly he was in no hurry. He seemed maddeningly in control, maddeningly content to go on kissing her like this for hours.

But something was building inside her. Something she didn't understand. Something hot and powerful and anxious. Something that with every wicked stroke of his tongue became more imperative.

Her moans became more insistent. The tentative circles of her tongue turned bolder and more demanding. She sank into him, pressing her breasts against the warm, rock-hard shield of his chest. And good lord, was it an impressive chest. She could feel every hard ridge, every steely slab, and every rock-hard bulge. She'd always admired his body, but there was something vastly different in admiring from afar and being plastered up against all that strength. He was big and powerful, and having all those muscles wrapped around her made her feel hot and heavy, and want to get closer.

Especially—the knowledge pooled between her thighs— that long, thick part of him that she could feel hard against her stomach.

She moaned and clutched. Pressed and rubbed. And still it wasn't enough. This feeling that had come over her wouldn't go away. It seemed to only grow stronger. The more he touched her, the longer her kissed her, the more she felt him against her, the worse the need became.

At least she was no longer alone. He was kissing her harder now—deeper—without as much smooth control. The stubble of his jaw scraped against the tender skin of her chin as his mouth moved over hers, plundering with raw intensity.

His groans were echoing her moans. His breathing was just as hard as hers, the hammer of his heart just as fast, and his skin just as hot.

She felt a burst of heady feminine pride and pleasure, knowing that she could do this to him. That he was just as affected as she.

His mouth fell to her jaw, and then to her neck, the wet heat of his breath making her shiver and shudder as he kissed a hot trail along her fevered skin. The hand that had been wrapped around her waist slid up to cup her breast, and the relief of the pressure was so acute, all she could do was moan and press herself deeper into the big, warm hand that seemed imprinted on her body.

He bent her back, arching her against him, kissing her again as he plied her breast with his wicked touch. Cupping and squeezing, pinching her nipple gently between his fingers until it drew to a hard peak.

Sensation exploded inside her. Oh God, how was he doing that? How could something feel so good? How could such big, brutish hands wield such exquisitely wrought pleasure?

She thought she'd died and gone to heaven. And then she knew she had when he replaced his hand with his mouth. Somehow he'd loosened the laces of her gown enough to slide his mouth under the edge of the fabric. The feel of his warm tongue circling her, before taking her gently between his teeth and tugging, sucking . . .

She cried out, a strange, pulsing heat pooling between her legs.

Her cry seemed to do something to him. He swore and the smooth, unhurried movements became more insistent, more purposeful.

She didn't know how it happened, whether she'd pulled him back or he'd pressed her down, but somehow she was lying back against the pillows, and he was stretched out on top of her—or half on top of her. For someone so big and presumably heavy, he certainly felt good. She liked having all that solid weight pressing down her—it gave her an odd sense of security and closeness.

She opened her eyes long enough to glance down and see his dark head bent at her chest as he continued to suck her deep into his mouth. But then the needle of pleasure was so intense she had to close her eyes again as another cry escaped from between her lips.

He was saying things, murmuring against her skin in Gaelic. She didn't need to understand the husky words to know that he was telling her all the things he wanted to do to her.

Her body shivered with wicked anticipation as his mouth covered hers again. He drew back once, long enough to look into her eyes. It was dark, only a sliver of moonlight slipping into the room from the shutters, but she could see the fierce emotion in his gaze. Emotion that made her heart catch and her breath quicken. His eyes were burning hot. He wanted her. She could see that. But it was more than want. It was a look of possession, a dark look of primitive intensity that made her feel as if he'd just staked a claim right through her heart.

By all rights his expression should frighten her. She knew what he wanted to do. Knew she should say something to stop him. Knew that what she wanted right now was impossible.

But the look entranced her. She couldn't turn away. Even when she felt his hand sliding under her skirt and guessed what he was going to do. Even when he touched her and

her entire body felt as if it had been shot through with a
bolt of lightning.

She gasped, trembled, every nerve ending standing on
edge as his finger lightly brushed over the tender place between her legs.

Oh sweet heaven! A rush of heat and dampness seemed
to gather there. If she had been able to think, she might
have been embarrassed and wondered at the strange throbbing. But then he touched her again and all she could think
about was how good it felt and how much she wanted him
to touch her more.

The light brushes of his callused fingertip weren't
enough. A soft sound escaped from between her lips—part
whimper and part plea. Her body was shaking with a
strange restlessness, as if wanting to move but not knowing how.

He touched her again, and finally she could no longer
hold back. She lifted her hips against his hand, unconsciously seeking the pressure that her body so desired.

He made a fierce sound that was almost a growl. His
face was dark and tense, his jaw clenched tight, as if the
measured strokes of his fingers were costing him every last
bit of his control. His gaze seemed to burn right through
her, singeing her with its intensity.

"God, you're beautiful," he said tightly. "I can't wait to
make you shatter."

Rosalin didn't understand what he meant, but she didn't
care because at last he was giving her what she wanted. He
was cupping her with his hand, rubbing her, and finally—
Oh God in heaven!—sinking his finger inside her.

He stroked her just the way he'd done with his tongue,
plunging and circling until the pleasure overwhelmed her.
Until the desire had nowhere to go. Until the gentle pulsing
became a hard spasming. "Robbie! Oh God, please!" She
arched under him, crying out, as sensation gripped her

body in an iron hold and finally let go, catapulting her into a celestial wave of pleasure so intense, so acute, so magical, she felt as if she'd glimpsed a piece of heaven.

Robbie. Watching her release, hearing her cry his name as pleasure swept over her, did something to him. It wasn't just the primitive response of his body—which had been stoked and primed to the breaking point—it was a feeling that centered somewhere in his chest and squeezed. The feeling that if he didn't have her, that if he didn't make her his, he was going to die.

God knew she was beautiful, with a lithe, sensual body that would make any man weak with lust. But he'd felt lust before and this raw craving, this bone-deep yearning, this all-encompassing need was like nothing he'd ever experienced. It came from a place so deep, buried so far inside him, he hadn't known it existed.

The feeling drowned out everything else. He didn't care who she was or why she was here. None of that mattered. All that mattered was that when she was in his arms he felt . . .

He *felt* something. Something strong and powerful and right.

The soft cries of her pleasure were still echoing in his ears as he started to work the ties of his chausses and braies. Sweat gathered on his brow as he held himself stiffly to the side, trying not to crush her with the full weight of his body.

She lay under him, soft and achingly sweet, her body weak and pliable from her release. So ready. His fingers were still damp from her slickness, from the proof of how ready she was for him.

He had to grit his teeth against the urge to sink inside when his erection bobbed free and the cool blast of night air hit the hot, turgid skin.

He didn't need to fist himself in his hand to test his readiness—he was so close he might explode.

He levered himself over her, settling himself between her thighs. Every instinct urged him to throw his head back and plunge inside.

She wouldn't stop him. She wanted this as much as he did. He could see it in her eyes.

He stilled. And there, through the pounding in his heart, the red haze of lust roaring through his blood and the desire throbbing hard between his legs, he heard something. A tiny voice that should have been drowned out by the primitive roar. A voice he told himself to ignore and that made him want to shout with pain and frustration. A voice that told him this was *wrong*. That no matter how much she wanted this, or he wanted this, he couldn't take her innocence.

But God, he wanted to. He wanted to so badly his body shook from the effort not to make her his.

She wasn't his and never could be. And Robbie apparently had more honor left inside him than he realized.

The small questioning tilt of the head that she gave him was the last shove. He wrenched away with a vile curse and turned away from her, as if that might clear his head and allow him to think.

But he wasn't thinking. His body was in too much pain. Every inch of him was throbbing with anger and frustrated lust. His heart was pounding so hard he couldn't breathe.

"What's the matter?" she asked. "Did I do something wrong?"

She tried to put a comforting hand on his shoulder, but he wrenched away, even the small touch too much to withstand in his present state. Seated on the edge of the bed, he bowed his head, willing the fire to stop roaring in his blood. But it wouldn't quiet. It was pulsing and hammering, needing someplace to go.

He needed to get out of here. Standing, he hastily refastened his clothing. He didn't dare look at her reclining on the bed in near-ravished disarray, knowing that the mussed hair, flushed cheeks, and swollen lips would be too much for him to resist. "I'm sorry," he managed curtly. "That should never have happened."

Ten

❧

That should never have happened, Robbie repeated to himself more than once over the long night. The harder question, and one he didn't want to ask himself, was how it had. He didn't lose himself in lovemaking like that. Ever. He was always in control. Always aware. Hell, he could be sucked deep in a lass's mouth, coming hard, and still be thinking about his next mission. But one minute he'd been kissing Rosalin Clifford, and the next he was almost inside her. He hadn't been thinking about anything else.

Robbie . . .

He forced himself to shut out the memory. But he'd never forget the sound of his name on her lips as she broke apart. That soft, sensual plea would haunt him for the rest of his life.

Bloody hell, what was wrong with him? How could he have forgotten who she was? She was his hostage, under his protection, and "Despoiler of Innocents" wasn't a title he was eager to add to his long list of sins. Even if she was Clifford's sister.

After waking Seton and instructing him to stand guard outside her door, Robbie sought the cold embrace of a winter's night, as much to chill his blood as to clear his thoughts. He passed the two men he'd left to guard the main gate and headed into the forest.

Robbie's expression didn't invite conversation, and they didn't ask him where he was going. He didn't know. But the dense, bone-chilling mist that had descended among the trees offered a strange comfort. The sharp brace of the cold air seeped in, penetrated, and eventually eased some of the tension coiling in his body.

Lust he knew how to remedy. A warrior spent too much time away from women to bother being shy about taking the edge off himself when the need arose, so to speak. It was the other emotions coursing through him, the equally fierce and intense emotions, that wouldn't be sated by a few hard pumps of his fist.

His desire for this woman went beyond lust. It had been strong enough to make him forget who she was—hell, he probably would have forgotten his own damned name, if she hadn't yelled it—and completely lose control. It had penetrated the haze of detachment that usually surrounded him when he was with a lass and made him feel things he'd never felt before.

But that wasn't what really concerned him.

He might be ruthless and merciless on the battlefield, but he'd always been a considerate bedmate. Yet even in his most youthful dalliances, before Wallace had raised his sword and Robbie had dedicated his life to the fight for Scotland's freedom, he couldn't recall ever being so gentle or tender with a lass. The reverence, care, and protective feeling that had come over him when he kissed her—*that* scared the hell out of him.

He didn't want anyone he took to bed to be different or special. And sure as hell not an Englishwoman—especially that particular Englishwoman. He had no intention of playing a part in some romantic tragedy, and that's all it could ever be between them.

With no particular destination in mind and still too restless to return to the manor and attempt to sleep, Robbie started to climb the Manor Hills toward Dollar Law. Though the dark shadow of the mountain was lost in the mist, it loomed over the valley like a vigilant watchdog.

By Highland standards the gentle, rolling hills of the Southern Upland range that dominated much of the Borders were relatively easy climbs. Dollar Law was one of the highest peaks in the area, probably coming within five hundred feet or so of the Cuillins, where the Highland Guard "trained" (more aptly, suffered), though well short of the great Ben Nevis. Still, by the time he reached the top, he was winded and feeling a burn in his legs.

As the summit was free of mist, he took a seat on the stones of the summit cairn and watched the darkness of night give way to the breaking of dawn.

By the time the first glimpse of sunlight appeared to his left, casting a soft orange glow across the valley below him, Robbie knew what he had to do. Rosalin Clifford could not stay. She might wish to not leave her nephew, but after what had happened—or nearly happened—her wishes no longer mattered. He had to do what was best for his mission, and right now, getting her far away from him was what was best.

He glanced toward the castle just visible beyond the trees in front of him. He would take her to Peebles as soon as she woke, and—

He stopped, squinting into the distance. Peebles Castle was less than ten miles away, and with the low mist it was difficult to see, but he'd glimpsed some kind of movement. A short while later he saw it again, only this time he'd seen the banners and unmistakable glint of silver that told him what it was.

He raced back down the hill and through the woods to the manor. Seeing the same men he'd left a few hours before, he shouted orders for them to ready the rest of the men.

Climbing the stairs to the chamber where he'd left the lass and the lad, he saw Seton perched in the same spot Robbie had been before he'd heard the noise that had taken him into the room.

His partner immediately got to his feet. "What's wrong?"

"English soldiers are heading in this direction from the castle. We need to go."

Seton swore. "You're certain it is us they are after?"

"Nay, but I'm sure as hell not sticking around to find out."

He knocked on the door, surprised when she immediately bid him to enter. Apparently, he wasn't the only one who hadn't slept much last night. Pushing open the door, he saw her sitting on a small stool by the brazier, her hands folded in her lap. She glanced up at him, and their eyes caught. He saw the question, saw the hurt, the confusion, and felt an unwelcome seizing in his chest.

Her skin was pale, her expression serene, her golden hair shimmering in the morning light. She looked so achingly beautiful, he knew he would remember her like this forever. Because this was where they would say goodbye. He wouldn't need to take her to Peebles Castle with the English heading this way.

"Wake your nephew," he said. "We need to leave."

She stayed perfectly still, barely reacting to his pronouncement. "I can't do that."

He crossed the room, took her by the elbow, and lifted her to her feet. "It wasn't a request, my lady. There is a party of English soldiers headed this way, and although I don't object to killing Englishmen, I'd rather not have you and Roger in the middle of a battle."

She wasn't looking at him and wouldn't meet his gaze. It was so unlike her, it made him uneasy.

He released her, dragging his fingers through his hair. "I'm sorry for what happened last night. I should never have—" He stopped. Christ, he felt like he was Roger's age, apologizing for stealing a kiss with his first lass. Except it hadn't been just a kiss he'd nearly stolen. "It won't happen again."

"I can't wake Roger because Roger isn't here."

It took him a moment to realize what she'd said. "What do you mean he isn't here?"

She lifted her chin, meeting his gaze full on. "I made a rope out of the bed linens, and he climbed out the window."

Robbie went completely still. His eyes searched her face. Surely, she couldn't be serious. That climb was at least a forty-foot sheer drop into a rocky ravine. The idea that the boy would take such a risk was so ridiculous, so preposterous, he didn't want to believe it.

But it was true. He could see it in the cool, unflinching repose of her face.

"Are you mad?" He exploded. "Do you have any idea how dangerous that was? The boy could have fallen to his death." It wasn't until the next thought struck that he realized he was shaking her. "*You* could have fallen to your death." *Bloody hell.* "That's it, isn't it? That was the noise I heard. You were on your way out that window as well?"

Even as she gave him a short little nod, the other truth was hitting him. Rage crashed down on him like a hot, black hammer with a crushing blow. His fingers tightened around her arm. "You did it on purpose," he snarled from between clenched teeth. "You deceitful English bitch, you threw yourself at me so I wouldn't discover the lad was gone."

She flinched, taken aback by his venom. "Nay, that's not how it happened. I was trying to stop you, but I didn't intend for that to happen."

"Didn't you? What else do you think would happen when you let a man kiss you like that? When you rub your body up against him like a practiced whore?"

Her eyes widened. "How dare you say something like that to me! You know I'm not—"

"I know you spread your legs eagerly enough, and that I

was a hairsbreadth from taking you up on your offer. A mistake on my part that I intend to rectify."

Her face paled, the delicate pulse below her neck fluttering. "You wouldn't! You swore you wouldn't ravish me."

A dark, wicked smile turned his mouth. "Who said anything about ravishing? With as hot as you were for it, I doubt I'll need to do much persuading."

He pushed her away so he wouldn't be tempted to prove it right now.

A flush stained her pale cheeks at the crude boast. "You weren't the only one who made a mistake. But I assure you it was never my intention to give myself to you to prevent you from learning of my nephew's escape."

He stood there seething, trying to control the anger racing through his veins. He couldn't believe that he'd allowed himself to be deceived by a beautiful face and siren's body. This was what he got for trying to be considerate and not pressing on to the camp. For not keeping them separated.

He should have anticipated treachery—she was English, wasn't she? And now, because of her, his weapon—his surety—against Clifford had slipped right through his fingers.

His gaze hardened. He might not have Clifford's heir, but he still had his sister. There was no longer any question of letting her go. Rosalin Clifford was coming with him, and after what she'd just done, her brother would be lucky if Robbie ever gave her back.

As horrible as her confrontation with Boyd had been, and as uncomfortable as the next few hours were while racing over the brutal countryside to escape their pursuers, Rosalin couldn't regret what she'd done. Roger must have reached Peebles Castle and been able to rally the soldiers to come after her. Maybe even Cliff. Whatever else happened, her nephew was safe. She would be grateful for that even as she feared for her own safety.

But if Boyd was trying to scare her, it was working. She'd never seen him so angry. That was why he was being so mean and had said all those hateful things, wasn't it? He wouldn't really force her to be his whore. And that's what it would be: force. In spite of his claim to the contrary, she wouldn't give herself to him like that again. Not after what he'd said to her and knowing what he intended. She wasn't that much of a fool.

She hoped.

She didn't know what was worse, how quickly she'd surrendered to him or how mistakenly he'd ascribed her motives. She *had* been trying to stop him from checking on Roger, but she hadn't planned to offer herself up as a distraction. It had just happened that way. She'd been just as caught up in the moment and surprised by how quickly things had spun out of control as he.

Did he honestly think she'd had any idea that a kiss could descend into *that* so quickly? She hadn't even known what *that* was. She'd had no idea a man's touch could rouse such incredible feelings in her. No idea she could become so swept away by passion that she would forget about everything else: her virtue, her position . . . good gracious, the fact that she was betrothed to another man!

Rosalin was ashamed by how quickly she'd succumbed and could only be thankful that he'd stopped before doing something that could not be undone. She still had her virtue, if not her innocence. She'd been naive and foolish, but now that she knew how easy it was to get caught up in the riptide, she wouldn't go near the water again.

No matter how "hot" she might be. His crude words still stung. How could a man who'd touched her so tenderly one moment treat her so coldly the next? She'd almost convinced herself that he might care for her a little. That maybe he felt the same strange connection that she did. That maybe her sixteen-year-old heart hadn't been wrong.

But his harshly spoken words had cured her of those illusions. She was an "English bitch." The enemy. His hostage. And if she let herself forget it, she could very well end
up his whore.

Still, she couldn't stand the idea of him thinking the
worst of her, and she had every intention of reiterating her
innocence as soon as his anger had cooled.

But even half a day later, after hours of the most perilous
riding she'd ever endured, up the steepest, narrowest
mountainsides and through the densest, darkest, most impenetrable forest, his jaw was just as hard, his mouth just
as tight, and his eyes just as narrowed as they had been
when he'd stormed out of the room.

Not that his black visage had ever been turned in her
direction. Nay, she didn't think he'd looked at her once
since they'd left.

None of the men had. Even Malcolm, Callum, and Alex
avoided her gaze. Whatever goodwill she'd earned after
the fire in the village was gone. The Scots took their cue
from their captain, and Boyd's anger toward her could not
be more clear. However it had happened, she'd bested their
hero in allowing her nephew to escape, and that could not
be forgiven. She was an English hostage. A *female* English
hostage. The lowest of the low. The fierce male Scot pride
could not withstand such a blow.

But the silence was oppressive. She'd never felt so alone.
By the time the first signs of the camp came into view, she
was so miserable—not to mention filthy and exhausted—
she would have welcomed a hovel, if it meant she could get
off this horse and escape their forbidding indifference.

Rosalin didn't know what she'd expected of the rebel
encampment—perhaps foxholes and scattered plaids over
the heather?—but it certainly wasn't the neat row of
Roman legionary-style tents leading up to a large sturdily
constructed wooden Viking-style longhouse that sprang
out of the thick forest along a rocky riverbed like a pictur-

esque faerie tale–looking village nestled in the tree-covered hillside. It wasn't exactly luxurious, but it was far from the image she had of the outlaw "hood" from which Robert the Bruce had earned his moniker of King Hood.

The forest itself, however, lived up to its frightening reputation. From the moment they'd entered the shadowy canopy of trees, she'd been waiting for one of Bruce's phantoms to jump out from behind a tree and shout "boo." It was easy to see why the English had ceded the forest first to Wallace and later to Bruce's men. The rebels could sit in ambuscade from virtually anywhere, and the narrow paths that wound through the forest would force the English soldiers to ride single file, leaving them even more vulnerable. The men of Ettrick Forest, like the legends of the outlaw Hood, were also known for their skill with a bow, a particularly deadly skill in this kind of environment with so many trees to hide behind.

She assumed they must have had scouts watching out because a handful of men—and a few women—were already standing outside to greet the returning warriors. From the cheers and lighthearted tone of their shouted greetings, she realized they were cheering the successful mission.

Rosalin hadn't expected women. But no sooner had they stopped and the men dismounted than she understood their purpose at camp, when the women ran forward to greet some of the men in a particularly friendly manner.

As no one seemed inclined to help her dismount, Rosalin was about to attempt to do so on her own, when she glanced at Boyd. One of the women had launched herself into his arms and was plastered to his chest. Her long, wavy pitch-black hair hung loose down her back as her head tilted back invitingly.

Rosalin must have made some kind of sound, because Boyd's eyes found hers right before he accepted the woman's welcoming kiss. Her quite thorough welcoming kiss.

Rosalin felt as if a horse had kicked her in the chest. *No!* she wanted to shout. *Don't. You can't.*

But he could. She held no claim on him, a fact he was making perfectly clear.

His arm was wrapped around the woman's waist loosely, as if it had been there many times before. The kiss also had a lazy familiarity that spoke of . . .

Oh God! The bottom dropped from Rosalin's stomach. She knew. They were lovers.

She turned away, fighting the suffocating stabs of pain through her heart that made her want to do something ridiculous like cry. A hot ball pressed its way up her throat and to the back of her eyes. But she blinked back the tears as she slid her foot into the stirrup and attempted to get down without her skirts tangling around her feet.

She would have fallen had someone not caught her around the waist from behind. Nay, not someone. She stiffened at his touch, knowing exactly who it was. His big hands nearly spanned her waist, closing around her like a warm vise, as he lifted her down effortlessly. Even without their bodies touching, she could feel the broad shield of his chest behind her and smell the warm scent of leather and spice that had become so familiar.

"Thank you," she said, not daring to look at him for fear that he might see how much his display with the woman had affected her. "I'm surprised you did not let me fall."

"As you are our only hostage now, that wasn't an option."

Her eyes narrowed, meeting the ice-blue gaze that riveted them. "Aye, my brother will not pay your blackmail if I am harmed—you might remember that."

His mouth tightened at the not-so-subtle reference to his earlier threat. "I think he'll pay to get you back whatever state you are in. You might remember that, my *lady*." He slurred the last word with obvious sarcasm.

She bristled. "You are wrong about what happened. For all your knowledge of *experienced* women, you should know the difference between practiced and not."

He smiled, and Rosalin immediately regretted her churlish words. By remarking upon the woman who'd just kissed him, she'd let him know that it had bothered her.

"This way, Princess," he said with a mock flourish. "Your palace awaits."

He started away, and with no choice but to follow, Rosalin ignored the curious stares cast in her direction and hurried after him.

At first she thought he meant to take her to the big longhouse, which she assumed served as their hall, but then he led her past the building to where there were a few more tents set up. Slightly larger than the others, she realized these most likely housed the king's lieutenants—perhaps even the king himself when he was present.

He stopped at the first tent. It was perhaps twelve feet square, with the middle of the pitched roof at least that high. Although the original natural wool would have been a brownish off-white, a protective coating of oil or wax to keep out the water had stained it yellow, and in places a dark-brownish black. Over a dozen hemp ropes supported the canopy from the outside, driven into the ground with large wooden pegs. Passing through the flaps that had been tied back, she saw the numerous wooden tent poles that gave the tent its structure.

Despite the afternoon light, it was fairly dark inside. But after Boyd lit the tall torches that flanked the entrance, she could better make out the interior.

Caesar was reputed to have traveled with his own mosaic tile floor in sections, and English kings had been known to outfit their tents as if they were a room in a palace with woven rugs, fine furniture, and silver and gold household plate. This tent was not so fine, but neither was it a crude hovel.

Her first impression was of well-tended orderliness. It might have been split down the middle with the two sides mirroring one another. They held box beds with some kind of mattress, probably made from straw, numerous wool blankets and a few furs, two wooden trunks for storage and extra seating, two tables, two stools, and two small braziers for warmth. The floor was covered in woven rushes. Other than a stray shield with a blue background and a band of red and white checks across it, a few candles, a pitcher, and a bowl for washing, there did not appear to be any personal items lying about that might give a hint about its occupants.

But she knew.

It was a warrior's tent, and the spartan, no-frills, nothing-to-distract-from-war interior fit Boyd perfectly.

"You can sleep there," he said, pointing to the bed on the left.

Since he threw down his plaid and helm on the other bed, she assumed it was his. Good God, he couldn't mean to sleep in the same room with her?

"Is there not somewhere else I might stay?"

"There is not. As you might have noticed, we are in the middle of the forest. I'm afraid accommodation is limited."

That wasn't what she meant and he knew it. He just enjoyed making her feel like a spoiled, cosseted princess. That was what he'd called her. She lifted her chin, glaring at him defiantly. "I just do not wish to displace anyone from their bed."

"If you are that worried, you can always share mine."

She stilled, staring at his face as if the granite facade might give her a clue as to whether he was serious.

His smile was cold and devoid of humor. "I thought not. Have no fear, my lady—Seton doesn't mind. He lives for that kind of gallant shite. Now, if there is nothing else, I have more enjoyable pastimes to seek out." His face hardened. "But I would caution you against another attempt to escape. Although you deserve to be in a pit prison for what you've done, I can find far less luxurious accommodations for you. There are no forty-foot walls, but even were you to get past the two men who will be guarding you—two of Douglas's kinsmen, by the way, so don't bother trying to wield your feminine wiles in that direction—the forest is not a place you will want to find yourself alone. Unless you like boars." His eyes found hers. "And phantoms."

A chill swept over her skin. His warning was well heeded. She was trapped and knew it. Douglas's men . . . She shivered. Suddenly, she didn't want him to go. Even angry and cruel, she trusted him. At least more than she did Douglases.

"Wait!" She stopped him before he pulled back the flaps. "Where are you going?"

"To celebrate a successful raid. Unlike you, I didn't get to take my release last night. So unless you want to suck my cock as Deirdre has offered to do, I will bid you good night."

Rosalin drew in her breath, shock permeating every fiber of her being. Even knowing that was what he had intended couldn't stop her from gaping at him. Was such a thing done?

The knowing challenge in his eyes answered her question.

Shock turned to a stabbing throb. She wanted to object. To tell him not to go. To tell him that if he let that woman touch him like that it would be over between them forever.

But how could something be over that had never begun?

Instead, she dropped her gaze and turned away from him. The handsome, noble warrior she'd watched from her window was gone, and she found she no longer wanted to look at the man who stood in his place.

Eleven

The sounds of the revelry continued well into the night. What were they doing? What was *he* doing? Was the woman really . . .

The black hole in Rosalin's chest seemed to grow larger and larger. Why did she care?

The taunting sounds filled her imagination and kept her awake until exhaustion—both physical and emotional—finally dragged her to sleep.

Boyd never returned.

Rosalin woke resigned if not refreshed. She would make do the best she could until her brother paid whatever ransom they demanded of him. What else could she do? Soon this would all be a distant memory. A distant, unpleasant, hurtful memory.

She nibbled on the remainder of bread, cheese, and dried mutton that had been brought to her not long after Boyd left—apparently, he hadn't completely forgotten about her—and started to explore her surroundings. Unfortunately, there wasn't any water in the ewer, so she could not wash. The comb and bar of soap resting nearby, however, taunted her.

Grime was a powerful motivator, and she'd just about bolstered her courage enough to face her Douglas jailers, when one of the men entered with another plate of food. This one containing, to her delight, what looked to be an apple.

Spine as stiff as a poleaxe, he marched into the room and set the trencher down on Sir Alex's wooden chest. He was probably only a few years older than Malcolm, but his dark visage and beard reminded her well enough of his "black" relative.

"Is there anything else you need?"

He spoke to the wall behind her in the most grudging voice she'd ever heard.

Her cheeks burned, but some needs could not be ignored. The idea of using the chamber pot in such a small, decidedly un-private area did not appeal to her. "I don't suppose you have a garderobe nearby?"

He still avoided her eyes, but she could see her question had discomfited him as much as it had her. "I'm to escort you around back for privacy when you need it."

She needed it. Her feet were dancing. The morning was cold and misty, but the breath of fresh air was welcome as he led her out and waited a short distance away while she tended her needs.

The rest of the occupants of the camp must have still been sleeping off their celebration, as it was very quiet and peaceful. She looked about, seeing some things that she hadn't noticed before. A few small outer buildings, what appeared to be a garden near one of them, the cluck of hens, a few sheep on the hillside, farm tools and a cart propped against the longhouse. She wanted to linger, but he led her back inside. Before he could leave, however, she asked, "I would like some water to wash—and a bath if one can be found."

His mouth tightened as if he wanted to refuse. "I will see what can be arranged."

A short while later, Rosalin was in heaven. A large wooden tub lined with linen had been brought in by two young warriors whose job it must be to tend the more menial labor. It was filled with cold water, but she didn't care. As soon as the men left, she tore off her clothes, reached for the soap and comb, and luxuriated in the sensation of being clean again.

For modesty's sake she'd left on her chemise, and after scrubbing like she'd seen the maids do, she emerged from the water feeling refreshed. But cold. Shivering and dripping wet, she realized too late that she'd neglected to ask for a drying cloth. Reaching for Boyd's trunk, which was the closest, she opened it to find a stack of neatly folded linens. She took one that was obviously meant for the purpose and wrapped it around her shivering body.

But with the soaking-wet chemise and nothing to change into, the cloth provided little in the way of relief. She had two choices. She could remove her chemise and don her smoky, travel-stained gowns again or she could borrow one of the freshly washed tunics she'd noticed in his chest. It wasn't a difficult decision.

A short while later, she'd hung her gowns and wet chemise from a few pegs in the poles that looked to be for that purpose and was sitting on Sir Alex's trunk, combing out her wet hair, clean and comfortably bundled in not only one of Boyd's tunics, but also a plaid she'd found tucked underneath. At first she'd thought it black, but it was actually shades of dark blues and grays. She wrapped it around her in a Roman fashion, knotting it on one shoulder and keeping it in place with one of the silver girdles she wore around her waist.

When Sir Alex entered the tent a few minutes later, however, he looked so shocked to see her in it, she wondered if she'd done something wrong.

Once his shock passed, he smiled. "I see you found some fresh clothing."

She blushed. "When I asked for the bath, I forgot that I didn't have anything clean to change into." She'd also removed her own clothes for the first time in years without a serving-maid, but she didn't want to mention that. "Do you think he'll mind?"

Sir Alex gave her a long, steady look. "If he does, tell him I said you could use mine."

For some reason, the prospect of her doing so seemed to amuse him.

"I'm sorry to disturb you—I just came in to get a few things." He grinned. "But you are sitting on them."

She gasped, jumping off his trunk. "It is I who should apologize to you for displacing you from your . . . um . . . room."

He pretended not to notice her embarrassment over sleeping in his bed. "It's a place to sleep, nothing more. As long as Douglas doesn't snore too loudly when he returns, I won't know the difference." His expression changed to one of concern. "You are all right?"

"As well as can be expected."

"He did not . . ." His voice let off, as if he were searching for the right words. "Hurt you?"

Heat crawled up her cheeks, guessing what he suspected. Was that what they all suspected? Did everyone think she'd given herself to him to let her nephew escape? No, they couldn't. But Sir Alex must have sensed something and guessed.

"I am fine," she said firmly. "Your friend is angry that my nephew was able to get away, but he has not hurt me. In any way," she added meaningfully. "I am exactly as I was when I arrived." Although perhaps a bit wiser.

He nodded. "I'm glad to hear it. Your inventiveness took us all by surprise. I'm not sure I would have gone out that window." He shook his head. "I've never seen Boyd so angry." He smiled. "Even with me. And other than your brother, I doubt there's anyone who angers him more."

"But you are friends. Why would he be angry with you?"

"I've committed the unpardonable sin, the one thing that can never be forgiven."

"What's that?"

"I was born in England," he said dryly.

"But aren't your lands in Scotland?"

"Most of them are now, although my brother held some lands in Cumberland and Northumberland. I've been raised in Scotland and fought on the Scottish side for every battle of the war, but it doesn't matter. In Boyd's eyes, I will always be English. I don't think even Wallace hated your countrymen as much as he does. Not without cause, perhaps, but it blinds him. He will never completely trust an Englishman."

He held her gaze, and she knew he was warning her. She nodded, telling him she understood. She'd sensed as much herself.

He must have seen something in her expression. "Don't worry, lass, it won't be much longer. A messenger has been dispatched to your brother. In a few days, this will all be behind you."

It was with considerable effort that Robbie dragged himself off the rush-strewn floor of the Hall, where he'd finally found sleep in the wee hours of the night, and ventured into the morning (or mid-morning) daylight. The sunlight cleaved his skull like a battle-axe. His stomach, which could weather even the worst of storms on Hawk's *birlinn*, tossed dangerously, threatening to remind him that the last goblet of whisky had probably been a bad idea.

Actually, the last *five* goblets of whisky had probably been a bad idea.

Like any Scotsman worth his salt, Robbie enjoyed his *uisge beatha*. But he couldn't recall ever enjoying it quite so much. Or with such purpose. If he were a weaker man, he might even think he'd been trying to drown his guilt in drink.

But he had no reason to feel guilty. Rosalin Clifford deserved his anger. She deserved a hell of a lot more after what she'd done.

So he'd threatened to make her his whore? So he'd

shocked the proper English lady with the crude suggestion that she suck his cock? So what?

Robbie rarely struck the first blow, but if someone hit him, he was sure as hell going to strike back. He didn't turn the other cheek. An eye for an eye, a tooth for a tooth—that was his religion. He was doing the only thing he knew how to do: fight back ruthlessly when wronged. The English had learned that the hard way. As he couldn't use his fists or his sword with her, he was using the one weapon he had left: his words.

He still couldn't believe he'd let a woman trick him like that. He didn't fall prey to feminine ploys or wiles. He'd thought himself immune to such pedestrian weaknesses. Undistractible.

Damn it, he'd even sensed something was wrong, but all she'd had to do was touch him and look up at him with that ravish-me mouth, and he lost his bloody mind.

Of course she'd known what she was doing . . .

But what if she hadn't? What if he was just being an arse?

She'd stung his pride, and he wondered how much of his anger was really because she'd managed to help her nephew escape under his watch.

He swore and raked his fingers through his hair, his nose wrinkling as the stench of last night's festivities and days of hard riding leached out of his skin.

He needed a good dunking in the burn. Perhaps it would clear some of the fogginess from his head. The foulness of his temper, he suspected, would not be so easily washed away.

With slightly more vigor, he rounded the corner of the Hall on the way to his tent and came to a sudden stop.

Bloody hell! His fists squeezed at his sides. He'd told Seton to stay away from her. But there was his partner, ducking out from beneath the flaps of the tent with a broad smile on his face. Whistling, unless Robbie was mistaken, as he rambled over to the next tent.

Black clouds darkened Robbie's already foul mood. Black *thunder*clouds. He stormed toward his tent. He would deal with Seton later, after he found out what was going on. But if she thought she was going to trick his partner like she had him—

He stopped. God's bones, was that what she was doing? Was that why Seton looked so happy and relaxed?

Robbie couldn't think. He could barely breathe. His heart was hammering in his head, causing his mind to spin out of control.

Iain Douglas started to say something but slammed his mouth shut, obviously thinking better of it.

Robbie strode past the two warriors, pushed between the flaps, and steeled himself for what he might find.

His stomach knifed when he saw her. There was nothing in her appearance to contradict his suspicions. In fact, it was the opposite. She was seated on Seton's bed combing her long, damp hair, her cheeks still flushed from her bath—or lovemaking—wearing . . .

Christ, she was wearing the plaid he wore on Highland Guard missions and, unless he was mistaken, one of his tunics!

As he entered, she glanced up with a gasp of surprise. Her eyes found his warily.

He ignored the stab of conscience. "What was Seton doing in here?"

His voice came out louder and angrier than he'd intended—and more accusing.

Her eyes widened and then narrowed with a glint of mischief. "What do you think he was doing?" she asked with a flip of her head. "I needed help with my bath."

He crossed the tent in two strides and hauled her up against him. "Do you think this is a jest, my lady? I assure you it is not. What did you do, take your 'offer' to Seton? Was he more amenable than I?"

She turned away in disgust. "You are a fool." He felt like it. A jealous one. "If you must know, he was in here to fetch a few items, presumably to bathe as I did." She wrinkled her nose. "You might consider doing the same. You carry the stench of your *celebrating*."

Her icy composure grated against his already flared nerves like sand on an open wound.

Robbie glanced toward the bath, a dangerous idea taking form. He stepped back, a slow smile curving his mouth. "What a brilliant idea."

He jerked the mail coif—the one concession he made toward heavy mail—over his head and tossed it on his bed. Next came the thick leather *cotun*. He'd been so eager to get out of there last night, he hadn't even taken the time to remove his armor. By the time he got to the linen shirt underneath, her eyes were two full moons.

"W-what are you d-doing?"

"What you suggested." He finished pulling the shirt over his head and threw it on top of the others. "Taking a bath. Would be a shame to waste the water."

She sucked in her breath, taking in every inch of his naked chest. His muscles tensed of their own accord, a natural reaction to being the recipient of so much study. Staring was putting it mildly. Gorging was better. And despite his anger, he felt himself warming under the heat of so much feminine appreciation.

Who in Hades was he kidding? It wasn't feminine appreciation, it was *her* appreciation. He'd never wanted to flex and strut around like some damned peacock in his life.

Only when he started with the ties to his chausses did she tear her eyes away. The delicate flush that had pinkened her cheeks drew pale.

"With me here?" She gaped. "You can't."

"I assure you I can. And you are going to help me."

"What do you mean, 'help you'?"

"I would have thought you would be familiar with the tradition for the lady of the castle to wash her important guests."

"That's an outdated tradition. No one does that anymore."

His eyes held hers. "We here in Scotland are a little backwards, as I'm sure your brother has told you."

She didn't protest any further, because by that time he was down to his braies. And with one quick pull of the ties, those were gone as well, and he was standing naked before her.

She went completely still. Except for her eyes, which were definitely moving. Aye, he was acutely aware of the slow travel of her gaze lowering. It was almost as if her eyes were touching him—stroking him—singeing a trail of fire on his skin, down his chest, over every band of stomach muscle, to the narrow path of dark hair that led to . . .

Her eyes widened as she took him in. All of him. It took some time.

Red palm prints of color stained her cheeks, but she didn't look away. The latent sensuality of her gaze, the unabashed maidenly curiosity, filled him with heat. He started to swell and thicken but sank into the cool bath before he'd come to a complete rise.

The tub was just big enough for him to be able to dunk his head. He came back up, hair slicked back, already feeling better. Sitting back, he slung his arms over the edge of the tub like a sultan from Outremer and glanced at her. She seemed to be frozen in place, staring at him as if she couldn't believe what he'd just done and didn't know whether she should look or turn away. She looked, and seemed particularly fascinated with the rivulets of water streaming down his upper arms and chest.

The cool water wasn't enough to stop him from hardening. If he weren't so angry, he might have debated the wisdom of pressing this further. But he was still angry—enough to play with fire.

He quirked a brow. "Well? Are you going to fetch the soap? There's a cloth for washing in the trunk." His eyes scanned her clothes. Bloody hell, he'd have to be more careful if he didn't want her to discover his role in the Highland Guard. "Which you must already know."

She hesitated, and he could see her indecision.

He'd never expected her to do it. He thought she'd refuse and tell him to go to hell.

He should have known better. She was a Clifford. She had more stubborn pride than sense and would not back down from a challenge. Bloody hell, how could the things he hated in her brother make him admire her?

Teeth clamped and eyes narrowed with determination, she stomped over to the trunk to fetch the cloth, and then over to the table where she'd left the soap. She knelt beside the tub, plunged her hand into the water (too damned close to a part of him that was aching for attention) to dampen the cloth, and after a vigorous rub of the soap, proceeded to attack his skin with an equally vigorous scrub. His chest suddenly felt like the rocks the laundress would beat the laundry against.

She started to scrub his arm. "These markings won't come off."

"It's a tattoo." One that he probably should have tried to hide.

"Of a Lion Rampant, and . . ." She drew closer, examining it with far too fine a comb. "Is that a spiderweb? And what does *Confido* mean?"

" 'I trust.' It's a reference to my clan's loyalty to the Scottish cause. It's engraved on my sword as well."

"So these are references to your clan?"

So to speak. The Highland Guard were his brothers. The Rampant Lion and spiderweb "torque" around his arm were the mark that bound them together. It was orig-

inally intended as a means of identification were the need
ever to arise (as it might have when Arthur "Ranger"
Campbell was sent to spy in the English camp), but the
knowledge of the mark had unfortunately fallen into
enemy hands with the death of William Gordon. He hoped
to hell she never mentioned it to her brother.

"Aye." Not wanting any more questions, he added,
"You're stalling."

Realizing she was staring, her cheeks heated, and she
resumed her scrubbing. There was nothing sensual in her
touch, nothing erotic, but still it affected him. Hell, "affected" was putting it mildly. Just the idea of her hands on
him was driving him mad. It wasn't the first time a woman
had bathed him, but it was the first time he'd ever been so
painfully aware of it.

Think of England, he told himself. He laid his head
back, closed his eyes, and tried to concentrate on everything he hated about the enemy he'd been fighting for almost half his life. Their overreaching kings, their pompous
superiority, their chivalric hypocrisy, their treachery, their
damned irritating accents . . .

But it wasn't helping. Closing his eyes only made his other
senses work harder. He could smell her warmth, the fresh
scent of the heather soap, the mint on her breath, the press
of every one of her soft, slim fingers on his skin.

Christ. He almost groaned.

He opened his eyes. Her golden head bowed forward as
she drew the cloth over his stomach, perilously close to the
heavy head of his cock, which hovered just beneath the water's edge.

He was about to put an end to it, when she lifted her
gaze to his. A gaze that was closer than he would have
liked.

"Does this please you, my lord?" she taunted with a sly
smile. "I'm afraid I've not much experience bathing men.

But it isn't much different than washing a pig before market."

Robbie was playing a dangerous game and knew it. The heat that sprang between them had just notched up quite a few degrees. But the pig comment had struck too close and demanded retaliation. "I think you missed a spot on my arm."

Their eyes held. He could see the green flare of temper and thought he'd won. But then her mouth pursed, and she slunk the cloth back into the water with renewed determination.

He knew the exact moment he'd made a mistake. Her movements slowed, and her hand gently started to slide the cloth over the bulge of muscle in a soft caress. He watched as her breath hitched and then quickened. As her lips parted and the glare of her eyes softened with arousal.

Their eyes met, and all the anger that had started this dangerous game fizzled away. A different kind of tension now snapped between them. His heart made a violent thump in his chest. A thump of awareness. A thump of question. A thump of expectation.

With the anger stripped away, he felt bare. More naked than he'd felt when he'd stripped in front of her. There was no hiding how much he wanted her. No hiding how much she affected him. No hiding that the attraction between them was so strong not even he could fight it.

Twelve

※

Rosalin knew she was in trouble.

For a while she was so furious, she was able to keep her mind off the body parts—the rather magnificent body parts—she was scrubbing. The stomach that looked as if it had been forged from steel like a centurion's breastplate, every band of ridged muscle hammered with perfect precision; the broad shoulders, solid chest, narrow waist, arms that bulged thick and heavy with muscle. There wasn't an ounce of spare flesh on him—every inch of his warrior's body had been honed and crafted for battle.

The strongest man in Scotland. Aye, he certainly looked the part. She feared no other man would compare. He'd ruined her—if not in fact, then in all the ways that mattered.

And then there was that other part of him. The thick, long column of his manhood that should have made her turn and run.

He wasn't the first naked man she'd ever seen—there was little privacy in even the largest and most luxurious of castles—but he was by far the most impressive. And he was the only one she'd ever wanted to look at. The only one she'd ever wanted to explore with her hands . . . her mouth. A flush rose to her cheeks as she thought of his taunt the night before.

When she lifted her head to see him watching her, everything seemed to change. They both knew it. It was as if the roar of battle, the clatter of swords, the tempest of wills suddenly went silent. In their place was the crackle of awareness, the magnetism of attraction, and the hammering of lust that rose to a deafening crescendo.

There was no pretense of indifference. He wasn't looking at her with distrust. He wasn't thinking of her as the enemy or as Clifford's sister. He was looking at her as if he wanted her. As if she were the only thing that mattered.

Her hand had slid to his stomach without even being aware of it. But he was. The line of muscles in his stomach clenched. His breathing was shallow, almost pained. His steely blue eyes watched her like one of her hawks.

He wanted something from her, but she didn't know what. Then his hips lifted ever so slightly, and she understood. He wanted her to touch him.

Their eyes held. She felt poised with indecision, her heart teetering on a precipice. It was a moment of decision. The point of no return.

But she couldn't go forward without knowing. "Did she . . . did you . . . ?" She couldn't seem to form the words. But she had to know whether he'd done what he'd said he was going to do with the dark-haired woman—Deirdre, he'd called her.

He didn't say anything for a long moment. It almost seemed as if he wanted to lie, as if he knew that what he said would be important.

If he said yes, it would have been over. She would have found the strength to stand and walk away from him. She would have known that she didn't matter.

But he told her the truth. "Nay, Rosalin," he said in a soft, low voice. "She didn't."

Her heart seemed to grow too big for her chest. Without any further hesitation, Rosalin lowered her hand.

Robbie's muscles clenched as he waited for the moment of contact, for the first tentative brush of her hand. The anticipation was nearly as sweet as—

Christ! The heel of her hand grazed the heavy tip, and he nearly jumped out of his skin. He groaned as sensation exploded from every nerve ending. Anticipation, hell! There was nothing as sweet as the feel of her hand touching him. And when she covered him with her palm . . . he gave thanks to every god he'd ever heard of, even as he prayed to a few nameless ones for strength. Biting back the pleasure, he had to fight the urge to thrust up into her hand.

A fight he nearly lost when she started to explore him, running her hand up his rock-hard length in a soft caress, petting him as if he were a wild beast. An analogy that wasn't that far off the mark right now.

It felt so good he couldn't stand it. The shy, maidenly fumblings were proving more arousing than the most practiced of strokings. Her innocent curiosity threatened to unman him.

"Oh God, sweetheart, you're killing me." The endearment slipped from his tongue so easily, it was hard to believe he'd never used one before.

Their eyes met, and she smiled shyly. He felt something jam in his chest. Something big and powerful and important. Something that should have given him pause, but instead only made him feel . . .

Shite, he swore, recognizing the feeling. He felt *happy*. It had been so damned long, he'd almost forgotten what it felt like.

"Tell me what to do," she said.

He didn't know if he could; every muscle in his body was clenched too tightly. Hell, he could have bounced rocks off his arse and stomach.

"Circle me with your hand," he managed through gritted teeth, grabbing the edge of the tub to steel himself.

His knuckles turned white.

He groaned, surging into her hold at the first press of her fingers closing around him. Blood pulsed—nay, exploded—through his veins. He could have wept, the blast of pleasure was so intense that had he been standing, it would have brought him to his knees.

"I can't," she said. "You're too big."

Her disgruntled tone would have made him laugh if he weren't so focused on trying not to explode. "Squeeze a little. I won't break."

Not yet—he hoped.

She did as instructed, and he nearly lost control right there as sensation shot through his spine, gathering at the base and hammering so hard it hurt just to hold it back.

This wasn't going to last long. "Stroke me, sweetheart," he whispered, covering her hand with his to show her how.

God, stroke me.

And she did. Quite effectively.

The gentle press of her soft, slender fingers around him, squeezing, milking, was too perfect. The pressure was too intense. A few hard pumps, and he couldn't hold back any longer. "That's it, love. Oh God, yes, right there . . . I'm going to . . ."

He should have closed his eyes and tossed his head back. Normally, that was exactly what he would have done. But he wanted to see her face. He didn't want to miss a damned minute of her introduction to the world of passion.

Their eyes met and held right at the moment that she brought him to the very peak of pleasure. When he was at his weakest. When he couldn't fight it, even if he wanted to.

A hard cry of pleasure tore from his lungs. He stiffened. He couldn't turn away, not even when the spasms wracked him and he started to come. Nay, especially not then. The pleasure she squeezed from his body seemed intensified, sharpened somehow by the connection. By a closeness he'd never felt before. By the tender feelings squeezing in his chest.

For the first time in his life when Robbie took his release, it was not his alone but shared with someone else, and the experience was unlike any other. It was bigger, more powerful, and more significant. The moment was too poignant and the look exchanged between them too meaningful.

He let her in, and when it was over, and the reality of what he'd done finally hit him, he didn't know how to get her out.

He bowed his head and swore, furious with himself.

Tell me I didn't just do that. Tell me I didn't just have Clifford's sister take me to release in her hand.

But he had, and in doing so, he'd let her slip under his guard. He'd let her know that he'd sent his leman away, that he hadn't wanted another woman. Only her. And as with Pandora's box, he feared what that knowledge now escaped would do to them both.

He looked up. She'd sat back from the tub a little and was still on her knees, eyeing him uncertainly.

He held her gaze unflinchingly and said, "I guess we're even now."

It took her a moment to realize what he meant. When she did, she flinched as if he'd slapped her. The look of hurt on her face was so acute, he had to turn away so that he wouldn't give in to the urge to pull her into his arms.

Pretending he didn't feel her eyes on him, he stood from the tub, strode over to his trunk, and proceeded to dry himself and don a fresh linen tunic and leather breeches with a cool efficiency he did not feel.

When he finished, he'd regained enough composure to face her. She'd moved back to sit on the edge of Seton's bed but was still watching him.

"I didn't deserve that," she said quietly, the condemnation in her beautiful green eyes giving him no quarter. "If you want me to hate you and think you as cold and unfeeling as you seem, you are doing a fine job of it."

For the first time in his life, Robbie felt like squirming. She was right. She hadn't deserved that. He dragged his fingers through his damp hair in frustration. Finally, he straightened and met her gaze head on. "It would be better for us both if you did."

She gaped at him incredulously. "You are serious? You think I will be better off if you say mean things so that I will hate you? That is the most ridiculous thing I've ever heard. Of all the misguided . . ." Her eyes flashed angrily, as she blinked up at him. "You arrogant beast! Do you do this with all your women so they won't fall in love with you, or am I the only one who needs such protection from your overpowering charms? Well, you needn't try to protect me from myself. I am quite capable of disliking you all on my own."

Now, he did feel like an arse. She was right, but only partially. It wasn't only she he was trying to protect.

"What would you have me do, Rosalin? You know as well as I that nothing good can come of this. You are my hostage, surety for your brother's truce and good faith."

"That does not mean we must be enemies. Can we not be civil to each other? You were friendly enough toward Roger—can you not treat me the same?"

Like a thirteen-year-old lad? God, she was young. "I don't know if that is possible."

"Why? Do you despise me so much?"

The look of disappointment on her face caused him to speak more bluntly than he might have. "Nay, I want you too much."

His honesty seemed to surprise her, and then—undeniably—please her. A slow smile curved her lips and a soft pink blush spread over her cheeks.

She looked sweet enough to eat. And God, he wanted to devour her—which only proved his damned point!

She tilted her head to one side. "You have never been friendly with a woman you wanted before?"

He'd never wanted a woman the way he wanted her, but he thought it better not to mention that. "Nay."

"Why not?"

He shrugged. "Women are for . . ." He didn't finish, guessing she wouldn't appreciate what he'd been about to say.

Her mouth pursed, however, suggesting that she'd guessed. "Women are for the bedchamber, is that it? But not worth your time for anything else?"

That was about the gist of it, but it hadn't sounded so bad when he thought it.

She made a sharp harrumphing sound and mumbled something about spoiled, too-handsome-for-their-own-good brutes that almost made him smile.

She stomped over to where he stood by his bed and put her hands on her hips. "Well, if it isn't too much trouble, I should like you to try."

He looked down at her and wanted to pull her into his arms so badly, his muscles ached from the restraint.

"Can you do that?" she asked.

When all he had to do was smell her and he wanted to toss her down on the bed behind them? "I don't know if I'm strong enough."

One corner of her mouth lifted in a wry smile. "From what I've seen, you are plenty strong."

He gave her a sharp glance. Naughty lass! That wasn't what he meant. And it wasn't going to help his restraint. "Not when it comes to you. We can't—" He stopped, trying to think of a way to say it less crudely. "I shouldn't have touched you the way I did or let you touch me the way you just did. It's dangerous. The next time, I might not stop. I don't seem to have much control when it comes to you. Nor do I wish to give your brother a reason to kill me that is deserved."

She shivered, but whether it was from fear or something else, he didn't want to guess.

"Does that mean you won't try?"

She looked so disheartened, he couldn't refuse. "I'll try," he said, even if he suspected it was going to kill him.

The broad smile that lit her face made him reconsider. He didn't suspect a damned thing; it *was* killing him already.

"Truce," she said, holding out her hand.

Reluctantly, he clutched her soft hand in his own. "Truce," he repeated.

Robbie had his truce with a Clifford, though he wondered how much this one was going to cost him.

Thirteen

❧

Rosalin saw little of him over the next two days. Apparently, Robbie's idea of a truce was to duck in long enough to grab some clothes, mumble a few words, and then disappear. He slept in the tent with her, but he waited until after she was asleep to creep in and woke before she was awake to creep back out.

In between, she tried to keep herself busy and do her best (without much success) to not perish of boredom. During the long hours alone, with only her none-too-friendly Douglas guardsmen for the curt exchange of words that passed as "conversation" (they probably thought something was wrong with her, she asked to go to the privy so often just to go outside), Rosalin was seriously considering mutiny. Or, as they weren't on a ship, open rebellion.

The first day, she'd attended to her person and her much abused clothing. She'd combed her hair until it was free of every last knot and tangle and fell around her shoulders in long, shimmery waves, and pounded and brushed her woolen gowns until they were free of most of the dirt. They still smelled of smoke, though, so she asked one of the dour Douglas brothers (she'd learned their names at least: Iain and Archie) to fetch her some dried heather and packed the gowns with it. By the following morning her chemise was completely dry and her gowns smelled good enough to wear again.

She'd never cleaned in her life, but by the second day,

she'd wiped every surface, tidied every furnishing, and practiced making the beds enough times to rival any of the maidservants at Whitehall Palace. She'd even mixed in some of the dried heather with the rushes to brighten the smell of peat that seemed to linger on everything.

While in the process of putting away the linens and plaid that she'd borrowed, Rosalin decided to take a peek through the rest of the trunk. Normally she wouldn't be so nosy, or show such a lack of regard for someone's privacy, but really it was Robbie's own fault. If he wasn't going to tell her about himself, then she was going to have to see what she could find out on her own.

Never far from her mind was his admission that felt like more of a confession: *I don't know if I'm strong enough.*

She knew he'd meant it as a warning—and it had been well taken. He was right: her brother would kill him. But the idea that *she* could weaken him so warmed her and sent a little—well, not so little—thrill shooting through her. It also provoked an urge in her to dig deeper, to see if maybe it meant something more. Fate had brought them together again, and she couldn't help but think there was a reason.

She didn't know what she expected to find, maybe a few mementos—a sprig of dried flowers or a lock of hair from a past sweetheart, a brooch or ring, *something* that hinted to his past—but that wasn't the treasure trove she uncovered when she dug through the stack of carefully folded linens, clothing, and armor, to the bottom of the trunk.

One by one, Rosalin pulled out leather-bound codex after leather-bound codex. There were seven in all, most containing multiple works. It was a small fortune in manuscripts ranging from Socrates and Plato to Augustine and the relatively new work of Father Thomas Aquinas, of whom there was talk of making a saint. They were scholarly works that did not belong in the war chest of a . . .

barbarian. Good gracious, he could rival her brother in his philosophical learnings!

There were also a few histories. She picked up one of the volumes, entitled *Historia Romana*, by someone named Appian of Alexandria. She paged through the thick pieces of parchment, scanning the carefully inked words in Latin. Picking up another, she was stunned to see that it was written in Greek.

Did Robbie really read these? If the well-worn bindings were any indication, it appeared that he did—quite frequently.

She was so enthralled by her discovery that she didn't hear him enter until he was standing right behind her. "What are you doing?"

She looked up guiltily from her cross-legged position on the ground before his trunk. It was quite obvious what she was doing, and his dark scowl reflected that knowledge, but she answered anyway. "I was bored."

His eyes narrowed. "So you decided to go through my belongings?"

"I was putting away the tunic and plaid I borrowed and happened to see these."

He gave her a look that suggested he knew otherwise.

He glanced around the tent, noticing the changes she'd made. "You aren't a serving maid, Rosalin."

"Nay, I'm a hostage," she said cheekily. Seeing his frown, she added quickly, "It's something to do."

He ignored her hint. "Aye, well, just make sure you make that clear to your brother when you come back with callused hands."

She picked up one of the books and started to flip through it again. "Why would you wish to hide these? They are wonderful."

"I'm not hiding anything. I just would have rather you had asked me first."

"Which I would have, had you been here. But as you've avoided me for the past—"

"I haven't been avoiding you. I've been busy."

She blinked up at him innocently. "Haven't you? Hmm. You must be *very* busy if you can't retire until after midnight and wake before dawn." She could see his temper flaring, and decided to switch subjects before she started to laugh. Teasing him was surprisingly fun. Holding up the codex she'd been leafing through, she asked, "Do you really read Greek?"

"Aye, a bit." He practically snatched it from her hand. "Have care with that. It's a rare partial manuscript of Roman history by Polybius."

She wrinkled her nose. "I've never heard of him."

He carefully placed the book back in the trunk and started to pick up the others to do the same. "Aye, well, I doubt many lasses are well versed in military history."

"And I doubt many Scottish warriors are well versed in Greek and ancient philosophy."

"You'd be surprised," he said dryly. "We aren't all barbarians." She glanced away so that he wouldn't see her blush. How had he guessed she'd had that exact thought? "We even have schools in Scotland, just like they do in England."

She ignored the sarcasm, focusing instead on what he'd said and the opportunity to learn more about him. She stood from the ground, shook out her skirts, and plopped down on the stool nearby. "So you went away to school when you were younger?"

He'd replaced all the books and seemed to be looking for something in his trunk. But he took the time to shoot her a look that said he knew what she was up to. "Aye. In Dundee."

"Is that near where you grew up?"

He sighed and turned to face her. "It is not." When it seemed that was all he intended to say on the subject, her disappointment must have shown in her expression. He continued with all the enthusiasm of having a tooth pulled. "I was born in my father's barony of Noddsdale, near Renfrew in Ayr, on the west coast of Scotland and was fostered in the Borders. Dundee is in the east of Scotland on the north side of the Tay. About thirty miles south of Kildrummy."

"That's quite a distance to travel for schooling."

"It's a well-known school, attended by young lairds and chieftains from all around Scotland. The vicar who taught me there—a man by the name of William Mydford— among other things, was an ardent military strategist. The 'pirate' warfare of which your countrymen often disparage us is actually traced to some of those books."

Her skepticism must have shown.

"Both Appian and Polybius wrote of Hannibal, the Carthaginian general reputed to be one of the greatest military strategists of all time. He was famous not only for his use of ambuscade, scorched earth, and for catching the Romans off guard by crossing the Alps, but also for teaching the Romans fear."

Rosalin had heard something of Hannibal. "He was also reputed to be unspeakably cruel."

He held her gaze. "By whom? The descendants of the Romans he defeated? Even Polybius, Greek by birth but Roman by affiliation, conceded that like most people he was probably good and bad."

She smiled. "So you went to school to learn to be a brigand?"

He shot her a look and seeing that she was teasing him, shook his head. "Nay, I was born knowing how to do that."

She scanned the leather-clad arms and chest. "Aye, I don't doubt it. You look as if you were born with a sword in your hand."

"I didn't need a sword until the English put one there. It

was never my desire to be a warrior. I would have been content—" He stopped suddenly, looking away, as if the memories had overtaken him for a moment but he'd been able to wrestle them back under control.

When he turned back to her, the good-humored teasing they'd shared a few minutes ago was once again carefully contained behind the determined, humorless facade. "School is where I learned to be a '*rebel*.' It's where I learned about justice—real justice, not the English version—the tyranny of oppression, and the principles of liberty and freedom that give Scotland and the community of the realm the ancient right and responsibility to anoint its own king and not be ruled by a foreign one."

Unwittingly, Rosalin's discovery of the books had raised the specter of all that was between them. The teachings in these manuscripts had fostered the fierce patriotism that gave him the single-minded determination to fight for Scotland's independence against her countrymen.

She was embarrassed to realize that she'd never given much thought to the Scots' side of things or that they might have their foundations in something so . . . scholarly. Indeed, they were likely the same philosophical underpinnings that her countrymen used to justify the war. She'd thought of the Scots as ruthless brigands, as backward barbarians. But what if . . . what if they had cause to fight? What if they had justice on their side?

Even the thought felt disloyal to her brother, not to mention treasonous to her king. But how could she ignore all that Robbie had told her about what happened to him?

It was disconcerting to think that the enemy were not uncivilized rebels who needed to be brought to heel, but educated warriors fighting for freedom and justice.

But she wanted to know what he'd been about to say. "What would you have been content with?"

He retrieved the item he'd been looking for from his trunk and slid it into the sporran at his waist. She'd caught only a quick glance, but it looked to be a curved piece of thin metal with a short handle.

Though her question seemed to have made him uncomfortable, he answered. "My brother Duncan had the love of battle like my father. I would have been content to till our land and raise our cattle. Before everything was razed, that is."

It took her a moment to process what he'd said. "You wanted to be a *farmer*?" This man who seemed to epitomize war and warfare?

His mouth hardened, as if her disbelief had offended him. "Aye. Well, the decision was taken from my hands when my father was murdered by your countrymen. I left school at seven and ten, joined the risings with my school companion and boyhood friend William Wallace, and never looked back." He nodded to the trunk. "Those books belonged to him, by the way."

She paled. *William Wallace, dear God!* Many English were just as horrified by what had happened to him as the Scots. "I'm sorry."

"For what? You didn't kill him." He said it matter-of-factly, but she sensed the deep emotion underlying the careless words.

"Perhaps not, but I'm sorry for everything you lost. The life you describe . . . It sounds nice. I shouldn't have said those things to you earlier—calling you a thug and a brigand. I didn't realize—" She stopped and looked at him. "I know little about the war or the history between our two countries, but with what you have told me, I think I understand now why you fight." She paused. "You had a brother?"

"Aye. Duncan was captured after the battle of Methven, not long before I was captured at Kildrummy. Unfortunately, he didn't have a guardian angel to rescue him and was executed before I could reach him."

She put her hand on his arm, her heart breaking for him. His father, his sister, his brother, his closest friends, his home and future. She didn't dare ask about his mother. "I'm so sorry."

He stared at her hand, as if no one had ever touched him with compassion like that before and he didn't quite know what to do with it. Eventually, he shrugged it off. "It was a long time ago, Rosalin. Now, if you'll excuse me, I have somewhere to be."

She jumped up. "Wait!" She couldn't let him go without trying. "I have something to ask you. A rebellion of my own, so to speak."

He looked at her blankly.

She bit her lip. "Is there . . . might I be permitted . . ." She drew a deep, exasperated breath and just blurted it out. "I'm dying of boredom in here with nothing to do. Might I be allowed some freedom to move about? You've made the danger of attempting to escape perfectly clear."

He gave her a long look. "You will give me your word you will not try to escape?"

Was he recalling the similar condition she'd made once?

She repeated the words he'd said to her from the pit prison. "My word is good enough for you?"

"It is."

She smiled. "Then you have it. I swear I will not attempt to escape while I am here."

He nodded. "Do not stray from camp without me or one of my men. It can be dangerous. And do not expect much from those at camp—as I've said, your brother is not a popular man in these parts. You'll not find many friendly faces."

Rosalin was so excited by the prospect of fresh air, she didn't care. "You will remove your watchdogs? I've had quite enough of the dour Douglas brothers. I don't like the way they look at me."

He took a step toward her, the muscles in his shoulders flaring. "Have they done something to offend you? If they've hurt—"

"No, no. Nothing like that. They've attended to their duty admirably under the circumstances. You can't blame them for frowning all the time—given who my brother is."

He relaxed, no longer looking like the God of War bent on destruction. "Good. I would kill any man who tried to hurt you."

The vehemence of his words startled her—as did the instinct. The primitive instinct of a man to protect a woman. Nay, not just a woman, *his* woman.

"I know," she said. And she did. Robbie Boyd would protect her with his life. She was safe with him.

But was she safe *from* him? Could he protect her from himself? For the longer she stayed here, and the more she came to know and understand him, the harder it was going to be to leave.

He considered her for a moment. "Very well. I will remove the guards."

She brightened at the unexpected concession. "Thank you."

Their eyes held for one brief instant, but it was enough to fill her chest with a strange warmth.

He gave her a curt nod and left.

Robbie winced when the blade nicked his neck. "Bloody hell, Malcolm, watch what you are doing. I've need of a shave, not a gulleting."

The lad grimaced as he carefully scraped the half-moon-shaped blade along Robbie's jaw. "Sorry, Captain. My brother is the barber."

Robbie drew his hand over the shaved area, a few fingers coming back with blood. "Aye, well, 'tis a good thing it's only a shave and not an arrow in my arm."

The lad frowned. "You could have waited for Angus to return with the Douglas. I don't know why you are in such a rush—they should be back any day. You've had a beard before."

"As I told you, it itches," Robbie said, too defensively even to his own ears.

What in Hades was he doing? The lad was right. He was used to being stubbled. He *liked* stubbled.

But not unkempt, and every time he looked at Rosalin, he felt like the damned barbarian she thought him.

She didn't belong here. He knew it, and everyone around him did as well. Each time she stepped out of the tent, it was as if a hush descended on the camp. Everyone stopped and turned toward her, watching her as if she were some kind of ethereal creature from another world.

With her fine—even if slightly stained—clothes, her refined English manners, and her pristine ice-blond coloring, she looked like she should be dancing under the candelabra of Whitehall Palace, not tidying his tent in the middle of Ettrick Forest. And after months of living with the "rustic" amenities of their headquarters in the heather, Robbie and his men looked like they should be thrown into the Tower of London for just daring to look at her.

His men might view her with varying degrees of animosity, but there was no denying her beauty, nobility, and innocence. Well, perhaps she was not so innocent, but he sure as hell shouldn't think about that.

Yet it seemed all he could do was think about that. *Robbie . . .*

Ah hell.

He must have sworn aloud.

"Is something wrong?"

"Nay, just hurry it up, lad."

He should be telling himself the same thing. Robbie knew he was playing with fire. The sooner the "Fair Rosalin" was gone, the better. She had him all twisted up in knots. He was afraid to sleep in his own tent, he was irritable and ill-tempered from lack of sleep, he was shaving in the middle of the day, he'd found himself bellowing at Iain and Archie Douglas for frowning, and he'd agreed to let a hostage—his means of bringing Clifford to heel—have free roam of the camp.

He'd also agreed to try to be nice—*friendly*. Christ, what the hell had he gotten himself into? He liked her too damned much already.

If their conversation earlier in the tent was any indication, she would know his life story before she left here. His schooling? Wallace? A farmer? For a moment he'd actually pictured himself with a wife and bairns running all around him. Pretty soon he'd be confiding in her how he'd come to join the Guard.

But it was her reaction that was the problem. Compassion, understanding, and a deep sense of justice were the last things he expected to find from an Englishwoman, let alone the paragon of *injustice's* sister. But Rosalin was still the same sweet girl who six years ago risked everything to right a perceived wrong. Wrapped up in a more sophisticated package, perhaps, but in all the ways that mattered, unchanged.

He wished he could say the same. But six years of war had hardened him. Focused him. Leaving no room for anything else.

For both their sakes, the sooner her brother agreed to the truce, the better.

Malcolm finished and handed Robbie a damp drying cloth to wipe away any stray hairs.

"That's an unusual blade," the lad said, handing it back to him. "Where did you get it?"

Robbie took it and slid it back into his sporran. "A friend of mine made it for me."

Magnus MacKay, known by the war name of Saint in the Highland Guard, wasn't just the toughest bastard Boyd knew, with more knowledge of the hazardous terrain of the Highlands than any other man, he was also skilled at forging unusual weapons, and on occasion, improving other everyday tools like the razor.

Ironically, he was also standing in front of him a few minutes later, along with Kenneth Sutherland, the newest member of the Guard, Ewen Lamont, Eoin MacLean, Arthur Campbell, and Gregor MacGregor. The six members of the Highland Guard had arrived with Douglas from Dundee. Douglas was one of the handful of the king's closest advisors who knew of the secret band of warriors—and their identities.

Right away Robbie knew two things: Bruce had a mission for them, and it must be an important one if it required nearly all of his elite Guard. Only Tor MacLeod, Erik MacSorley, and Lachlan MacRuairi were absent.

They stood on the edge of camp in the clearing that they used for practice, where Robbie had greeted them when he'd been informed by the scouts around camp of their arrival.

"What's the occasion?" MacKay said with an eye to Robbie's jaw, exchanging grasps of the forearm by way of greeting. "I can't remember the last time I saw you cleanshaven."

Robbie swore inwardly, cursing the impulse that would give his brethren even a whiff of a scent to follow. They were tenacious curs, every last one of them. If they connected his shaving with Rosalin's presence, he would never hear the end of it.

"It was at your wedding, Saint," MacGregor offered helpfully.

Robbie shot him a glare. "The only reason you know that was because you're still angry about the lass. I know it's hard for you to believe, but not all women prefer a pretty face."

Even after seven years, MacGregor hated being reminded of his dubious distinction of being known as the most handsome man in Scotland. For a warrior as skilled with a bow as he was, it was particularly galling to be known for something so embarrassingly *un*-warriorly.

MacGregor shot him a glare. "Sod off, Raider."

Seton looked as if he might say something, but reconsidered after Robbie gave him a look that promised retribution if he did.

Douglas wasn't as circumspect. "I hope this doesn't have anything to do with our hostages? The king was troubled by the taking of the lass. I told him it hadn't been intentional and that you intended to let her go. But he's made you personally responsible for them both."

"Too bad, too," MacGregor added. "I would have liked to see the Fair Rosalin. If even Douglas here conceded her beauty, the lass must be sensational."

Why the hell did Robbie suddenly feel the urge to make that face of his not so pretty? Masking the annoyance he felt at MacGregor, he turned back to Douglas. "Aye, well, there's been a change of plans."

Douglas's face darkened. "What kind of change of plans?"

"The lad got away."

There was a moment of dead silence as the men stared at him. Robbie Boyd didn't make mistakes like that.

"You let Clifford's son escape?" Douglas spit out, giving voice to what all of them were thinking.

"I didn't *let* him do anything. The lad shimmied down a forty-foot-long rope from the garret of Kirkton Manor in the middle of the night and made it to Peebles Castle before I realized he was gone."

Douglas was furious. "Was no one standing guard? How the hell did you let this happen? He's Clifford's heir, for Christ's sake!"

Robbie wasn't used to being taken to task like a wet-behind-the-ears squire—even if in this case, it was deserved. "*I* was standing guard, and if you have a problem with my abilities we can put them to the test on the practice yard."

Douglas didn't take him up on the challenge and backed off. "But you still have the lass?" he said.

"Aye."

Douglas was looking at him as if he knew there was more, but sensed that he'd pushed Robbie about as far as he could.

Excusing himself, Douglas left to see to his men, who had gone to the Great Hall to find food and drink after the long ride.

As soon as he'd gone, Robbie turned to MacKay. "I assume you are here for a reason?"

The big Highlander nodded. "Aye. You and Dragon need to gather your things. We'll need to leave as soon as possible if we are to make it by nightfall."

"Where are we going?"

"Lochmaben. We've received word of a shipment of silver from Carlisle heading north to pay the garrison at Stirling. The coin will be heavily guarded—the English aren't taking any chances of it not getting through."

"Your information is reliable?"

"Extremely," Lamont interjected. Hunter's new wife, the former Janet of Mar, had worked with a source inside Roxburgh Castle who had never been wrong, and Robbie assumed from Lamont's confidence that was where the information had come from. They'd taken to calling their informant the Ghost.

"The English have taken a few of our lessons to heart," Sutherland added, "and have set up a diversionary shipment going to Caerlaverloch. Chief, Hawk, and Viper are monitoring the coast, just in case, but we intend to intercept them before they reach Lochmaben for the night."

"How many?" Seton asked.

"We're not sure," Lamont said.

"Possibly as many as fifty," MacLean said with a shrug. Robbie lifted a brow, anticipation for battle already surging through his veins. "What are the rest of you going to do?"

He even managed to get a chuckle out of Arthur Campbell at that. The famed scout was one of the quieter members of the Guard.

Robbie was just about to send his brethren to the Hall to get some food while he and Seton headed off to Douglas's tent (where he'd removed from prying eyes the distinctive armor he wore on Highland Guard missions), when MacGregor let out a low whistle.

"Christ almighty, if that's your hostage, I think I'm going to start joining you on your raids."

Robbie followed the direction of his gaze, seeing Rosalin hurrying out of the Hall, looking as if the devil were on her heels. She must have seen Douglas. If the bastard had scared her—

He stopped, thinking of another bastard. "Stay the hell away from her, Arrow."

He might have growled.

MacGregor wasn't the only one to look at him. The other Guardsmen eyed him with varying degrees of lifted eyebrows and understanding.

"Is that the way of it?" MacGregor said slowly, considering him. "Clifford's sister? Of all the women in the world to finally catch your eye! I can't wait for Hawk to hear about this."

Robbie silently swore every foul word he could think of. Since when had he become so transparent? He clenched his jaw. Since the moment Rosalin Clifford had ended up tossed over his lap.

"The lass is my hostage, nothing more. My temporary hostage. But yours is not a face most lasses forget. I think you'd probably rather not have her brother learn of your presence in camp."

It was a good excuse, but not one any of them believed.

MacKay stayed back while the others strode off. He

gave Robbie a pitying look. "I've been there," he said. "And so have most of the others. I think only Chief and Hawk escaped the curse."

"What curse?"

MacKay's mouth hardened. "The curse of that damned face. Bloody hell, my wife threatened to have Arrow watch over her if I wouldn't when she came on our missions."

Robbie gave an involuntary shudder. No man would want his wife in that kind of proximity to MacGregor. "It's a wonder you didn't kill him."

MacKay smiled. "I made him pay on the practice yard, and enjoyed every bloody minute of it."

"You could have done something about the face."

MacKay shook his head. "I tried, damn it, I tried. But I think Arrow's mother dipped it in the same water that Achilles's mother used. He heals without a scratch."

Robbie laughed and went off to fetch his things. A mission was exactly what he needed to remind him of what was important. Rosalin Clifford may have distracted him, but it wasn't going to get in the way of what he had to do.

Fourteen

❧

Rosalin had her freedom, but she was too scared to use it. After coming face-to-face with the Black Douglas, she'd scurried back to her tent like a frightened mouse. Three hours of waiting later—with no Robbie appearing to reassure her—she decided that she was being ridiculous. Robbie had told her Douglas wouldn't harm her; she would believe him. She was also hungry. The removal of her guards meant she would have to fetch her own food.

Mustering her courage, she wrapped her plaid around her shoulders and headed out of the tent into the cool evening mist. From her experience so far in Scotland there seemed to be little else: morning mist, midday mist, and evening mist. Today, the gloom was heavier than usual, almost seamlessly switching back and forth between a drizzling, dreary rain.

Remembering the reaction her arrival in the Hall had caused earlier—and the discomfort of being stared at by so many—Rosalin decided to seek out a smaller number of curious-wary-angry gazes and headed toward the camp kitchens, which had been set up against the back wall of the Hall. A wooden roof protected the pots and fires from the rain and snow, but the walls that enclosed the area were only on three sides and didn't go all the way up, offering little insulation from the cold and wind.

It was a crude but efficient setup. In addition to the pots

hanging in fires, there were a few tables to prepare the meals and a large bread oven constructed of stone.

Apparently, the women at camp weren't here just to be companions for the men. They were also serving maids for the meals. One woman looked up as she approached and whispered something to the dark-haired woman standing beside her.

Rosalin's foot seemed to stutter mid-step, and she nearly stumbled. It was the woman who'd kissed Robbie. Deirdre.

A pit of dread sank to the bottom of her stomach, and her courage faltered. The last thing she wanted to do was be confronted by an angry mistress. After years at court, Rosalin was under no illusions about women. They could be every bit as cruel and ruthless as men. Perhaps more so.

But she forced her feet forward and her chin up. She was Lady Rosalin Clifford, sister of one of the most important barons in England. She did not cower and run.

Usually. But she was painfully aware that none of that mattered here. Her rank would afford her little protection with these women. They didn't care who she was, they only knew *what* she was: English, a hostage, and the sister of the man who was probably the most hated in Scotland.

A third woman had joined the first two by the time Rosalin drew close enough to hear them. Of course they were speaking in Gaelic, so she couldn't understand a word. From the way the two other women deferred to Deirdre, however, Rosalin guessed that she must be in charge.

She was older than she'd appeared at first glance. At least a good handful of years beyond Rosalin and the other two girls, who appeared closer to her own two and twenty. She was prettier, too, than she'd realized, possessing the kind of bold sensuality that Rosalin could never hope to emulate. With her dark hair and eyes, high cheekbones, and wide mouth, Deirdre's features were sharp—almost exotic-looking—making Rosalin suddenly feel drab and uninteresting by comparison.

And then there was her figure. Rosalin wrapped her plaid around her chest self-consciously. She could never hope to compare in that arena. Buxom and curvaceous were putting it mildly.

The two younger women were also brown-haired, albeit lighter in complexion and eye color, but not as fair of face. There was a sullen, downtrodden look to them that spoke of hardship. Deirdre had it as well, but hers was better hidden behind the sharp edge of maturity. There was little this woman hadn't seen, and Rosalin didn't know whether to pity or envy her for it.

The three women must have been clearing the dishes, as a stack of used trays, trenchers, goblets, and pitchers had been deposited on one of the worktables. Two large tubs of water set out next to it suggested that they were about to start washing.

Rosalin came to a stop in front of the table opposite them. She looked down at the dirty dishes, a wry smile turning her mouth. "It seems I've missed the meal."

She assumed they would speak English, but the blank expressions and awkward silence that followed made her wonder.

Finally, Deirdre responded. "Fetch the lady something to eat, Mor," she said to one of the girls at her side. Then to Rosalin, she said, "The cook has just taken in a few more trays. If you like, I will have Mor bring it to you there."

Her tone was more matter-of-fact than friendly or deferential, but free of the malice or resentment Rosalin had feared.

Rosalin shook her head. "If it isn't too much trouble, I think I will take it back to my tent." A loud roar emitted from the Hall behind them. "I should not wish to disturb their celebration."

"They are not celebrating—no more than any other night when ale and whisky are plentiful." She studied Rosalin's face with a scrutiny that made her wish she could read minds. "But you are probably right. They are not the most reasonable in this state." Rosalin took that to mean her Englishness would not be appreciated—or rather, would be even less appreciated than normal. Deirdre eyed her askance. "Iain is not fetching your meals?"

Rosalin shook her head. "Robb—" She blushed, and quickly corrected, "The captain has given me permission to move around the camp."

Deirdre lifted a brow at that. "He has? Hmm."

Rosalin didn't know what that "hmm" meant, but it didn't seem as if she agreed with Robbie's decision.

Rosalin tried to explain. "I threatened to die of boredom, which would make me quite useless as a hostage."

The faint hint of a smile lifted one corner of the other woman's mouth. "You do not need to defend him to me, my lady; the captain makes his own decisions. I would not think to question them."

Rosalin was aware of a subtle undercurrent and realized Deirdre was probably referring to other decisions as well—such as the one that had taken him from her bed.

Feeling a tightening in her heart, Rosalin was suddenly anxious to leave. In spite of the woman's unexpected equanimity, she was painfully aware of the man who was between them. The man Deirdre had had, but Rosalin . . . never would.

The truth hit her with a blow. She understood what Deirdre must have known from the first. Deirdre didn't resent her because she didn't fear her. *I'm not a threat to her.* Rosalin might have distracted him temporarily, but eventually she would go, and when she did . . .

Rosalin saw her thoughts mirrored in the woman's eyes. When she did, he would go back to Deirdre's bed.

Her stomach turned, and it took everything she had to hold back the hard press of tears that sprang to her eyes. It had taken Robbie's mistress to make her see what was so obvious. There could never be anything meaningful between them. She was *temporary.* A means to an end. When he'd exacted what payment he could from her brother, she would be sent back and undoubtedly never see him again.

Fortunately, the girl—Mor—chose that moment to return with a small tray of food. Rosalin took it from her and recovered her composure enough to thank her. "I will return the tray when I am finished."

"The morning will be soon enough," Deirdre said absently, already turning her attention back to the stack of dishes in front of her.

Rosalin started to walk away with her tray, but then turned back. "I should like to help while I am here. If you think of anything I can do."

The girl who had been silent while Rosalin spoke with Deirdre said something to the other women in Gaelic. By her tone, Rosalin guessed that it wasn't very nice. Mor covered her smile with her hand, but Deirdre said something sharply back that sobered both girls quickly.

Again, Rosalin was aware of being scrutinized and assessed.

"I presume you are good with a needle."

Rosalin nodded. Most noble ladies could be counted on to have the skill.

"Well, it isn't tabards or tapestries, but there is always a stack of linens to be mended."

Rosalin smiled for the first time since she'd left her tent. "That sounds perfect. Thank you."

Whether it was her smile or her gratitude, something seemed to make Deirdre uncomfortable. She brushed off her thanks. "Aye, well, the captain will have to agree to it when he gets back."

The smile fell from Rosalin's face; she stilled. "The captain is gone?"

Her distress was so obvious even Deirdre must have felt sorry for her, as there was pity in her eyes. "Aye, he rode out a few hours ago."

"When will he be back? Where did he go?"

The other woman shrugged. "I don't know. I should think a day or two."

"Is Sir Alex here?"

"Nay, he left as well."

Panic started to crawl up inside her. The goblet on the tray started to rattle. He wouldn't have left her *alone* with . . .

"Then who is in charge?" she asked, her stomach twisting as she anticipated the answer.

"The Douglas."

Blood was no longer dripping down Robbie's arm, but each hard fall of his horse's hooves jarred his ribs and sent a blast of pain through his side, serving as a visceral reminder of the dangers of distraction. For nothing else could explain the uncharacteristic mistakes he'd made that had enabled the enemy to get in two clean blows: the first, a blade across the shoulder that had struck with enough force to slice through his steel-studded leather *cotun* to the skin below, and the second, the crushing blow of a mace across his side that had broken more than one rib.

He would like to say that it was because the mission had been more difficult than any of them expected—the fifty men they'd faced had been a highly skilled combination of English soldiers and hardened mercenaries who hadn't given up their silver easily—but he knew that wasn't the reason.

It was Rosalin. She was the distraction. He couldn't shake the feeling that something was wrong. He told himself that there was nothing to worry about. He'd left Douglas in charge and made it damn clear that if any harm should befall her, if she even complained of a quiver of fear, he would hold him accountable. He was fairly sure he'd threatened Douglas with enough bodily damage to deny his new wife any pleasures in the marital bed by removing certain necessary parts with a dull spoon, but Robbie couldn't remember his exact words.

Rosalin would be fine, he told himself. He'd been gone only half a day.

Which didn't explain why he and Seton were currently galloping through the forest in the middle of the night, and not celebrating their successful mission with the rest of the Guard by sleeping and tending their injuries in a cave not far from where they'd won their hard-fought victory.

I should have told her I was leaving. He didn't know why he hadn't, except that he'd been trying to convince himself after the uncomfortable conversation with his brethren that she didn't meant anything to him. That he wasn't beholden to her.

Seton swore behind him. Robbie heard the sound of a branch snapping as he turned with the torch.

"Christ, that almost took my head off," Seton said. "Either slow down or hand me the bloody torch."

"Or you could try to keep up."

Seton threw him a black glare. "It's pitch-black out here, thick with mist, and well past midnight. After nearly twelve hours of riding, with only a few hours' break to fight a damned battle, my horse is a little tired. Hell, *I'm* a little tired. Are you going to tell me why we are killing ourselves to get back to camp tonight rather than enjoying a much deserved rest with the others?"

Robbie set his mouth in a hard line. "I want to get back."

"That's bloody obvious; the question is why. Are you worried about the lass?"

"Douglas won't let anything happen to her." He said it almost as much to himself as he did to Seton. Robbie trusted Douglas with his life—and had done so more than once. But it was Robbie's responsibility to see to Rosalin's safety, and he didn't like delegating it to anyone else. Even a trusted friend.

"But?"

Seton knew him too damned well. "But hell if I know. Something just doesn't feel right."

It was a testament to their long partnership that the explanation not only satisfied him, it also seemed to make Seton nearly as anxious to return as he.

Robbie wasn't like Campbell. He didn't get feelings about things. The implicit trust of Seton's reaction surprised him. It probably shouldn't have, but it did.

The closer they drew to camp, the worse the feeling grew. By the time they passed the first sentry it was probably two or three in the morning, and Robbie was stretched to the breaking point. Every rustle of leaves, every gust of wind, every hoot of an owl or sound of nightlife grated against nerves that were already frazzled and on edge.

"Everything looks all right," Seton said in a low voice.

It did. The sentries were at their posts. The camp was dark and quiet. The faint scent of peat from the fires wafted through the air.

Then why the hell did he feel like he was about to jump out of his damned skin? Why did he have to fight the urge to race through camp like a madman and tear open the flaps of the tent to assure himself that she was all right?

When they turned the corner around the Great Hall and the second row of tents came into view, he was about to heave a sigh of relief when he caught the flicker of something in the trees.

"What's that?" Seton said.

Robbie didn't take the time to answer. He snapped the reins and kicked his mount forward, plunging into the darkness toward the light. A moment later he heard the sound of a soft cry that sent a torrent of ice rushing through his veins.

The man came out of nowhere.

After hours of tossing and turning, telling herself there was no reason to be scared, and certainly no reason to hold her breath like a terrified child every time someone walked past the tent, Rosalin finally found sleep only to wake up a few hours later with a pressing need that could not be ignored.

Everyone is abed. There is no reason to worry. No one will harm you. But just knowing that Robbie wasn't here lent a new vulnerability to her situation. She hadn't realized how much his presence reassured her. How instinctively she knew that he would protect her. Without him, she felt like she was sitting in a den of hungry lions without a sword and shield.

After attending to her business in a matter of a couple of very relieved minutes, she was making her way back to the tent when a man stepped out from behind a tree to block her path.

Her heart jumped, and she let out a startled cry that strangled in her throat. The candle dropped to her feet.

He loomed over her, a dark, forbidding shadow. He wasn't exceptionally tall, but he was thick and heavily built. The pungent scent of drink accosted her as he bent down and picked up the candle.

"What do we 'ave 'ere," he slurred, holding it up to her face, "a new whore?" The burr of his accent was so deep, it took her a moment to realize he was speaking English— the Northern English common at the Borders.

Her blood turned to ice. She opened her mouth to protest, but he'd already slid his arm around her waist and jerked her up against him.

"Let me go," she said, trying to push away.

"What the 'ell?" He pushed her up against a tree and lodged his forearm against her throat. "You're fucking English."

Holding the candle close to her face, he gave her the first clear look at him and the cold, black eyes that looked at her murderously. It was the face of nightmares. A thick scar sliced through his heavy brow across a squashed nose and disappeared beneath the edge of a thick beard. The legacy of a sword or battle-axe blade, it gave a menacing edge to an already brutish appearance. When he opened his mouth and sneered, his big, yellow teeth reminded her of a boar's tusks. That was what he looked like—a big, ugly boar, with thick, wiry black hair and a flat squashed nose.

But it was his heavily lidded eyes and the way he was looking at her that sent chills racing through every corner of her body. She struggled to free herself, but it only made him lean in harder, pressing the forearm laid across her neck and cutting off her breath.

His face was so close, she could smell the sour scent of whisky on his breath. "Who the 'ell are you?"

"Hostage," she managed to get out in a soft breath. "Boyd."

She wasn't sure whether her words had penetrated the drunken haze.

They had, but not in the way she'd hoped. His mouth curled in an ugly sneer. "An English bitch as a hostage? A whore, more like." His hand covered her breast and she tried to cry out as fear stiffened every inch of her body. "I hope the cap'n taught you something. Let's see 'ow much yer worth."

She could see the intent in his eyes and renewed her struggles. She clawed at the arm across her neck. "He'll kill you," she managed.

He caught her hands and pinned them up over her head, the soft skin of her wrists digging into the bark. But it was nothing compared to the pain and horror of having his body pressed against hers. She twisted against him, trying to break free, wanting to retch nearly as much as she wanted to breathe.

"Boyd?" he laughed. "He hates the English as much as I—"

A noise behind him made him turn. A dark figure plunged out of the shadows on a horse. As he leaped down, his cloak flying like the wings of a demon behind him, Rosalin caught a glimpse of his face and nearly fainted. Beneath the darkened nasal helm there seemed to be only emptiness.

Her scream was strangled even though the man's arm was no longer at her throat. He'd turned to defend himself, but he could barely get his hands up before the battering ram of a steel-gauntleted fist came crashing into his jaw with enough force to send him flying through the air a few feet before landing with a thud on his back.

The dark, cloaked figure was standing over him a moment later, pounding him into the ground with powerful blow after powerful blow.

She'd seen something like it once before. "Robbie!"

The word escaped from between her lips as if in answer to a prayer.

He paused long enough to glance at her. Beneath the shadow of the terrifying mask she could just make out his familiar features. But his expression was one she'd never seen before. It was fierce and menacing, without a hint of mercy. It was the face of a warrior in the heat of battle, the face of one of the most feared men in Scotland.

He turned back to finish what he'd started. *He's going to kill him!* Despite what the man had been about to do, Rosalin didn't want the brute's death on her soul—or on Robbie's.

She knew she should try to stop him, but someone else did it for her. Another cloaked figure emerged from the darkness on horseback. As he wasn't wearing a helm, however, the blond hair identified him.

Sir Alex jumped down and swore. Crossing the distance toward the men, he pulled Robbie off. "Christ, Raider, you'll kill him. He's one of ours."

Sir Alex had Robbie's arms pinned back. Robbie twisted, attempting to break free with a quick movement of his arm that might have had Sir Alex on his back, too, if he hadn't managed to block it.

Robbie said something to Sir Alex in Gaelic, but Rosalin didn't need to translate that particular curse. "He deserves it," he said, breathing hard. "He was going to hurt her."

Sir Alex looked at her and when their eyes met, she knew he didn't need to ask how the man was going to hurt her. The graveness of Sir Alex's expression made her think he also knew about Robbie's sister.

The commotion had alerted the occupants of the next tent, and Rosalin didn't need to see his face to know that the Black Douglas was one of them.

"What is going on out here?" Douglas said, two of his men coming up behind him with a torch.

If Sir Alex hadn't still been holding him back, Rosalin knew that Robbie would have launched himself at his friend. "This is how you watch over her? You fucking bastard, I should kill you for letting this happen."

The man with the blackest heart in Scotland seemed taken aback by the vehemence of Robbie's anger. His gaze shifted to her—still crouched up against the tree and undoubtedly pale and terror-struck—and then to the man lying still on the ground behind Robbie. His expression changed to one of grim understanding.

The Black Douglas swore, repeating one of the words Robbie had just used, and dragged his hand through his sleep-rumpled hair. "Uilleam just arrived with a missive from my wife. I didn't think to tell him about the lass. He didn't know who she was." He turned to address her. "I'm sorry, my lady. That should never have happened. If you were hurt it's my fault, and I shall take full responsibility for the mistake."

She was so stunned that the Black Douglas was apologizing to her that it took her a moment to respond. She shook her head. "He didn't hurt me." Her voice came out scratchy, and she rubbed her bruised throat unconsciously.

Robbie growled like a ferocious wolf and surged forward with such power and force that Sir Alex couldn't hope to hold him back.

Instinctively the Black Douglas squared to meet the attack, but by this time Rosalin had collected herself enough to intervene. She rushed forward to intercept Robbie, putting a gentling hand on his arm.

She swallowed hard through the pain to clear her throat. "Really, I'm fine." He looked down at her, and the deep emotion burning in his gaze made her heart flip high in her chest. "Please," she whispered. "It was a mistake."

Though her brother would undoubtedly like nothing more than for these two men to beat each other to a pulp, Rosalin just wanted it over. She wanted to curl up against the black leather-clad chest, bury her head against his shoulder, and feel safe again.

She didn't know who moved first, but one minute she was leaning against him and the next, he'd swooped her up into his arms and started to carry her back to the tent.

"You and I are going to talk tomorrow," he said to Douglas as they passed.

The big man nodded grimly. "I'll see to Uilleam—and your horse."

The conversation sounded far away. Rosalin had already burrowed her head against him, closed her eyes, and let the relief of being safe in his arms overtake her.

Robbie didn't want to let her go. Ever. Cradling her in his arms, her soft body warm against his chest, was unlike anything he'd ever imagined. The wave of emotion that rose inside him, crashed over him, and threatened to drag him under resembled tenderness, but it was bigger and far more powerful.

This was his fault. He never should have brought her here. It was his job to protect her, and if she'd been hurt, he never would have forgiven himself.

God, when he thought of what could have happened, it made his stomach turn. Bile climbed up the back of his throat. His sister's face passed before his eyes.

He squeezed Rosalin closer, the pain of his broken ribs nothing compared to the burning pain in his chest. God, she smelled good. He pressed his mouth against the silky softness of her hair, inhaling the faint scent of lavender.

Not ready to relinquish her yet, he entered the tent and carried her toward his bed. Sitting with his back against the wall, he held her so that her head was resting against his chest like a pillow. He pulled off his helm and tossed it at the foot of the bed.

The movement caused her eyes to open. He watched her brow furrow as she took in his face. "You've been fighting," she said, reaching out to brush a cut on his cheek. His body reacted to the soft touch, tensing. She tried to wipe the smudges from his face. "How did you get all this soot on your face? When I first saw you, I thought you were a ghost." She glanced at the helm and shuddered. "Or a demon."

Knowing she was treading close to dangerous waters, he took her icy fingers in his hand and brought them to his mouth. "Go to sleep, Rosalin. It's been a long day. We'll talk in the morning."

Her eyes met his with a look that cut right through his chest. "You won't leave me?"

He shook his head. The word "never" rose to his lips, but he pushed it back. That was a promise he could not make. "Not tonight. Now sleep, sweetheart."

She did as he bade, falling asleep with a contented smile on her face that made him feel like not the strongest but the luckiest man in Scotland. Slowly, it warmed the coldness that had been burning inside him since the moment he'd seen her pressed up against that tree, until he, too, slept.

Fifteen

Rosalin drew the needle through the linen for the final time, made her knot, and used the scissors she'd borrowed from Deirdre to cut the thread. Holding the tunic up to the sunlight (that she'd begun to lose hope of ever seeing again) streaming through the Hall window, she admired her handiwork. Although not quite as good as new, there was no longer a large, gaping tear across the upper sleeve. From the rust-colored staining around the tear that remained even after washing, she suspected it had come from a sword blade.

" 'Tis a fine job," the woman sitting beside her said.

Rosalin smiled, pleased by the compliment. "Thank you, Jean. The light in here is a vast improvement to the tent."

Ironically, despite the closeness she'd shared with Robbie a few nights ago when she'd fallen asleep in his arms, she'd made greater inroads with the women of camp than she had with its leader. Robbie had already gone when she woke that next morning, and their conversations since had been brief and mostly in passing. The women, however, were slowly starting to include her in their conversations.

The mending had helped. The first bundle of clothing that had arrived from Deirdre she'd attempted to mend in the tent. But after a long day by candlelight, she'd sought out natural light the next day—and company.

Rosalin had walked into the Hall three days ago, pulled

up a bench in a corner near a window, and quietly went to work on the basket of mending. The women ignored her for the first day, but by the second, curiosity got the better of a few of them. By the third day, she'd begun to learn something of them as well. Though she wouldn't exactly call them friendly, they were for the most part polite, and one or two of them had even taken to sitting beside her while she worked—like Jean.

The girl couldn't be much older than eight and ten, but her natural dark-blond prettiness had already begun to dull under the ravaging weight of struggle and strife. Like Rosalin, most of these women had lost their parents at a young age. Unlike her, however, they hadn't had the fortune of a generous guardian to take care of them. With the men in their life either off to war or killed by the destruction around it, they'd been left to fend on their own.

As fallen women weren't exactly a subject of polite conversation, Rosalin had never given much thought to how or why someone would choose a life of sin. It was deeply distressing to learn that for many of them, choice was not a part of it. When the men in your family had been killed, your village had been razed, and there was little work to be found (and even less if you were a woman), you did what you must to survive. Worse were the girls like Jean, who'd been forced into the life by rape.

In truth their stories were heartbreaking. As was the matter-of-fact way they were told, as if the unfairness wasn't only expected, but accepted. No matter what the church might say, Rosalin couldn't find it in her heart to condemn them. Indeed, she couldn't help but feel grateful that fate had not forced her to have to make a similar "choice." Birth, rank, and a caring brother had afforded her the protection these women did not have. It was humbling to think how easily their fate could have been hers.

It was a hard life. From what Rosalin could see, the women worked all day keeping the camp running smoothly and stayed up most of the night pleasing the men. Different men. A few fortunate ones like Deirdre and Mor had been "claimed" by one of the leaders, but the other women like Jean moved from bed to bed each night.

"I don't know what we will do when you go, my lady," Jean said with a shy smile. "You have saved us about two weeks' worth of mending in a few days."

Rosalin felt a strange pang in her chest at the thought of leaving, but she knew it could be any day. It had been over a week since they'd arrived in the forest, and the envoy that had been sent to her brother to negotiate for her release could return at any time. "I have been happy to do it," Rosalin said. "It has given me a way to pass the time."

"Aye, well I suspect when word gets out of your fine work, you will have plenty to keep you busy while you are here."

Suddenly, the smile fell from the girl's face and a troubled look crossed it. Rosalin turned to see what had caused the reaction and noticed that two of the other women had come into the Hall to start preparing for the midday meal.

Agnes was one of the older and more experienced of the women, and from what Rosalin could tell, closest in rank to Deirdre. The second woman, Mary, had a sad, empty-eyed look to her and drank enough ale and whisky to put a man of Robbie's size on his back, but she never appeared drunk. Except for Agnes, the other women at camp seemed to avoid her. If there was a rank among the women, Rosalin would put Mary at the bottom of the heap.

It was only when she turned in their direction that Rosalin realized what had caused Jean's reaction. A large, angry-looking bruise covered Mary's right cheekbone.

Suspecting what might have been the cause of the injury, Rosalin felt outrage spark inside her. She turned to Jean. "Who did that to her? Did one of the men strike her?"

Jean shook her head and put her finger up to her mouth to quiet her. "Please, my lady, do not say anything. You will only make more trouble for her. It's Mary's own fault. We tried to warn her. Fergal gets a little rough when he's drunk, but she wouldn't listen and went with him anyway. He's the only one who will take her now."

"What do you mean?"

Jean's mouth hardened with distaste. "Last time we went to the village at Corehead for supplies, she caught the eye of one of the soldiers in the nearby garrison. Fancied herself in love with the Englishman, she did. Until she got herself with child and he kicked her out of his bed."

Rosalin gasped, her eyes widening with alarm. "She's pregnant?"

Jean shook her head. "Nay, she lost the child not long afterward. You wouldn't guess it by looking at her now, but she used to be quite a favorite among the men." She shrugged. "But no one wants an English whore." She blushed. "Meaning no disrespect, m'lady."

Rosalin didn't care about that. "That is no excuse for someone to hit her."

Jean looked at her as if she were either the most naive person in the world or the stupidest. "Fergal isn't so bad, my lady. Not when he's sober, at least. I'm sure he'll make it up to her—which is why she'll not thank you for interfering."

Reluctantly, Rosalin took Jean's advice and returned to her mending. She understood the precariousness of Mary's position and didn't want to do anything to make it worse for her, but the unfairness of it ate at her. The woman had lost a child. Must she now endure a beating in silence? How long must she serve penance for the mistake of falling in love with the wrong man?

If the question resonated a little too loudly, Rosalin didn't want to hear it.

Rosalin was still fuming an hour later when she carried the stack of linens back to her tent to prepare for the mid-

day meal. It was wrong to hit a woman—*any* woman—
and Mary needed someone to stand up for her, even if she
would not herself.

The brute should be punished, and it went against
Rosalin's nature to stand aside and do nothing—say
nothing—when she saw someone treated so unfairly.

Not paying attention to her surroundings, she startled at
the sound of a loud roar coming from the other side of the
building where the men practiced. Curious, she back-
tracked a little, following the sound of the cheers and yells.
Once she'd turned the corner, she saw a large gathering of
men—what appeared to be nearly all the forty or so men
in camp—in a small clearing. They were standing in a
loose circle watching something.

She scanned the area for Robbie but didn't see him.
Suddenly second-guessing the wisdom of her current pur-
suit, she started to turn around when she caught a glimpse
between two of the men of what had them so riveted.

She froze. Everything froze—her heart, her breath, her
step. Indeed she was rooted to the ground with . . . shock?
She wasn't sure, but whatever it was, she couldn't tear her
eyes away from the display in front of her. It wasn't just
that Robbie was naked to the waist—although that alone
would probably have been enough—he was also being attacked by a half-dozen men wielding swords, coming at
him from different directions. And he was winning without a weapon or even a shield to defend himself—only his
hands.

She must have walked forward, because she found herself edging between two of the men to get a closer view.

Sweet heaven, she'd never seen anything like it! Highland
wrestling she'd heard of, but this was different. She didn't
know how to describe it except that he was tossing grown
men—seasoned warriors all of them—around as if they
were pesky gnats. They couldn't get close to him. As soon
as they made their move, he'd evade them with a twist of

his body, a block of his hand, a jab of his knee, even a kick of his foot. They ended up keeled over in pain or on their backs.

It wasn't until the men chanted for "Seton" that anyone gave him a contest. Sir Alex had obviously been trained in the same fighting style, because he matched the strange moves with nearly equal precision. It was brutal, but strangely fascinating to watch—almost like a vicious, violent dance.

Rosalin felt as if her heart was in her throat, as if she were a hairsbreadth from raising her voice to tell them to stop as they exchanged blows and blocks, jabs and twists, kicks and flips. It seemed as if it could go on forever, even though both men were obviously tiring. Finally, Sir Alex made a quick move toward Robbie, trying to land a jab of his elbow in Robbie's ribs. She gasped when she realized why: a large part of Robbie's left side was black and mottled with bruising.

But Robbie had anticipated the move. He twisted, taking the blow with his right side, jabbed Sir Alex hard under the chin with his elbow, and cut behind his feet to land him on his back.

The crowd erupted in a roar.

Robbie grinned and reached his hand down to help his friend up.

Sir Alex stared at it for a minute, cursed prodigiously, but eventually took it.

Their interaction was so much like that of brothers that she almost laughed.

"You're too impatient," Robbie said in a way that made Rosalin think it hadn't been for the first time. "And predictable. I knew the ribs would be too much for you to resist."

"It's your only damned weak spot," Sir Alex muttered in frustration.

Robbie just grinned. But looking at that broad, chiseled

chest, Rosalin had to disagree. Even with the bruising, there wasn't a weak spot on him.

Almost as if he could read her thoughts, he turned and saw her standing there. It seemed that everyone else saw her standing there as well, because the raucous laughter suddenly stopped with all the sublety of a clap of thunder.

A blush rose to her cheeks. Robbie frowned but walked over to her. "Did you need something?"

Being confronted by well over six feet of half-naked man seemed to tie her tongue. After a flustered moment of staring at his chest, which seemed to cover most of her field of vision, she forced her gaze up to his eyes. But not before noticing the cut on his arm. "You're hurt!"

"It's nothing."

Suddenly aware that everyone was watching them—and listening—she said, "I need to speak with you."

He frowned. "Did something happen?"

She looked around self-consciously, shifting the stack of linens in her arms. "Please, it's important."

He held her gaze for a moment before turning to his men. "We will resume after the midday meal." He glanced at a few of the men, who wore proof of their time on the ground in the layer of mud covering their backsides. "Some of you look as if you need time to wash."

The men laughed and started to hurl insults at one another as they dispersed.

Plucking his shirt and *cotun* from a nearby rock, Robbie donned the first and tossed the latter over his arm.

As much as Rosalin was reluctant to see that spectacular, gleaming chest all covered up, it did clear her head.

He offered to carry her bundle as well. She thought about it before handing it over. "You might as well. I believe the top one belongs to you anyway."

He ignored the pointed reference to the injury he had not told her about and took a quick glance at her work. A brow lifted as he examined the stitches. "Christ, how did you do that? It looks as if the cloth was rewoven on the loom. I can barely see the stitches, they are so tiny."

Recalling what he'd once said to her when she'd questioned him about his skill in sneaking up on her, she said, "Practice." One side of his mouth lifted, but then fell when she added, "I'm also quite proficient at tending wounds and making poultices."

He shot her a look. "It's nothing, Rosalin. A scratch."

She clamped her jaw. That was no scratch. Heaven's gates, were all men so stubborn? Her brother was the same way when he was injured. "Even a 'scratch' can turn putrid and cause death if not tended."

"I would not deprive Clifford of the pleasure so easily."

They'd almost reached the tent, but she stopped in her tracks and spun to face him. "That is not funny."

The thought of her brother killing him—or him killing her brother—made her ill.

"It was not meant to be. I simply point out that my death would be one of Clifford's—your countryman's—great pleasures."

She knew what he was trying to do, remind them both of the circumstances by forcing a wedge between them, but she wasn't going to let him. "It would not be mine."

She held his gaze challengingly, daring him to deny the connection that ran between them. A connection that neither war nor her brother could sever.

He sighed and shook his head. "It's been tended."

"By whom?"

He gave her a look that made her wish she hadn't asked. "Oh," she said, her mouth snapping closed. Deirdre.

He held the flap back while she entered the tent and climbed in after her. Putting the stack of linens on Sir Alex's trunk, he then went to his own and removed a drying cloth and soap. Obviously, he, too, meant to wash before the midday meal. "What is it you wished to speak to me about?"

"Have you ever struck a woman?"

"Bloody hell, of course not! Why would you ask such a thing?" He looked distinctly offended.

"It's not uncommon."

He frowned. "Perhaps not, but only weak men hurt those who are unable to defend themselves. I am not weak."

She would not argue that. "What of those under your command?"

His eyes narrowed, a dark cast coming over his handsome features—not unlike the one she'd seen the night he battled Uilleam. "Where is this coming from, Rosalin? Did someone hurt you?"

She shook her head. "Not me."

His anger dissipated and comprehension dawned. "One of the other women?"

She nodded, all of her frustration bursting out. "It isn't right. Drunkenness isn't an excuse for brutishness. I was taught that men are supposed to protect ladies, not hurt them."

He held her gaze steadily. "You do realize why these women are in camp, Rosalin? They are not ladies."

She jutted out her chin. Did he think her that innocent? "Yes, but one sin does not justify another. What the women do doesn't make it acceptable to beat them. Or do you think a woman you take to your bed for pleasure is not worthy of consideration?"

He held up his hand as if to fend off her attack. "I do not think that way; it's just that I am surprised you do. Whores are usually beneath the regard of most noblewomen."

"Well, not mine."

He studied her appraisingly, making her wish she knew what he was thinking. "I can see that."

"So do you condone men under your command who beat women?"

"I do not. Who was it?"

She bit her lip. "I cannot say."

"Why not?"

"The woman will be harmed if he is punished." He looked so confused that she added, "Her place here is . . . tenuous."

"Ah, the Englishman's whor—" He stopped, seeing her expression.

"Don't call her that! It's not her fault that she fell in love with the wrong man. The heart does not see battle lines."

He held her gaze for only a moment, almost as if he, too, wanted to avoid thinking about the subject too carefully. "Perhaps not, but neither can you fault the men for not wanting to bed with her. Should I order them to do so?"

She frowned. "Of course not."

"Then what would you have me do?"

"I don't know, but it isn't right. She lost her child—is that not punishment enough? And now she is forced to subject herself to a drunken brute's temper and cannot raise her voice to complain at all for fear of losing her place in camp?"

"The sword of justice does not always fall fairly, Rosalin. Take it from someone who knows."

She looked up at him, her big, luminous green eyes bright with outrage and frustration, and Robbie felt something in his chest turn over and then tug. Hard, and with too much persistence to ignore.

He was in trouble, and every day that passed it was getting worse. He wanted her so intensely, all he had to do was catch the barest hint of her scent and he stiffened up like a lad about to tup his first maid.

Her proximity was driving him mad. Everything about her was driving him mad. He didn't dare look at her hands, for if he did he would remember those soft white fingers wrapped around his . . .

Bloody hell, a few minutes of pleasure had resulted in days of torture.

Not that he would regret it. How could he regret what had been one of the most erotic, sensual, and intimate moments of his life?

She seemed to be the only one in camp unaware of his torment. Douglas looked at him as if he were mad, Fraser with amusement, Deirdre with accusation, and Seton with warning. He'd threatened to slip his dagger between Robbie's ribs if he touched her.

His partner meant it, too, and though Robbie didn't usually get intimidated (having to catch ten spears aimed at his head during MacLeod's aptly named "Perdition" training came to mind as an exception), he'd seen Seton's skill with a dagger enough times to not summarily dismiss the threat.

At first Seton's place on the team might have been a gratuitous gesture due to Bruce's friendship with Alex's brother Christopher, but Boyd had to admit his partner's skill would have earned him a spot today. He could wield a dagger with deadly accuracy and quickness that was unrivaled among any of the Guard. Hell, among any warriors Robbie had ever seen.

He frowned, thinking of their contest earlier. Seton had also become far more adept at the hand-to-hand combat than Robbie would have believed possible. He wasn't as strong as Robbie, but he was quicker. And younger. If he ever learned to control his patience, he might actually give Robbie a real challenge.

But it wasn't Seton's threat that worried him now. It was this other feeling. This bigger feeling that seemed to be growing in his chest and overtaking everything else. The feeling that made him want to slay every dragon for her so he wouldn't have to see this look on her face again.

Rosalin Clifford felt too keenly. That was her problem. And it would only bring her disappointment and frustration. He should know. One day she would learn the hard truth that she could not right every wrong in the world. He was almost glad he wouldn't be around to see it. Almost.

But that didn't mean he was untouched by her outrage on behalf of the lass. And he couldn't help but think of his sister. If someone like Rosalin had been there to stand up for Marian, maybe she wouldn't have felt that there was no other road but the one that led off a cliff.

"I'm sorry," she said, putting a hand on his arm. He forced himself not to look at it. "I did not mean to raise bitter memories. Of course you know of what I speak."

Her head was tipped back to look at him. The soft scent of lavender permeated his senses. She was standing so close, all he had to do was bend his head down and his lips would be touching hers.

Fire roared in his blood in anticipation. His eyes flickered over the too-beautiful features, the wide green eyes, the dark, long lashes, the red lips and velvety-soft skin, and all he could think about was watching those lips part, those lashes flutter over half-lidded eyes, those creamy cheeks flush as he brought her to the peak of pleasure with his hands—and his mouth.

God, he wanted to taste her. He wanted to slide his tongue between her legs and ravish her until she bucked and arched. Until she broke apart and came into his mouth with a hot rush. He could almost taste her on his lips. Feel the warm silk of her honey sliding against his tongue.

He almost groaned. Desire coursed through every vein in his body, reverberating like a drum. And she heard it. Sensed it. Her eyes grew hazy. Her mouth opened in a soft gasp of anticipation.

He leaned into her, feeling the soft shudder that rippled through her as if it were his own.

His heart pounded. His muscles tensed. His fists clenched against the temptation. The temptation he had to resist.

With a muttered curse, he stepped back. "I need to bathe

before the meal." He didn't wait for her to respond before stalking out of the tent.

He wasn't running away, damn it. It was self-preservation.

But he didn't know how much more of this he could take. It couldn't be much longer, he told himself. The envoy to Clifford would return at any time, Clifford would agree to the truce—what else could he do?—Rosalin would leave, and Robbie would be one step closer to achieving the only thing that mattered: winning the war and freedom from English rule.

Freedom from men like her brother.

His jaw hardened. A few more cold dips in the burn would get him through this. If only the memories were as easy to wash away from his body as the lust.

Sixteen

❧

Robbie entered the Hall a short while later—clean, if not more relaxed—and was surprised to see Rosalin seated at one end of the trestle table next to Seton. Douglas, *not* surprisingly, was at the opposite end.

He knew she was still uneasy around Douglas, even though his friend had stopped looking at her as if she were Satan's spawn (or in this case, his sister). He took a seat on the other side of Seton to act as another barrier. It wasn't because he didn't think he could take sitting next to her for a couple of hours. He couldn't be that weak.

Bloody hell.

He spent most of the meal conversing with Fraser and trying to ignore the easy conversation between his partner and the woman who was driving him to distraction. What in the hell were they talking about? Why were they whispering? Why was she laughing so much? And why did he care?

Because Seton was right. Robbie was jealous. Deeply and irrationally jealous. He might not be able to have her, but he couldn't stand the thought of someone else having her—and sure as hell not the partner who'd been a thorn in his side.

He was saved from doing something embarrassing—like bellowing at them to stop making so much noise—by the appearance before him of one of the serving women. As the lass leaned over to refill his tankard of ale, he caught sight of her cheek.

A reflexive surge of rage rushed through him at the sight of the large, angry-looking bruise. Instantly he understood Rosalin's outrage.

The lass had spilled a couple of drops that ran over the edge of the table into his lap, and glancing at his expression, misunderstood the source of his anger. She looked terrified. "I'm sorry, my lord. I will fetch a cloth to clean it up."

He snagged hold of her wrist before she could move away. She was fine-boned like Rosalin, and the fragility only made him more furious. But feeling her tremble with fear forced a gentleness into his tone. "The ale is nothing. My concern is for your injury. Who did this to you, lass?"

Though he was not speaking loudly, quite a few of the occupants of the room had taken notice of the conversation, including the man he suspected of striking her. Fergal Halliday was a minor laird from nearby, and good with a sword, but he also had a vicious temper when drunk.

His suspicions were confirmed when her gaze darted nervously and unconsciously to the man in question at the far side of the Hall. "No one, my lord. It was me. I . . ." She seemed to try to be thinking of something that would explain the bruise that was clearly caused by a hand. "It's so silly," she said with a forced laugh. "I tripped a few nights ago on my way back to my pallet and hit the edge of the table."

He caught Rosalin's eye. It was a poor excuse. And were it not for Rosalin's warning and the lass's own pleading look, he would have said so and demanded the truth from her. But Rosalin was right—she had been punished enough. He would not take her livelihood from her. Fergal would be dealt with as well. As Captain Robbie could make his life hell for the next week or so.

He released her arm. "An unfortunate accident indeed,"

he said slowly. "I hope that it will not happen again. You will come to me if it does." He held her gaze so there could be no doubt of what he spoke. "No woman should suffer such abuse, and you can be assured it will not be tolerated. You are welcome here, lass, and I hope no one makes you think otherwise."

Her eyes widened with shock. It was clear she was so unused to kindness that she didn't know how to react. Slowly the edges of her mouth started to curve, and by the time the smile reached her eyes they were shining with gratitude.

"Yes, my lord. Thank you, my lord."

She hurried away, obviously uncomfortable with the attention.

Robbie glanced toward Rosalin. It was a mistake. He'd had many admiring stares from women—his reputation and popularity at the Games had earned him more than his share—but none had ever felt like this. None had ever made the air in his lungs expand and his chest swell. None had ever made him feel like the most important man in the room. And none sure as hell had ever made him want to keep that look shining in her eyes forever.

A man could get used to that look.

A man could learn to crave that look.

A man could do something stupid for that look.

But damn it, Bruce needed Clifford's agreement, and Robbie couldn't do anything to jeopardize it. And what he wanted from Rosalin Clifford would sure as hell jeopardize it.

Right now they had momentum, and Clifford's resistance could easily change that. Not only might it encourage others to follow, but it would stop the progress Bruce was making in retaking his castles.

Robbie forced his gaze away. God's blood, where was that messenger? He should have been here by now.

Gulping down the remaining ale in his cup, he got to his feet. He had to get out of here.

Before he could start down the aisle to the door, it was thrown back and the very man he'd wanted to see came striding toward him. The man he *thought* he'd wanted to see. But the stone of dread that sank in his chest when he recognized the envoy told him otherwise.

Clifford's agreement to the truce had arrived. Robbie's gaze slid to Rosalin, and the weight in his chest started to burn. He was going to have to give her back.

The Hall had been cleared while Robbie, Sir Alex, the Black Douglas, and a handful of other men talked to the envoy. Rosalin paced nervously outside the door to learn her fate.

She had no doubt her brother would do whatever it took to free her, but how soon would she be forced to leave?

She stopped in her tracks. Blood drained from her face. *Forced?* Was that what it had become? Did she actually want to *stay* with the rebels, living in a tent in the godforsaken wilds of the most inhospitable countryside she'd ever seen, with one of the most hated men in England? A man whose very name conjured up whispers of demons? The man whose head her brother longed to see on a pike over the gates of his castle?

It was so inconceivable, so impossible, it couldn't be true. Of course she wanted to go back to England. To her pretty, clean dresses, her luxurious castles, her comfortable life with the family who loved her.

Her brother's family. Not hers. Though she loved them with all her heart, they would never be hers. She would have a life with . . .

The realization hit her with such force it nearly knocked her down. Sir Henry. God in heaven, how could she have forgotten about the man she was supposed to marry?

But forgotten him she had. Utterly and completely. Her

stomach started to toss so violently, she had to sit down on one of the stairs. Wrapping her arms around her waist, she tried to calm the sudden maelstrom raging inside her. What was she going to do?

The door behind her slammed open and the men started to pour out. She glanced up and saw Robbie in the doorway. From his clenched jaw, tight mouth, and dark gaze, she knew something was wrong.

She came to her feet anxiously. "What is it?"

"Your brother is a bloody bastard!"

Her heart started to pound, and her teeth caught her lower lip nervously. "What did the message say?"

Ice-cold blue eyes bit into hers, as if it were somehow her fault. "He's playing games. Games I've been on the other side of before. I just never thought he'd play them with his precious sister." His eyes narrowed. "Or is there something you aren't telling me? Perhaps you are not as close as I have been led to believe?"

Her brow furrowed. "We are very close. What do you mean by games? And what has he done before?"

His jaw clamped even tighter. It was clear he wanted to tell her, but something was holding him back.

The urge to tell her apparently won out. "When we were taken at Kildrummy it was under a truce. Your brother had given his word that we would be negotiating a surrender. I didn't want to agree, but Nigel Bruce and Seton insisted your brother could be trusted. As soon as we lifted the gate and walked outside to meet them, the English attacked. We were arrested, Nigel Bruce was taken to Berwick and executed, and the rest of us were cast in irons. You know the rest."

"You must be mistaken. My brother would never do something so dishonorable."

"Are you really so sure of that? It is war, and I'm sure he justified his perfidy with that. Our mistake was in trusting the word of an Englishman—any Englishman."

The look in his eyes sent a chill down her spine. It was a warning. Whatever Cliff's reply, it had reminded him of who she was and all that lay between them.

She straightened her spine and lifted her chin to him. "If what you say is true, my brother didn't know anything about it."

"He said the same—swore to it up and down. So much so that I refrained from killing his men when I had the chance, believing him when he said we would be treated fairly. You saw the results of that. Your brother does not deserve your stalwart defense."

"You don't know him the way I do."

His gaze held hers steadily. "I could say the same to you."

Rosalin had to look away, the turbulence in her stomach returning. He was right. She didn't know Cliff as an enemy, but she refused to believe he would have been involved in something so dishonorable. Her brother was a knight, and he took great pride in the chivalric code. There had to be an explanation.

She glanced back to him. The sun had gone down, passing behind the Hall and casting his features in angular shadows. He looked hard and unyielding, every inch the formidable Enforcer. "What else did the messenger say? Did my brother agree to the truce?"

Boyd's mouth tightened. "Yes and no. He will agree, but only if I parley with him in person."

Rosalin paled. For the second time in that short afternoon, her heartbeat took an anxious leap. "No! You can't do that. It's too dangerous."

"I thought you trusted your brother. Surely such a renowned knight would not do something as treacherous as setting a trap for me?"

Her cheeks flushed angrily at his taunting challenge. "It's not my brother I worry about. There will be other men around. They could capture you when you leave. Or follow you."

He lifted a brow. "If I didn't know better, I'd think you were worried about me."

She felt the strangest urge to tap her finger against that steely chest and maybe give it a good shove. "Of course I'm worried about you, although right now I'm wondering why. You make it difficult for someone to—" She stopped suddenly.

He tipped her chin back to look into her eyes. "To what, Rosalin?" His voice held an odd huskiness.

She scanned the depths of his gaze, looking for something. "To care about you."

She felt him stiffen. He stared at her so intently for a moment that she thought she was drowning in him, spinning in a whirlpool of emotions.

She thought he would pull her into his arms.

Instead, he dropped his hand from her face. "You would be foolish to do so."

Disappointment cut through her like a sliver of jagged glass. What had she expected? A return declaration? Some kind of indication that she was not alone in her feelings?

All he cared about was the war and defeating the English. There wasn't a place for anything—or anyone—else in his life. He was consumed by one thing and one thing only: seeing the English pay for what they'd taken from him.

And she'd listened to him—at first. But something had changed. Something had made her think that there might be room for something else in his heart. Room for her. Now she wasn't so sure.

"When will you leave?" she asked, her throat squeezing.

"Immediately. I want this over as soon as possible."

She flinched, the words sinking between her ribs like a dagger. It took everything she had not to let him see how much pain he'd caused. A healthy dose of that Clifford pride held her upright. "God's speed, then. I will anxiously await your return."

"Rosalin, hell, that's not what I meant."

He tried to reach for her, but she turned away from him, holding her spine stiffly to hide the trembling in her shoulders, and walked away as regally as the princess he'd once accused her of being.

Seventeen

❧

Robbie had been waiting for this moment for six years. But the long aisle of Melrose Abbey was not the battlefield he'd had in mind in which to face his enemy.

Clifford was waiting with three of his men near the carved wooden screen and altar, beyond which only monks were permitted. Robbie started down the south aisle with three of his own men flanking him. He'd brought a dozen men, but only Fraser, Barclay, and Keith had accompanied him inside the abbey. A few more waited outside, while the rest were spread out around the village keeping an eye out for any sign of a trap, and readying for their escape should it be necessary.

Robbie didn't expect anything, but with the English he'd learned to be cautious.

By agreement, both parties had left their weapons at the door. Though drawing swords in the holy place would be sacrilege, Clifford had insisted, with a not-so-subtle reference to Bruce's killing of the Red Comyn six years before in a church. The "barbarous" act had begun Bruce's bid for the throne and had also served to get him excommunicated.

Robbie didn't object. He wasn't the one who would need a weapon if their parley took a bad turn.

Besides, as long as Robbie held Rosalin, he had everything he needed to win this particular battle.

The tables had been turned. Robbie was no longer a

prisoner under the yoke of his jailor's bidding or a rebel supporting a king on the run. This time Robbie held all the power, and they both knew it.

He had dreamed of the day he would have the pompous bastard under his heel. The English and their bloody superiority! For too many years they'd treated the Scots like serfs in their own kingdom, like recalcitrant subjects and scurrilous rebels. Seeing a little humility on any English lord's face—especially Clifford's—was something Robbie had been looking forward to for a long time.

One day soon the English king would be forced to recognize Scotland as an independent nation, but for now Clifford's acquiescence would satisfy.

The fall of their footsteps on the tile floor echoed in the cavernous nave of one of Scotland's greatest abbeys. Built in the shape of St. John's cross, the abbey's thick stone pillars and walls rose more than forty feet above him, limned and decorated with brightly colored paintings they complemented the thousands of small pieces of glass stained and meticulously cut and fitted into lead to fill the enormous arched windows, of which there must be fifty.

It was impressive. Awe-inspiring. A modern marvel of architecture. The kind of place you wanted to crank your neck back and look around, picking out the different saints and scenes from the Bible.

But Robbie's gaze was fixed right in front of him. On one man.

Lord Robert Clifford looked much the same as the last time they'd met face-to-face. His blond hair had darkened, there were a few more scars on his face, and he was a few pounds heavier with muscle, but the patrician features, cold eyes, and shimmering chain mail and spotless tabard with the red stripe and blue-and-yellow checks of the Clifford arms were all the same.

One thing was different. This time Robbie noticed the resemblance to his sister.

When their eyes met, Robbie felt as if someone had landed a fist in his gut. Christ, they were the same color. He might have been looking into Rosalin's eyes.

Shite. He had to look away. Mouth clenched tight, he came to a stop a few feet away.

The two men faced off in silence. This moment had been a long time in coming. Much had changed, and they had six years of fighting between them, but they were both keenly aware of what had happened the last time they'd met. Robbie could still hear the condemning words. *"Take him to the pit."*

He'd been so damned surprised. Maybe that was what had angered him the most. He'd actually let himself believe Clifford. He could have killed Clifford's men while defending his friend, but he hadn't. He'd expected justice—or at least the pretense of it.

Blood rushed through him at the memories, and the heat of anger flared through his veins. Anger, but not the hatred that usually roared through him at the mention of Clifford. Hatred that had become as much a companion to Robbie as the armor he wore.

By all that was holy, he should want to smash his fist through that perfectly straight set of teeth and wrap his hands around the bastard's throat until the breath strangled from his lungs. Clifford's treachery had led to the death of many of Robbie's comrades, including Thomas, and he'd been only hours away from taking the rest of them. Clifford had been a thorn in Robbie's side, a symbol of his hatred of the English, for a long time.

But he felt no such urge. What the hell was wrong with him?

Still, they did not shake hands, and the tension in the air was palpable.

Boyd realized he was being subject to just as much scrutiny, but the cold eyes—the cold *green* eyes, damn it—gave no hint to Clifford's thoughts. It was one thing he didn't share with his sister, although in this case, Robbie wished he did. Rosalin's expressive eyes gave her thoughts away—

Damn it, he had to stop thinking about her. But it seemed all he could do. ". . . *care about you*." Christ, why the hell had she said that? He didn't want her to care about him, and hearing the words had forced him to acknowledge something he wanted to ignore.

He'd reacted badly and regretted his harsh words. But she'd caught him off guard. What the hell was he supposed to do? She knew the circumstances as well as he did. There were few things less insurmountable than the sister of an English baron—an English *overlord*, no less—and a Scot "rebel," fighting for Bruce. Hell, climbing the highest peak of the mighty Cuillins in the winter with his hands tied behind his back might be easier.

The best thing for them both would be getting this over as quickly as possible.

To that end, he broke the standoff. "Clifford," he said with a sharp nod. "As you insisted on this meeting, I assume you have something to say."

Clifford's icy demeanor cracked. "Damn right I have something to say. As if burning people out of their homes and stealing their goods aren't enough, you abduct my son and my sister? What the hell kind of barbarian are you?"

Robbie felt a flicker of the familiar rage. "The kind that holds your sister, so if I were you I'd give caution to my words. Need I remind you of the cages where the Countess of Buchan and a fourteen-year-old girl spent a couple of years of their lives thanks to your king? If you want to talk barbarians, perhaps you should look closer to home." The knight's flush told him his barb had been well aimed. "Your sister and son were my *hostages*—and have been treated with every consideration. Too much consideration, it seems, as it enabled your son to escape. As for the raids, you have only yourself to blame. My envoy came to you with terms, which you refused."

"I hardly call two thousand pounds terms. I call it bloody robbery."

"Call it whatever the hell you want, but it's the cost of peace—and of getting your sister back. Two thousand pounds is a pittance compared to the wealth the English have plundered, looted, and pillaged from *my* country."

Clifford's mouth fell in a hard line. Robbie could see the anger he was forcing himself to contain, see the frustration, and finally see the acknowledgment that Robbie had been waiting to see for a long time. He had no choice but to submit.

"You will have your truce," Clifford said, every word pulled through clenched teeth.

Although the result had been a foregone conclusion, hearing the words felt good. At least it should, but for some reason Robbie didn't feel the satisfaction or the sense of victory he wanted. Because beneath Clifford's anger, beneath his frustration, beneath his acknowledgment, Robbie also saw something else: his helplessness. Helplessness born of the love he had for his sister and the fear he couldn't quite hide. It made Robbie uncomfortable. Uneasy. *Unsatisfied.*

He also knew what it meant, and that thought—the knowledge that he had to give her back—made him feel something that he feared was dangerously close to what Clifford was feeling.

The gaze that met his wasn't cool at all, but pained. "Rosalin is safe? She has not been harmed?"

Robbie should torture the bastard and let him think the worst. God knew, he deserved it. But he found himself telling him the truth. "She will be returned to you exactly as I found her—without even a bruise. I give you my word."

"Roger said as much, but damn it, she's a gently reared lady, unused to such harsh conditions." Robbie didn't like thinking about it any more than Clifford did. "When?"

"As soon as—"

But Robbie's words were cut off when another man—a knight, by the look of him—pushed his way forward. "Your word? What kind of assurance is that?" He looked down his nose at Robbie with an expression so dripping with condescension and disdain, it could have filled a slop bucket. "Why should we believe the word of a man who is no better than a brigand? How do we know he hasn't had his vile hands all over her?"

Clifford looked more annoyed by the man's interruption than Robbie. "I told you I will handle this."

The knight persisted. "I must have assurances—"

"Sir Henry," Clifford said. "Shut up."

Robbie stared at the man Clifford had identified as Sir Henry with cold calculation. Though the knight's words and attitude had angered him, Robbie had heard them too many times before to let it show. But there was something about this man that set his teeth on edge. He was nearly Robbie's height and only slightly slimmer in build, though he was at least a handful of years younger. He reminded him of someone. But with his dark hair and light eyes, it could be half the members of the Highland Guard— including himself. The thought should have amused him, but for some reason it only made him frown.

"Have we met?" Robbie drawled with an indifference that he knew would grate.

It did. The knight flushed angrily. "If we had, you would not be standing here, but rotting in a grave somewhere."

Robbie quirked a brow. "Bold words. Care to prove them?"

Sir Henry stepped toward him. "Aye, any time. Just as soon as you return my betrothed."

It took a moment for the words to sink in, and when they did, no amount of training could have hid Robbie's shock. He probably wore the look of a man who'd been shot in the back with an arrow. He might as well have been.

It gave the other man the advantage—the momentary advantage. He sneered knowingly. "I'm not surprised she did not tell you. Probably thought you'd try to exact your payments from me as well. We are to be married at the end of the month, and I will have assurances that you have not touched her."

Robbie wasn't containing his anger any longer. It was snapping through him dangerously, ready to explode. She'd lied to him—or as good as lied to him. *Betrothed*, damn it? While she'd been lying in his arms, letting him put his hands on her—putting her hands on him—she was going to marry another man. *Care about you.* God, he felt like a fool.

He was tempted to tell Sir Henry exactly what they'd done—and exactly where his hands had been.

"What if I've had my hands all over her?" Robbie couldn't resist taunting. "What will you do then?"

The other man's eyes flared with rage. "You bastard, I'll kill you."

He would have launched himself at Robbie, but Clifford wisely held him back. "These men are here under truce, de Spenser. You will not break it."

"What's the difference this time, Clifford?" Robbie said. "Age give you a sense of honor?"

The slight flush on the other man's face was the only sign that the barb about what had happened at Kildrummy had found its mark. "I have agreed to your terms. Your word that Rosalin is unharmed will satisfy. Robert Bruce will have his truce and his two thousand pounds."

"And as soon as he gets it, you will have your sister."

Clifford's face went white. "But that could take weeks. I will need time to get that coin together. You said as soon as I agreed—"

"That was before you insisted on this little meeting,"

Robbie said. "Now I think I will need more surety to ensure that you keep the terms of our bargain."

Clifford surged toward him, but held himself back by the thinnest of restraints. "I know why you are doing this, and if you hurt her, by God I'll kill you!"

"You tried to do that once before. What makes you think you will be any more successful this time?"

Clifford's face turned so red, Robbie thought he was going to explode. But the knight had more control than Robbie probably would have had under the circumstances and bit back whatever it was he wanted to say. "Go. You will have your truce and your money as soon as they can be arranged. You have given me your word my sister will not be harmed. I will hold you to it."

"That isn't good enough," Sir Henry de Spenser sputtered. "I demand assurances that he has not forced himself on her."

Clifford turned to the younger knight. "One more word and you won't need assurances for anything."

Whatever de Spenser saw in Clifford's eyes caused him to sober—and curb his tongue.

Clifford turned to Robbie. "You will give your word?"

"I will."

He would not force himself on Rosalin. That he could promise. But with the tumult of emotions raging inside him right now, that was about all he could.

Rosalin sat on a rock, savoring the simple pleasure of the warm sunshine on her hair and face. Birds chirped in the distances and the fresh scents of the garden floated past her nose with the gentle breeze. A faint—a *very* faint—hint of spring was in the air. For the first time since she'd come north, it was warm enough to be outside without two layers of wool, and she wore only her slightly less stained light-blue under-gown over her chemise.

She bent over to one of the plants at her feet—a

hearty-looking kale—and cleared a few leaves from the meticulously tilled earth around it. In addition to cole-worts, there were onions, parsnips, turnips, carrots, and a smattering of hearty herbs that had managed to withstand the cold winter.

The vegetable garden had been a surprise. She'd stumbled across it the day after Robbie left on her way to return the pile of clothing to Deirdre. It was a small patch of ground, no more than fifteen feet by ten, tucked away behind the last tent on the outskirts of camp. A surprisingly sophisticated wattle fence had been erected to prevent the hares, wild cats, boars, wolves, and other animals who inhabited the forest from disturbing it. Well tended, ordered, and peaceful, this place seemed a small oasis in the wild, unfriendly countryside around her. She loved just sitting here, surrounding herself with . . . *him.*

She knew right away to whom the place belonged. Robbie Boyd hadn't forgotten as much of his past as he wanted to believe, and to Rosalin, this small garden carved out in the trenches seemed proof that there was still a battle to be won inside him.

A farmer? Who would have thought that the strongest man in Scotland and one of the most feared and violent warriors in Christendom was not only a scholar but also a would-be farmer. Maybe she shouldn't have been surprised. The physical, outdoor, get-your-hands-dirty work fit him.

Though he was a laird with a barony in Noddsdale and other lands in Renfrew and Ayr, managing lands and tenants wasn't how she saw him. If the war hadn't come, he would have done his duty as laird, of course, but she pictured him in less lordly pursuits, roaming the countryside on foot, shirtsleeves rolled up around those tanned, muscular forearms, lending a hand to his tenants, whether it be with a plow or a hammer. Perhaps with a son or two alongside him, he would bound up the hill to the fortified farmhouse after a long day's work to greet his wife and the rest of his children with a smile and a hard kiss.

What if she were that wife?

The image caught her with a hard pang of longing. To someone who'd never had a home of her own and who'd marked the passage of time by the few opportunities she'd had to see her brother, the simple pleasure of such a life seemed a faerie tale.

It *was* a faerie tale. The war had come, and there was no going back. There were no "what ifs." There was only the future. Yet this garden—like his kindness to Mary that day in the Hall—gave hope that some of it might come true.

She wanted to love him. She feared she already did. The question was whether he could ever love her back.

"I thought I might find you here."

The voice caught her unaware, and she jumped. Recognition followed, and she turned with a laugh to see Sir Alex standing at the gate. "I'm afraid you caught me dreaming."

He smiled. "I just wanted to make sure you didn't miss the midday meal by falling asleep out here again." His smile fell, his mouth twisting slightly. "With the temper Boyd's been in lately, I fear if you lose an ounce, he'll probably accuse me of dereliction of duty and letting you starve."

Rosalin rose from her rocky perch and crossed the garden to the now open gate. She wanted to make light of what he'd said, but there was a bitterness to Sir Alex's tone that she could not ignore.

She put her hand on his arm and looked up into his eyes. He had been so kind to her, and she genuinely liked the handsome young knight turned rebel. In many ways, it would have been so much easier if he had been the one to catch her eye. They were much alike. "Is it really so bad between you?"

The question seemed to take him aback. He appeared to contemplate it for a minute, and then shrugged. "Not all the time. On a mission or in the heat of battle it doesn't seem to matter as much. But once the battle is done our differences aren't as easy to hide. He doesn't respect me—as a warrior, as a compatriot, as a friend—and never will."

He took her hand, gallantly tucking it in the bend of his elbow as if they were at court, and started to lead her back toward the Hall.

"That's not the way I see it," she said with a sidelong glance. "He trusts you—more than he realizes. I watched you two fight together at Kildrummy, and even then I saw it. Now it's even more so. In truth you seem more like brothers. Is there not a way you could try to put your differences aside?"

Sir Alex appeared to give serious consideration to her words. Eventually, he shook his head. "It's too late for that. It used to bother me, but now I realize that no matter what I do it will never change. He's too far gone. The only thing he cares about is making the English pay for what they've done and to him. I'm standing in the way of that."

"Because you were born in England?"

"It's more than that. It's because of what I stand for. I remind him of things he wants to forget." A wry smile turned his mouth. "I'm a conscience at a time that it's not convenient to have one."

"What do you mean?"

"I won't turn a blind eye to the raiding, the pillaging, and the war of terror being waged along the border by both sides. I guess what it comes down to is that we have a different line in the sand. He's willing to do whatever it takes, and I'm not. Boyd will never respect someone who isn't willing to give everything to the fight for independence. He thinks I'm naive and sees my 'knightly' ways as a relic of the past at best and as hypocrisy at worst. Perhaps it is to some, but it isn't that way to me. I need to be able to look myself in the looking glass when this is all over. This used to be about what was right, but Boyd has lost sight of that. Now it's just as much about punishing the enemy and exacting retribution for everything that they've taken from him."

"I don't believe that. I know he is driven—"

"Driven?" Sir Alex made a sharp sound of laughter. "That's one way of putting it. It's the only thing that matters to him. The *only* thing."

If he was emphasizing it for her benefit, Rosalin didn't want to hear it. "That's not true. I think many things matter to him. You do, the people here, and I'd wager the other phantoms." *Me*, if he would admit it to himself.

Sir Alex's face went utterly still. He stopped and took her elbow. "What did you say?"

She bit her lip, looking up at him uncertainly. "Robbie is part of Bruce's phantoms."

His voice was very low and deliberate. "Did he tell you that?"

She shook her head and shrugged. It made perfect sense. If she were selecting men to form a band of extraordinary warriors, she would certainly include the man reputed to be the strongest. "It wasn't very difficult to figure out after the night in the forest when he appeared out of the darkness with that ghastly helm and blackened face to save me from the Douglas soldier. I suspect you are one, too." She looked at him for confirmation, but the stony countenance revealed nothing. "Is the Black Douglas as well?"

Sir Alex stared at her intently. "Have you told anyone else of your suspicions?"

"Of course not!"

"Then promise me you will not voice them again to anyone—even Boyd. *Especially* Boyd."

His fingers had tightened and his face had grown so dark she almost didn't recognize him. She nodded, a little fearfully. "Why?"

"Because it's dangerous."

Rosalin's eyes widened at that. They continued walking. She was more disturbed by Sir Alex's comments than she wanted to let on. Not about the phantoms, but about Robbie's determination to win at all costs. Sir Alex was right—it was hard to reconcile the Devil's Enforcer with the noble warrior she remembered.

But maybe they weren't so far apart after all. Though she loved her brother and understood he was doing his duty, she'd come to sympathize with Robbie's cause—if not his methods. In the quest to win at all costs, he'd lost sight of what he was fighting for. But recently she thought she might have helped him remember.

He might not be the knight in shining armor riding in on a white steed that she'd created in her mind, but she refused to believe he was the empty black shell of vengeance that Sir Alex suggested, either.

Just as they were about to enter the Hall she turned to him. "You are wrong, Sir Alex. I think he is still greatly affected by right and wrong. I think that's why he fights so hard. He might act ruthlessly and harshly when he has to, but he won't do anything truly dishonorable."

Alex held her gaze steadily. Her impassioned defense perhaps had revealed more than she wanted it to. "Don't give yourself false hopes, my lady."

"What do you mean?"

"I've known Robbie Boyd a long time, and he will let nothing get in the way of winning this war. *Nothing.* When the time comes, he'll send you back. He needs Clifford's cooperation, and this is the only way he'll get it. Do you think your brother would agree to a truce and to the payment of two thousand pounds if Boyd didn't have you to hold over his head?"

He wouldn't, although she hadn't wanted to think about it. Her brother was just as stubborn and single-minded as Robbie. If it weren't for her, he would never agree.

If she'd been harboring a secret hope that when the time came Robbie would not be able to send her back, that he would stop seeing her as a weapon to use against Cliff, that he'd want to hold on to her just as strongly as she wanted to hold on to him, she knew she'd been deluding herself.

He would send her back, and then what? Would he forget all about her? Fight for her? Or worse, do nothing?

Rosalin didn't have long to ponder the question, for no sooner had they sat down to eat than the door slammed open, and Robbie and the men who'd gone to meet her brother stormed into the Hall.

She had to clutch the edge of the wooden trestle table to prevent herself from jumping up from her seat. But the moment of relief she felt upon seeing him safely returned died when their eyes met. His burned with an unholy rage that turned the blood racing in her veins to ice.

Unconsciously, she leaned toward Sir Alex, who was seated beside her. If anything, the movement only served to make Robbie's eyes burn even darker. He crossed the distance of the room in a few strides.

"You're back," she said softly.

Her heart clenched as his eyes bit into hers. Something was wrong. Very wrong. "Come with me," he demanded.

She'd never seen white lines around his mouth like that. Her pulse raced wildly. "I haven't finished my meal."

"What's this about, Boyd?" Sir Alex said, getting up protectively at her side.

It was the wrong thing to do. Robbie looked like he might level his friend with his fist rather than just his gaze. Instead, he reached over the table and plucked Rosalin from her seat. She was so startled, all she could do was gape as he carried her out of the suddenly silent Hall.

Eighteen

✣

She'd turned him into the bloody barbarian some accused him of being, but Robbie didn't give a shite. He'd controlled his rage for the long journey back to the forest, but the moment he'd seen her there sitting with Seton—looking so damned beautiful it made his chest squeeze—the tethers had broken free.

His jaw clenched and blood roared through his veins as he stormed out of the Hall through the forest to his tent. He was careful not to look down at her. Her soft scent was torture enough. As was the way she wrapped her hands around his neck and seemed to burrow against his chest, tucking her cheek against his shoulder.

She didn't say anything. Just went with him calmly. Bloody hell, didn't she see how furious he was with her? Couldn't she tell that he was at the end of his damned rope? Shouldn't she be shaking with terror and begging to know what was wrong?

Obviously she trusted him too much. The foolish chit thought he wouldn't hurt her.

Damn her for knowing me so well.

Cradling her against him, he ducked through the tent flaps and stood at the entry, letting his eyes adjust from the sunlight.

"Are you going to put me down and tell me what this is all about?" she asked gently.

He looked down for the first time, seeing that beautiful

face staring up at him. The pang in his chest nearly cut off his breath. She looked so innocent—so guileless—but she'd been lying to him from the start.

Jaw locked, he put her down and set her firmly away from him. "What this is about? How about the fact that you lied to me?"

Her brow furrowed with confusion. "I have never lied to you. Does this have something to do with my brother? Did he refuse your truce?"

"Nay. Clifford agreed to everything."

Her face fell. What was wrong with her? Why the hell did she look disappointed?

She turned away from him. "Then why are you angry? You have everything you wanted. You can send me back and get on with your war."

That was exactly what he should do, damn it. But for the first time in a long while, he was thinking about something other than war. When he'd made his demand of Clifford to hold on to her until he received the money, he'd been thinking of one thing and one thing only. "Your brother agreed readily enough, but your betrothed," he said as he took a step toward her, "your *betrothed* had need of some assurances."

He had the satisfaction of seeing every drop of blood slide from her face. Guilt froze the no-longer guileless features. "S-sir Henry was th-there?"

He didn't know whether it was wanting to make the trembling stop or anger that made him grab her elbow and bring her up hard against him. "Aye, he was," he said in a voice not far from menacing. "And he didn't seem all that happy to learn that his affianced might have been spending time in my bed." Her eyes widened, but she didn't say anything. No protest. No "how could you tell him such a thing?" Nothing. "Why did you lie to me, Rosalin? Why didn't you tell me you were to be married?"

Something cracked in his voice. Something that went beyond anger. Some kind of emotion he didn't want to acknowledge.

Whatever it was, she heard it. Her eyes softened, and her voice was soothing. The type of soothing voice his mother had used when he'd taken a tumble as a young boy. "I didn't lie to you. Nor did I mean to hide it from you." A pink blush stained her cheeks. "I simply did not think of it—or of Sir Henry."

Robbie was no fool. He might not be an expert on such matters, but he'd wager Sir Henry would give MacGregor some competition—and not with the bow. "Sir Henry might be a hotheaded arse, but he is not the kind of man a lass is likely to forget."

She tilted her head, studying him. "He's quite handsome, yes, but in truth he is but a pale substitute for another."

The spark of rage at the mention of "handsome" died as the truth hit him. *Christ.* No wonder the knight bothered him so much. He reminded him of someone, all right—himself. A younger, prettier version of himself, that is.

She stepped toward him. "Did you not see it?"

He didn't say anything, but simply watched her as a deer watched the hunter's bow. She was moving closer, wielding a weapon far more dangerous than an arrow: desire. He wanted her with every fiber of his being, and her closeness—her softness—was prodding every primitive instinct in his body.

"I'm ashamed to admit it," she said, putting her palm flat on his chest and tipping her head back to look at him. It burned—the place under her hand, his chest, everything. "But I didn't think of him at all."

She was slipping in under his defenses, digging under his skin. Somehow he needed to find the strength to push her away. "Bloody hell, Rosalin, he is the man you are going to marry!"

A tiny furrow appeared between her delicately arched

brows, and then shook her head. "I can no longer marry Sir Henry."

Bitterness flooded him. "I told him nothing, Rosalin. Your knight will have no cause to break the betrothal. I made you come, but I did not take your maidenhead."

She appeared not to notice his intentionally crude language. "It's not because I think he will break the betrothal. I will not marry Sir Henry because I am in love with someone else."

Robbie saw red. "Who?" he demanded, taking her by the arm to haul her up against him once more. "Damn it, who?"

But he didn't need to ask. All he needed to do was look in her eyes and the answer stared right back at him. *Me. She means me.*

Longing rose inside him with a fierceness of which he wouldn't have believed himself capable. He wanted to believe it, wanted to take what she offered, sweep her up in his arms and make love to her, whispering promises he could not keep.

But it was impossible, damn it! Why couldn't she see that? Why did she have to make this so damned hard? She was wrong about what she felt, making a young girl's mistake of confusing lust with emotion.

He backed her against the thick support beam with a slam that shook the tent, pinning her with his body. He wedged her legs between his, letting her feel the proof of his words. "This isn't about love, Rosalin. It's about lust." He circled his hips, grinding himself against her crudely but bloody effectively. A bolt of lust surged to the heavy, throbbing tip.

She gasped, but not with shock—with something else that made every inch of his already hot and pulsing skin tighten and flame even hotter.

God, she wanted it. Wanted *him.*

Wrapping her arms around his neck, she stretched against

him—into him—and lifted her mouth to his, even as he bent to take her lips in a ravenous kiss.

He groaned at the contact. Felt his body roar with pleasure as she opened her mouth to him. He sank in his tongue with no pretense, no caution, stroking her hard into his mouth, and pressing his body into hers as he let her feel the force of his desire pounding between them.

And she was kissing him back. Kissing him back in a way that made his head buzz and his blood pound. Kissing him back in a way that made him want to slow—linger—over every sweet caress. Take his time and show her . . .

Love, he heard her voice taunting him.

Damn it, no! He tore away with a growl. Lifting one of her legs to wrap it around his hip, he nudged himself into position. "Can you feel what I want to do to you, Rosalin?" He moved again, circling his hips hard and trying not to think about how good it felt. How the heavy tip of his erection was poised at her cleft. How the pressure was coiling at the base of his spine. How only a few layers of fabric separated him from making her his.

Not mine, damn it.

He stared into her eyes. "I want to fuck you so badly I can't see straight, but that's all I want. What we have is lust—do not confuse it with anything else."

Rosalin knew what he was doing, but it didn't lessen the sting. His crude words in the face of her declaration of love hurt—hurt a lot.

She almost believed him.

"Is that right?" She looked into his eyes and saw the heat—not just of lust but of something else. A slow-burning emotion that he would not name, but which she knew was there. She could feel it in every stroke of his body, in every sweep of his tongue, in every achingly tender touch and caress. He cared for her. "Then show me." She tightened the leg wrapped around his waist and brought them closer, returning the intimate circling. "Show me that's all you want. That this is only about . . . what did you call it, fu—?"

He cut her off with a hard squeeze, his voice low and dangerous. "Don't say it."

She quirked a brow. "Why? Are you trying to convince me, or yourself?" Very slowly she enunciated the forbidden word.

His face darkened thunderously as he pressed into her harder. The fullness, the weight of him, made her stomach do a funny little flip and her pulse quicken. She remembered how he felt in her hand and wanted to feel him . . . inside her. Not just to prove a point. She wanted the connection. The closeness. The intimacy of joining her body with his.

"Damn you, you don't know what you are saying."

"I know exactly what I'm saying. If all you want is my body, take it. I'm giving myself to you. Without conditions attached. Walk away when it's all over."

His eyes narrowed as if this were some kind of trick, but she could see the flames of desire snapping wildly. "You don't know what the bloody hell you are talking about. Your brother would kill me."

"I know exactly what I'm talking about. I feel this . . . *lust*, too. My brother has nothing to do with it. Besides, since when did the Devil's Enforcer start worrying about an Englishman's ire?"

Tension snapped between them like wildfire. She could feel the fierce pounding of his heart and the taut flex of barely restrained muscle as her hands skimmed the hard bulges of his chest and arms. She would never tire of touching him. Of feeling the hard, unyielding strength sizzling under her palms. For even beneath the leather and linen, the heat radiated.

"Show me, Robbie." He was holding himself so still, Rosalin knew she had him at the breaking point. "Or perhaps it wouldn't be so easy to walk away after all? You know what I think? I think you care about me. Your gentle touch doesn't lie."

Rosalin should have known that Robbie Boyd was not a man to back down from a challenge. He would fight to the bitter end. With his hands. And sweet heaven, what hands!

"Gentle?" he laughed mirthlessly. "What I feel for you is far from gentle. It's rough and primitive and wicked—very, very wicked."

Rosalin gasped as he reached for the edge of her skirt and lifted it. A moment later his hand was between her legs, cupping her possessively. Heat flooded her as one finger slipped inside. She cried out at the unexpected flood of pleasure, as warmth and dampness pooled to his touch.

Then he did something that did shock her. Something very wicked indeed. He spun her around, clasping her hands over her head to rest on the wooden pole. Flipping up her skirts, he wedged himself between her legs from behind and slid his right hand around to dip his fingers between her legs again.

A thought flashed in her head. Was it possible . . .

A hot blush flooded her cheeks. His hips were moving against hers in a way that left no doubt as to what was possible.

The pressure—the friction—was incredible. She strained against his hand, against the thick bulge sliding against her, and against the fierce sensation building inside her.

He leaned down, his tight, husky voice breathing close to her ear, as he continued his deft strokes. "What if I came into you like this from behind, my fair Rosalin. Would you like that?"

If the unevenness of her breathing and the frantic pulsing between her legs were any indication, she feared she would. Quite a lot.

He groaned as her pleasure communicated itself to him in a very warm and silky way.

"Is this gentle?" he said. She felt another blunt finger slip inside her, stretching her. Then another. "How about this?"

Releasing his hold on her hands pinned above her, his left hand started to explore her body. The feel of one of his big hands cupping her breast, squeezing her, pinching her nipple between his fingers, even as others plunged in and out of her body was too much.

She moaned, arching against him, pressing her hips back to meet his feigned thrusts. "Aye," she whispered between bated breaths. Surprisingly it was. No matter how hard and rough he wanted to make it, there was an inherent tenderness to his touch that he could not hide.

He swore angrily, as if he, too, knew the truth. His movements slowed, his strokes becoming softer and more drawn out, as he, too, succumbed to the pleasure of the intimate touch. "God, you feel so good," he groaned, rubbing some of her dampness with soft little circling motions of his thumb. "So warm and wet for me. But I'm going to make you even hotter—and wetter."

Any embarrassment she might have felt was lost in the cacophony of other emotions swirling inside her. Her breath—her whimpering moans—quickened at a frantic pace in keeping with the plunging of his fingers. She felt her body lift in expectation as passion took hold. As her desire and love for this man entwined in the perfect whirlpool of sensation.

His hand took her higher and higher. A fever spread over her skin. "Oh God, Robbie," she begged helplessly.

He held her there. Right at that perfect place, until she couldn't take it anymore and broke apart. "That's it, *mo ghrá*. Let me feel your pleasure."

The spasms rocked her, pulsing through her body in sharp wave after wave. His hand was still holding her when the last ebbs had flowed from her body.

She glanced over her shoulder and lifted her hazy gaze to

his. His blue eyes were hot and penetrating, his face a hard mask. "What does *mo ghrá* mean?"

He was holding her so closely, she swore she could feel his heart stop. For a moment she thought he actually looked ill, but then his features once more schooled into hard impassivity. "It means 'my beautiful one.' "

To her surprise, he let her go. To her even greater surprise, she didn't fall to the ground in a boneless pool. "What about . . . Are you not . . . ?" Her cheeks flushed hot.

His face was drawn so tight, he almost looked to be in pain. "What you want is impossible, Rosalin. I'll not take your virginity to prove it. You wanted pleasure; I gave it to you. Do not make anything more of it."

Rosalin stared at him, stunned and more hurt than she would have thought possible. For a moment she felt a flicker of doubt. Was lust truly all this was to him? Was she imagining things that weren't there? Or was he just being stubborn and intentionally cruel to push her away?

Perhaps she should let him. Heaven knew it would be easier. She did not delude herself. A future for them seemed unlikely, even if they both wanted it. But she wouldn't let him go without a fight. Not this time.

"I see," she said softly. "Thank you for clarifying it for me. Now I shall know the difference."

His hands clenched. "What difference?"

"To compare. When I return home."

The pulse below his cheek jumped. He was furious, but determined not to show it.

She smiled, as if she hadn't noticed. "When am I to leave?"

"As soon as your brother delivers the silver. A week, maybe two."

She feigned concern, a small frown gathering between her brow. "And should I feel this desire again before I go, what then?"

"What the hell do you mean, 'what then'?"

Rosalin knew she really shouldn't take such pleasure in angering him, but then again, he'd hurt her. "Should I seek you out or someone else?"

He stiffened. His dark gaze rested on her for a long, angry pause before flickering to the bed. Rosalin suspected she was one nudge away from being tossed on that bed and very thoroughly ravished.

A proper, gently born lady really shouldn't be feeling such a wicked thrill at the prospect.

But when his gaze landed on hers again, it was narrowed with understanding. "It won't work, Rosalin. You will not goad me into changing my mind."

He turned and ducked out of the tent before she could reply.

We'll see about that, Rosalin thought smugly. She intended to goad him into quite a lot. It seemed she, too, could be quite merciless when fighting for the right cause.

Robbie walked away while he still could. Before he did something rash like toss her down on that bed and give her exactly what she'd asked for. The lass trusted in his honor more than she should. He wasn't one of her damned knights.

Someone else. Bloody hell! The goading words still set primitive fires roaring through his blood.

He pushed a branch out of the way, snapping it, as he made his way through the forest to what was fast becoming his new favorite haunt: the ice-cold burn that ran behind the camp. He needed to cool off. One part of him in particular.

He was furious—not with her, but with himself. In his effort to prove that she meant nothing—that all he felt was lust—he'd only served to prove her point.

He couldn't do it, damn it. He couldn't even pretend. He'd tried to be crude and rough, but the moment he touched her something came over him. A powerful feeling that drugged his senses and dragged him into some kind of sensual haze, where all he could think about was bringing her pleasure.

Her responses hadn't helped any. Damn it, she was an innocent, proper English *lady*. She was supposed to be shocked by his playacting from behind. Shocked as in horrified, not shocked as in awakened with far-from-maidenly curiosity.

She wasn't supposed to dissolve against him, arching into his hand, pressing her sweet little bottom against his sorely abused cock and making soft, breathy whimpers of pleasure to egg him on. She wasn't supposed to be so damned *hot*. He'd been one wiggle of those shapely buttocks away from unmanning himself and coming along with her.

Young, innocent, and English did not apparently mean meek and easy to maneuver. Nor did they seem to preclude enjoyment in the baser pleasures. Someone should have warned him.

The whole thing had left him in the unusual position of feeling distinctly overmatched. As if he'd shown up to battle with a pike to find out he was facing a siege engine.

He'd expected her to take his word for it—not to press. He sure as hell hadn't expected a perfectly executed counterattack that would have made Striker proud. The lass had developed an uncanny ability to identify and take advantage of his weaknesses. All of which seemed to be related to her.

Wasn't *she* supposed to be the one who was inexperienced? Yet he seemed to be the one left flailing in the dark, ill equipped to navigate the intricacies of a lady's mind. Truth be told, he'd never gotten that far before. He'd had many relations with women, but never a relationship.

He stopped suddenly, as if he'd run into a wall. Was that what this was? How the hell had that happened?

He didn't know, but it had. She'd insinuated herself into his tent, his thoughts, his life, and somehow along the way, she'd begun to matter.

Nay, he realized. She'd always mattered. He'd been doomed from the moment she'd opened the door to the pit prison. Not that it would change a damned thing.

As he was only a few feet away from the burn, he quickly divested himself of his armor and clothing and dove in.

He tried not to shriek like a five-year-old lass as the cold water closed in around him, driving icy needles into his skin. Robbie might be from the west coast of Scotland, but he didn't seem to possess the inhuman ability to acclimate to the cold water that his brethren from the Isles did. MacSorley, MacRuairi, and MacLeod could swim in this shite for hours. Robbie did what was necessary and then got the hell out.

Having effectively chilled the unspent lust from his body, he washed quickly and climbed up the rocky banks.

With the roaring in his ears quieted, he could finally hear the other voice—the far quieter one—whispering in his ear. The one that told him he'd acted badly. That she hadn't deserved to be treated like a whore. Nor had she deserved the harsh words uttered in an attempt to push her away.

She'd told him that she loved him, for Christ's sake. He might not have wanted to hear it, but he should have shown some consideration for her feelings. Lasses were fragile, emotional creatures. Not cold, unfeeling bastards like him.

He owed her an apology.

He'd just finished strapping the baldric he wore across his shoulder for his sword when he heard a sound. He tensed, instantly primed for battle. But then, recognizing the footsteps, he moved his hand from the hilt of his sword.

"You're supposed to whistle," Robbie said with annoyance as his partner came into view. "I could have taken your damned head off."

Seton shrugged. "You knew it was me. Besides, I wanted to make sure you were alone." He gave him a pointed look. "What in the hell was that show in the Hall all about? Fraser said Clifford agreed to the truce."

"He did."

"Then why were you so angry with Lady Rosalin?" Robbie didn't say anything. "Does it have to do with Sir Henry de Spenser by any chance?"

Robbie shot him a warning glare. "Leave it, Dragon."

But the young knight had never heeded caution. That was part of the problem. "Not this time. I won't let you hurt that poor girl. What you are doing to her isn't right. She's young and fancies herself in love with you, and you are confusing her with your . . . whatever the hell you want to call it. When you send her away you are going to break her heart. So leave her be."

Robbie wanted to be angry. He wanted to tell Seton to bugger off, but he couldn't. His partner wasn't saying anything he didn't already know. His chest was squeezing so tightly his lungs were burning. He could barely get the words out. "What if I care about her?"

Seton held his stare, and for once it felt like their positions were reversed. It wasn't without sympathy that his partner gave him the cold, unflinching truth. "If you care about her, you'll leave her be. Unless you are prepared to throw away your chance for a truce and the king's two thousand pounds?"

Robbie's mouth clenched in answer. Never.

"Even if you were, are you prepared for what would come after? If you think Clifford wants your head now, how do you think it will be if you try to take his beloved sister? He'll never let you have her. Christ, Raider, you should know better than I that what you want is impossible."

He did, which was why he'd never let himself consider it. Even if he could put aside the fact that she was English and Clifford's sister—which he wasn't sure was possible—a connection with him would be too dangerous. Anyone close to him was a target. Hell, look what had happened to his sister. He wouldn't put her in that kind of danger.

"If it means anything, I'm sorry," Seton said.

Surprisingly, it did. Robbie nodded in acknowledgment.

"Are you sure it is wise to keep her here until Clifford arranges the payment?"

Wise? Nay, but he couldn't let her go. Not yet. "I don't trust Clifford. What's to prevent him from reneging on our deal as soon as we return her?" Robbie stopped his partner before he could speak. "And don't say 'honor'—we both know how far that goes with Clifford."

Seton didn't argue. He'd done all his arguing years before, and it had resulted in their being taken.

They started to walk back, and had just reached the farthest tent when they saw Malcolm running toward them. Immediately Robbie's gaze went to his tent, but it appeared undisturbed.

"What is it, lad?" he asked.

"The Douglas said to come quickly. There's something wrong with one of the horses."

Not understanding the urgency, Robbie and Seton nonetheless made haste to the old bothy on the opposite side of camp that served as a barn for their few horses and livestock.

No sooner had they entered the old stone-and-turf building than Douglas turned to him. He was kneeling on the ground near Fraser's horse, who appeared to be in distress. "Did you feed the horses oats when you were in Melrose?"

Robbie frowned. "Of course not," he said. They barely had enough grain to feed their people, let alone the horses. Their mounts subsided on dried grasses for the most part.

"Well, someone did," Douglas said, pointing to a pile of dung.

Robbie took a step closer and saw that he was right.

Mixed into the normal manure he could see the telltale sprinkling of the light tan-colored groat about the size and shape of a maggot. There weren't many—only a few—but enough to . . .

Ah hell. Enough to *track*.

Some horses—often older one's like Fraser's—had trouble digesting whole oats. In this case, they were fortunate or they might not have discovered the ruse.

He swore and met Douglas's gaze. "Ready the men."

"Where are you going?" Douglas yelled after him.

Robbie didn't take the time to respond. A minute later, when he was standing in his empty tent, his heart, which had been somewhere near his throat, dropped soundly to the floor.

Rosalin was gone.

Nineteen

❦

Rosalin barely stifled the scream that rose to her throat when the armed knight appeared in front of her.

Not long after Robbie left, she'd gone to the garden to think. There had to be some way to make this work, assuming that she could get Robbie to admit there was a "this." Also assuming that he could accept her being English. And being the sister of his greatest enemy. And her being English. She knew she'd already said that, but it probably bore mentioning twice.

And then there was her brother and the king. Edward was fond of her, but he wouldn't sanction a match between the butter girl and Robbie Boyd, let alone the sister of one of his leading barons. There was no hope for it. Robbie would just have to forcibly marry her. That would be the story at least.

But could she convince Cliff? Aye, it wouldn't be easy, but she knew he loved her more than he hated Boyd.

She would just have to make sure Robbie didn't give him cause otherwise. The raiding and personal war between them would have to stop. She would not make friends of enemies, but surely they could come to some sort of agreement with her serving as surety?

When the war ended something more might be possible, but right now a fragile peace was all she could hope for. Perhaps more than she could hope for.

It was in the midst of this planning—or probably more

accurately, fantasizing—that the soldier appeared. He slipped silently from behind the foliage to stand before her, his mail glimmering in the fading sunlight behind him. Fortunately, he'd raised his helm, and his face (and a moment later the red-and-white check arms he bore on his tabard) identified him, preventing her from alerting the rest of the camp to the presence of Sir Henry de Spenser's top household knight.

"Sir Stephen!" she gasped. "What are you doing here?"

It was a silly question. She could guess exactly what he was doing here, but the shock had not yet left her, and it was all she could manage under the circumstances.

"We've come to rescue you, my lady."

"We?" She looked around.

"Sir Henry and the rest of the army are not far behind. I was sent ahead to scout, but when I saw you . . ." His voice dropped off as if he couldn't believe his good fortune. "I can't believe the rebels left you alone like this!"

Her mouth went dry. Dear God, she couldn't let this happen! Men would die. Men like Sir Stephen.

Sir Stephen de Vrain was one of Sir Henry's closest friends, and her favorite among his men. He was a handful of years older than she—closer to Sir Henry's age of six and twenty—and though not classically handsome, he had a pleasing countenance with sandy-brown hair, rich hazel eyes, and an easy smile. It was the smile that had charmed her.

Robbie would kill him if he found him here. She could not let that happen. "You must leave. If they find you here, they will kill you."

He glanced around uncomfortably. "Aye, you are right. Let's go."

"But I . . ." Her voice fell off. She didn't want to go. "I cannot leave yet." He looked at her as if she were half as crazed as she felt. "I gave my word not to escape when they permitted me free roaming of the camp."

He smiled then. "'Tis admirable of you, my lady. But there is no dishonor in breaking a promise to a rebel."

Rosalin cringed. The statement was so in keeping with what Robbie had told her, she was ashamed for her countrymen.

The sound of raised voices put a swift end to their conversation. "Come, my lady," he said, taking her by the arm. "We must away."

She tried to pull her arm back. "Wait! I don't want to go."

But Sir Stephen wasn't listening to her protests. The sound of approaching footsteps spurred him to action. He hauled her against him and started to drag her off through the trees.

Rosalin tried to dig in her heels and push away, but it was no use. He wasn't as tall and muscular as Robbie—few men were—but he was strong. She put up as much of a struggle as she could without screaming, knowing that to do so would be a death knell for the knight. As soon as they were out of immediate danger, she was certain she could convince him to let her go.

She hadn't counted on the horse waiting a few yards away.

She was leaving him.
Robbie wasn't thinking about losing his hostage—and the means to bring Clifford to heel—or the fact that the English had managed to outwit him and discover their camp, or that God-knew-how-many men were probably trying to surround them right now. All he could think about was that the woman who told him she loved him not two hours ago was leaving him. Walking away—just as she'd taunted him—as if what had happened between them meant nothing.

It was what he wanted. He just hadn't expected it to feel as if an iron claw were ripping a gaping hole across his chest. As if his insides were being torn out and twisted on a rack. As if the last flicker of light had just gone out inside him.

His jaw hardened with the sharp edge of bitterness. Of the betrayal that he had no right to feel.

But God's blood, if she thought to escape him so easily, she would learn differently.

His men had already been alerted and were readying for battle. He called for a horse, and a minute later he plunged through the trees and shrubs after them.

The knight had a head start, but Robbie held the far greater advantage: he knew the terrain.

In his haste to get away, the Englishman had made a wrong turn that ended in a ravine and had to backtrack, enabling Robbie to catch up with him. He pulled up alongside them at a full gallop.

Fresh rage surged through him when he saw how hard Rosalin was fighting to hold on to her seat behind the knight. If she fell off at that speed . . .

Damn it.

The gaze that met his was full of terror, but also something else. A desperate plea that echoed the words she shouted to him above the din of thundering hooves. "Don't . . . h-hurt . . . please!"

It was far too late for mercy, if he'd ever had any. He lifted his sword.

The knight was concentrating on trying to get away but must have caught the glint of the blade out of the corner of his eye. He turned. Beneath the helm, his eyes widened with fear. The knight reached for his own sword—almost knocking Rosalin off—but it was too late.

Robbie started to bring his hand down, and would have cleaved the bastard in two if Rosalin hadn't done something that took ten years off his life. Minimum.

His blade had barely begun its descent when she screamed, "No!" and launched herself toward him.

He had to make a split-second decision: kill the knight or let her fall and be trampled underneath the pounding hooves.

He didn't hesitate. His sword clattered to the ground as he caught her around the waist and pulled her to safety in front of him.

She sagged against him, looping her arms around his shoulders and burying her face in his leather-clad chest. From the way her back was shaking, he knew she was crying. From terror or relief, he didn't know. Probably both. Hell, he didn't blame her.

His hand went to her back. He rubbed and muttered soothing words as he drew his horse to a stop, while the soldier galloped away. He was forced to let him go. For now. Crushing her to him, he inhaled her, taking her in and trying to assure his still-thundering heart that she was all right.

It wasn't long, however, before the memory of her walking away intruded.

The hammering in his chest came to an abrupt stop. He unlatched her from his chest and pulled her back to look at her. Swollen, tear-stained eyes stared up at him, and he felt his lungs clench. Aye, his *lungs*, damn it. But he forced the sensation away, hardening his expression as well as whatever the hell else he'd been clenching.

"Were you so anxious to get away that you would kill yourself to do so?"

Her eyes widened a little at his tone. "I wasn't trying to get away. I just didn't want you to hurt him."

His hold tightened on her, his anger going black. Who was she protecting? "God's blood, was that de Spenser?"

She shook her head. "Nay, one of his household knights. Sir Stephen has always been kind to me—"

"Enough." He cut her off, swinging the horse around to retrieve his sword. "You gave me your word, though why I should be surprised a Clifford did not keep it, I don't

276   M o n i c a   M c C a r t y

know. I don't have time for this. I'm sure *Sir Stephen* did
not come alone."

She bit her lip and nodded. "He said the others were not
far behind."

That put a swift end to the conversation. He raced back
to camp at an only slightly slower speed than upon which
he'd left.

The camp was in a state of organized upheaval. Douglas,
Seton, and Fraser had already taken charge, gathering
what supplies and belongings they could and seeing to the
men and the handful of women.

Robbie immediately went to work alongside them, duty
and experience temporarily quieting the tempest of divergent emotions storming inside him. Anger. Hurt. Betrayal.
He focused on the anger. It was easiest to understand.

Fraser would see to the women's safety, while Douglas
and Robbie led the attack against the Englishmen. Seton
would have charge of Rosalin. Robbie gave his instructions in Gaelic to forestall any protests from Rosalin, who
watched him anxiously with big, accusing eyes that made
him feel as if *he* were the one to blame. Surprisingly his
partner didn't argue, but just gave a grim nod in response.

He left Rosalin under Seton's watch, while he returned to
his tent to retrieve what he could. The tents could not be
saved—there wasn't time enough—but he packed his books
and as many garments as he could from his trunk in leather
bags. They would be hidden nearby and retrieved later.
Seton had already gathered anything that could connect
him to the Highland Guard, including his armor.

No more than five minutes after they'd arrived, Robbie
was ready to leave.

He could no longer avoid those hurt eyes. "Seton will see
you safely away."

The color faded from Rosalin's face. "You are leaving
me?"

"Ironic, isn't it."

She frowned. It took her a moment to understand. "I told you I wasn't trying to leave—"

"Do not worry." His mouth curved in a semblance of a smile. "I don't imagine this will take long."

She gazed up at him, apprehension making her face look pale and frightened. He forced himself to be immune. She'd made a fool of him enough already.

"What are you going to do?"

"Give them the battle they came for."

Fear leapt to her eyes. "No! You mustn't—"

"Take her," he said to Seton, her pleas for her country-men falling on deaf ears. Or maybe not so deaf. They had drawn the battle between them again. How could he have forgotten which side she stood on?

He didn't look back as they rode off. All of his attention was once again focused where it should be: on the war and killing any Englishman who got in his way.

Rosalin was silent for most of the journey. The speed at which they were traveling didn't leave much opportunity for questions. In addition to Sir Alex, Callum, Malcolm, and one of her former jailors, Archie (dour Douglas brother number two), made up the party of men who had been charged with the task of seeing their hostage to safety.

As best she could tell from the position of the setting sun, they rode east for the first few miles—crossing a deep corrie thick with trees and brush that looked impassable until a narrow path was revealed—and then headed north for hours in the darkness.

For once she welcomed the hair-raising speed, stomach-knotting terrain, and bone-deep exhaustion of the jour-ney, as they kept her mind from dwelling all night on the grim countenance she'd left behind.

The way he'd looked at her, the change in his expression, the change in *him* had been dramatic. Cold, merciless, impenetrable. It was a glimpse of the ruthless enforcer, the heartless raider, the man who'd laid scourge across the Borders. The man she'd convinced herself no longer existed.

Her pleas, her attempts to reach him, had slid off him like water on steel. The connection and deepening emotions she'd put so much store in had been unable to penetrate the shield that had gone up around him.

He'd been furious. He'd refused to believe that she hadn't left voluntarily. Given how it had looked, perhaps she could understand. She'd tried to explain, but clearly he wasn't in any mood to listen to her.

What bothered her was how quickly he'd assumed her guilt and how incapable he thought her of honor. Shouldn't he have trusted her a little? At least enough not to immediately discount her explanation?

Sir Alex's warning that he would never trust an Englishman—or woman—came back to her. She'd hoped Robbie thought her different. She'd just told him she loved him—how could he think she would leave him so easily? Obviously he hadn't believed that either. What more proof could she give him?

The tangle of hurt and disappointment was exacerbated by fear. She was terrified of what was happening, of the battle being waged by the men they'd left behind in Ettrick Forest.

No matter how he appeared, Robbie was not invincible. As hurt as she was by his coldness before she left, the thought of him being hurt or—God forbid—killed made it feel as if she were riding with an icy claw wrapped around her chest that every once in a while squeezed.

But as much as she feared for him, most of her fear was for the men who must fight against him. Though she intended to break the betrothal with Sir Henry when she returned, she did not want to see him or any of his men killed. And Robbie's face as she'd ridden off had left no doubt of his intentions.

Her stomach twisted with fear and anxiety through the long night. It must have revealed itself on her face, for not long after dawn broke Sir Alex rode up next to her. "Try not to think about it, my lady. We will find out what happened soon enough."

She nodded, a lump growing in her throat as the emotions she'd kept bottled inside all night threatened to erupt at his show of compassion. "I'm not sure I want to know. Whatever happens, I fear the result."

His gaze held hers with understanding. " 'Tis often how I feel. It is not easy having friends on both sides and constantly being caught between the two. With my lands so close to the border, it's a position I've faced many times myself."

"How do you deal with it?"

"I don't. Not very well at least."

"I can't bear the thought of anyone being hurt. What do you think has happened?"

He gave her a sad look, as if he knew what she wanted to hear but wouldn't lie to her. "If Boyd catches up to them, your brother's men are dead."

She paled, feeling ill, knowing he was right. And if Robbie did kill them, it would make it that much harder for her to convince Cliff to agree to a match between them.

But Sir Alex was wrong about one thing. "Those were not my brother's men—they were Sir Henry's."

"I thought you only saw one. How can you be so sure Clifford did not have a part in it?"

She didn't know, but she was. "Cliff wouldn't do something so risky." So *rash*. "Something that would put me in danger like that."

Sir Alex studied her for a long pause. "I hope you are right, my lady. If Boyd believes your brother has broken the truce . . ." He let his voice fall off.

An ominous chill swept over her, making her skin prickle. She didn't want to ask. "What?"

Sir Alex's mouth fell in a hard line. For a moment, he looked just as grim and forbidding as Robbie had before she left. In that instant she saw not the Golden Knight, but the hard edge that had made Sir Alex part of the band of rebels.

"I don't know. But he will use whatever weapon he has at his disposal to make sure it doesn't happen again."

Me. He means me.

Rosalin shook her head. "He won't hurt me."

"Nay, not physically, but I fear—" He stopped. "Have care, my lady. That is all I'm saying. If you put yourself in the middle of this battle, you cannot win."

He spoke like a man who knew what he was talking about.

Rosalin was surprised that he'd guessed the direction of her thoughts so easily—were her hopes for the future so transparent? If the sympathetic look Sir Alex was giving her was any indication, they must be.

Embarrassed, and not a little discouraged, she was glad when one of the men riding ahead turned and said something to Sir Alex in Gaelic, pointing in the direction of a small village that had just appeared in the distance.

In the soft light of early morning, with the swirls of mist gently dissipating like smoke from a pipe, the village on the grassy strath below them looked almost enchanted— like something from a mystical bard's tale.

Straddling both sides of a wide, winding river, the stone and thatched cottages appeared so quiet and peaceful. The slate roof of a sizable church with a turreted tower in the center of town rose high above everything else. She scanned the buildings again. For a village of this size, there should be a castle. She felt her first whisper of premonition when her gaze snagged on a large empty area not far from the church on the banks of the river. Except it wasn't empty, she realized. From the distance, she could just make out large piles of stone scattered haphazardly about.

"What is it?" she asked.

Sir Alex turned to her, his expression strangely blank. "We're almost there."

"Where?"

He paused. "Douglas."

Her eyes widened in horror, as her stomach took a sharp dive. He might as well have said hell. For a Clifford, the village of Douglas was tantamount to the same thing. Her brother had tried for years to hold this land—and its castle—making plenty of enemies along the way.

"Castle Dangerous" it had been called by the garrisons sent by Cliff to hold the Douglas stronghold, and for good reason. Three times the Black Douglas had attacked and burned his own castle, including the infamous episode of the "Douglas Larder" that she knew Robbie had been involved in. The last had occurred about a year ago, and the castle had been destroyed—by Douglas himself. How could Robbie send her here, into the very heart and dominion of her family's greatest enemy?

"You have nothing to fear, my lady," Sir Alex said, trying to ease her rising panic. "You will be safe here."

"Safe? Surrounded by people who would probably like nothing more than to sink a dagger into my back?" She gave a harsh, bordering on hysterical, laugh. "I did not try to escape, but it seems Robbie is making sure of it. Am I to be thrown into a pit prison after all?"

"You will be treated with every consideration. I know it seems hard to believe, but trust me, you have nothing to fear. Joanna Douglas is not like her husband."

A short while later, when Rosalin was welcomed to Park Castle like a long-lost relative (replete with gasps of horror at what she'd been through and concerned pats of her hands) by a woman who was as beautiful and sweet-looking as her husband was dark and frightening, Rosalin was forced to concede Sir Alex was right: Joanna Douglas was nothing like her husband. In truth, she seemed more like the cherub she resembled than the devil's consort. Perhaps he'd abducted her?

When she accidentally blurted out her suspicions, however, Joanna had laughed and patted the round swell of her pregnant stomach, assuring her that although their courtship had been a difficult one, it hadn't come to that. James wasn't really so terrifying, she'd insisted. When Rosalin grew to know him better, she'd see that.

Rosalin couldn't think of what to say that wasn't rude, so she did not respond.

Like a baby chick, Rosalin was scooted under the caring wing of her hostess, given a bath, fresh clothes, a hot meal, and a warm bedchamber in which to rest. Indeed, were it not for the placement of that room in the highest part of the tower and the guard stationed at the bottom of the stairwell, Rosalin might have been a treasured guest.

Despite her exhaustion, however, she found she could not rest. She had to see Robbie. Leaving a message with Lady Joanna that it was important that she see him as soon as possible, Rosalin watched for his arrival from the window of her tower chamber.

Twenty

It was after midday when Robbie and his men rode into the bailey of Park Castle. After hours of riding with only an empty stomach and sore backside to show for it, he was in a foul mood. The heat of battle was pent up inside him, eager for an outlet.

The English bastards had turned tail and run. With the element of surprise gone, they'd apparently decided not to chance an attack. Like frightened hares, they'd raced back to the garrison at Peebles, with Robbie and his men hard on their heels.

Any thought that Clifford might not have been a part of it was eradicated when the gate opened. Even from a distance, he'd recognized the red stripe and blue-and-yellow checks of one of the soldiers in the bailey.

Furious at being denied the battle promised him, Robbie had debated lying in wait for the English to emerge. But he didn't have the men or supplies. Once he gathered both, he would exact his retribution on Clifford for breaking the truce he'd only just agreed upon.

Robbie had anticipated a trick, and he'd gotten one. Clifford had brought him to Melrose and tampered with their horses' feed to follow him back to camp and attempt a rescue of Rosalin. Robbie had to admit it had been a cunning plan, but it was also reckless. If it failed—as it had—Clifford was putting his sister at risk. Unless . . .

Robbie's jaw clenched. Unless Clifford thought there *was* no risk. Unless he was certain Robbie wouldn't harm her.

Some of his anger turned inward. Was that it? Had Clifford seen too much? Or had the lad, and reported it to his father? Either way, Robbie knew knowledge of his feelings for Rosalin weakened his position.

If being denied his quarry and having possibly given Clifford an advantage weren't bad enough, Robbie had had to listen to Douglas's thoughts on the matter for much of the journey.

"Clifford isn't going to get away with this. I knew nothing good would come of having that lass at camp. You should have let me send her to Douglas right away as I wanted to."

Robbie tried to rein in his temper. Douglas could be as bad as Seton, though they argued from opposite sides. "And how would that have changed anything? They still would have found our camp when we returned from Melrose."

His friend gave him a hard look. "Aye, but they wouldn't have found the lass. God's blood, Boyd, they almost had her, and we would have let the means of bending Clifford over our knee slip away. Losing the lad was bad enough, but giving the chit freedom to move about the camp unguarded? What the hell did she do to get you to agree to that? Suck your—"

Robbie reached over and grabbed him by the throat, nearly lifting the powerfully built knight off his horse with one hand. The red haze of pure rage swirled before his eyes. "Say it and I'll break your damned teeth." The horses had come to a stop. Douglas could have tried to break free, but he seemed too intent on watching Robbie. "You can criticize me all you like—some of which is deserved—but do not disparage the lass. Despite her unfortunate relatives, she is an innocent in all of this—and a lady."

Realizing the other men had stopped to gape at them, Robbie let his friend go.

"So that's how it is," Douglas said, his voice stunned. "Bloody hell, I almost feel sorry for you."

Robbie gave him a fierce stare. "You don't know shite."

"I know you've changed. A couple of weeks ago you would have jumped at the opportunity to retaliate against Clifford, not try to think of reasons not to."

Robbie's fingers clenched the reins so tightly his knuckles turned white. "What the hell are you suggesting, Douglas? Are you questioning my commitment to the cause?"

"Nay, I'm questioning your commitment to the lass."

"I want her. But I can control my damned cock."

"You're so sure about that? I think this is about more than bedding."

He wasn't sure at all, but hell if he would tell Douglas that. "She's English. I don't think I'd need to explain that to you. Hell, what if Joanna had been English?"

It took Douglas a long time to respond, and when he did it wasn't the answer Robbie expected. "It wouldn't have made a damned bit of difference."

Given the source that admission was surprising, to say the least. It was akin to heresy, and Robbie didn't know what the hell to do with it. Realizing this conversation had gone on long enough, he urged his mount forward with a flick of the reins and a clip of his heels.

But Douglas wouldn't let it go. "Whatever your feelings for the lass, she cannot be trusted. You can't let this go without retaliation."

Robbie didn't need reminding about Rosalin's broken vow. She had been leaving willingly . . . hadn't she?

He frowned. "I don't intend to. The lass and Clifford will both be dealt with. But how I do that is up to me. The king put me in charge."

Douglas gave him a hard look. "Aye, you don't need to remind me. Just make sure you don't let your feelings for the lass interfere. I don't need to tell you how much is riding on this."

Robbie clamped his mouth closed. No, he didn't. Robbie was well aware that the king needed not only Clifford's truce, but also the coin that would enable him to evict the English from Scotland's castles and tighten his grip on the throne.

Needless to say, the sight of Park Castle was a welcome reprieve from the past long, frustrating, ire-inducing almost twenty-four hours. After dismounting and following Douglas up the motte and into the old tower house, Robbie was looking forward to a hot meal, a substantial draught of ale, a bath, and a preferably quiet and dark place where he could get at least a few hours of sleep before riding out again.

Joanna Douglas arranged the first three in short order, but the fourth would have to wait. As would Rosalin's request. Assured by Joanna that Rosalin had been well taken care of, he made his way into the Hall to fill in Seton and the others on what had happened, as well as make plans for a retaliatory attack.

But after hours of listening to the back-and-forth—with Seton urging caution and Douglas demanding widespread destruction that would have put Bruce's "Harrying of Buchan" a few years ago to shame—Robbie's mood was even fouler than when he arrived. Damn Clifford to hell! It was a curse he'd wished on the bastard for years, but this time there was an added fervency for what he'd done to his sister. Instinctively, Robbie knew how much it would hurt Rosalin when he did what he had to do.

Perhaps it was with this in mind that he declined the request to attend her. The last thing he wanted to hear was an impassioned defense of Lord Robert Clifford—not in his present state of mind.

* * *

Rosalin saw Robbie ride in with the others, but her sigh of relief was mingled with trepidation at what that might mean for Sir Henry and his men.

She waited—and waited—pacing anxiously across the room, as the beam of sunlight slowly retreated inch by inch from across the floor back out through the window until it was gone.

From the maidservant who'd brought her tray of food she'd learned that the men were meeting in the Hall. Lady Joanna hadn't confined her to her chamber, but Rosalin knew that she would not be welcome below.

It was after hours of anticipation, then, that she finally heard the deep, familiar voice and heavy footsteps as Robbie climbed the tower stairs. The feminine voice she recognized as that of their hostess.

She waited, hands twisting, for the door to open. Instead the voices dropped off, and a few minutes later a door closed below her. She could just make out the soft footfalls descending the stairs. Lady Joanna must have been showing him to his chamber—not hers.

Rosalin sucked in her breath, her chest on fire. Apparently, he would not even do her the courtesy of answering her plea to see him. She knew he must be exhausted—she was, too—but didn't she warrant a few minutes of his time?

Before she could think better of it, she raced out of her chamber and down the flight of stairs. Pausing before the door, she knocked—in case she'd been wrong about what she heard—and heard the familiar voice respond, "I said I don't need—"

He stopped when she threw open the door. She thought he swore, but she was too distracted to notice. He was obviously in the process of undressing as he was naked to the waist, barefoot, and his hands were on the ties of his leather chausses.

She swallowed. Hard. A hot flush consumed her body.

Forcing her eyes away from the wide expanse of hard cut steel, she gave her tongue a moment to untie. Fortunately, the shock seemed to be mutual.

"You shouldn't be here," he said, recovering first.

She gave a sharp laugh, realizing what he meant. "I think it's rather late to start worrying about propriety, when I've shared your tent for two weeks. I needed to see you."

His hands went to work retying the ties he'd been loosening moments before. The chausses hung loosely on his hips, and she couldn't help but follow the trail of dark hair that disappeared beneath the edge of the leather at his waist. His stomach was as flat and hard as the rest of him, with tight bands of muscle layered across it.

"Joanna informed me of your request."

His voice knocked her from her temporary stupor. Her eyes met his accusingly. "And you couldn't spare me a moment of your time?"

His mouth tightened, and now she could see the hard lines etched on his face that she'd missed before. He looked tired and agitated—edgy in a way she'd never seen him before. "Nay, I decided to exercise a modicum of discretion for once. I am not fit company for a *lady* right now, Rosalin, and rather than say something out of temper, I thought it better to wait until that temper had cooled."

She felt a little shiver of trepidation at the emphasis on the word *lady*, understanding what kind of woman he might be fit for. Though everything about him boded forbidding and unassailable, she took a step toward him. "I was worried about you."

Her concern barely registered. "As you can see, there was no cause. Your brother's men declined to take the field against us."

"Thank God." She didn't bother to hide her relief. "But it wasn't Cliff's men, it was my fian—" She stopped, seeing his darkening expression. "It was Sir Henry's."

His mouth tightened, his eyes burning hot into hers. "I do not wish to talk about this with you, Rosalin, but suffice it to say your brother was involved—unless there is another baron with a red stripe and blue-and-yellow check arms? I saw one of his men myself when we chased your betrothed back to Peebles."

Rosalin's eyes widened a little at his claim, but she pushed away the twinge of uncertainty. She shook her head. "Cliff might have been there, but he wouldn't have had anything to do with this. He wouldn't put me in that kind of danger."

"But your betrothed would?"

She felt the heat rising to her cheeks. It felt disloyal to Sir Henry, but she had to make him understand. "Sir Henry is a great knight, but he is young, proud, and I think sometimes overly bold," which sounded better than rash. "I suspect he acted out of worry for me and did not give thought to the consequences." He seemed to consider her words, and she pressed on. "I did not break my word to you, Robbie. I wasn't trying to leave."

"Then why were you walking away with him?"

"I wasn't walking away. He was dragging me. Could you not tell the difference?"

His frown told her he was remembering. "If you were being forced, why did you not shout for help?"

"Because I did not wish to see you kill him. I hoped to be able to convince him to let me go as soon as we were a short distance away. I did not count on the horse. The man was my friend. Can you not see the dilemma I faced? Would you have stopped to ask him questions before lifting your sword against him?"

His silence was answer enough.

It wasn't right that she was forced to defend herself like this, and some of her anger started to break through. "I had just confessed my feelings to you. It might have meant nothing to you, but it meant something to me."

"You are young, Rosalin. This will all seem very different once you return to England."

She couldn't believe he was trying to talk her out of how she felt. "I'm old enough to know my own feelings, and if you need proof I have six years of it. I never forgot you, and we'd met but for a few minutes. How do you imagine I will now? I love you, Robert Boyd, and if I had my wish we would never be apart."

For one moment she thought her words had penetrated and that he might reach for her. But he held his hands rigid at his sides, clenching and unclenching. "You might get your wish," he snarled. "For a while at least."

"What do you mean?"

"I mean your brother broke the truce, and I do not intend to let that go without a response."

Her calm, rational approach fell by the wayside. She rushed toward him and placed her hand on his arm. "No! You can't do that! Have you not heard what I said? Cliff didn't do this, and if you retaliate with a raid or exact some sort of other vengeance against him there will be no chance."

He looked down at her, the handsome lines of his face drawn taut. He grabbed her by the shoulders, as if to keep her back. "No chance for what?"

Tears blurred her eyes; her throat burned. She barely got the words out. "For us."

Their faces were only inches apart, his looking down, hers tilted back. He'd shaved, but the shadow of a beard already darkened his jaw. His chest seemed to radiate heat and the faint hint of pine-scented soap. Her desire for him reached up and grabbed her by the throat, squeezing.

She was not the only one affected. Robbie seemed pulled as tight as a bowstring, the steely muscles in his body flexed and taut. "There *is* no 'us.'"

She quirked a brow at him. Couldn't he feel how closely he was holding her? Her breasts were crushed against his chest and her hips were wedged solidly against his. "Then what is this, Robbie? Tell me why you are so angry if this means nothing. Tell me why your heart is racing as fast as mine. Tell me why you are fighting so hard for control."

"You know why, damn it."

"Aye, you want to—how did you so eloquently put it? Fuck me so badly you can't see straight. As I recall, I offered that to you as well, and you refused."

His voice fell to a low growl, which she ignored. "Because I was trying to protect you, damn it."

That dainty brow arched again. "How noble of you. I'm sure my future husband will be very pleased."

His hands tightened. "Rosalin . . ."

But she didn't heed the warning. "I think you were protecting yourself. I think you didn't make love to me because you know it would be different. You would feel it in *here*," she tapped her finger against his chest, "and then it wouldn't be so easy for you to let me go."

At last the tightly held control seemed to snap. "Easy? How can you think any of this is easy? I've thought of nothing but how difficult it was going to be to watch you go since practically the first moment I took you. You have no idea how much I wish the circumstances were different, but they aren't, and I live in the real world, Rosalin. Not some damned fantasy where the war is a mere inconvenience or the hatred your brother and I bear each other is overcome by a handshake. And I will not let my feelings for you interfere with what I have to do."

Despite his anger, Rosalin felt a ridiculous gurgle of happiness. She knew it! He'd admitted he had feelings for her. Feelings that she suspected ran far deeper than he realized. It made her even more certain she had to stop him from doing something that her brother would not ignore. But how would she get through to him? "All I'm asking is that you do not act precipitously. Make sure my brother broke the truce before you retaliate." She placed her palm on his chest, savoring the fierce pounding of his heart. "Please, Robbie—it's only a few days."

Robbie held himself perfectly still, but emotion was sparring and sparking inside him like a violent lightning storm. God's blood, she didn't know what she was asking! He wouldn't compromise his duty and what he'd fought for for over half his life for anyone. His family's death had to mean something.

Every instinct cried out to strike back at Clifford. Strike back hard, in the only way the English understood. And what did she offer in return? A dream? A hope? A damned faerie tale?

He'd never asked for this. But for a moment he wanted what she offered with an intensity that shook him.

"Please," she said, leaning closer. The dream beckoned in the honeyed temptation of her mouth. *Kiss her. Take her. Make her yours.*

He grabbed her by the shoulders, mostly to keep her at a safe distance, but also because he couldn't go another minute without touching her. From the moment she'd burst into the room—hell, from the moment he'd tossed her over his lap—all he could think about was putting his hands all over her.

But that wasn't what she was asking for. *Us. A future.*

What she wanted he couldn't give. He released her and took a step back. "I've made my decision."

"But—"

He cut her off. "Don't. Do not try to put yourself between me and my duty."

Her eyes flashed angrily. "This isn't about your duty. Be honest about that at least. Your duty is to secure the truce—a truce you have in place, but which will be jeopardized if you attack without cause. If you have a duty here, it is to make sure you are right. This is about vengeance and the personal battle you have with my brother—the path straight to hell that you both seem intent on traveling down. He strikes, you strike back, he strikes back harder. Right, wrong, everything else is immaterial."

His fists clenched. What the hell did she know about any of this? He wouldn't expect her to understand. She was *English*. "We tried it your way for years, and look where that got us. An English puppet on the throne, English lords in our castles, and innocent Scots hung in barns. The English ignored our cries for justice for years." He leaned closer. "But you know what, Rosalin? They are listening to us now."

Her eyes scanned his face. She must have realized he wasn't going to change his mind, because she brought out the last weapon in her arsenal—and it was a powerful one.

Tears glistened in her eyes and she grabbed hold of his arm as if it were the last lifeline of a sinking ship. "Please, Robbie, I'm begging you to reconsider. It's only a few days. Won't you do this for me—for us?"

The soft press of her breasts against his arm, the intoxicating rose scent of the soap that permeated the air around her, the gently parted lips that were lifted in sweet invitation were a full-out assault on his resolve. The walls were closing in. The bed loomed out of the corner of his eye.

She shouldn't have come here like this, damn it. He'd warned her. He was hot and restless and in desperate need of the relief she so innocently offered.

Or was it innocent?

He stiffened, recalling the time her nephew had escaped. "It's not going to work this time, Rosalin." A confused wrinkle appeared between her brows. "First you offer yourself to save your nephew and now your brother? Is that the bargain?" She let out a sharp gasp of outrage, her eyes shooting to his. But he wasn't done yet. He moved his hips against hers suggestively—crudely. "Should I take you up on it this time?"

She stared at him as if he were the lowest piece of scum,

and at that moment he felt it. Instinctively he tensed, waiting for the slap that he no doubt deserved.

But she wouldn't let him off so easily. Coolly—icily—
she pushed away from him. "What I offered, I offered
freely and without condition. You are just too damned
blind to see it. Go ahead and have your war, Robbie. If
that's all you want, you will have it. I'm done fighting you.
I'm done fighting *for* you."

She meant it. He could see it in her eyes.

Let her go.

His heart hammered in his ears. Muscles he didn't even
know he had strained against the urge to reach for her.

She waited for what seemed an eternity, her eyes on his
face, watching for some kind of sign.

If that's all you want . . .

The muscle in his jaw ticked. Blood roared through his
veins, pounding. But he stood perfectly still against the
storm.

She turned.

To hell with it. It wasn't all he wanted at all. He caught
her wrist before she could spin away.

Their eyes met. "Damn it, Rosalin, I want *you*." He
didn't know exactly what that meant, except that it meant
something.

She lifted her chin and threw the gauntlet down right at
his feet. "Then take me."

He couldn't let it sit there. Not this time. Every man had
his breaking point, and the beautiful woman who looked
up at him with her heart in her eyes and dared him to refuse what she offered was his.

Robbie didn't snap or lose control; he simply threw the
reins up in the air and let them fall where they may. He'd
had enough. He would have her and be damned.

Twenty-one

Robbie drew her into his arms and did what he'd been aching to do since the moment she'd walked into the room. His mouth fell on hers with a deep groan. It was as if a dam had broken and all the passion, all the emotion, all the desire he'd bottled up inside was set free the instant his lips touched hers.

God, they were soft. And so damned sweet he didn't know how he could have resisted for so long. Why had he? If there were voices in his head trying to remind him, he wasn't listening to them anymore.

He was too busy kissing her. Tasting her. Sliding his tongue deep into her mouth with long, slow strokes that she parried with strokes of her own.

It was incredible. The lass was a quick learner, God help him.

He could have gone on kissing her like this forever. But the longer and more thoroughly he kissed her, the fiercer her response grew and the hotter his blood fired. Heat radiated off him. And then there was that other pounding, the one against his stomach that was growing harder with every stroke.

He could taste her need, her hunger, feel the urgency building, and it sent flames licking through every corner of his body. The moans, the little whimpers echoed in his ears, ripping what control he had left to shreds. She was clutching his arms, his shoulders, trying to pull him closer, but their bodies were already plastered as close as they could be without . . .

He swore against her mouth. Once the image was there it would not be dislodged. Skin to skin. Naked tangled limbs. Sweaty sheets. Him sinking inside her. The ultimate closeness. She wanted that. And God, he wanted it, too.

Swinging her up in his arms, he carried her over to the bed. He broke the kiss only long enough to set her down and slide in next to her. He wasn't going to give either of them time to think.

Perhaps she had the same thought, because the moment her head touched the pillow she was reaching for him again. Circling her hands around his neck to bring his mouth down on hers. Bring him down on top of her. He let her feel his weight while he savored the incredible feel of that soft, curvy body under his.

But it wasn't enough. Not now. Not with the image blaring in his head. He was moving faster now. His lips slid to her jaw, her neck, to the tender place below her ear that made her shiver, to her throat, and finally to her breasts.

The rapid beat of her heart and uneven catching of her breath hammered in his ears, egging him on faster and faster. Too fast. But she didn't seem to care. She was right there with him.

Her hands were in his hair as he worked the laces of her gown and then her shift—neither of which garments he'd ever seen before. Only the thought of having to explain to Joanna how they'd become ripped prevented him from tearing both off her.

"Hurry," she breathed, her impatience matching his own.

He muttered an expletive. Christ, she was killing him. His normally deft fingers felt twice as big and were practically shaking. Hell, they *were* shaking. So much for experience. When it came to Rosalin this was all new.

No skin had ever felt so soft, no lips had ever tasted so

sweet, no one had ever smelled so damned good, and no woman had ever made him this hot.

But it was more than that, and he knew it. Even if he didn't want to think about it. For the first time in his life, he was making love to a woman with more than his cock.

Finally, he had both the gown and chemise underneath loose enough to take her beautiful breasts in his mouth. He cupped her, squeezing gently as his lips closed over one taut nipple. He sucked it gently, circling it with his tongue and plucking it between his teeth. She gave a soft cry and arched into his mouth, her fingers tightening their grip on his hair. His whole scalp tingled as pleasure poured over him in a hot wave, dragging him under.

He wanted to strip her naked and worship every inch of that creamy white skin. But he wasn't going to last five minutes. Not like this. Though he had to at least try.

"Oh God, Robbie . . ."

The soft plea took his intentions to go slow and ground them to dust. He gave her what she wanted and sucked her hard into his mouth. She was so beautiful, so damned responsive, it drove him wild. He couldn't get enough of her. He ravished her breasts with his lips and tongue. Teasing, laving, sucking until he felt her body tremble with the promise of pleasure.

He wasn't going to make her wait.

Rosalin knew what she was doing—she hoped. It was the biggest gamble of her life. But the reward . . .

The reward would be a lifetime of happiness.

He loved her. She was sure of it. It was right there in his kiss. She'd pushed him with far more confidence than she'd felt. She'd never seen him so near the end of his rope. Yet when he kissed her, instead of rough and punishing, his lips had been soft and gentle. Did he realize how he cradled her against him? How his big, battle-hardened hands caressed her skin as if she were a delicate piece of porcelain?

She had to make him see the truth before it was too late. She'd already offered him her heart, so she'd gambled with the only thing she had left: her body.

On some level she knew it was a fool's wager, that she should value her virtue more highly, and that if he truly cared for her, she would not need to prove her love. But on the other hand, nothing had ever seemed more natural—or right. And somewhat brazenly, she admitted that she wanted the experience for herself. That no matter what the result, she wanted to know what it felt like to be joined with the man she loved.

And from the moment his mouth fell on hers, hungrily and with purpose, she knew there would be no turning back. The knowledge was a little overwhelming—frightening even. She was a virgin, and although she knew the basics (she'd seen more than one couple mating under a blanket in a crowded, dark Hall), she also knew there would be pain. But Robbie would have care for her innocence. She trusted him without reservation.

He would make it good for her. And she hoped she would make it good for him. She wanted desperately to please him.

But as she'd neglected to take advantage of the potential tutors she had at her disposal at camp, she had little knowledge of how to do so. All she had was instinct. She gave over to the desire, holding nothing back, and returned his kiss with all the passion he'd awakened inside of her.

She ran her palms over his arms and shoulders and down his back, the way she'd dreamed so many times of doing. He growled at her touch, the muscles flexing under her fingertips. His body was a thing of beauty. Sheer masculine perfection. Smooth skin pulled tight over rock-hard muscle, lean and chiseled. There was not an inch of extra flesh upon him, just slab after slab of perfectly delineated muscle. His arms were bulging with strength, his stomach flat, and his waist narrow. He was so hard. So solid. And so hot. His skin was practically burning under her fingertips. Fevered. And the fever infected them both with its scorching heat.

She sensed the change that came over him when he lifted her toward the bed. His kiss became rougher and more carnal, leaving her no doubt of his intentions.

His big hands covered her body, her breasts. And then his mouth . . . his mouth was sucking, and she thought she'd died and gone to heaven. Tiny needles of pleasure shot to her toes and heat rushed between her legs. She felt the same hot restlessness she'd felt last time, right before he'd touched her with his fingers.

She desperately wanted him to do that again, so she arched against his mouth on her breast, lifting her hips with a gentle press.

He made some kind of tortured sound. It might have been an oath, but she was too lost in the haze of pleasure to notice.

Cool air washed over the skin of her legs as he tossed up her skirts. His mouth ravished her breasts, the scratch of his beard burning—marking—a trail on her sensitive skin.

He lifted his head from her breast. When he sank his finger inside her, she cried out. The damp skin of her breast prickled in the cool air.

"God, you feel good."

Her half-lidded eyes fluttered. But then he stroked her again, and any response she might have made was lost in the wave of sensation that crashed over her.

His voice was tight and strained. "Damn it," he growled fiercely. "I can't wait much longer."

Neither could she. She arched into his hand with a cry as he stroked her again. And again.

Then suddenly his hand was gone and he was holding her by the hips. If she'd had any inkling of what he intended to do, she was sure she would have objected. She would have locked her thighs tightly together and refused the wicked kiss. She would have been properly shocked and traumatized for at least a full minute. At least.

Certainly longer than the two seconds of stunned stiffness she'd managed before dissolving like a complete and utter wanton against his mouth. His glorious mouth. *There*. Between her legs. Kissing her. With his warm, soft lips and his tongue. Yes, with his tongue. His incredible, talented tongue that made her arch and moan, and then shudder and cry out in pure sinful delight. It came over her in molten wave after molten wave, flooding her body with heat.

When it was over, she was a puddle of sensation, warm, soft, and ready. She opened her eyes as he moved himself into position over her. His handsome face was tight and drawn with something resembling pain. A thin sheen of sweat had gathered on his brow.

She looked down. Somehow he'd managed to loosen his chausses and braies, and his manhood bobbed hard between them. His very sizable manhood. Some of the flush from her cheeks paled.

"I don't want to hurt you," he said through clenched teeth.

She lifted her gaze back to his. "I know."

The trust in her eyes nearly felled him. Robbie wanted to deserve that trust, but if the size of the erection pounding against his stomach was any indication, it was seriously misplaced. The way he felt right now—that his skin was two sizes too small and that his entire body was on the verge of exploding, that the only thing he'd wanted to do when she was shattering against his mouth was sink into her and join her, that she was the most beautiful thing he'd ever seen in his damned life—if he didn't get inside her in about two seconds he was going to do something he'd never done before. Ever. Even when he'd been a lad.

"I'm not sure . . ." He couldn't finish.

Her face grew serious. "No promises, Robbie—I know that."

He frowned. "That's not what I meant." Whether this was a good idea no longer mattered. "It's just that I want you too much, and it can be painful the first time for a lass."

An adorable smile curved her mouth and the soft pink flush crawled back up her cheeks. She gave him a shy look from under her lashes that hit him somewhere in the vicinity of his ribs. Above his ribs, actually. And maybe a little to the left.

"Well, then perhaps we should get on with this and get to the second time."

And then she did something that put an end to talking—and just about everything else as well.

She slid her hand down the front of his chest, trailing her fingers over the flexed muscles of his stomach, and touched him. She took him in her sweet little hand, wrapped her soft fingers around him, and gave him a perfect squeeze that made him suck in his breath as pleasure shot from the base of his spine. He made a pained sound, gritting his teeth against the fierce sensations and the nearly over-whelming need to let go.

But he didn't. God help him, he somehow managed to keep his body under control. But for how long, with her touching him like this?

She remembered too well how he'd taught her to stroke him. Remembered how to squeeze and milk with long, hard pumps that went from base to tip.

He had to make her stop.

He didn't want her to ever stop.

His heart hammered. The muscles in his arms almost buckled as he fought to keep himself propped over her as she tortured him with her sweet stroking. It felt so good, he just wanted to . . .

He felt himself pulse and knew he couldn't let it go on. The first time wasn't the time to test the limits of his control. "Now, sweetheart," he said tightly. "I need to be inside you."

Their eyes met. She unwrapped her hand from around him and let him guide himself into position. He parted her legs, letting the soft skin of her thighs rest against his. They were both still half-dressed, and her skirts were bunched up around her waist. He was tempted to rip them off her once again but didn't think he could take one more delay.

Next time, he swore. Next time he'd take his time and do it slow and easy. But right now, all he could think about was being inside her.

She sucked in her breath when the fat tip met the silky flesh. Or maybe that sound was his, since his entire body seemed to be hit with a bolt of lightning at that first incredible contact. It took everything he had not to sink into her. To just let the sensation roll over him in wave after shuddering wave.

Their eyes met, and he could see the twinge of fear creep up behind the sated haze. A fresh wave of tenderness rose in his chest. Leaning over, he kissed her. Gently, and with all the emotion burgeoning from deep inside him. From a place he hadn't known existed. He murmured soft words against her skin. Told her it would be all right. Told her he would care for her. Told her to trust him. He would make it good.

Even if it bloody well killed him. That he said in Gaelic.

He rocked his hips against her slowly, letting her get used to the feel of him between her thighs. Letting the thick tip tease and circle until she started to squirm against him. Until she was soft and wet and breathing hard and her hips started to lift, seeking more friction.

Every second was exquisite torture. Somehow he found the strength to hold back when every instinct in his body was clamoring to sink into that tight silken glove.

Instead he turned the rocking to a slow push.

Tight. Oh God, she was so tight. That was his first thought. The second was that she was warm and wet. The third was that his head was going to explode, he was so out of his mind with pleasure. That he'd never felt anything so good in his life. That every inch, every gasp, every minute their eyes stayed locked together he was flying closer to heaven.

He paused only once. He gazed into the big, beautiful green eyes that locked on his. Some last vestige of conscience managed to seep through, and he gave her a look in silent question. He would have found the strength to pull back if she'd asked him to. But she didn't.

"Please, Robbie," she whispered softly.

He didn't hesitate again. With a hard thrust, he took her.

Mine. The knowledge was fierce, primal, and too overwhelming to deny. A lightning bolt of pleasure shot up his spine, gripping him from head to toe.

Her cry of pain tore through his pleasure like a jagged knife. He soothed her as best he could, peppering gentle kisses on her face and lips and holding himself completely still—which might have been the hardest thing he'd ever done—until her shock eased.

She stared at him, trying to blink away tears.

"I'm sorry, *mo ghrá*," he said, kissing the salty dampness from her eyes and lashes. "I would take the pain from you if I could."

Her smile was tremulous at best. "It's not so bad," she said so bravely, he almost laughed.

"Hardly a testament to my lovemaking skills, but I promise it will get better."

"Anytime soon?" she squeaked, her voice high-pitched.

He brushed aside a silky lock of golden hair that had

become tangled in her lashes. "Aye," he said huskily, right before his mouth covered hers. If it killed him, he would bring her pleasure.

He'd never had to seduce a woman before, but he did so now. He kissed the pleasure back into her body with long, soothing strokes of his tongue and mouth. He teased, enticed, and told her wordlessly exactly how he would love her with his body.

Slowly, he could feel her tension ease. Her fingers were no longer clutching the bedsheets at her side but were wrapped around his shoulders. And then they were clutching him. Gently at first, and then more insistently. He loved to feel her delicate fingers digging into his arms. The visceral sensation of her pleasure heightened his own.

He tried not to think about how good it felt. How good *she* felt. How her body gripped him like a tight, hot glove. Or how incredible it was going to feel when he could move. When he could slide in and out, hard and deep.

But she was making it damned difficult. Her body was so soft and sweet and warm. And welcoming. Aye, he could feel her opening for him. Feel the tight clamp of her muscles begin to soften and dampen around him.

When she started to press her hips against his, he knew he had to move. Slowly at first, and then faster as she responded, lifting her hips to meet his thrusts. The kiss started to fall apart as their moans and groans increased in urgency, as his breathing became more erratic and took second place to the far greater need building in his loins.

But it wasn't just his loins. Nay, the need for her was elemental. It permeated him, flesh, bone, and soul. There was no part of him she'd left unclaimed. He wanted her with everything he had—and even with things he didn't have.

His thrusts lengthened, deepened, and quickened, echoing the breathy little gasps of surprise she was making every time their bodies slammed intimately together. Despite the erotic picture that presented, he couldn't tear his eyes from her face.

She was the most beautiful thing he'd ever seen in his life. Her cheeks were flushed pink with arousal, her lips gently parted, and her eyes soft with an aching tenderness that bound them together in a way he'd never imagined. In a way he'd not thought himself capable of.

He'd had lots of good swiving before. Hell, even lots of great swiving. But he'd never had perfect swiving. And that's what this was: perfect. It was the way she moved with him. The way they moved together—as one. It was a sensual rhythm unlike any other. But he knew it was more than that. He'd never felt so connected with a woman. Never had her pleasure been his own. He could feel it building in her. Feel as the heat and sensation started to gather and twist. Feel the pressure coiling and knew exactly when it was about to unwind.

He sank deep inside her and stilled.

Her eyes widened in sensual shock a moment before the soft cries of pleasure tore from her lungs and her body started to shudder under him. And then through him as her pleasure became his.

But it was her whispered words that pushed him over the edge. "I love you."

His chest squeezed and then expanded. With a feral cry from between clenched teeth, he clutched the soft curves of her bottom, holding himself deep as he circled his hips, grinding every pulse, every spasm, every hard jolt of pleasure that crashed over him in blinding wave after blinding wave of shattering sensation.

His mind went black. If he didn't know it was impossible, he might have though he passed out for a minute, so intense was the blast of sensation that overtook him. The roaring in his head was so loud that when it finally quieted—when the last drop of pleasure had been wrung from his body—the room sounded unnaturally still.

All he could hear were the heavy sounds of heartbeats and the uneven fall of breaths. Realizing he'd collapsed on top of her, and was probably crushing her, he rolled to the side and tucked her under one arm. She rested her cheek on his chest, with her tiny palm pressed right above his heart, while he let his cheek rest atop her silky head.

Neither of them said anything. What more was there left to say?

He wasn't even sure he knew what the hell had just happened. Cataclysmic. Life-changing. Awe-inspiring. They were all too mundane to describe the experience.

It had been so much more than he'd imagined—and what he'd imagined had been pretty damned spectacular. Instinctively he'd known it would be good between them— their attraction had been too charged from the start for it not to be—he just hadn't anticipated the rest. The feelings of tenderness that had gripped him. The feelings that hadn't come from anywhere close to the vicinity of his groin. They'd been much deeper and much more powerful. They'd come from a part of him he hadn't been sure existed anymore.

But he didn't know what it meant. Or, more important, what the hell he was going to do about it.

When Rosalin was a young girl, not long after her parents had died, she'd gone chasing after Cliff and some of his friends on a hunting trip. She ran after them for miles, over hills and through valleys, as quickly as her little legs would carry her.

By the time she'd caught up with them, she'd been exhausted. Every limb, every bone, every muscle in her body felt as if it had been strained and stretched to the breaking point. Cliff had been furious that she'd followed them, and she'd been sore for weeks, but the sense of accomplishment had made everything worth it.

It was the most physically exhausted she'd ever been.

Until now. But like then, it had been worth it. Every minute of it.

Well, maybe not *one* particular minute of it.

As she lay strewn across his chest, trying to find the energy to breathe—let alone think—Rosalin winced at the memory. That minute had hurt quite a lot. But the sharp twinge had faded quickly—thankfully—and it had been replaced by a dull soreness and a wonderful sensation of being filled. Possessed. Claimed. Primitive words, perhaps, but it didn't make them any less meaningful or significant. What they'd just done had bound them together in a way she never could have imagined. In a way that could not be undone.

If she'd thought she loved him before, she knew it now for certain with every fiber of her very sore, exhausted, and aching being. She didn't need to worry about it being perfect. It *was* perfect.

She belonged to him not because he'd taken her maidenhead but because of the connection they'd forged together. She would never forget the look in his eyes as he'd held himself deep inside her and let himself go. The sharp poignancy of the moment would be burned in her heart forever. A man did not look like that at a woman whom he did not care about—care *deeply* about.

A woman whom he did not love.

For a moment, the hard mask had dropped and revealed the vulnerable man underneath. The man who wanted to love but didn't know how. The man who'd had so much taken from him that he'd told himself he didn't need it anymore. The man who needed her, even if he might not realize it yet.

Lost in her thoughts and caught up in the sense of euphoria that had overtaken her, it took a few minutes for Rosalin to realize how quiet it was. How quiet *he* was.

A prickle of unease tried to worm its way through her happiness, but she wouldn't let it. Nothing was going to interfere with this moment. He was probably just as moved by what had happened as she. And probably just as tired.

With that thought, Rosalin snuggled in closer to the warm bare chest, let his spicy masculine scent wash over her, closed her eyes, and succumbed to the exhaustion.

Long after Rosalin fell asleep, Robbie lay awake in the darkness. Part of him wanted to savor every minute he had of holding her in his arms. The other part needed time to think. It wasn't until he'd decided what to do that he allowed himself to rest.

Just before dawn he carefully crept out of bed, dressed, and made his way downstairs to put his plan into motion. When he was done, he returned to the room to wait for her to wake so he could tell her what he'd done.

Twenty-two

Rosalin was still asleep. Instead of being bundled up against him, she'd taken one of the pillows and was hugging it to her chest. She looked as sweet and contented as a child, her beautiful face soft in repose, her small fist resting near her strawberry-red mouth, and her golden-blond hair streaming out behind her in wavy, tumbled disarray. Robbie had covered her last night while she slept, but he knew that the half-naked skin beneath the coverlet was every bit as velvety and baby-soft.

Unable to resist—and admittedly feeling a bit put out over a damned pillow—he removed his boots, *cotun*, and shirt, and crawled back into bed beside her. Carefully extracting the pillow from her hold, he felt a satisfied swell in his chest when, after a kittenish mewl of displeasure, she slid back into his arms with a contented sigh.

God, he could get used to this. She was so warm and soft, and she smelled like a bed of roses—a bed of well-ravished roses. His chest ached from just the simple pleasure of holding her. He hadn't felt at peace like this in years. Maybe ever.

Stroking her hair, he watched the gentle rise and fall of her chest on his for as long as he could—until the first rays of sunshine captured the strands of gold in their shimmery light. Then, he knew he could not wait any longer.

He gave her a gentle shake. "Rosalin."

Her long lashes fluttered open. Still groggy with sleep,

her gaze found his. Slowly the confusion cleared, and a broad smile curved her sensually bruised lips. "Good morning."

His chest tugged. She looked so damned happy. He would do just about anything to keep her that way. But he feared "just about" might not be enough.

The lass was too perceptive. Before he could respond, her smile fell. She propped herself up a little on his chest. "Is something wrong?"

"You need to return to your room."

She drew in her breath, her eyes widening as if his words had somehow hurt her. "You're sending me away?"

There was something small and vulnerable in her voice that made him frown. Unintentionally, he'd struck a tender spot. She'd been sent away before, he realized. If the hurt in her eyes was any indication, perhaps quite a lot. He knew little of her childhood other than what he'd been able to piece together. She'd been orphaned young and sent to live with the Earl of Hereford. Clifford was the only sibling he knew about. Because of her rank and wealth, the esteem of her guardian, and her brother's position, Robbie had assumed her life had been easy. But privilege and favor, it seemed, did not replace a family.

Any more than war did. But it was the only way he knew, the only way he could make the deaths of the people he'd loved mean something.

He squeezed her tighter. "Nay," he said, wanting to ease her fears as quickly as possible with a kiss on her head. "Or at least only temporarily. It's almost morning, and unless you want the entire castle to know what we've been doing, you should return to your own bed before someone comes to check on you."

Her relief was visceral. He could feel it in the relaxing of her muscles as his thumb gently caressed her back while he held her.

She lay her cheek back down on his chest. "I don't mind."

"Well, I do." He lifted her chin to look into her eyes. "I will not have you maligned or subject to slurs for what I have done."

"For what *we* have done," she corrected. "I knew full well the consequences, Robbie. You do not need to protect me from them. I am not ashamed of what we did. No promises, remember?"

His mouth hardened. Aye, he did. But that didn't ease the frustration at being unable to make them—or assuage his guilt for taking her innocence. Guilt that for a man who purported not to worry about honor weighed surprisingly heavily. What a damned mess!

He told himself that at least he had not put the truce in jeopardy. Technically, he'd kept his word. He had not forced her. Although he doubted Clifford would appreciate the distinction. Nor would he if their roles were reversed.

Why the hell did he care? Clifford had wanted to kill him before. If Clifford kept his side of the bargain, Robbie would keep his: Rosalin would be returned to her brother unharmed. Nothing had changed. All this had done was make their parting more difficult.

Suddenly, her expression changed. She sat up, her eyes quickly darting from his chausses to the clothes that he'd discarded on the chair in his rush to climb back into bed with her. "You've been up."

It was not a question, but he nodded anyway. "Aye."

She waited, watching him silently, but he knew what she was asking.

"I sent Seton and Douglas with a message for your brother demanding an explanation."

Given their divergent interests, by sending both of them, he hoped to get an accurate answer. It also meant neither of them would guess what had happened, and he would be free from their judgment for a few days. Seton would be enraged. Why did he dread his partner's finding out so much? Since when did Seton's opinion matter? They never agreed on anything. But maybe this time, it was justified.

Her eyes widened to fairly insulting proportions. "You did?"

One side of his mouth curved. He supposed he deserved her shock. "Aye, you will have your few days."

She looked at him as if he'd just handed her the heavens. "You did this for me? For us? Does this mean . . ."

Robbie didn't know what it meant. He'd done it partly for her, and partly to ease his guilt. Hell, what he'd done to her last night could be considered retaliation enough.

But he knew what she was asking, and he wouldn't give her false hope.

She was already stretched out against him, but he drew her in tight and snug. Their eyes met. "It means we have a few days until they return, that is all. But beyond that . . ." He looked at her intently. "I have to do my job, Rosalin. No matter what that entails."

She nodded. "I understand."

Did she? He wasn't sure she did. Too much was resting on this. His duty would always come first. And he had no idea how he could reconcile the feelings he had for her with the determination to win Scotland's freedom and punish the oppressors that had driven him for years. For so long nothing had mattered in his life but war. He still wasn't sure there was room for anything else. How could an Englishwoman—even one sympathetic to his cause—fit in with that? "I don't know if I can give you what you want."

She blinked up at him. "But you care for me."

He wouldn't deny it. But caring wasn't what she wanted. She wanted a future.

"Then is this about my brother? About me being English?"

"Yes. No." He raked his fingers back through his hair. "Christ, isn't that enough?"

"It doesn't have to be. This can work, Robbie. I know it can. Just give it a chance."

When she looked at him like that, she could almost make him a believer. "I'll try."

She beamed up at him, and he felt something hot and tight catch in his throat. His chest swelled so hard it felt like it was going to explode. It had been so long since he felt anything like this, it took him a moment to realize it was happiness. Happiness that was so big and powerful it almost felt threatening.

All he could do was kiss her, which, as she was already halfway up his chest, simply required a little lifting of his arms to drag her up the other half.

He groaned at the warm, willing taste of her and at the sensation of having her stretched out on top of him.

Aye, he liked that. Liked it a whole hell of a lot.

His hand slid down her back, coming to rest on the gentle swell of her buttocks. He held her against him, letting her feel him thicken and lengthen as his tongue licked deeper and deeper into her mouth. She was like the sweetest ambrosia and he couldn't get enough.

But when she moaned and started to squirm, he had to pull away. "Christ, sweetheart, there isn't time."

She gave him a mischievous grin, but it was the glint in her eye that alarmed him. The glint that was far too wicked for a lass who'd just lost her virginity. "Are you sure?" She was still draped on top of him, and he swore the little vixen circled her hips against him purposefully. "I was rather hoping you would make it up to me."

His eyes narrowed. "What do you mean 'make it up to me'?"

She gave a careless shrug. "You know, about the second time being better than the first."

He flipped her on her back and came down on top of her to pin her with his body so quickly, all she could do was gasp in shock.

"How did you do that?" she demanded, half outraged and half awed.

He smiled slowly. "Practice." His combat skills were being put to unexpectedly good use. He glared down into her eyes. "What do you mean 'better'? I'm not sure what you were expecting, but *that* was bloody spectacular."

She had the impudence to appear surprised. "Was it? How should I know when I have nothing to compare it to? But if you aren't up for the challenge, I understand."

She started to try to roll out from under him, but he wasn't about to let her go anywhere. No self-respecting Scotsman would let a slur like that go unpunished.

Taking her wrists, he pinned them above her head and proceeded to kiss, lick, and rake his teeth gently against her neck until she started to shiver and shudder.

"Oh, I'm up for it," he whispered huskily in her ear. "*Very* up for it." He slid his length up and down between her legs until she wasn't just shivering and shuddering, she was shaking. "Perhaps we have time for a lesson after all."

"Very well, but don't take too long."

His gaze met hers with a wicked gleam of his own. "Aye, well in that case I suspect you are going to be disappointed."

He intended to punish her with the torture of anticipation.

Only when he saw the amusement twinkling in her eyes did he realize he'd been maneuvered. But by that point he was already circling one very pink and very tight nipple with his thumb, she was making those breathy little gasps, and he no longer gave a shite.

Rosalin was close. The feel of him big and deep inside her—filling her—as she rode him like a stallion was unlike anything she'd ever imagined. It was wild, freeing, and strangely empowering, knowing that she was in control of the powerful warrior beneath her.

He held her hips, guiding her as she rode the thick club of his erection up and down, taking him deep and hard, finding the perfect rhythm for her pleasure.

It had started out slow. Languorously slow as she wanted to savor every sensation, every thick inch of his body stretching and filling hers. But then it had quickened, until she was moving over him at a frenzied gallop.

When her pace reached the breaking point, she arched her back and cried out as her body started to fly. She was shaking and shattering, chanting his name in a soft whimper as the flood of heat rushed free.

She thought the sensation couldn't get any sweeter, but she should have known better. The hands that were gripping her hips brought her down hard on top of him. He held her there, grinding her against him until she shattered again. It was deeper this time, and even more powerful. "Yes, oh God, yes, Robbie . . . !" She was mindless with passion, consumed by the pleasure overtaking her.

He was, too. She could feel him straining beneath her, the big body fighting for control. "That's it, *mo ghrá*. Christ, I can feel you squeezing me—"

He stopped, tensing right before he let out a roar and his pleasure shot deep inside her in hot, pulsing spasms.

She collapsed on top of his naked, hot, and slightly damp chest into a boneless, syrupy heap. She couldn't have found the strength to move even if Hannibal himself were knocking at the gate. She smiled, thinking that Robbie would appreciate her analogy.

She lay there in complete and utter contentment, savoring the simple pleasure of the heavy rise and fall of his chest under her cheek.

The past two days had been some of the happiest in her life, but this was her favorite of all. This was what she would remember forever. Being curled up on top of him, every inch of her body weary and sated from his lovemaking, his steely arm wrapped around her as if he would never let her go, with the heavy beat of his heart reverberating like a drum through her. She felt utterly connected and utterly contented.

"Well?" The deep, powerful voice held a note of expectation, and something else that she treasured for the gift it was: teasing.

She schooled her features into blank repose and managed to find the strength to tilt her face to meet his gaze. "I stand corrected. It *was* possible." When he'd rolled her into his lap and told her what she could do, she hadn't been so sure.

"And?"

She nodded, seeming to consider. "Yes, definitely an improvement."

He cocked a brow, challenging her assessment. Her stomach flipped. God, he was handsome. He looked every inch the brigand with his bed-rumpled hair, piercing blue eyes, dark stubble, and bruised right cheek, sustained in some kind of skirmish when he'd been riding out yesterday. There was a small cut, too, and she suspected he'd taken a blow to his still injured ribs as well, but he'd refused to let her "fuss" over him. Stubborn brute.

He told her little of what he'd done the past two days they had been at the castle. He rode out every day, she assumed to scout and do whatever it was he did to enforce the king's authority in the Borders. In the afternoons, he and his men practiced in the yard. Only at night did he come to her.

She feigned ambivalence. "How many times is that now? Three? Four?" *Five.*

His eyes narrowed, but she saw the glint of amusement. "I guess it depends on how you want to look at it. By my last count, eight."

Rosalin couldn't prevent the heat from rushing to her cheeks. The rogue! He was counting how many times he'd made her shatter!

She harrumphed and pursed her mouth primly. "Ah yes, well, maybe by the time you get to ten it will be, what did you call it . . . *enjoyable*?"

"*Spectacular*, brat." He gave her a playful swat on her backside. "You do wonders for a man's confidence."

Her mouth twisted to hold back a smile. "I wasn't aware you needed an improvement in that area. From what I can see from the window when you are practicing, you have plenty of confidence boosting going on out there."

He frowned until he realized to what she was referring, and then a broad smile curved his mouth.

The boyish grin slammed right into her heart. If she ever needed proof of how much he needed her, it was right there. For a moment, she could almost see what he might have been like had war not stolen everything away from him. Happy, relaxed, teasing.

"You're jealous," he said, looking much too pleased with himself.

"Don't be ridiculous."

She tried to toss her nose up in the air but he caught her chin. The amusement was gone from his expression. "You have no reason to be, Rosalin."

Admittedly, he'd paid little attention to the steady flock of women who seemed to find any manner of duties to attend to in the yard whenever the infamous Robbie Boyd was training with his men. But it was still difficult for her when the other women were out there, and she was once again watching him from a window. Only at night did he belong to her.

"I know," she said. "But can you blame me? They are free to watch you, while I am . . ." She shrugged. "I feel like I'm at Kildrummy again."

She could tell he didn't like the comparison. "I'm trying to protect you. It is safer for you in here when I cannot be with you."

"That's exactly what Cliff used to say."

He *definitely* didn't like that comparison.

But he surprised her with his response. Actually, he shocked her speechless. "Well, he was probably right. You had no business being in Scotland at such a time. What was he thinking to let you come?"

It must be snowing in hell: Robbie Boyd was in agreement with Lord Robert Clifford. It would be cause for celebration if the subject of that agreement weren't locking her up in a tower. He was staring at her, apparently waiting for her to answer. She pursed her mouth. "He didn't exactly agree to let me come visit."

He had an extremely discomfiting way of remaining dauntingly expressionless yet still conveying danger. "What do you mean?"

"My guardian, the earl of Hereford, was ordered to Scotland by the king, and I convinced him to take me along."

"Into the middle of a war?" he roared, his expression no longer so expression*less*.

"The war was over at the time, if you'll recall. Or at least it was thought to be over. Bruce's men were scattered. Bruce himself had fled Scotland."

"Aye, I seem to recall the period," he said dryly.

She bit her lip, embarrassed. Of course he did. "The countess and a number of other ladies were going; I saw no reason why I shouldn't join them. I hadn't seen Cliff in almost two years, and I missed him desperately. I knew he would keep me safe—and he did. Just like I know you will keep me safe."

He held her gaze, and she knew he was thinking of what had happened—or nearly happened—that night at camp with Uilleam. And no doubt about his sister. "Not always." His voice was oddly thick.

"No, not always. But no one is safe always. Even locked in a tower," she added with a wry smile. "And that is not a way to live."

He didn't say anything for a minute, and then switched the subject. "How old were you when your parents died?"

She propped her chin up on his broad chest and stared at him. It seemed like an innocuous question, but she got the feeling it was anything but. "I was four when my father died. My mother followed him to the grave before the year was out."

He appeared surprised—and troubled. "I didn't realize you were so young. There were just you and your brother?"

She nodded. "There were other babes, but all but one were lost in the womb or infancy. I had a brother who was a year older than me, but he died about a year before my father. Each death took a little of my mother's heart, and after my father died I think she just lost the will to go on." She smiled. "I missed her—or maybe the idea of her—for a long time. But in truth, Cliff was more of a mother to me. Mother, father, and brother all rolled up in one. I followed him around everywhere; I don't know how he tolerated it."

"But you were separated?"

She nodded, her face shadowing at the memory. "They had to drag me crying and screaming out of his arms when I was sent to live with the earl. I didn't understand why I could not be with Cliff while he went to squire. I was too young to understand about rights of wardship and marriage. But the de Bohuns were kind to me, and Cliff visited or sent for me when he could."

Absently, he twisted a lock of hair around his finger. "You were lonely, though."

She frowned, slightly taken aback by the observation. But then she shrugged. "Perhaps a little. More after I returned from a visit, especially after he married Maud and had the children. But with Cliff in the north and me in London, it had been some time since I'd seen any of them. I was only allowed to travel because of the wed—"

She stopped, feeling his muscles tense, and caught her

bottom lip with her teeth, cursing the inadvertent reminder.

"Because of your wedding?" he finished, surprisingly calmly.

She nodded, and peered into his eyes intently. "I meant what I said, Robbie. I will not marry him. No matter what happens."

Their eyes held. It was one of the rare times in the past two days that she'd referred to the uncertainty of their future—or whether they even had one. By unspoken agreement they'd avoided any discussion of what would happen when the Black Douglas and Sir Alex returned. It was as if neither one of them wanted to disturb the fragile peace they'd constructed around them with talk of retaliation, truces, her brother, or the war.

Did he want a future with her? He'd shown her in countless ways with his tenderness and gentleness that he loved her. But he'd never actually said the words. Nor, she was painfully aware, had he mentioned marriage.

Whatever his intentions were, Rosalin did not want to push. She knew she needed to give him time. He might not realize yet what he wanted. What she'd tried to do the past couple of days was show him how wonderful it could be, shower him with love, and make him see all that he'd been missing. How there was more to life than war. How he could still do his duty, fight for Scotland's independence, and carve out some happiness for himself. And how she could be a part of that.

There was more to him than the brutal war machine bent on vengeance, striking without thought. The reprieve he'd given her had proved the man she remembered still existed. But she was painfully aware that reprieve was only temporary. The men could return at any time.

Would he send her back or did he love her enough to fight to keep her, even if she was English and Robert Clifford's sister? Her deepest fear was that he would never be able to reconcile the two. And worse, that maybe he wasn't keeping her in this tower just to protect her but also because he was ashamed of her. That a relationship with an Englishwoman somehow diminished his reputation as the freedom fighter who despised all things English.

She tried to ignore the stab of disappointment when he didn't respond to her vow not to marry Sir Henry. Instead, he started to roll off the bed. "I need to return to my chamber." After the first night, he'd come to her.

"Already?" she asked, trying to hide her disappointment with a smile.

He saw through it anyway. "I'm riding out at dawn. Besides, I do not want to give Lady Joanna any reason to suspect that I am not enjoying the fine bed in her mother-in-law's chamber."

Rosalin suspected it was too late for that. She suspected Lady Joanna knew exactly whose bed he was enjoying.

She watched him dress in silence, wishing that their worlds did not feel so apart. The one he shared in here with her and the one he shared out there with everyone else that required strapping on armor and swords. Her eyes moved from the bruises on his ribs to the one on his face. "I hope you will not be returning with any more 'scratches'?"

One corner of his mouth lifted. "Not today, unless they are wielded by farm implements."

She gazed at him questioningly.

He grimaced. "One of my duties for the king is to listen to the disputes of the people when he cannot, which means a long morning listening to a bunch of squabbling between neighboring farmers."

"The Devil's Enforcer meting out justice?"

Her incredulity seemed to amuse rather than offend him. "Aye, well, it's only one of my duties—a very small part. My reputation is not in any danger."

She'd sat up in bed to watch him, and she realized his

gaze had fallen to her very thin chemise. Although he did not seem to possess a modest bone in his body (admittedly with good reason) and came to her bed completely naked (not that she was complaining), sensing her modesty, he had not pressed her to remove her chemise. But if his heated gaze on her barely covered breasts was any indication, she suspected that patience was almost at an end.

"Have you heard of the legal term *quid pro quo*?"

She translated the Latin in her head: this for that. She wrinkled her nose. "Nay."

He grinned. Perhaps if she hadn't been so excited by his next words, she would have noticed how slyly. "How would you like to go on a short hike later?"

She practically jumped out of the bed. "Really?"

That smile deepened. "Be ready at about three."

She nodded excitedly. "I will be."

He started out the door, but at the last minute he turned. "And Rosalin." Her eyes met his. "Make sure not to wear anything with too many ties."

She was left to ponder that for the remainder of the day.

Rosalin spun on him angrily, eyes flashing and hands on her hips. "You should be ashamed of yourself, Robert Boyd. You tricked me and brought me up here under false pretenses."

Robbie tried not to laugh, but she looked so adorable and outraged it wasn't easy. He gestured to the valley below them. "I promised you a short hike and a beautiful view. Did I not deliver both?"

If looks could kill, he'd be dead right now. "It's breathtaking. But you know very well it's not the view. It's the payment you've demanded in return that's the problem."

He shook his head, *tsk*ing. "I wouldn't use the term 'payment'; it sounds too . . ."

"Underhanded? Strong-arming? Unscrupulous?"

He grinned. "I was going to say formal. I prefer *quid pro*

quo. I give you a little something of this, you give me a little something of that. Everyone's happy."

"I'd hardly say stripping down naked in the middle of the day outside where anyone can happen upon us is 'a little something.'"

"We are up on a hilltop, surrounded by trees, with no one around for miles." A slight exaggeration, but he would hear anyone who tried to sneak up on them. "I thought it would be fun."

"Fun?" she exclaimed, practically sputtering. "Fun for *you*, you mean."

He had to grin at that. Damned right it would be fun for him. Even the thought of all that naked skin bared to his eyes in the sunlight made him hard. He shrugged as if it didn't matter. "That's all right. I thought you were more adventurous, but if you are too embarrassed by whatever it is you are intent on keeping hidden under that shift, we can return to the castle."

Aye, and he'd be lying dead with two very green daggers in his chest. "You are a horrible man who deserves every bit of your ruthless reputation."

He grinned harder. When it came to having her naked, she was probably right. He waited with surprising patience, when all he wanted to do was rip those clothes right off her and taste every inch of that naked skin. He was rewarded. A moment later she started furiously working the ties of her gown. She was calling him all kinds of names under her breath, but he didn't care. His pulse had stopped and his breath seemed lodged in his lungs as piece after piece of clothing fell at her feet.

He was in awe.

He was in rapture.

He was in . . .

Oh hell, he was in trouble. The past few days had been like a dream. He felt himself caught up in the magical web she'd spun around him and didn't know how he was going to get out. Didn't know whether he *wanted* to get out. Though he knew he shouldn't be encouraging her fantasy of a future between them, like Icarus to the sun, he was powerless to stay away from the warmth in her eyes. And the heat. That, he sure as hell couldn't stay away from.

She paused when she reached her shift. Their eyes met. The anger that he'd counted on to make her forget her embarrassment had faded. She looked at him uncertainly. But he was too far gone—and too damned aroused—to have pity.

"Take it off, sweetheart. I want to see every inch of you." His voice was husky and dark and full of sensual promise.

"What about you?"

She was stalling, but as his being naked worked with his plan, he let her get away with it. He removed his weapons first, then his leather armor and boots, and finally his shirt and braies. As always, he was conscious of her eyes on him when he undressed, which only added to his arousal. By the time he was standing naked in front of her, his cock was so hard it was practically pounding a hole in his ribs.

She might have been a maid a few days ago, but the heat in her gaze as her eyes roamed over his naked body was anything but innocent. When she got to his manhood and stopped, and unconsciously licked her bottom lip, he had to grit his teeth against the surge of lust that pulsed through him.

If she ever realized the sensual power she wielded over him, he feared she could have him following her around like an eager pup with one crook of that slender white finger.

"Is that better?" he challenged.

Her eyes skated over him again, getting that soft, heavy-lidded look of arousal that he'd come to crave. She gave a quick nod and with a deep breath, lifted the linen chemise over her head and let it drop in a pool at her feet.

He sucked in his breath, his eyes slowly scanning the delicate feminine curves of the lithe beauty before him. Christ, she was even more beautiful than he'd imagined from the pieced-together views he'd managed. Her legs were long, her waist slim, her breasts firm and perfectly round. And her skin . . . It was incredible. As smooth and flawless as freshly churned cream. He knew the baby-softness, the velvety feel, and when he dared to run the back of his finger over her breast, he groaned.

Realizing her cheeks were pink and her eyes had dropped to her feet, he cupped her chin and forced her gaze to his. "You are perfect, *mo ghrá*. There is no cause for you to be embarrassed."

But she was. And as jittery as a filly before a storm. Not a bad analogy for what was to come.

"Make love to me, Robbie," she whispered.

It was the sweetest plea he'd ever heard, and one he sure as hell wasn't going to refuse. "Aye, my lady. I intend to." In one smooth motion, he swept her up into his arms, cradling her like a child. Although the sensation set off by the contact of her naked skin to his left him no doubt of her womanliness.

She laughed in surprise and gazed up at him with so much emotion in her eyes it made his chest hurt. He bent down to pick up the plaid she'd worn around her shoulders and carried her toward the large tree.

She latched her arms around his neck. "You'll hurt your ribs carrying me like this."

"My ribs are fine. And the day I can't carry a slip of a lass like you is the day I'll resign my title at the Games forever."

She grinned. "I suppose there are a few benefits to that title of yours—other than the more obvious ones."

He had no idea what she was talking about. His brows knit together in question.

She rolled her eyes and shook her head. "You'll get no more compliments from me. I'm sure you are well aware of how the ladies view that impressive physique of yours."

He grinned wickedly. "Oh, that."

"Yes, *that*, you wretch." She swiped at him, but as he decided at that moment to put her down on the plaid he'd spread out on a bed of leaves, she missed.

He grinned down at her. "You hit like a lass."

"I *am* a 'lass,' in case you hadn't noticed."

He gave her a long, hot look up and down. "Oh, I've noticed."

He bent on one knee and leaned over her. She looked so beautiful it took his breath away. Naked, in a bed of leaves, hair spread out wildly behind her, she looked like a wood nymph in some kind of erotic dream. Except it wasn't a dream. This was real.

The moment of playfulness was gone. "There is only one lady whose opinion matters to me," he said truthfully, bringing her hand to his lips.

She smiled, the knightly gesture obviously surprising her as much as it did him.

He kissed her then. Gently. Tenderly. Giving free rein not just to the passion, but also to the powerful feelings that seemed to give it much more force.

He worshipped her body with his mouth and tongue, leaving no inch of her unclaimed. Her skin was like the sweetest cream, and he drank her in like a man dying of thirst. Like a dying man. That's what she was—ambrosia for his soul.

He feasted on her, burying his face between her velvety thighs and lapping her creamy softness. He licked and nuzzled, flicked and sucked until her beautiful breasts arched into the sun and her thighs tightened around his neck. He held her to his mouth as she shattered, crying out his name.

When she could open her eyes, he gave her a wicked grin. "I told you it would be fun."

She gave him a look that made him feel like he was an incorrigible lad of about five. But then a decidedly wicked gleam appeared. "It's certainly about to be." Their eyes met. "I should warn you that I can be quite merciless as well."

He smiled, genuinely amused. "You can?"

She nodded and lazily started to run her soft fingertips over the hard-muscled bands of his stomach, her wrist passing dangerously close to the powerful head of his erection. She was teasing him, and he didn't think he liked it. Or rather, he liked it too much.

She pushed him onto his back with a gentle shove and rolled on top of him, straddling him. At first he thought she would impale herself on him again, but instead, she started trailing soft little kisses down his chest. Down his chest and over the same bands of muscle she'd just teased.

His stomach dropped. Could she intend . . .

"Do you remember what you told me that first night at camp?"

He swore. His heart started to pound with something akin to fear. "Nay."

The look she shot him from his stomach, her mouth achingly close to his cock, called him a liar. "You told me I could suck your . . ." She blushed, unable to get the word out.

Oh Christ. Every muscle in his body jumped. Hell, his skin jumped—or he jumped out of it. He had to fight to keep himself from grabbing her. All he could manage was a groan.

"I think I should like to," she whispered.

And then she kissed him. She moved her soft, pink lips over the big, fat head of his cock and slowly lowered her mouth.

He did jump out of his skin then. Every ounce of blood pounded through his body. He'd never been so aroused in his life. He wouldn't have moved if the entire English army were climbing up that hill.

He prayed for strength. But God wasn't giving him any.

And she was just as merciless as she'd promised. She brought him to his fucking knees.

"Show me," she whispered, holding him in her hand.

And he did. He lifted her head over him and told her how to milk him. How to lave him with her tongue and take him deep in her throat and pump the length that wouldn't fit with her hand. He watched her take him in her warm, moist mouth, watched as those beautiful pink lips stretched around him, until he felt the first pulse ratchet through him. And then he took her with his body, making love to her under the trees as if he could hold on to this day forever.

Twenty-three

❧

Forever was over too damned soon. When they returned to the castle at dusk, Robbie was informed by one of the guards that Seton and Douglas were waiting in the Hall.

He probably should have sent Rosalin upstairs, but she ran ahead of him so excitedly, he didn't have the heart to call her back.

He was only a step or two behind her when she burst into the Hall and rushed toward Seton. "Was it as I said, Sir Alex? Did my brother explain that he had nothing to do with the attack in the forest?"

Robbie already knew the answer. One glance at Douglas's black visage told him.

"Aye, my lady," Seton answered. "It was as you said." He turned to face Robbie. "Lord Clifford knew nothing about de Spenser's plans to attack the camp. In fact, he was furious. Before we arrived Sir Henry had been reprimanded, ordered back to England, and," he looked back at Rosalin, "the betrothal dissolved."

Rosalin shot him a very pleased "I told you so" look.

Seton frowned, his gaze sliding back and forth between Rosalin and Robbie. Robbie swore inwardly; his partner was too damned perceptive. A trait that came in handy on missions, but not right now.

Robbie turned to Douglas. "Are you sure?"

"Where Clifford is concerned? Never. I don't trust the bastard." His gaze shot uncomfortably to Rosalin, and his mouth thinned as the next words seemed pried out of his mouth. "But he seemed in earnest. He's worried about his sister. He wants her back. He told me to remind you of your promise."

Robbie's jaw clenched. He didn't realize it until Seton's eyes narrowed on him again.

Fortunately, Joanna Douglas, who had been visiting her family that afternoon (one of the reasons he'd decided to slip away with Rosalin), picked that opportune moment to arrive.

"You're back!" She raced into her husband's waiting arms. He spun her around (having care for her round stomach), kissed her, and smiled—the latter causing Rosalin's eyes to round in surprise.

"Miss me, *mo ghrá*?" Douglas asked.

Joanna laughed. "Perhaps a bit. How was your journey to Peebles?"

Douglas restored his dark visage with a frown. "Not well. Seton was just filling in Boyd and the . . ."

"Lady Rosalin," Joanna provided helpfully, sending Rosalin an apologetic smile for her husband's rudeness.

But Rosalin was so happy, she didn't appear to notice.

"There's more good news," Seton said with a hard look at Boyd. "Clifford will have the silver by the end of the week." His gaze turned to Rosalin. "You will be going home soon, my lady."

Robbie hoped he was the only one who noticed the despair that dulled the excited sparkle from her eyes. "That is good news indeed." She managed a smile, and Robbie knew she was struggling not to look at him.

He was glad she didn't, as he didn't have an answer for the unspoken question in her eyes.

After Lady Joanna left to see to the evening meal, Rosalin excused herself to return to her chamber. Robbie wanted to follow her, but he needed some time to think. He watched her leave the room, but when he looked back,

it was to see Seton watching him. Watching that grew
steadier and darker as the evening progressed.

Robbie tried to ignore it, but he knew that sooner or
later there was going to be hell to pay.

It came sooner. The meal was barely under way when
Seton cornered Robbie on his way back from relieving
himself of some of the Douglas ale. He'd gone outside
rather than use the third-floor garderobe—a decision he
was now regretting.

More distracted by his thoughts than he realized, in the
shadowed torchlight, Robbie thought the man who stepped
out in front of him was one of the guardsmen on patrol.
When he was slammed up against the stone wall of the
castle with a forearm across his throat, however, he realized his mistake.

"Tell me you didn't do what I think you did." Seton
jammed his arm harder for emphasis. "Tell me."

Seton's mouth was pulled pack in a feral snarl and his
eyes pinned Robbie with murderous rage. Robbie had seen
him angry more times than he could count—hell, half the
times he'd purposefully incited the anger—but never like
this. Which could explain Robbie's slower-than-usual reaction, and the fact that he didn't break the arm that had
him pinned when he shoved up against it and twisted to
the side to free himself.

Although he had to admit it might not have been that
easy. He rubbed his throat, staring at the other man in the
shadowy darkness. Seton hadn't worn mail since the early
days of training, but his arm had felt as if it were covered
in it. Hell, *made* of it. Seton might not be built as powerfully as Robbie, but he was bigger and stronger than most,
with years of hard-wrought battle muscle on him. Robbie
had realized it, but not with quite so much force.

Annoyed, he glowered back at his partner. "You can
think whatever the hell you like, but I don't have to tell you
a damned thing."

"You're right. You don't. I already know the truth. I just didn't want to believe it. I didn't think even you could be so dishonorable as to defile an innocent lass. But you proved me wrong, you bloody bastard!"

Robbie was ready for him this time. But cornered as he was between the staircase and the river with the castle at his back and Seton at his front, there wasn't enough room for him to maneuver and completely evade the powerful fist that came pummeling toward his teeth, or the one that followed with a quick uppercut to his jaw from the left. Robbie retaliated with a hard blow of his own to the gut and a knee to Seton's side that pushed him back far enough for Robbie to get in better position.

One of the guardsmen came rushing over, but Robbie yelled at him—all of them—to get back to duty.

The distraction gave his blood a moment to calm. "You don't want to do this," Robbie warned Seton. "You won't win."

"The hell I don't. Someone needs to fight for that girl's honor. I won't let you get away with this. You might be the strongest man in Scotland, but that doesn't make you right—or invincible."

Robbie was used to Seton's shiny-armor shite, but something about it this time angered him—maybe because it was deserved. "You always have to be the sanctimonious knight, don't you, Seton? Even when it has nothing to do with you."

"It has everything to do with me. You've shamed all of us with what you have done. You've made us into the brigands and barbarians they accuse us of being. She was our hostage, not a means of retribution. Do you hate Clifford so much that you have to ruin his sister?" Seton was seething now, fists clenching at his sides, circling and waiting for an opening. "The same sister who saved our lives? What the hell is wrong with you?"

Robbie wasn't as immune to his partner's jibes as he

wanted to be. All the guilt he'd been trying to bury the past few days bubbled to the surface—nay, it roared to the surface. His chest pinched uncomfortably. "This has nothing to do with Clifford."

"The hell it doesn't. It's always about Clifford or the English."

Seton's certainty planted a seed of doubt in his own mind. But no, damn it, it hadn't been about revenge. "I told you I cared about her."

"If you truly cared about her, you would have kept your bloody hands off her and returned her a maid. You knew nothing could come of this, but still you took her innocence. That isn't care, that's selfishness. Maybe if it were lust I could understand. But I know you too well, and you've never been consumed with anything other than vengeance. The only thing you care about, the only thing you've ever cared about, is destroying the English. I just didn't think you'd use an innocent lass to do it. Do you even have a damned conscience anymore?"

The question seemed to hang uncomfortably in the air, even though it was clear that Seton didn't expect an answer. Instead he attacked, spinning and whipping his leg around in a sweeping kick that would have taken Robbie to the ground if he hadn't been the one to teach him the move himself. It did, however, knock him off balance enough for Seton to land a hard hit to the side of his head. A blow that snapped Robbie's head back and sent blood trickling from his ear. A blow that left no doubt of Seton's intent. This was no training, no sparring and grappling between partners. This was all-out war.

The rush of battle surged through him. The next time Seton attacked, Robbie was ready. He blocked the blow that came toward his head with his arm, turned, and using Seton's momentum flipped him onto the ground. He inflicted a few more blows while trying to get a knee down on Seton's chest. But Robbie had taught his partner well.

Seton was able to angle his body away enough to avoid solid contact, while at the same time hooking his foot around Robbie's leg to knock him to the side.

Robbie turned it into a roll and sprang back to his feet. Seton had done the same and came at him again. They exchanged jabs, punches, and hard strikes of the knee until they were both breathing hard, bloody, and bruised.

It was the longest fight Robbie had had in years. He tried to end it by leaving his injured side open, but Seton refused to take the bait. He was using his strengths—his quickness and youth—against Robbie, and for once, showing patience. Seton was proving a formidable opponent, and under different circumstances Robbie might have been proud of it. But right now all he wanted to do was shut him up.

The verbal jabs Seton was getting in in between those of his fists were landing just as hard. "What the hell did she do to deserve this? She helped us, and this is how you repay her?" Seton followed the question with a blow to Robbie's ribs that would have broken a few more bones had he not twisted out of the way.

Hooking Seton's feet, he tried to wrap his arm behind his back, but Seton dropped, turned, and jabbed the arm free with an elbow first to his stomach and then to his eye. In response, Robbie lifted his knee hard into Seton's face, hearing an unmistakable crack.

"Was it worth it, Raider?" Seton taunted, blood pouring from his now broken nose. "Was your revenge against a woman part of your plan?"

Robbie's muscles flared, guessing what he was about to say. "Don't say it."

Despite his battered face, broken nose, and bloody mouth, Seton smiled. "What? The truth is ugly, isn't it? Did ruining this girl make up for what was done to your sister?"

Robbie snapped, rage turning to mad fury in an instant.

He went from wanting to shut Seton up to wanting to kill him.

He lost control and went after Seton with everything he had, losing all patience in the effort to destroy his opponent. It was the very lesson he'd imparted on Seton hundreds of times not to do, but which he ignored, confident that his physical strength would win in the end like it always did.

No one could beat him. No one. He was proving it, too, pummeling Seton with blow after blow from every direction, hammering him to a bloody pulp.

But still his partner would not admit defeat.

Finally, whipping his leg around in a hard kick, he sent Seton to the ground on his knees. Robbie wrapped him in a chokehold with the crook of his right arm from behind. He moved his left hand into position at the back of his head. A few seconds of pushing and squeezing and Seton would lose consciousness.

It was one of Robbie's most overpowering moves. No one could defend against it. He was too strong. Once his arms became locked and the other hand went into position, there was nothing an opponent could do.

Or so he thought. He had his left hand into position at the back of Seton's head and was about to start pressing forward, when Seton reached up, grabbed Robbie's two smallest fingers, and snapped them back hard. Hard enough to break them. Robbie let out a grunt of pain—there was a reason one of the most painful and effective means of torture was done with fingers. He released his left arm just enough for Seton to lever that arm down. With the added pressure of his other hand, Seton used the momentum to turn Robbie completely around and down on the ground with a hook to his leg. He pressed down on Robbie's back with his knee, pulling his arm back with enough force to almost pop it out of the joint. The pain was indescribable. Pinned, Robbie's arm was fully ex-

tended, and Seton had leveraged his body so that all his
weight locked against it. If Robbie moved, his arm would
break. "Concede."

Robbie gritted his teeth until tears were in his eyes. Rage
and disbelief converged in stubborn refusal.

Seton extended his legs to stretch the arm infinitesi-
mally, but enough to make Robbie groan.

"Don't make me break it."

Seven years of Robbie's trying to grind him into the dirt
had given Seton's words a biting edge. Robbie did not
doubt that he would do it.

Still, he resisted until black spots appeared in his eyes,
sweat poured down his face, and his teeth felt like they
were going to shatter from clenching. But eventually he
uttered the words he hadn't spoken in over fifteen years.
Since the man who'd taught him everything he knew about
fighting, his father's former henchman, Cormal, had
bested him. "I concede."

Seton let him go and Robbie felt the air surge back into
this lungs. He rolled to his side, cradling his shoulder and
arm until the pain receded to a bearable throb and burn.

He heard Seton struggling to his feet, but his partner's
equally battered state didn't make Robbie feel any better.
The rage that had given Seton the opening was still snapping around inside him dangerously. He'd lost. To Seton.
He couldn't bloody believe it.

By all rights, Seton should be gloating, but all Robbie
could see when he stood and faced him was cold condemnation. "I'm done making excuses for you. I can't do this
anymore. Find yourself another partner."

For seven years Robbie had longed to hear those words.
Their pairing in the Highland Guard had been ill fated
from the beginning. Still, he was surprised how much the
words grated. "I made a mistake. Is that what you want
me to say? I'll fucking marry her, if that will assuage your

knightly sensibilities. God knows that would be revenge enough on Clifford."

The shocked cry that had risen to her lips when Rosalin saw the two bloodied men died in her throat—and then in her heart.

She froze as Robbie's words washed over her in an icy veil of hurt and disbelief. She didn't know what was worse—to hear the words of marriage she'd so longed to hear uttered so crudely, or to hear that marriage linked to revenge on her brother.

He didn't mean it, she told herself. He couldn't mean it.

"How do you plan to do that?" Seton said. "She's a *hostage*, remember? Clifford will never let you have her, and if you attempt to keep her, he'll come at you with everything he has—which he might do anyway if he discovers what you've done. Do you think he'll keep the truce if he learns you've violated his sister? You know how important this mission is. You were supposed to be keeping the Borders under control, and instead you are going to unleash a firestorm. Just when the king is getting a foothold in the Tayside, he's going to have to come clean up your damned mess."

"He didn't violate me." Rosalin spoke in a whisper, but both men turned to her as if she'd announced her presence with the boom of a death knell. "And as I told Robbie before, I have no intention of telling my brother anything. Your truce is perfectly safe."

She lifted her chin, tried to control the shaking that threatened to consume her limbs, and descended the stairs as regally as a . . . princess. Both men watched her approach with varying levels of discomfort—Sir Alex with embarrassment and Robbie with two things she'd never thought to see on his face: shame and fear. He should be feeling both for what he'd just said.

"I decided to come down for the evening meal." She

looked at Robbie and despite her hurt, felt her heart lurch
at the sight of his face. "When I didn't see you inside, I
changed my mind. On my way back upstairs, I heard
someone shout." She eyed them both, taking in every
bruised, bloody, and battered inch of them. They looked
horrible. Noticing the unnatural position of Robbie's fingers on his left hand, she had to force her feet not to move
to him. "I don't need to ask what you were fighting about.
I heard."

Sir Alex recovered first and stepped forward. "I am
sorry you had to see this, my lady. Sorry for all of this. You
never should have been here in the first place. If you wish
to return to England now, I will take you."

Rosalin's breath caught in surprise. She looked at
Robbie, expecting him to argue, but his mouth was
clamped shut. He didn't seem to want to meet her gaze.
What did it mean? What had happened here? Why wasn't
he trying to reassure her? And why was he looking so
guilty?

He cared about her—loved her—this couldn't be about
revenge on her brother. He hadn't meant it. A couple of
hours ago he was teasing her and they were making love in
the sunshine.

She turned to Alex and shook her head. "Thank you, Sir
Alex, but that is not necessary. I do not wish to return to
England." Out of the corner of her eye, she saw Robbie
relax. The relief on his face told her she'd been right: he did
care. The question was how much. A question that could
not be answered with Sir Alex standing in watch. "Would
you give us a few moments, please?" she asked him. "I
think there are some things Robbie and I need to discuss."

Sir Alex looked as if he wanted to disagree, but after a
long glance at Robbie, he headed off toward the river, presumably to clean himself up.

As soon as he was gone, Rosalin couldn't wait any longer. She crossed the distance to Robbie in a few steps and put her hand on his battered face. "Are you all right?"

He pulled away—jerked away, actually. "I'm fine, Rosalin. I'm not a child—I don't need comforting."

She flinched. Were his words not enough, now he needed to rebuff her concern?

He swore and dragged his fingers—the uninjured ones on his right hand—through his hair. "Damn it. I'm sorry. This isn't your fault. None of this is your fault. It's mine. I'm not sure how much of that you saw or heard. We fought. I lost and said some things I didn't mean."

What hadn't he meant, that he was going to marry her, or the reason? Suddenly her mouth dropped open, realizing what else he'd said. "You lost?"

She wished the words back when his face darkened. To say that it had to be a blow to his pride was an understatement, and the damage to his pride was obviously as raw and battered as his body.

His shoulders tensed. "Aye. He said some things to make me angry, I lost control, and he took advantage of my mistake, but that is no excuse. He beat me. Damn it, he beat me."

"Surely you've lost before?"

"In that kind of contest? Not in a long time."

Rosalin was quiet for a moment, watching the emotions war on his face. "What is really bothering you, the fact that you were beaten or that Sir Alex was the one to do it?" He gave her a hard look that told her the question had struck a nerve. "Somehow I don't think if it had been the Black Douglas you would be so angry."

His jaw hardened until the muscle in his jaw ticced, which she took to be agreement.

She took a step closer to him and put a hand on his arm, relieved when this time he did not shake her off. "I heard what he said about not being your partner anymore."

Belatedly, she remembered she wasn't supposed to know

about his part in Bruce's phantoms, but he didn't appear to notice. "It's for the best."

"I feel to blame. I know Sir Alex was trying to defend my honor, but I never meant to get between you."

"You didn't. This has nothing to do with you—not really. The problems with Seton and me have been building for a long time."

"But he's your friend. I know how difficult—"

"He isn't my friend." He looked at her as if she were mad. "He's bloody Eng—"

He stopped so suddenly, the silence that followed seemed as loud as a clap of thunder.

"English," she finished softly.

He swore and tilted her chin to meet his gaze again. "That's not what I meant, Rosalin. I'm just angry. I say a lot of things I don't mean when I'm angry."

"Like about marrying me to take revenge on my brother?"

He grimaced, which due to the injuries on his face must have caused him some pain. "Aye, like that. I didn't mean it."

"Which part? Marrying me or doing so out of revenge?"

Everything seemed to still: the cool breeze in the night air, the flicker from the torchlight shadowing his face, the sound of their breathing, even the drum of her heartbeat. Her eyes scanned his stony expression, looking for some kind of crack, some kind of softening. She was doing exactly what she hoped she would not have to do—push— but with Cliff about to fulfill his side of the truce, time was running out.

He cupped her face with his good hand—the one bloodied only at the knuckles—and stared down into her eyes. His expression did soften then, and she felt hope swell in her chest. "God knows, I have no right, and it would be a foolish thing to do for many reasons, but aye, if it were possible, I would marry you. The idea of sending you away . . ." His voice grew so tight, it cracked. "It's killing me. I would love nothing more than to tell your brother to go to the devil, but too much is resting on this damned truce. We're close, Rosalin. I can feel it. I can't do anything to jeopardize that. It's too important." He paused. "I can't let their deaths be for nothing; I can't let them down."

Of course he couldn't. She understood, probably more than he realized. But it was what else he'd said that caused happiness to swell inside her like a big ball of sunshine. A broad smile curved her lips. "Do you mean it?"

Wariness flickered back into his gaze. "Wait, sweetheart—don't get carried away. Did you hear what I said? Only if it were possible."

"I heard what you said." He wanted to marry her. He did love her. Needing to be in his arms, she buried her head against his leather-clad chest and waited for his arms to wrap around her. They did. Even dirty and with the stench of battle upon him, she savored the warmth and masculine strength. But realizing he was probably confused, she pulled back. "It *is* possible, don't you see? I will write to my brother."

For the second time in less than five minutes he looked at her as if she were crazed. "Just like that, and you think he will welcome me into the family?" He laughed without any humor. "It would be a cold day in hell before Clifford sanctioned the marriage of his sister to a 'rebel' Scot."

She shook her head. "You are wrong. My brother loves me and will do anything to see to my happiness."

"But he *despises* me. He will never agree to a marriage between us. I can think of only one person in Christendom who he would be less likely to betroth to his beloved sister—and Douglas is already married. You don't understand, Rosalin—you have not been a part of this."

"It is you who do not understand. I do not deny the truth of what you have said. He will be angry at first, refuse, and probably try everything he can think of to talk me out of it. But once he understands that I love you, and that you lo—um, care about me, he will agree."

If he noticed her slip of the tongue, he didn't show it. "How can you be so sure?"

"Because I know one thing: the love he has for me is stronger than the hate he bears you."

"I wouldn't be so sure of that."

Her heart pinched. She stared up at him, and for a moment she felt a flicker of doubt. Love was stronger than hate. If he loved her, he would know that—wouldn't he? She gazed up at him and said solemnly, "But I *am* sure of it. Let me write Cliff, and you'll see."

He studied her face, and she could sense him relenting.

"What harm is there?" she pressed. "The worst he can say is no. He won't do anything while you have me."

He didn't look so convinced.

The pad of his thumb ran back and forth over her bottom lip. "I don't want you to be disappointed."

She brightened, sensing victory. "I won't be. I may have to go to him when the truce is settled and persuade him, but eventually he will agree."

From the way his arms tightened, she could tell he didn't like that idea. His lowered his mouth to hers in a brief caress that followed the trail of his thumb. She suspected only the cuts and bruises prevented him from deepening it.

When he lifted his head, his eyes met hers. "Write your letter, Rosalin, and we will see what your brother has to say."

Twenty-four

The wait for Cliff's response seemed interminable.

Rosalin knew it was partly because Robbie had not been to her solar since the night of the horrible fight with Sir Alex. She'd slept in his arms after he'd washed and had someone tend his wounds, but they had not made love. She'd assumed it was due to his injuries, but now, two days later, she suspected it had more to do with Sir Alex and his not-so-subtle condemnation.

Whether Robbie wanted to admit it or not, whatever had happened in the yard that night had kept him from her bed. He blamed his removal from the tower on some problems with his men, and later on the return of the elder Lady Douglas (James's stepmother) and Douglas's sister Elizabeth, but Rosalin knew it was more than that. The realities that he'd been able to ignore while Sir Alex and Douglas were away were now staring at him full force. Neither man hid his feelings on the matter.

Rosalin understood that his friends' disapproval weighed heavily on him, and it only made her more eager for her brother's response. Even though Robbie spent as much time with her as he could when not busy with his duties, she missed the closeness and the reassurance of sleeping in his arms.

The only consolation was that he seemed just as miserable about the arrangement as she. The longing in his eyes when he looked at her almost managed to quiet the doubts that had risen from his harsh words to Sir Alex. Almost.

With the return of the Douglas ladies, Rosalin's confinement to the tower was not quite as lonely. Elizabeth Douglas was charming, beautiful, and as refined as any lady of Rosalin's acquaintance in England—in other words, she couldn't have been more *unlike* her terrifying brother. At one and twenty Elizabeth was sophisticated for her years, and Rosalin wasn't surprised to learn that she'd spent much of the last decade in France.

In some ways it made her as much of an outsider as Rosalin. Elizabeth had been uprooted from her friends—including Joanna—at a young age and returned to Scotland a stranger. Whereas Rosalin longed for the quiet, simple life of the countryside, she could tell that Elizabeth missed the excitement of her life at the French court.

But Rosalin wondered if there was something disturbing her. Elizabeth spent an inordinate amount of time staring out of the window as if expecting someone to come riding into the yard.

The elder Lady Douglas was polite, but she seemed to share her son's feelings—if not his animosity—toward Cliffords. As she'd spent most of the time in bed recovering from an illness she'd suffered while traveling, however, her stepdaughter was free to spend as much time as she liked with their "hostage." Joanna had taken to joining them after the midday meal to sew for an hour or two before she had to return to her duties.

Today they were in the solar Joanna shared with her husband on the second floor above the Hall. It was the most spacious chamber, with an enormous four-poster bed, a large fireplace, two large cushioned chairs, a desk, a bench, and two small windows that overlooked the courtyard. As in the other solars, the furnishings were surprisingly fine and comfortable for the castle of the family of a man who was supposedly an outlaw.

Since Cliff's garrison at the nearby destroyed Douglas Castle had been sent home the year before, he had not attempted to fill it again. The English garrisons in the surrounding areas made periodic sweeps of Douglas, but Elizabeth told her they were more for show than anything else. The rebels left when warned and returned as soon as the English soldiers were gone. Cliff and King Edward might not agree, but the land had effectively been conceded to the Scots.

Elizabeth was asking about Rosalin's previous trip to Scotland when the door suddenly burst open and the Black Douglas stormed into the room. Like Robbie, he had a way of making a big room suddenly feel small. Unlike Robbie, however, it made Rosalin's skin tingle with fright, not excitement.

She did her best to sink into her chair and disappear. But it wasn't necessary, Sir James Douglas only had eyes for his wife. He strode over and leaned down to brush a kiss over her cheek. "I'm sorry to disturb your *rest*, but I wanted to let you know that I'll be riding out for a few hours."

From the way he said *rest*, Rosalin could tell he was displeased to find his wife out of bed. The Black Douglas's tender affection toward his wife still took some getting used to. Around Joanna, he seemed almost human.

Joanna brushed off the reprimand with a roll of her eyes. "Is something wrong?"

Rosalin didn't miss the way his gaze slid in her direction. "Nay, just a short scouting trip. I'll be back before nightfall."

Joanna frowned, looking as if she wanted to question him further. But she must have sensed that he would not elaborate with Rosalin in the room and let the matter drop.

"No standing on your feet for too long today, *mo ghrá*," Douglas said sternly, but with something in his voice that bespoke real concern. "You should not overtire yourself. You need to rest."

Joanna reached up and put a hand on her husband's glowering face. "I'm fine, James. The babe is fine."

Their eyes held, and something so strong and powerful passed between them that Rosalin had to turn away, feeling as if she were intruding.

A moment later, the terrifying warrior left the room and Rosalin could breathe again.

Joanna must have noticed her reaction. She smiled. "You have nothing to fear from my husband, you know. He would never hurt you. He would never hurt *any* woman."

Although she sensed that Joanna spoke true, Rosalin had heard too many terrifying stories and was too cognizant of his hatred toward her brother to ever be completely relaxed in Sir James Douglas's presence. The same could be said for Robbie, she realized, but he was different. She'd seen the noble side of him before she'd heard the stories.

"Jamie has always had a chivalrous streak," Elizabeth said. "Remember when we were caught on the other side of the burn near Boradleeholm, and the swell made it too wide to cross, and he and Thommy decided to carry us—"

She stopped so suddenly that Rosalin looked up from her needlework. Elizabeth's faerie-princess-beautiful face looked as if it were made of ice and about to crack.

Joanna covered the awkward pause. "Aye, they carried us across. I remember."

Elizabeth recovered and managed a small smile. "It was a long time ago. We were children." She seemed to be telling herself this.

"Aye, but the important things do not change," Joanna said softly.

Elizabeth met her sister-in-law's gaze for an instant, and then turned away as if she didn't want to hear whatever she was trying to say. She turned to Rosalin. "Jo is right. You have nothing to fear from my brother—reputation notwithstanding." She smiled cheekily. "Besides, with the way Boyd looks at you, I suspect he'd kill James for frowning at you the wrong way."

Rosalin tried not to blush but couldn't help but be pleased that Elizabeth had noticed. Elizabeth stood near the window peering out into the yard. "Your Boyd is quite handsome in a fierce, imposing sort of way. Every time he arrives with James he causes quite a stir. All the young women from the village are quite put out, you know. There's been a lot of talk."

"Gossip, you mean," Joanna said sternly. "You should not listen to the maidservants, Lizzie."

Rosalin was dying to ask her what they were saying but managed to refrain.

Elizabeth moved away from the window, and Rosalin had to resist the urge to jump up and change places with her, realizing that Robbie was probably outside.

"How else would I learn anything?" Elizabeth grinned.

They spoke of other matters for a while, but eventually Rosalin managed to find a way to ask Joanna something that had piqued her curiosity the first time she'd heard James Douglas greet his wife, and then again today. "Joanna, what does *mo ghrá* mean?"

Joanna smiled. "It's a term of affection—an endearment. It means 'my love.' "

Rosalin felt her heart rise up high in her chest and lock in her throat, cutting off her breath. *My love.* Not "my beautiful one." The sneaky devil! He'd lied to her! *Lied!*

And she'd never been more happy in her life. He did love her. Her unease about his reasons for marrying faded away, and all that remained was happiness and excitement. She couldn't wait for Cliff's response to arrive.

Robbie felt as if his soul had been trapped halfway between heaven and hell, and the devil and God were battling over his fate. The wait for Clifford's response was agonizing. The separation from Rosalin was unbearable. Literally. As in he couldn't bear it any longer.

To hell with Seton! To hell with Douglas! He wasn't going to waste any more of whatever time he and Rosalin had left together. God willing, it would be longer than a day or two.

As much as Robbie told himself that he must be half-crazed to let himself get carried away with the futility of her writing to Clifford, he couldn't help being moved by her certainty and absolute belief in her brother. Robbie wanted to believe her. Wanted to believe it was possible. So much so that he'd gone against his instincts and done something he'd never thought he'd do in this lifetime: trusted an Englishman, or rather, woman.

Married? Christ, he still couldn't believe it. Three weeks ago, the thought would never have crossed his mind. Even after what had happened between them, he'd never thought it possible. But Seton was right. He'd acted selfishly. He'd wanted to make her his, when he knew damned good and well she couldn't be. He had to at least try to make it right. He just hoped to hell he wasn't making a huge mistake.

Seton had been right about a lot of things, it turned out. And now Robbie's future hinged on the good graces of Sir Robert Clifford. The whole world seemed to have turned upside down.

With a plan in place for how he could right at least part of it, Robbie waited for his opportunity. Getting her alone wasn't easy with Elizabeth Douglas seemingly tied to her hip, but the moment Joanna and Elizabeth appeared in the Hall to prepare for the evening meal, he slid up the stairs to Rosalin's chamber. She rarely ventured into the Hall unless she was certain he would be there.

She was turned away from the door, looking out the window, when she bade him enter. "Just put the tray on the table," she said.

Instead, he slid his arm around her waist and lowered his mouth to whisper in her ear, "Looking for someone?"

She yelped and spun around. "You startled me!" He grinned, and she put her hands on her hips. "As a matter of fact, I *was* looking for someone. I heard from Lady Joanna that Sir Thomas was expected in the next few days."

He was beginning to understand why Douglas got so prickly every time Joanna mentioned Randolph's name. He would have to keep her far away from MacGregor. He pulled her up hard against him and said darkly, "That isn't funny, Rosalin."

His warning tone had no effect on her grin and her eyes twinkling with mischief. "I disagree. I find it quite humorous. What is it about Sir Thomas that makes all the rest of you flare up like prickly bears? His handsome face? Those gorgeous blue eyes? The knightly—"

He stopped her with a kiss. A long, searing kiss that left them both flushed and breathing heavily.

"God, I missed you," he groaned, sliding his mouth around to devour her neck.

He cupped her breasts and started to work the ties of her gown. "Wait," she said, looking up at him. "Did my brother's response arrive—is that why you are here?"

He shook his head, sorry to disappoint her. "Nay. I'm here because I couldn't stay away any longer." The feel of her body pressed against him was driving him wild.

But she pushed him back. "Why *did* you stay away?"

He'd hurt her, he'd realized—unintentionally. "I was trying to do the right thing."

"Because of Sir Alex?"

He stiffened. "No."

She didn't believe him. "You have to talk to him."

He clamped his jaw closed. "There is nothing to talk about."

But she was right. The rift between him and Seton had

never been so wide; the tension between them was so thick it seemed about to explode. He knew he probably owed him some kind of apology, but he kept waiting for Seton's anger to die down like it always did. Except this time it didn't. What really confused him, though, was why Seton hadn't told anyone he'd bested him. Robbie would have thought he'd be shouting it from the damned parapets. God knew he had every right to. Robbie had been hard on him over the years. Maybe too hard, he acknowledged grimly.

"Saints, you are stubborn!"

She looked so put out he had to smile. "Aye. It's one of my more endearing qualities."

She let out a sharp laugh and shook her head. "Is that right? I'd hate to see the less endearing ones."

He pushed her back up against the stone wall, pinning her hands to the sides of her head. "Do you want to keep talking about all my good qualities or should I show you a few?"

Her eyes flared with heat. "What did you have in mind?"

He moved his hips against hers, letting her feel exactly what he had in mind. "This, for one."

Heat poured through his body and he groaned. It had been too long. She made the sweetest little gasp, and he was about to lean in and kiss her neck again when he heard a sound that made him glance out the window to his right.

He frowned.

"What is it?"

"Seton and Douglas. Damn it, I thought we'd have more time. They should have been gone for a couple more hours."

He peered harder into the distance as they neared, and tensed. They were riding too fast. Something was wrong.

He turned back to her, the disappointment probably as keen on his face as it was on hers. Leaning down one more time, he gave her a swift kiss. "We'll have to resume this later."

She nodded. He was almost to the door when she said, "Wait! Do you think it could be something from my brother?"

He stopped, turning to look at her. "Perhaps."

A few minutes later, when he met an arguing Seton and Douglas as they rode into the courtyard, he learned that it *was* a response from Clifford—just not the one he'd imagined.

Robbie clenched his fists, squeezing through the pain of his broken fingers in pure animalistic rage.

By God, Clifford would pay for this!

Robbie had heard the kind of story related by the lad so many damned times it should no longer affect him. The ordinary day. The happy, unsuspecting villagers going about their business. The first prickle of alarm when the soldiers are sighted. And the sheer terror and chaos that follows when the first sword starts to fall. But the horror of it always struck him anew. And this time it was worse. So much worse. This time he was to blame.

The lad was about Malcolm's age and was fighting to hold back the tears as he described what he'd seen. "They were killing everyone, my lord. Women, children—it didn't seem to matter. They blamed us for helping you. Said we were all rebels for keeping your camp supplied in the forest. Someone told them about the, uh . . . your women. The men were pulling them out into the street when my ma put me on the horse and told me to ride and try to find the Douglas. I didn't want to look back."

"But you did?"

The boy nodded and looked away. He'd already told them what he'd seen, and the images were still burning vividly in Robbie's mind. Deirdre and the other women from camp being . . .

His stomach turned as bile rose to the back of his throat. Raped and probably killed because of him. How could he have let this happen? How could he have been so stupid?

"That's when I saw the other soldiers riding toward me and I thought I would never get away. There were hundreds of them, swarming all over. I've never seen so many weapons."

"Clifford's men," Douglas provided, even though Robbie had heard it before. The boy's description of their arms had left no mistake. As had the description of Sir Henry's and his men. Apparently, Rosalin's betrothed hadn't been sent back to England after all.

But he was going to wish he had been.

"This happened yesterday?" Robbie asked the boy.

He nodded.

Probably right after receiving Rosalin's letter. She'd been right. Clifford's first reaction had been anger. And look what it had cost them.

The lad had obviously reached the end of his tether. He'd been through hell and looked it. But he'd told them everything they needed to know. Robbie thanked the boy and sent him away to get some food and rest.

"I got here as soon as I could, my lord," the boy said. "Do you think . . ."

Robbie wanted to lie, but the boy deserved the truth. He'd left his mother and younger siblings behind to ride for help. Robbie shook his head. There was no chance to save them. The villagers were dead and Corehead was no doubt burned to the ground.

The tears were falling unheeded now. "But you'll do something, won't you?" the boy asked.

"Aye, lad, I will." He would strike back and strike back hard in a place that would hurt.

He exchanged looks with Douglas, and the other man nodded. They'd been through this so many times before, he knew exactly what to do. Douglas left the Hall to start readying the men. Robbie was about to follow when Seton stopped him. It was the first time the other man had spoken to him directly since their fight.

"What are you going to do?"

How his partner—*former* partner—managed to convey disapproval in a flat tone, Robbie didn't know. But he did. "What the hell do you think I'm going to do? You heard what they did."

"But it doesn't make sense. Why would Clifford do something like this?"

Robbie's jaw locked. Because Robbie had believed Rosalin when she said her brother would do anything for her and let her write him. "He had a reason."

"What the hell did you do?"

The accusation snapped the last thread of Robbie's temper. "I fucking listened to you, that's what I did! I tried to make it right, and look what happened. I let her write Clifford and open discussions—isn't that what you are always wanting to do? Well, this is what you get from English negotiations. So if you have anything else to say, say it, or get the hell out of my way."

"I'd tell you not to do anything rash, but I'd be wasting my breath. So which English village will feel the sword of your retribution this time?"

Robbie steeled his gaze, guessing at what the reaction would be. "Brougham."

Seton flinched, shocked. "By God, I thought you cared for her. That is her home."

Robbie gritted his teeth. "It isn't Rosalin's home, it's *his* home. This has nothing to do with her."

"It has everything to do with her. She might have spent most of her life in London, but that is where she was born. She will never forgive you. I hope to hell you know what you are doing."

"I do. We are leaving within the hour—be ready."

Seton shook his head. "I told you I'm done. I won't be a part of this."

The gauntlet had been dropped. "I could order you to go."

"You could, and I'd refuse."

They stared at one another, facing off as they'd done so many times before. But Robbie knew this time it was different. This time Seton wasn't going to back down. Robbie should throw him into the damned pit prison. "Fine. You can stay here and guard Rosalin."

"You mean pick up the pieces of the heart you are about to break."

Robbie's eyes narrowed, refusing to be goaded. "There'll be plenty of time for me to put it back together."

"What do you mean?"

"It means she will get her wish. She won't be going back. I'll marry her as soon as I return. Let's see how Clifford likes *that*."

For the second time, Rosalin caught the end of a conversation she wished she hadn't heard. Elizabeth had come up and told her the men were leaving. Rosalin had raced downstairs beside her and stumbled into this . . . nightmare. *Won't be going back . . . marry her as soon as I return.* Words she'd hoped to hear, but not like this. She didn't understand. What could have happened?

Robbie looked over and saw them standing there. His face was a mask of black rage, and his eyes when they landed on her were as hard as onyx. He looked cold and unyielding, and so remote he might have been standing on a distant island.

"You are leaving?" she asked.

His eyes bit into her with . . . anger? Blame? Resentment? God, no, she must be imagining it. "I am."

She took a step toward him. "But why?"

He didn't say anything, but just continued to stand there

with that horrible look on his face. Her gaze slid to Sir Alex. He looked just as enraged. "Tell her, Boyd. You owe her that at least." He held out his hand to Elizabeth. "Come, Lady Elizabeth. Lady Rosalin will wish to hear this in private."

Left alone—at least as alone as they could be in the corner of the chaotic Hall—Rosalin approached him cautiously. "Tell me what has happened."

"What has happened?" he repeated. She could see the muscles flare in his shoulders and knew he was fighting for control. "What the hell did you write your brother?"

She drew back from the blast of anger. "Exactly what we discussed. That I wanted to stay in Scotland. That I was happy here. That I'd fallen in love and asked him to agree to a meeting in person under the color of the truce."

"Aye, well he refused."

She frowned. "I told you he might. But I will be able to convince him."

"It's too late for that. God, I can't believe I let you talk me into this."

She reached out and put a hand on his arm, but he was impervious to her touch. "Please, won't you tell me what happened?"

And then he did. In cold, brutal detail until the blood leached from her face, her stomach dropped, and her knees turned to jelly.

"No," she whispered. It was too horrible to contemplate. She'd come to think of some of those women as her friends. *Jean. Oh God, poor Jean!*

It couldn't be true . . . could it? For a moment she felt a sliver of uncertainty. She knew her brother but not the military commander, the man who despised Robbie Boyd and had made it his mission to capture him. Cliff would have been angry, but to do something like this? No. She refused to believe it. Rosalin was under no illusions about her brother's ruthlessness in war, but he wouldn't sanction the killing of children and the rape of women. No matter how angry. And above all, she was absolutely certain he wouldn't do something that could hurt her. There had to be an explanation. "There must be some mistake. Cliff wouldn't—"

"Don't say it!" He wrenched his arm away. "I don't want to hear another damned word about what your sainted brother would or wouldn't do. If I'd listened to my gut, none of this would have happened. I knew better. I can't believe I let you talk me into this. I told you it would never work. You cannot reason with English dogs."

Rosalin tried to control her frantic heartbeat. Tried to tell herself he was angry and didn't mean it. But it was getting harder and harder to make excuses for him. Harder and harder to be understanding in the face of his cold distrust. "There has to be some explanation. Send someone to—"

"No!" His voice fell like the crack of a whip. "No explanations, no couriers, no bloody messages. Your brother will have my reply. The only reply he will understand."

Rosalin had never seen him like this and didn't know what to do. How to break through. How to reach him. "Please, Robbie, don't do anything rash. Don't do anything in anger that cannot be undone. Lashing out like this . . . it is wrong."

"Christ, you sound exactly like Seton. I don't need either of you to be my bloody conscience."

Like Seton. Rosalin reeled from the truth. Why had she never seen it before? She *was* like Sir Alex and that's how Robbie would always see her. As English. As someone incapable of being fully trusted. Robbie and Sir Alex had fought for seven years together and he still refused to see him as a friend. In seven years would she still be waiting for him to realize that he loved her?

What if he never did?

A sinking sensation settled low in her gut. She felt the

happy future she'd imagined slipping away from her like the hazy figment of a dream.

She had to get through to him. "Don't you? Do you even stop to ask whether it's right or wrong anymore? Or maybe it no longer matters. Maybe it is only about who can inflict the most pain. What happened to all the principles in those books you love?"

His mouth tightened. "I'm not going to defend myself to you."

"Then defend it to yourself."

His silence was answer enough. Rosalin scanned his face, looking for a crack. Looking for anything to tell her she hadn't been wrong. Where was the man who read philosophy, who kept a garden because it reminded him of a simpler, peaceful time, who helped save a village from fire, and who stood up for a woman most men would think beneath his regard? She'd convinced herself that that despite the ruthless shell, at his core, he was still a man of honor, still a man capable of knowing right from wrong. But she was wrong. All that mattered was vengeance and the single-minded determination to win at all costs, justified or not. "So you are going to fight back with a raid in England? Will you kill children and rape women as well?"

The mouth that had kissed her not an hour ago drew hard and menacing. He took her by the elbow and hauled her up against him. "Don't push me, Rosalin. I've been pushed today about as far as I can go. Unlike your countrymen I do not slaughter innocents, but your brother will feel the pain close to home. Have no doubt about that."

It took her a moment to realize what he meant. But she knew him too well, knew the way he thought, and her stomach knifed in horror. She gazed up at him incredulously. "Not Brougham. Dear God, please tell me you aren't going to attack the only place in this world that was ever a home to me. How could you hurt me like that?"

He released her and backed away. "This has nothing to do with you."

Every word felt like a betrayal. It *was* a betrayal. God, what a fool she'd been! She'd thought if she loved him enough, she could pull him back from the black abyss he'd been sinking in. She'd convinced herself there was more to him than the ruthless raider. But what if there wasn't? What if this was him?

"This has *everything* to do with me, and if you don't see that now you never will. When you hurt him, you hurt me. I know you want to pay someone back for your friends and for the people in the village, but this isn't the way. This is wrong. I'm begging you not to do this. Give Cliff a chance to explain."

Nothing. No reaction. No softening of his gaze. No relenting. Her words did not even dent the steely shell. He was breaking her heart and didn't even care.

"You will not sway me, Rosalin. Not this time."

"Do I mean so little to you then? God, I thought you loved me. *Mo ghrá.*" Her voice broke, emotion tightening like a hot ball in her throat. "You called me 'my love.'"

He looked surprised, and maybe even a little embarrassed by her discovery. But if she was expecting a declaration, she was to be disappointed. Brutally disappointed. "My feelings for you are irrelevant." *Irrelevant.* How little she mattered to him. He might as well have tossed her heart on the ground and walked right over it. "Stop trying to force me to choose between you or your brother. If you want any chance for this to work, I told you not to put yourself in the middle of it."

Tears of frustration stormed to her eyes. "I *am* in the middle, don't you see that?" Just like Sir Alex, she was caught between the two sides. "I will always be in the middle."

"You are wrong. When we are married your allegiance will belong to me—only me."

"So what do you intend for me to do, carve your name across my heart? Renounce my country, king, and family? None of it will change the fact that I will always be English and I will always be a Clifford."

"Don't bloody remind me."

He had no idea how much his thoughtless comment hurt. How it seemed to epitomize the very futility of a future between them. "I knew how hard it was going to be to make this work, but I thought the challenges would be worth it. Despite what you may think, I am not a romantic fool living in a fantasy world. I knew what I was asking of you. I knew how difficult it would be for you to see past my being English and Robert Clifford's sister. But did it ever once cross your mind to think about what *I* was giving up to be with you? Do you think I want to leave my friends, family, the man who has stood by and protected me for my whole life, and the life I had in England to come to live in a hostile, unforgiving land—a country at war—where I know no one? Where I must be locked in a tower for my own protection? Where the moment I open my mouth I'm viewed with hatred and suspicion—even by the man who I'm giving up everything to be with?" She paused, just as surprised by her outburst as he. Realizing she was shouting, she lowered her voice. "What about our children, Robbie? What will you tell them? Will you turn them against their uncle?"

Obviously, the thought had never occurred to him, and he seemed to be having a difficult time working it out in his own mind. "Our children will be Scot."

"And half-English."

His jaw clenched as if the sheer force of his will could make it untrue. "I will not discuss this with you now."

"If not now, then it will be too late." She moved toward him, giving him one last chance to make it right. "Please, Robbie, I'm not asking you to trust my brother, I'm asking for you to trust *me*."

He gave her a long look. Some of her words must have gotten though, because for a moment he seemed to be wavering. But then his expression once again shuttered. He shook his head. "I did, and look what happened."

Rosalin stared at him in disbelief. "So this is my fault?" Anger rose inside her. Anger and outrage. "I've told myself to be patient because I know what you've been through. I understand why you might view my countrymen with such loathing and distrust—God knows you have good reason—but I am tired of trying to prove to you that I am worthy of your trust. I have never given you a reason not to trust me, but every time I think I've finally gotten through to you, something happens and you assume the worst. Whether it's me supposedly tricking you to set Roger free, allegedly lying to you about being betrothed, or breaking my word to escape with Sir Henry's men. Well, I'm not going to do it anymore. Either you trust me or you don't. My brother did not do this. I'm asking you to wait to hear from him before you seek your vengeance."

He turned away, cold and implacable. "You ask for too much."

He drove the final nail into her heart. This wasn't the man she loved. She wondered if that man ever existed. "No, it is you who ask for too much. You expect me to sit by and watch as you destroy my home—my family? I won't do it." *Too far gone.* "Sir Alex tried to warn me that only one thing mattered to you—you tried to warn me yourself—but I didn't want to listen. I convinced myself that you needed me. I told myself you loved me. That I could make you happy."

"You have." He made it sound almost like a concession.

She drew a deep breath. "But you will not make *me* happy. You are not the man for me. When I was sixteen, I fell in love with a noble young warrior who I watched do everything he could to save his friends under the worst conditions. I convinced myself that he was still there. But you were right. He no longer exists. War changed you. You've seen too much. You will never go back. You are too blinded by hatred to take the gift that is being offered you, and I'm done trying to make you see. Go. Have your vengeance, Robbie. But know that you are killing any chance of a future between us."

"I thought you heard. You aren't going back, Rosalin. We will be married as soon as I return."

"I will not marry you. Not if you go through with this. I will not be a weapon to be used against my brother whenever he does something you do not like."

His eyes narrowed. Without seeming to realize it, he took her by the arm and hauled her up against him. "I do not take to threats, Rosalin—or ultimatums. You will marry me, damn it."

She looked up at him, seeing the cold fury imprinted on the handsome features. "I thought you did not force women?"

His icy expression cracked. All at once he seemed to realize what he was doing. He dropped her arm. "You are overwrought," he said, perhaps trying to convince himself. "Eventually you will understand that I did what I had to do."

Just as eventually he would see that she had done what she had to do. She turned her back, not wanting to see him walk away from her. "Goodbye, Robbie."

Her heart squeezed as if wringing the last drop of her love to land in a pool at her feet.

He hesitated. She wanted to think him warring with himself. She wanted to think that he finally understood the truth of what she'd been trying to tell him. But his will—his hatred—was too strong.

He walked away, and with him, took the last embers of hope. It felt as if he were cutting her apart limb from limb. The pain—the heartbreak—was excruciating. She stood there until the sound of hoofbeats faded away into the distance.

Perhaps she'd been naive, and it was too much to expect that love could heal wounds as deep as his. Robbie had reasons for his hatred and distrust. But he'd let them consume him to the point that he struck back without questioning, and with a ruthlessness that enabled him not to care who he hurt in the process. Even her.

Rosalin had had enough. Enough of Scotland. Enough of war. Enough of loving a man who didn't have the capacity to love her back. It was time for her to let him go. She went to find Sir Alex.

Twenty-five

❧

Robbie and a force of nearly fifty warriors, including Douglas and twenty of his best men, crossed into England near Gretna. They skirted the heavily defended fortress of Carlisle to the west, taking cover in the forested countryside, and passed the old Roman wall at Burgh by Sands near the Solway Firth—the place where King Edward I had met his timely end five years before. It had taken them nearly a day of hard riding to get here, and it was still another twenty miles to Brougham.

A raid so far south of the border would have been a fool's gambit a few years ago. But the tide had turned, and last year Bruce's raiding parties had traveled across much this same countryside. Nonetheless, the raid was not without substantial risk. But Robbie had hours to consider every detail and plan for any contingency.

He was ready.

Or at least he should be. But every hour that took him from Douglas increased his unease and the growing sense of doom hanging over him. He couldn't get the sight of Rosalin's stricken face out of his mind or the sound of her voice out of his head.

It is wrong . . . You are not the man for me . . . Killing any chance of a future between us.

He'd told himself she'd spoken in anger and desperation to turn him from his path. That she didn't mean it. But the farther they rode from Douglas, the more he feared she meant every word. It was like a weight pressing down on his chest, making it hard to breathe.

Damn her for doing this to him. Damn her for making him question his resolve! He could not let such a vicious attack go unanswered. Clifford had to pay.

An eye for an eye . . .

But she'd been so certain, damn it. Robbie ran through the lad's account over and over in his mind, looking at it from every angle. The boy had identified the soldiers' arms, Clifford's men were there—there could be no doubt of that—but other details had been less explicit. The lad had been terrified. It had been chaotic. He'd escaped in the first few minutes. Enough to see what was happening, but had he gotten the entire picture?

Robbie grimaced angrily. What the hell was he doing? Was he looking for any excuse to turn from his course? She was making him weak, making him lose focus. If she was going to be his wife, she needed to learn she couldn't interfere. And she would marry him.

Wouldn't she?

My home . . . How could you hurt me like this . . . ? I thought you loved me.

Love? What the hell did he know about love? But something was making him second-guess himself. If he did this, he knew he would lose her. And the thought was making his pulse race with something akin to panic.

Bloody hell.

He didn't realize he'd spoken aloud until Douglas turned to him. If there was anyone whose face was blacker than Robbie's right now it was Douglas. Robbie hadn't missed the argument he'd had with Joanna as they prepared to ride out and guessed that she didn't approve of the course they'd set either.

"What is it?" Douglas said, looking around. They'd stopped well south of the wall to water the horses in one of the many lochs—or lakes, as the English called them—in the area. It was dark, and they planned to get some sleep before resuming their journey in the morning. The attack would come in the afternoon, giving them cover of darkness in which to get away. At least that had been the plan.

"We need to go back," Robbie said.

Douglas was incredulous. "You are calling off the attack? Damn it, Boyd! What the hell is wrong with you? What did she say to you?"

"I'm not calling off the attack," Robbie said. "At least not yet. But I need to make sure the lad was right about what happened. We need to go to the village and see the truth for ourselves."

Douglas eyed him skeptically. "This is because of the lass, isn't it?"

He would not deny it. But that was only part of it. "Bruce is counting on this truce with Clifford, and if there is any chance of holding on to it, it's my duty to do so. No matter how much we personally hate the bastard."

"And if you learn Clifford was responsible?"

"We will be back."

There were a few grumbles. The men weren't happy to be denied a chance to exact retribution for what had been done to the women and the villagers, but Robbie was their commander, and they trusted that he would not be doing this without a good reason.

He hoped to hell he had one.

It was a few hours after dark the following day when they neared Corehead, the small village tucked deep in the heart of the hills and forests of Ettrick, from where Wallace had gathered men to launch his first attack on the English nearly sixteen years before. As they crested the hill, Robbie got his first glance of the devastation. He expected to see the village razed to the ground, with nothing remaining but embers and the gruesome evidence of the slaughter that had occurred.

That wasn't what he saw.

Douglas swore, and they exchanged a glance. From this vantage, nothing appeared to be amiss. There were no blackened burned-out shells of buildings and no bodies piled up along the street. Indeed, although it was quieter than usual, he could see that there were a few people milling about.

Robbie's heart started to hammer.

As they drew closer, he could see a few signs of an attack. Broken shutters, tumbled fences, a few shattered pots and trampled gardens, but it appeared the whole-scale devastation that seemed certain from the boy's account had not occurred.

Word of their arrival had spread quickly, and the villagers began to gather along the high street as they approached. To his shock and relief, he saw Deirdre and the other women coming out of one of the buildings.

"I don't understand," Douglas said.

"Neither do I," Robbie answered grimly, but he had the first inkling that he'd nearly made a big mistake.

From Deirdre and the village reeve he learned just how horrible a one. The lad had been correct in what he'd seen; he just had not put it together correctly. The first party of soldiers—de Spenser and his men—had arrived *ahead* of Clifford's soldiers. Sir Henry and his soldiers had cut down nearly a score of villagers and were pulling Deirdre and the other women out of the cottage where they'd taken refuge, to tie them up and rape them for their crime of whoring with the rebels. They would have all been killed and the village set to flame—there was no doubt of that, Deirdre said—but Clifford and his men arrived and put a stop to the carnage. At first they all assumed he was there to raid as well. A few villagers tried to resist before they understood that Clifford was actually there to save them. Clifford arrested de Spenser and his men and took them back to Berwick for punishment.

Robbie listened to the accounts of the attack with a

growing sense of shame, realizing the magnitude of the mistake he'd nearly made and what it might have cost him.

Had he really almost destroyed the only place that had ever been a home to Rosalin? Razed an entire village without cause? Christ, he felt ill. She would have never forgiven him. For good reason. What the hell had he been thinking? Thank God he'd realized the truth before it was too late. Before he'd done something that could not be undone.

He was suddenly anxious to return. More than anxious. There was a voice in the back of his head shouting "hurry." He needed to get back and apologize to her, and aye, probably to Seton, too. It seemed he did need a conscience. For today had shown him just how far he'd strayed from the young warrior who'd raised his sword alongside William Wallace to fight against injustice.

On the third night after riding out of Park Castle, Rosalin and Sir Alex paused on the south bank of the river Tweed, looking across the wooden bridge to the steep White Wall on the opposite bank and the aptly named "Breakneck Stairs," which wound up the hill to Berwick Castle.

She turned to look at the man who had risked so much to bring her here. He'd proved more of a friend than she could ever have imagined, safely leading her through the harrowing war-torn countryside.

"Are you sure about this?" she asked. "You can still leave me here and return."

Sir Alex's jaw was locked in grim determination, as it had been since the moment she'd come to him asking to be taken back to her brother. She'd been trying to talk him out of what he intended since the first night, when they'd stopped to sleep a few hours and she'd watched in horror as he took a knife to his arm. The arm where he had—or used to have—a marking much like the one Robbie had.

Now the lion rampant tattoo had been obliterated by deep
scores and slashes through his flesh.

As she suspected, Alex had been part of Bruce's phantoms. The markings would identify him as such, and he
knew what the English would do to him to get him to identify the other members of the secret band of warriors.

She suspected excising the markings from his flesh would
be far easier than excising his friends from his memories.
She knew how difficult this was for him. She could see it in
his increasingly darkening expression with every mile they
passed. He was resolved, and in many ways just as stubborn as Robbie. She just prayed Sir Alex didn't come to
regret what he was about to do. There would be no going
back. For either of them.

He shook his head. "I've made my decision. I've had
enough of the secret warfare and pirate raids. God knows
I've tried, but I no longer have the stomach for it. Half the
time I felt like I was fighting against my own side anyway.
Maybe this way it will do some good."

"What do you mean?" How could him turning against
his friends do them any good?

"Maybe I can help end this war by working from the
other direction. Instead of fighting against the English, I
can fight from within—through reason and negotiation."

It was a lofty goal and hard for Rosalin to argue against,
as she was leaving for similar reasons. But although she
could understand Alex's decision, she knew Robbie and the
others would not. Whatever the reasons, Robbie would see
Sir Alex's defection as a personal betrayal. And on top of
her leaving, she suspected that it was going to be a bitter
blow for him to swallow—whether he would admit it or
not.

Why was she still worried about Robbie's feelings when
he'd treated hers with so little regard? Even though she
knew that she was doing what was right, it didn't make the
heartbreak any easier. If only her love could be as easily cut

from her heart as a tattoo. She would gladly take the temporary physical pain over the ongoing desolation of hopelessness. Wounds from a knife she would recover from. But she knew she would never completely recover from this, and the scars, she feared, would be both lasting and deep.

"Are you sure *you* want to do this?" Sir Alex asked softly.

She wasn't sure at all. But it had to be done. Rosalin glanced across the black river at the flickering torchlight on the other side. She took a deep breath, feeling the hot swell of emotion tighten in her chest. God, why did it have to hurt so much? She nodded, and without further hesitation, they rode across the bridge.

It was morning when Robbie stormed into the yard of Park Castle. He'd ridden as if the devil were nipping at his heels, unable to quiet the voice inside him. *Hurry!*

But the moment he glanced up into the tower window, he knew it was too late. His heart sank like a stone in a bottomless well. Darkness crashed down on him. She wasn't looking down at him from the window. She wasn't there.

A fear that was confirmed moments later when Joanna Douglas met them in the Hall.

"Where is Rosalin?" he demanded, fear already slashing his voice with a harsh edge.

"Watch it, Boyd," Douglas said. "I know you are angry, but don't take it out on my wife."

But Joanna did not shirk from his anger. "I don't need you to defend me from overbearing brutes, James. I'm quite used to them and displays of black temper."

Robbie winced. Had he really thought her too sweet?

She turned back to answer him. "I assume at Berwick Castle by now. She and Sir Alex rode out not long after you left."

Though part of him had known it, the news still shook him. How could she be gone, damn it? He had to explain.

He had to apologize. He had to tell her how wrong he'd been.

You drove her away.

Douglas swore. "And you just let them leave?"

Joanna's sweet blue eyes turned glacial as her gaze leveled on her husband's. "I did."

From her tone, she seemed to daring him to say something more.

Douglas clamped his mouth shut. Apparently, after the mistake they'd narrowly averted, he'd decided to cut his losses with his wife. Joanna had been right. Rosalin and Seton had been right. And they all knew it.

Robbie clenched his fists, the raw emotion lashing around inside him like a whip. Anger. Disbelief. Despair. It needed a place to go, and he struck out against the only other person he could blame besides himself. How could the man who'd been his partner for seven years betray him like this? "I'm going to kill him."

Joanna lifted a delicate brow. "Sir Alex?" She shook her head. "I fear that might be difficult."

"What do you mean?"

"He left you something." She pointed to the small solar off the Hall that Douglas used to conduct estate business. "It's in there."

Robbie closed the door behind him as he entered the room, grateful a moment later for the privacy when he opened the plain burlap sack to see the darkened nasal helm and plaid.

He flinched. For the second time in the space of a few minutes, he felt the hard slap of shock. And it stung—bitterly.

Seton had finally done it. He'd left the Guard and defected to the English. Robbie didn't know why he was surprised. Hadn't he expected Seton to betray them for years? He was a bloody Englishman. How could Robbie have trusted him, even a little?

Ah hell. Barely before he'd finished the thought, the truth hit him hard. That was exactly what had driven her away. She told him that he would always see her as English—as Clifford's sister—and never be able to fully trust her. She'd accused him of being blinded by vengeance. She was right. His inability to see the sweet, caring woman who was offering him her heart had made him lose the best thing that had ever happened to him.

I thought you needed me.

He did need her. He hadn't realized how much until now. She'd seen something in him that he'd almost forgotten was there. He thought her fierce sense of justice had reminded him of someone once, and now he realized who it was: him. Once he'd fought for the right reasons. Once he'd stopped to ask whether something was right or wrong. Winning didn't have to come at the expense of honor, and somehow along the way, he'd forgotten that. But she'd brought it back to him.

Of course she'd left. He'd given her no reason to stay. When he thought of how many times she'd offered him her heart and he'd offered her nothing in return, he wanted to empty his stomach. She'd been willing to give up everything for him, and the only thing she'd asked for in return—his trust—he'd been unwilling to give her.

She loved him, and . . .

He dropped to a bench as the sickening truth crashed down on him.

He loved her. Of course he did. He'd known it and hadn't wanted to accept it. He'd been too scared of what it might mean and too scared of having to send her back. And by refusing to admit it, he'd achieved the very thing he'd feared: he'd lost her.

He would never have given her back. If her brother didn't agree he would have found another way. He knew that now. But she didn't. And he'd lost the chance to tell her.

Seton had accused him once of being dead inside. He

wished it were true so he didn't have to feel the black emptiness opening up within him.

He put his head in his hands and tried to think, tried to hold on to the edge of the cliff to prevent himself from slipping into the chasm of darkness that was his future.

How in the hell was he going to get her back?

Twenty-six

Rosalin and Sir Alex's sudden appearance at the castle gate had caused something of an uproar—to put it mildly. She had been crushed in her sleep-roused brother's overcome embrace, while Sir Alex had been surrounded by soldiers and very nearly tossed in the pit prison until she'd threatened to jump in there with him. Instead, he'd been taken to the guardhouse. After days of questioning, he had been ordered to London to make his case to the king in person.

Saying goodbye to him, and then watching him ride out with a small army of her brother's men, was the hardest thing she'd done since leaving Douglas. Sir Alex was her last link to Robbie, and seeing him go felt like the final break. The sense of loss was profound, though God knew, Robbie didn't deserve her heartbreak or her tears. She should hate him for what he'd done. Each morning she expected her brother to call for her, to give her the horrible news that would all but ensure it.

But two days passed, and then three. Plenty of time for a messenger to have arrived from Brougham, bringing news of the attack. It wasn't until the fifth day, when the soldier her brother sent after she'd told him of the attack returned, that she was called to Cliff's solar to hear the hideous truth.

Her brother had his back to the door and was staring

into the small fireplace as she entered. He appeared to be deep in thought.

She braced herself, expecting the worst.

He turned, his hands clasped behind his back. "There has been no attack."

He might have toppled her to the floor. She swayed, flinched, or did some odd combination of the two. "What?"

Cliff met her gaze, and she could see the worry in the green eyes that were so like her own. Since she'd returned, her brother had treated her as something akin to a delicate piece of porcelain, assiduously avoiding any mention of subjects that might cause her distress, such as her abduction, Robbie Boyd, or the letter she'd written him. He knew something was terribly wrong but was waiting for her to explain.

"Brougham has not been attacked. Boyd must have discovered what really happened at the village in time."

Cliff had explained everything about the attack, validating her trust in him. Not that it mattered. Or did it? Why had Robbie changed his mind? What had turned him from his course? And most important, what did it mean?

She must have paled or looked as if she were going to faint, because Cliff crossed the room, took her by the elbow, and helped her sit on one of the cushioned benches before the fire.

She couldn't seem to think. "You're sure?"

He nodded.

"But why?"

Her brother gave her a long look. "I suspect you can answer that question better than I."

Before bringing Sir Henry and the other prisoners back to Berwick, Cliff had sent a message to Robbie explaining what had happened in the village and agreeing to meet in one week's time (to discuss the contents of her missive and the exchange of coin), but it would have arrived after they both left.

"I'm not sure I can. Robbie was so determined. I tried—begged him—to turn from his course, but he refused." Tears swam before her eyes as she stared up into her brother's grim face. "It was horrible."

He swore and sat down beside her, tucking her under his arm while she sobbed, the way he used to when she was a child. "The bastard doesn't deserve your tears, little one. And he sure as hell doesn't deserve *you*."

That only made her sob harder.

"Tell me what happened."

And she did. Well, most of it at least, leaving out the more intimate details, although she suspected Cliff filled in the gaps well enough. When she was done, his mouth was pulled in a hard, angry line. "I'll kill him."

"No! Please. I just want to forget any of this ever happened."

She took the folded square of linen he handed her and dabbed her nose and eyes.

Cliff's expression was no less fierce, but his voice softened. "Are you sure about that, Rosie-lin?" He stopped. "I've fought against Boyd for a long time, and I've never known him to hesitate. But something caused him to pull back, and I suspect that something was you."

Rosalin sniffled and took a deep breath. She shook her head. "Even if he changed his mind about the attack, it doesn't matter. It would never work. Who I am will always be between us. I cannot be with a man who does not trust and love me."

He squeezed her tighter and sighed, as if a great weight had been lifted off him. "I hate to see you in pain, but I won't say I'm sorry to hear that. You can't see it now, but this will be for the best. Anything between you would have been all but impossible."

Rosalin blinked up at him. "But not impossible?"

He looked away, his mouth pursed as if he'd tasted something unpleasant. It was much the same look Robbie got when her brother's name was mentioned. "I want you to be happy, but handing my sister over to that barbarian would be asking a lot. And I would never have done it if I wasn't certain that he could make you happy. The brigand would have been hard pressed to prove it to me." He squeezed her one more time and kissed the top of her head. "Forget about him, Rosie-lin. He doesn't deserve you."

"I'll try," she promised. "And Cliff?" He looked at her. "Thank you for not trying to make me hate him."

His mouth lifted. "Hell, if I thought it would work, I would have. But I suspect that battle was lost years ago."

"What do you mean?" He cocked a brow and held her stare. The blood slowly drained from her face as the truth dawned. "You knew?"

He shrugged. "Not right away. It was the guards who gave it away. I knew there had to be a reason Boyd didn't kill them. God knew, he had every reason to, so I suspected someone had helped him. From the way your breath stopped and face paled every time he was mentioned, it didn't take me long to realize who that might be."

"Why did you never say anything? You must have been so angry with me for betraying you."

"In truth, I was rather relieved." His jaw hardened as if from something unpleasant. "It evened the score."

Rosalin was shocked when she realized what he was saying. "Did you trick them into surrendering, Cliff? I refused to believe it of you."

"I didn't—at least not intentionally. The king didn't tell me what he had planned. I gave my word the meeting would be held under truce not knowing they would be arrested. They wouldn't have been able to hold out much longer and the result would have been the same, but I didn't like that it had been done at the expense of my honor. I was ashamed of what had been done, but had to do my duty." He smiled crookedly. "You saved me from having to make a decision I didn't want to make."

Rosalin was stunned. "I can't believe you knew all these years and never said anything."

"I suspected why you did it and hoped you'd forget." He smiled ruefully. "I guess that didn't work very well, did it?"

She shook her head, emotion balling up in her throat again. "What am I going to do, Cliff?"

"I don't know, little one, but we'll figure something out. It will get better."

If only she could believe him.

When the two thousand pounds arrived from Clifford a week after Rosalin and Seton left, Robbie wondered if his desperate plan might actually have a chance of working. Clifford could have reneged on the truce, but he hadn't. That and the letter agreeing to meet that had arrived a day too late had to mean something.

Robbie rode north to Dundee with Fraser and a handful of other men to bring Bruce the much needed coin, but also to speak with MacLeod. If his plan was going to work, he was going to need the help of his brethren.

He didn't inform the king of his intentions, suspecting Bruce wouldn't agree. But unsanctioned missions involving wives (or God willing, future wives) were hardly unusual for the Guardsmen. MacLeod himself had ordered one to rescue his wife at the beginning of the war, so Robbie expected a sympathetic ear.

Still, it had taken him a few days to persuade the leader of the Highland Guard to agree. But a week after he'd arrived in Dundee, Robbie and the nine other Guardsmen were standing in the forest near Berwick Castle going over the final details of his plan. Actually, he was going over the details, and they were doing their damndest to talk him out of it.

"It's bloody suicide, Raider," Lachlan MacRuairi said. "Just because we've managed to get out of there before doesn't mean we'll be able to do so again. It took me over two years to free my wife from that hellhole—with a failure that nearly got us captured. If you are imprisoned there is no guarantee of a rescue. I've been in that pit prison, and believe me, you don't want to spend much time there."

Robbie remembered, and if there was anyone in the Guard who knew about getting in and out of dangerous places it was MacRuairi.

"It won't come to that."

I hope.

Eoin MacLean, the tactician of the group, stared him down. "So this is your plan: walk into Berwick Castle, ask to see Clifford, tell him you want to marry his sister, and hope he doesn't toss you in the pit prison or hang you with the nearest rope?"

"Sounds about right."

"You must be bloody crazed," MacLean said with disgust.

"So you've said before," Robbie said. "All of you. But I know what I'm doing."

He was doing the only thing he could think of to try to get Rosalin back. He was going to prove to her that he trusted her. *My brother loves me and will do anything to see to my happiness.* Robbie hoped to hell she hadn't been exaggerating, because he suspected this was going to put that "anything" to the test. For the second time, his life was going to be in Clifford's hands. Although this time he was putting it there himself.

Hell, maybe he *was* crazed.

Erik MacSorley, who'd been prodding him for the better part of the week, grinned. "I didn't take you for the grand gesture type, Raider. But if this doesn't work out, I'll sail you down to London. I hear King Edward has a couple of sisters, and with your penchant for Englishwomen . . ."

Robbie told him what he could do with his ship, and the big West Island chieftain—who looked more Viking than

Scot—laughed. But for once, Robbie didn't mind being the butt of his jokes. MacSorley's lighthearted jesting relieved some of the heaviness weighing over them all at Seton's betrayal.

Unlike Robbie, the other Guardsmen had been stunned. Hell, he'd been stunned, too, but just hadn't wanted to admit it. They all knew Seton struggled at times with the secret warfare and the less knightly aspects of this war. They also knew that he and Robbie had never gotten along, but no one had realized how bad it had become.

They'd all taken the blow personally. The loss of William Gordon was still an open wound. Though the circumstances were vastly different (Gordon had died in an explosion while on a mission), the sense of loss was the same. Circumstances had made them as close as brothers—closer—and they were all feeling the absence of one of their own.

No one had said anything, but Robbie sensed that some of the others—Sutherland, MacKay, MacLean, and Lamont, who were closest to Seton—put some of the blame on him. Probably rightly so. But it didn't change the fact that Seton had betrayed them.

"What if she's not there?" Sutherland asked.

Robbie didn't want to think about that. It was one (of many) of the weak points of his plan. There was every likelihood Clifford had put her on the first ship bound for London.

"She will be," Robbie said with more certainty than he felt. "And if she's not, I hope you have plenty of powder."

Though not as experienced as Gordon had been with black powder, Sutherland had become proficient enough to provide distractions when the Guard needed them.

The newest member of the Highland Guard gave him a sharp glance. "Aye, though I'd rather not have to use it."

"Me, too," Robbie said dryly.

It was time to go.

"We'll give you twenty-four hours, Raider," MacLeod said. "If you aren't out by vespers tomorrow night, we're coming for you."

Robbie nodded. He'd tried to talk them out of a rescue, but it was the condition upon which MacLeod had agreed.

MacRuairi, who'd had nearly as many problems with Seton as Robbie, gave him a hard look. "If you see Seton tell him to go to hell, before you stick one of his damned daggers in his back like he did to us."

Robbie didn't know what he would do if he came face-to-face with his former partner, but it wouldn't be pretty. "I'll pass on the message."

He left the forest on foot and without his armor and weapons, hoping he would need them to fight his way out of here later.

Thirty minutes later, after he gave his name to the guard at the gate, Robbie's trust in Rosalin was put to the test.

Twenty-seven

Irony worked in mysterious ways. Two days after her conversation with Cliff in his solar, Rosalin had decided to keep herself busy by helping the nuns at the hospital at St. Mary's Priory. On the first day, she met not one but two young women who were heavy with child. One had been abandoned by the man she thought intended to marry her, the other had been raped when rebels raided her village.

Rosalin discussed with the abbess the possibility of setting up a special home for women who found themselves in such circumstances. The abbess was immediately amenable to the idea. The need was great, but the hospital was equipped for travelers and the infirm, not as a sanctuary for women with child. With Rosalin's patronage and financial support from her brother, the priory would have a place to send them.

The irony arose a few days later, when Rosalin realized she had missed her menses for the first time in the eight years since she'd begun them. Were it not for her brother, she might have needed one of those beds. Not that she relished informing Cliff of her condition. There would no longer be any question—if he had any—of what had happened between her and Robbie.

Once she got over the immediate shock and fear of what it meant—she would be disgraced and a harlot in the eyes of the Church—she felt a small glimmer of happiness kindling in the darkness of her despair over losing Robbie. A

babe. *His* child. He had given her a family after all.
Someone who needed her for love and protection. It might
not be the family she'd dreamed of, but she knew better
than anyone that they could make do. She was going to
love this babe with all of her heart and be happy.

Nearly two weeks after she'd arrived at Berwick, Rosalin
was at the hospital, finalizing the details with the abbess
and trying to figure out how she was going to tell Cliff
about her predicament without having him send an army
to kill Robbie, when she heard the first whisper.

"Captured."

She paid it no mind until about an hour later, she heard
another. "Devil's Enforcer," one of the nurses said.

Rosalin froze. Trying to maintain as much dignity as she
could—even though she'd clearly been eavesdropping—
she asked the woman, "Did you say something about the
Devil's Enforcer?"

"Did you not hear, m'lady?" the young novice said.
"They've captured Robbie Boyd."

Her heart stopped and sank at the same time. "Who has
captured him?"

The girl gave her an odd look. "Why, your brother, my
lady."

Rosalin barely heard the last word. She was already out
the door on her way back to the castle. By the time she
burst into her brother's solar, she was out of breath,
flushed, and her brow damp with perspiration. "Tell me it
isn't true."

Cliff lifted his head from the document he was studying
and sighed. "I guess you've heard."

"So it is true? You've captured him?"

"Not exactly."

"What do you mean, not exactly? Is he here or isn't he?"

"He's here, but I didn't capture him. The bast—man,"
he corrected, "walked in here of his own accord."

"He did *what*?" she screeched incredulously.

Her brother shook his head. "He walked in here demanding to see me."

"And what did he say?"

"I don't know. I thought I'd give him time to think about it for a while."

Rosalin narrowed here eyes. "And where is he doing this thinking?"

As if she didn't already know. Cliff could be every bit as ruthless as the "brigands" he complained about. "In the pit prison."

"Cliff! How could you?"

His mouth hardened. "He's lucky I didn't string him up by the bollocks for what he did to you. One night in the pit prison won't kill him. Unfortunately."

"I want to see him." Seeing his expression, she added, "And don't think about refusing."

"I wouldn't dream of it," he said with heavy sarcasm. "Why wouldn't I want my little sister within arm's reach of one of the most dangerous men in Scotland?"

She stared at him until he relented.

"Very well, I'll have him brought up to the guardroom. But I'm warning you, Rosalin, I'm not making any promises. I've waited too long for this day."

What time was it?

Robbie blinked into the pitch-black darkness, wondering at the wisdom of his plan. He'd anticipated the possibility of spending some time in the Berwick pit prison; he'd just hoped to speak to Clifford before being unceremoniously dumped into a hole.

As he was alone, he assumed that meant Seton had convinced them of his earnestness. His mouth hardened, not wanting to think of his former partner.

How much time did he have left? He had no way of knowing precisely without the aid of daylight, but he suspected only an hour or two at most. If Clifford's curiosity didn't get the better of him soon, Robbie's Highland Guard brethren would be here to break him out before he even had a chance to plead his case.

Assuming they *could* get him out.

At least they would know where to find him, he thought wryly. MacRuairi was intimately familiar with the place, having spent some time here a few years back after helping free his now wife from captivity.

Robbie was more relieved than he wanted to admit when he heard someone fumbling with the latch. A few moments later, the door was thrown back and a rope lowered. With his injuries, it took him longer than it should have to pull himself up the ten feet or so to the top.

Chained manacles were slapped around his wrists by two grim-faced but silent soldiers the moment he stood outside the opening. Without explanation he was dragged outside the small anteroom, through another room, and pushed through an arched doorway into what looked to be the guardhouse at the main gate.

He heard a familiar gasp the moment he stumbled inside and he jerked his head up with surprise. *Rosalin!* Their eyes met and all the fear, all the longing, all the love he had for her hit him with the force of a thunderbolt.

A moment later when she looked to her right with a scowl, Robbie's expression hardened as he became aware of the other person in the room.

"What did you do to him?" she demanded to her brother.

Clifford—the bastard—shrugged with a smirk he didn't bother to hide. "A few of my men were a little overzealous when he identified himself at the gate last night. After what he's done, he should consider himself lucky."

"Go to hell, Clifford."

"If anyone is going there soon it won't be me. I'm not the one in irons."

Rosalin frowned. "Take those off him, Cliff. I told you he wouldn't hurt me."

Clifford met his gaze; they both knew the chains weren't for her protection. "I don't think so," the other man said. "Let's hear what he has to say first."

Rosalin took a step toward him. She looked so damned beautiful it took his breath away. But there was a fragility to her in the paleness of her cheeks and dark shadows under her eyes that hadn't been there before, and any punishment Clifford might have meted out couldn't compare to the guilt he felt knowing he'd been the one to put it there.

He half hoped she'd rush into his arms and tell him that she'd missed him. But she didn't, and he had no right to expect it. Not after their last parting.

For once, the expressive eyes that had always seemed a window into her thoughts were shuttered to him.

He couldn't have lost her. He wouldn't countenance it. She'd given him her heart, and he wasn't going to let her take it back.

"What do you want, Robbie?" she asked.

"You."

Clifford made a low growl and took a threatening step toward him, but Rosalin caught him by the arm. "Please, Cliff. I want to hear what he has to say."

Clifford gave her a long look before moving back. "It had better be good."

Robbie ignored him and looked at Rosalin. He would have preferred to say this without an audience, but he supposed he should be glad he was getting a chance to speak to her at all. He'd expected to have to plead his case to Clifford.

"I'm sorry. I should have trusted you. I made a mistake, and I'm here to try to make it right."

He turned to Clifford and squared his jaw. "I want to marry your sister."

"No."

Robbie gritted his teeth together. The bastard was enjoying this. "Rosalin said you would do anything to make her happy. She asked me to trust her. I do. That's why I am here." She made a sound, and he turned to see her eyes widen with surprise, and then slowly start to shine with what he hoped was the first glimmer of forgiveness. He turned back to Clifford. "Was she wrong?"

Clifford turned to Rosalin. "Christ's cross, Rosie-lin, why the hell did you tell him that?"

"I never thought he would do something so foolhardy."

"Or romantic," Robbie put in.

He wasn't sure whether she heard him. "I did give him my word," she said to her brother.

Clifford made a face, and then glared at Robbie. "She wasn't wrong. I just don't think you can make her happy."

He crossed his arms and gave Robbie a smug smile, as if challenging him to convince him.

Robbie's fists clenched. He felt the manacles straining around his wrists and thought it was probably smart that Clifford had kept him chained. But a glance at Rosalin took the fight out of him. If they were going to have any chance, he and her brother were going to have to find some way to put years of hatred behind them.

He took a deep breath. "I don't know if I can either, but I love her, and I swear to you I will spend every minute of my life trying—even if that means putting aside our enmity. She loves you, and I won't do anything to get in the way of that. You protected her and looked after her when others in your position might not have, and for that you deserve credit." His gaze met Rosalin's. "I want you to be my wife because I love you—it doesn't have anything to do with him or revenge. It never did. I was just too blind to see it. If you want to spend the next fifty years singing his damned praises, I'll listen. I might not agree, but I'll listen. Our children will call him uncle."

"Oh Robbie." Something sharp and tender sparked in her eyes, and the next moment she was in his arms—or at least as much in his arms as he could manage with the chains. The feel of her all soft and warm pressed against his chest released something inside him. He felt as if a dam had broken, and all the fear, all the longing, all the love he had for her came rushing out. He tucked her satiny head under his chin, pressed his lips on her hair, and let the warm scent of roses wash over him.

There was so much he wanted to say, but the emotion was too thick in his throat.

Clifford made a sharp scoffing sound. "I'm not convinced yet."

Rosalin unwrapped herself from his chest to turn on her brother. "Cliff, what more do you want from him? He put his life in your hands because he trusted me, and I'll not have you—"

Clifford held up his hand, cutting her off. "I have a few conditions."

Rosalin's eyes narrowed suspiciously. "What kind of conditions?"

Clifford's gaze softened. And at that moment Robbie knew he'd won. She was right: her brother her loved her more than he hated Robbie. He wanted her happiness, even if it was with the man he'd been trying to capture for years.

"That he promises to bring you to England as often as you like. I want my children to know their aunt, and I need to see for myself that he keeps his promise."

Rosalin turned to Robbie.

"Agreed. As long as it can be done without putting Rosalin in danger."

Clifford nodded.

"What else?" Robbie said.

"You name your firstborn son Clifford."

Robbie froze. He looked at the other man as if he were mad. Rosalin laughed and elbowed him in the ribs. "He's teasing you, Robbie."

Christ, he'd probably permanently damaged his heart, it had stopped for so long.

Clifford smirked. "As it appears I'm going to have to suffer the humiliation of letting you escape again, your reputation is going to suffer as well. Whatever story I come up with to tell Edward, you aren't going to dispute it."

"I suspect I will play the dastardly villain in this tale?"

The other man smiled. "Of course."

Robbie swore. "Agreed. I doubt my reputation can get any darker."

"I wouldn't bet on it."

Rosalin scowled at her brother. "Bride abduction should suffice, Cliff. No embellishing."

He made a face, but didn't argue. "I assume you can find your way out?"

Robbie nodded. He should have some help soon. "Aye."

"Then make good use of the time I'm about to give you." He turned to Rosalin. "Give me a hug, sweetheart."

Rosalin ran into his arms, and Robbie felt his chest squeeze as he watched them. The bond between the two siblings was strong, and he swore he would do his damnedest never to interfere with that again.

No matter how much it killed him.

After a long moment, Clifford let her go. He gave Robbie one more look. "Hurt her again and not even Bruce's phantoms will be able to protect you."

Despite the irony of that particular threat, Robbie believed him.

A moment later the door closed behind him.

Rosalin had been overcome with emotion since the first moment he'd been pushed into the room. It had taken everything she had not to run to him, especially when she'd seen the damage inflicted on him by her brother's soldiers.

Then, realizing that he'd surrendered to show his trust

for her . . . it was too much. But the breaking point, the point when she knew he really loved her, was when he'd vowed to let her talk about Cliff—even alluding to the children he didn't know he was having.

She crossed the room, putting her hand on his cheek. "Your poor face."

He grinned. "I'll let you fuss over me all you want, once we are out of here. But first . . ."

He slid his hands onto her hips and brought her against him. The next moment his mouth was on hers and he was kissing her with passion that bordered on desperation.

She wrapped her arms around his neck and crushed her body to his, needing to feel his heat and strength.

He groaned, kissing her deeper, sweeping his tongue in her mouth with long, ravenous thrusts.

Her body ignited with heat, her skin drawing tight and prickly, her nipples hardening, and dampness gathering between her legs in a pool of molten need.

He cupped her bottom, holding her against his hardness. The desire became overwhelming. Her body started to move against his, seeking the sweet relief of friction.

He tore away with an oath. "God, you are killing me. But we need to be ready, and I doubt your brother left us here so I could take you in his guardroom with these." He lifted his chained manacled wrists.

"Ready for what?"

"You'll know it when you hear it. What time is it?"

She looked at him quizzically. "I don't know. It was near sunset when I came in. They will be calling for vespers soon, I'd imagine. I forgot about the manacles. How are we supposed to get out of here with your hands chained?"

He smiled, stepped on the chain with his feet, and pulled until his muscles seemed strained to the breaking point— but it was the iron that snapped. He'd broken the chain in two. He laughed at her expression. "It's a little trick I learned to impress the lasses." Rosalin wasn't even going to comment on that. "But we'll have help."

"The other phantoms?"

His expression went utterly still. He just stared at her.

"Did you not think I would figure it out?" She shook her head. "Really, Robbie, I'm not blind. I've seen you fight. I've seen the markings and the demonic-looking helm. I heard Sir Alex call you Raider once. I figured that was your war name. It's appropriate, by the way."

He was still stunned. "How long have you known?"

"A while. Sir Alex told me I shouldn't tell you I knew."

His expression darkened. "The traitorous bastard probably hoped you'd tell your brother. God knows it won't be a secret much longer."

From his expression, she could tell that he'd taken Sir Alex's defection even harder than she'd anticipated. "He didn't betray you, Robbie. He just stopped believing in the same things. He will keep your secrets, just as I would have kept them."

"There are other ways—"

"You mean the tattoo? You need not fear discovery that way. He removed it—or obliterated it, really."

The information didn't have effect that she'd hoped. Instead of allaying his fears of betrayal, it only seemed to make the betrayal worse. As if the markings were some kind of sacred bond that Alex had just run a knife through.

"He's in London," she said, knowing he was too proud to ask. The sting was too raw right now, but she hoped over the years to help him understand and accept what Sir Alex had done. *Years* . . .

"Did you mean it, Robbie?"

"What part, *mo ghrá*?" He slid his hands around her waist again and drew her in tightly. His voice grew husky. "That I love you? Aye, I meant it. And I intend to do everything I can to prove it to you until you never have to ask again. You were right—I need you. I didn't realize how much until I arrived at that village and knew how close I'd come to making a horrible mistake and realized how far I'd strayed from the man I used to be. I'm going to be that man again, Rosalin. And if I forget, you will be there to remind me."

She smiled, tears of happiness filling her eyes. "I believe you. You must love me if you agreed to let me sing Cliff's praises. I can be quite long-winded, you know."

He shuddered, getting that sour-distasteful look on his mouth.

"And when you complimented him, I had no doubt of it."

"The hell I did!"

She laughed. "I wish you could have seen your face when he said you would have to name our son Cliff. Although it does have a nice ring to it."

He rolled his eyes with a groan. "Christ, Rosalin, don't even jest about it. I still haven't recovered."

She took his hand and put it on her stomach. "I suppose there is close to nine months to decide."

Robbie was an exceptionally smart man, but it took him a minute to realize what she meant. His face lost every drop of color. He stared at her with something resembling horror in his eyes. Then his face crumpled. If she'd ever doubted his ability to feel emotion, she never would again. He looked like a man who'd been shattered. He held her tightly, and she could feel his chest shaking.

"I'm sorry. Oh Christ, I'm sorry. I never thought . . . I should have thought. You would have paid the price, and I could have lost you both."

She knew the way his mind worked, and he was probably twisting it in some way to think about his sister. She put her fingers on his mouth to stop him from saying any more. "I love you, Robbie. It's not the same. And you came for me in time. In rather dramatic fashion, I might add."

She jumped when she heard a sound like thunder.

"That's our signal," he said, taking her hand. "Time to go."

Cliff had taken care of the soldiers at the door. Smoke was everywhere and people were running all over the bailey. It was remarkably easy to slip around the buildings unnoticed in the chaos. Near the pit prison Robbie let out a sharp whistle, and two men appeared a moment later.

Though she'd seen Robbie in his phantom garb before, the sight of two giant warriors in those faceless looking nasal masks startled her.

"It's all right, *mo ghrá*. They are friends."

"I see your damned fool plan worked," one of the men said dryly, and then bowed to her. "My lady."

Robbie hugged her closer to him possessively. "Aye, Chief."

Rosalin gave him a secret smile. "I thought it was rather romantic."

"Smart lass," Robbie said with a grin.

"We'd better go," the second warrior said. "This isn't the first time we've used this particular distraction, and we don't want to overstay our welcome. It was good of you to not make me go into that damn hole again, though."

Robbie winced. "Aye, well, I did get a chance to sample Berwick's finest accommodations for most of the last twenty-four hours. I can see why you aren't anxious to return. I'll need help with these," he said, holding up his hands.

The second man removed something from the sporran he wore at his waist, and in seconds the iron manacles fell to the floor.

They made their way to the postern gate, where four other phantoms were waiting for them. The men exchanged a few gestures and Robbie shook his head. A few minutes later, Rosalin realized why, when the two men who'd stayed to guard the gate were knocked out by hard claps to their helms with the pommel of a sword rather than killed. A few moments later, she was whisked into a waiting *birlinn*.

She was helped in by another man wearing a bow across his shoulder.

"So this is your Englishwoman," he said with a low whistle of appreciation.

Robbie wrenched her fingers rather forcibly from the other man's gauntleted hand. "Stay the hell away from her, Arrow. I mean it. That face of yours won't look so pretty when I'm done with it."

Rosalin was surprised when the other man replied under his breath, "I should be so lucky."

They took a seat on one of the wooden storage chests near the back of the boat.

In all, including Robbie, she made out ten shadowy figures. To a one they were big, muscular, and menacing-looking. Indeed, were it not for Robbie holding tightly to her waist, she would be terrified.

The man holding the ropes that controlled the sail looked to Robbie. He grinned, his teeth gleaming white in the moonlight. "Glad you could join us, Sir Robert."

"Sod off, Hawk, and sail. Get us the hell out of here," Robbie said, but there was something in his voice that sounded like embarrassment.

She looked up at him, her brows drawing together. "Sir Robert?"

Aye, he looked distinctly uncomfortable. Boyishly uncomfortable, like Roger had when discussing the girl from Norham. "It's nothing."

She waited patiently.

"It was a stupid idea."

She continued to wait. As she suspected they had a long boat ride ahead of them, she had all night.

He sighed. "I was trying to think of ways to prove to you how I felt." Their eyes met in the darkness. "The king has been offering to knight me for years. I finally accepted."

For her. He'd done that for her. She knew how he felt about knightly codes and chivalry, but he wanted to show her that he was still the young warrior she remembered. He didn't need a knight's spurs to prove it to her, but she was moved nonetheless. "Oh Robbie, that is sweet."

He cupped her chin, tipped her head back, and placed a tender, almost reverent kiss on her lips. Despite the cool sea air, a swell of warmth rose inside her.

But apparently, she'd spoken too loud.

"Aw," the captain said from behind them. "That is sweet, Raider."

Robbie swore.

"What's wrong?" she asked.

"He's never going to let me hear the end of this."

"Is that so bad?"

"You have no idea." He shook his head. "But it's worth it. You are worth it. If I can make peace with your brother, I can put up with that arse's prodding for a few hours. There isn't anything I wouldn't do for you. Anything."

Rosalin couldn't resist teasing him one more time. "Clifford Boyd. It has a nice ring to it, don't you think?"

He shuddered, and then kissed the teasing words right from her mouth.

Epilogue

❧

Kilmarnock, Ayrshire, Dean Castle, All Saints' Day, November 1, 1312,

Rosalin had vowed she wouldn't scream, but the cramping, stabbing pain took her by surprise. How could something so wonderful hurt so badly?

The sound tore from her lungs, and there was nothing she could do to stop it.

It was happening much faster than she'd expected. Too fast. She desperately wanted Robbie to be here. But he was away on a mission, and "Cliffy," as she called their unborn child, had decided to make his appearance a few weeks early. A messenger had been sent to Douglas when her first cramps had begun last night, but Rosalin didn't know whether it would reach her husband in time.

The last months of marriage had brought her more joy than she could have imagined. The king had given Robbie some land and an old tower house in Kilmarnock for his faithful service, and they stayed there as much as they could when they weren't at one of the royal castles with Bruce and the other phantoms. She still called them that, even though she knew they referred to themselves as the Highland Guard.

She'd become close with the other wives. There was something about secrecy and the danger of the missions their husbands undertook that created a special bond among them. They were united in fear when they were gone, and in relief when they returned.

But the woman she'd become closest to was Helen MacKay, formerly Sutherland. When "Angel" wasn't accompanying the phantoms on a mission, she spent most of her time at the nearby abbey in Ayrshire with Rosalin, helping to set up the refuge they'd established for unwed women who were with child. Helen's skill as a healer made them a natural team.

It was Helen who tended her now. And Helen to whom she voiced her fears. "Will he make it in time?"

The other woman squeezed her hand. "The babe will be here when he is ready. Whether his father arrives in time or not, I don't know. But it will be all right; just keep breathing."

Tears sprang to her eyes. "I want him here." She sounded like a petulant child, but she couldn't help it. Selfishly she needed him. She needed his strength to get her through this. The hardest part of being married to a warrior was the time he spent away. Not that she would change it for the world. She was so proud of Robbie. He was still more brigand than knight, but hatred and vengeance no longer drove him.

"I know you do. He will be here if it is humanly possible—or superhumanly possible, knowing him. But he left me here to take care of you." Helen smiled. "Although *left* is probably not the right word."

"Ordered?" Rosalin managed between pained breaths.

"Aye, that's better."

Rosalin's face darkened with worry. "You should be there with them."

What if something happened to one of the Guardsmen and Helen wasn't there? Rosalin would never forgive herself.

Helen lifted a brow. "Do you think your husband would be of any use to them if I wasn't with you? He'd get them all killed, which is why they all insisted I stay here with you. Besides, I have a secret." She smiled conspiratorially. "I won't be going on many missions for the next nine months or so."

Rosalin's eyes widened. "Oh Helen, a child? That is wonderful!" She managed to hug her friend for a moment before another pain took hold. She was still breathing hard when she asked, "So Magnus finally convinced you?"

Helen smiled. "He's been patient. More patient than most men would have been. We've been married for over three years. But, nay, it wasn't Magnus. It was seeing all the children at Dunstaffnage during Beltane." She shrugged. "I realized I was ready. I love my work, but I want to be a mother, too. I hope I can do both. If I waited for the war to end I might be an old woman."

Bruce was slowly increasing his hold on the throne, but they were still waiting for the decisive battle.

"Of course you can do both," Rosalin said. "I'm so happy for you." But then another pain wracked her and her face contorted in a grimace. When it had finally passed, she added, "Although after seeing this so many times, it's hard to believe you would ever put yourself through it."

"The rewards are worth the pain."

"Says the woman not screaming like a banshee with sweat rolling down her face."

Helen laughed. "And still you manage to look beautiful."

Rosalin didn't even deign to respond. For the next hour, pains grabbed hold of her stomach and held. They became longer and more frequent in duration. She was exhausted but excited, knowing that after the long wait their babe was almost here.

"You have to start pushing," Helen said.

"No, please not yet. Robbie wants to be here."

"Trust me, you are better off that he's not. Men are no use in the birthing chamber."

Suddenly, they heard a sound outside. Helen rushed to the tower window and smiled. "It appears you will get your wish after all."

Rosalin returned her smile until another pain took hold, and she cried out.

A moment later her husband burst into the room. He looked horrible and wonderful at the same time. He was caked in dirt, his *cotun* flecked with God-knows-what, his eyes were wild, and his face was taut with fear. But she'd never been so happy to see him in her life.

He rushed to her side, kneeling at the edge of the bed. "God, Rosalin, are you all right?"

"I'm having our baby."

Some of the fear slipped from his face, and he managed a small smile. "Aye, *mo ghrá*, I can see that. Or hear it, rather."

"It hurts."

He looked at Helen.

"She's fine," the other woman assured him. "Now that you are here—"

But she didn't get a chance to finish. Robbie glanced over at the floor to the pile of bed linens that had been removed after her water broke, and blanched.

He started to sway, and Rosalin grabbed his arm. "If you swoon, Robbie Boyd, I swear to you I will tell Hawk, and you will never get a moment's peace. And then I will tell my brother. How do you think it will sound in England if it becomes known that the strongest man in Scotland faints at the sight of a little blood?"

"*Your* blood. It's *your* blood." But the threat had worked. He looked more solid and some of the color was returning to his face. "And I wasn't going to faint."

Rosalin and Helen looked at each other and laughed.

"I told you they were useless in the birthing room," Helen said, and then looked at Robbie. "If I have to set up a bed for you, I'm not going to be happy."

Robbie scowled at her. "I can do this. Please, I want to be with her."

He held Rosalin's hand as the next pain grabbed her, and the next. Somehow having him there helped. It still hurt like Hades, but the edge didn't seem quite so sharp.

When it was time to push, Helen told him to make himself useful, and he supported Rosalin from behind as she bore down.

She lost track of time. It seemed to go on forever. She didn't think she'd ever been so relieved when Helen said, "Almost there. One more big push."

Rosalin gritted her teeth, with her husband whispering encouraging words in her ear, and called on every last ounce of strength to deliver their son into the waiting arms of her friend.

The angry little cry a moment later was the most beautiful sound Rosalin had ever heard. Tears sprang to her eyes.

There were tears in Helen's eyes as well. "It's a boy, and he is perfect."

Rosalin felt the relief in her husband's body as well as her own. They looked at one another wordlessly, at an utter loss.

After detaching the babe from the placenta and tying the cord, Helen bundled the child in a soft wool plaid and handed the red, squalling infant to Rosalin.

He had a downy tuft of dark hair, but that wasn't what provoked her to say, "He looks like you." She looked up at her husband, who was staring at the child as if he'd never seen anything so magnificent. "He certainly has your temper."

Robbie stroked the baby's tiny head with the back of his finger. His voice was thick when he said, "What shall we call him?"

She smiled. "I thought . . ." He gave her a look that said "don't say it." But she'd always known exactly what they would call him. "I thought Thomas."

Robbie held her stare, and the emotion that passed between them was sharp and poignant with the memories. Their child would bear the name of the friend who had unknowingly brought them together. Every time they looked at their son, he would remind them of the love that had been so hard fought and won. At all costs.

AUTHOR'S NOTE

Sir Robert Boyd is probably the most well-known historical figure of the Guardsmen I will write about. He plays a large part in the Wars of Independence, fighting alongside both William Wallace and Robert the Bruce, with his name mentioned a number of times by the important chroniclers, including both Barbour and Blind Harry. Blind Harry refers to Boyd over twenty times and calls him "wise and strong," which inspired his place among my Highland Guard as the strongest man in Scotland.

I debated on whether to make Boyd a Guardsman because there is so much known about him (except—conveniently—whom he was married to), but he is such a compelling figure I couldn't resist. To me, he is the William Wallace type of freedom fighter and serves as an important link connecting Bruce's cause to Wallace's.

Boyd was probably born a few years earlier than I suggested, about 1275. His father (or possibly his grandfather) was a hero of the Battle of Largs in 1263, and the family was rewarded with land and a barony in Noddsdale in Ayrshire. Boyd's father, also Robert Boyd, is said to have been one of the Scottish nobles who were called to a meeting by the English and treacherously murdered at the "Barns of Ayr" (an event immortalized in the movie *Braveheart*). In reprisal, Wallace later trapped the English garrison in the barns and set it on fire. I combined the events in the novel for Boyd's father's death.

Wallace is said to have left Boyd in charge of his army when he was away, helping the Boyd clan earn its motto of "Confido," as well as their nickname of the "Trusty Boyds" for their loyalty to the Scottish cause for independence. Boyd fought faithfully beside Wallace, his boyhood companion, and some suggest his kinsman, until the latter's death in 1305. Boyd was also one of the early supporters of Robert the Bruce and fought (loyally) alongside him for the duration of the war, even serving as one of his commanders in the key Battle of Bannockburn, which will feature in a future book.

As Blind Harry says of Boyd at Bannockburn (*History of the Counties of Ayr and Wigton, Vol. III*, by James Paterson, Edinburgh, 1866):

"Ranged on the right the Southron legions stood,
And on their front the fiery Edward rode,
With him the experienced Boyd divides the sway,
Sent by the King to guide him thro' the day."

Boyd may also have been with Bruce and Sir Roger de Kirkpatrick at Greyfriars Monastery in Dumfries in 1306, when Bruce stabbed John "The Red" Comyn before the altar, launching his bid for the crown.

The schooling and military history leanings I give Boyd in the novel are actually based on Wallace's early life. Wallace was reputed to have quoted Hannibal and attended school first in the Stirling area at Cambuskenneth Abbey where his uncle was a clergyman, and then at a popular school in Dundee, taught by William Mydford, who is believed to have fostered Wallace's fervor for liberty. Interestingly, Wallace met Duncan (MacDougall) of Lorn and Neil Campbell (Arthur "Ranger" Campbell's brother) at school in Dundee. Both would later join him in his rebellion.

The works by Polybius and Appian probably didn't make

their way west until the fifteenth century. The Latin translation of Appian wasn't until 1477.

Boyd's sister Marian in the novel is fictional, but his brother Duncan was captured and executed in 1306. Around this same time, Boyd was taken prisoner at Kildrummy but managed to escape. How he managed to do so is lost in the mists of time, but it was what sparked the idea for Rosalin.

Rosalin is the fictional sister of Sir Robert (de) Clifford, first Baron (de) Clifford, who is one of the most important English commanders in the War against Scotland. Clifford's mother was a great heiress, and while the genealogical charts aren't consistent (they never are), most suggest he was an only child. Clifford's father died fighting in Wales when Clifford was seven or eight, and his wardship was held by the king's brother Edmund of Cornwall, the Earl of Gloucester, and eventually King Edward I.

Clifford's military career in Scotland began in 1296 with raids in Annandale (Bruce lands) and Annan, and he appears in many battles over the years until his death at Bannockburn in 1314. But he is probably most remembered for his enmity with Sir James "The Black" Douglas. The fight over the Douglas lands would launch a feud between the Cliffords and Douglases that would last for over one hundred years.

Although Clifford was fighting the Bruce "rebels" in Scotland at the time of the prologue in *The Raider,* his name doesn't appear in the siege of Kildrummy. Kildrummy probably wasn't garrisoned but was immediately dismantled after Edward, Prince of Wales (the future Edward II) and Aymer de Valence (the future Earl of Pembroke) lay siege to it. It was the treachery of the blacksmith Osborne (see *The Viper*) that was responsible for the castle's fall, Boyd's imprisonment, and Nigel Bruce's subsequent execution.

Clifford was, however, at Berwick Castle during the

time of Bruce's raids in 1311 and 1312, having been appointed Keeper of Scotland South of the Forth on April 4, 1311, which made him the perfect brother for my fictional heroine.

There is really no chivalrous way to spin the Bruce raids in 1311 and 1312. They were basically a campaign of blackmail (sometimes with hostages) to support his kingship and fund the costly war. If the money was not paid, the English were threatened with "fire and sword." However, with the exception of the raid in Durham in 1312, which was led by Edward Bruce and the Black Douglas, the Bruce raiders did not typically kill anyone unless they resisted. Even the *English* monks at Lanercost Abbey made note of this in their records of the period.

The enormous two-thousand-pound figure for the truce between Boyd and Clifford is based on the actual amount paid by Northumberland in August 1311.

At the time of *The Raider,* Bruce was laying siege to the castle at Dundee, which would eventually fall and be destroyed in May 1312. Key to understanding the reason for the raids is remembering that although Bruce had a hold on Scotland north of the Tay at this time, the south was still occupied by English garrisons. It was clearing these garrisons from Scotland's important castles (and usually the destruction of the castle afterward) that marks the period between 1311 and 1314. But laying siege to castles and paying men beyond their hundred days of service was expensive, the royal coffers were empty, and Scotland was devastated after years of war. Without the raids, Bruce wouldn't have been able to get a foothold in the south and evict the English who were so deeply entrenched there.

Boyd, James Douglas, Thomas Randolph, and Edward Bruce were the king's key lieutenants in the south and the men more often than not leading the raids in England. How you viewed them (whether hero or terrorist) was largely an issue of perspective, i.e., on which side of the border (called the Marches at the time) you lived. For example, Douglas was known as "Good Sir James" in Scotland, but in England he was reviled as "The Black Douglas."

Similarly, from our modern perspective there is nothing heroic in hostage taking. But in medieval times, it was basically institutionalized and an accepted part of warfare. We've already seen it with David, the young Earl of Atholl, in *The Recruit,* who was held as a hostage most of his young life by the English king as surety for his father's good behavior. That David came to sympathize with his hostage takers was also very common and actually served a purpose as a bridge between the two sides when the hostage was returned.

It appears uncommon for something bad to happen to the hostage even when a deal was reneged upon. David is a good example of that as well. Even when his father rebels and is eventually executed, the boy is not harmed.

The most famous example is probably the great English knight William Marshall. He was held by King Stephen as a youth and famously avoided death when his father broke his promise and taunted the king that he still had "the hammer and anvil with which to forge still more and better sons."

Men—of course—were vastly preferred, but there were some examples of women serving as hostages.

I couldn't resist the temptation to name Rosalin after her illustrious relative. The famously beautiful "Fair Rosamund," who captured the heart of King Henry II and became his mistress, would have been Rosalin's great-aunt three times over.

Finally, although I have Rosalin giving birth at Dean Castle in Kilmarnock in the epilogue, the old Balliol lands were not formally given to Boyd until after Bannockburn. Dean Castle would be built by his son, Thomas, and their descendants would be the future Earls of Kilmarnock.

Coming soon!

Look for
the next novel in Monica McCarty's
Highland Guard series!

THE ARROW

Published by Ballantine Books